The Moonstone and Miss Jones

The Moonstone and Miss Jones

JILLIAN STONE

BRAVA

KENSINGTON PUBLISHING CORP.
www.kensingtonbooks.com

BRAVA BOOKS are published by

Kensington Publishing Corp.
119 West 40th Street
New York, NY 10018

All Kensington titles, imprints, and distributed lines are available at special quantity discounts for bulk purchases for sales promotions, premiums, fund-raising, educational, or institutional use. Special book excerpts or customized printings can also be created to fit specific needs. For details, write or phone the office of the Kensington special sales manager: Kensington Publishing Corp., 119 West 40th Street, New York, NY 10018, attn: Special Sales Department; phone 1-800-221-2647.

Brava and the B logo are Reg. U.S. Pat. & TM Off.

ISBN-13: 978-0-7582-6898-3
ISBN-10: 0-7582-6898-X

First Trade Paperback Printing: October 2012

10 9 8 7 6 5 4 3 2 1

Printed in the United States of America

Chapter One

FRANÇAIS TÉLÉGRAPHE AND CABLE
4 SEPTEMBER 1889 11:10 AM
DX MARSEILLES PHAETON BLACK
CPT AMERICA JONES
C/O CHERBOURG LE HAVRE CALAIS

SHANGHAIED IN SHANGHAI STOP MEET ME
BELOW STAIRS AT THE OLD FLAT

"I SWEAR I'LL SEE PHAETON BLACK HANG FROM A YARDARM." America Jones crushed the wire in her fist and tossed the message aside. The crumpled paper bounced along the bustling street of Le Havre in carefree ignorance of her angry heart.

Her boatswain, Ned McCafferty, flattened one side of his mouth into a thin line. She knew his grimace well. The very one he used to hide his amusement so as not to provoke her. "I wouldna' advise ye string up Mr. Black, Cap'ain Miss, not in y'er condition."

She sighed. "I suppose it defeats the purpose of chasing him halfway around the world. Perhaps I will torture him first." She'd do it, too, except the devilish man would have her strip down to camisole and pantalettes and swish a riding crop about.

America stepped off the curb and crossed Rue Dauphine. The harbor breeze stirred memories of Phaeton on a balmy Polynesian night. Bare-chested, a trickle of sweat ran down his torso. America caught her breath as a surge of arousal coursed through her body. "Drat!" He had entered her mind for a mere moment and rekindled her passion. And something else—an awful, unbearable yearning.

"First, I suggest ye catch him, lass." Ned purposely fell back and swept up the discarded telegram. He opened the crumpled paper and read aloud. "Shanghaied in Shanghai. Stop." His mumble followed on behind her as she turned the corner and set a brisk pace in the direction of the Port Authority. She tossed a glare over her shoulder. "I thank you kindly not to read my personal messages."

"Hold on there, Cap'ain. He might have been shanghaied—or worse."

She stopped in her tracks, brows knit together. "What are you saying, Ned?"

He removed his cap to scratch his head. "Stop and think now, Miss. Say your Mr. Black was kidnapped. Might of taken him a good while to get a message off ship."

"What if—might have? Just like a man to give Phaeton the benefit of the doubt." Hands on her hips, she leaned into Ned's face. "And he *might have* run off." America caught a lower lip under her teeth and chewed, a nervous habit which Phaeton often provoked, especially when she was cross. And she was thoroughly vexed at the moment.

Had Ned and Phaeton formed a bond during the voyage? She certainly hadn't noticed. But then why would she? She'd danced around the deck of the *Topaz* like a giddy young girl in love. Too deliriously happy, she supposed.

The wretched truth of it was she'd never been happier in her entire life. Not even when Papa was alive had she known such contentment and genuine affection from a man. While it lasted. America wound a circuitous path around dockworkers and drays. She missed him. These last weeks had been a misery without Phaeton by her side.

And in her bed.

America exhaled a deep sigh. Her eyes moistened and she blinked hard, refusing to cry a single tear for the man. "I suppose we'll find out the truth soon enough."

For some weeks now she had sensed they were closing in on

the rapscallion. Once aboard ship she'd give the order to make ready. They'd shove off under a full moon, have a skim across the channel, and up the Thames. The *Topaz* would make Port of London before morning—quick as you please.

Phaeton's wire had been held at the telegraph office for several days, but the cable had been sent from Marseilles. Might it be possible the *Topaz,* fast as she was, had nearly caught up with his ship? Her heart thumped erratically in her chest. She revisited his cryptic words. Shanghaied in Shanghai? It had been his first and only communication since his disappearance. What was she to make of such a message? Just like Phaeton to be clever in such a dire moment. In fact, the more life threatening the situation, the more amusing he often became.

Whether it be abandonment or abduction, she'd get to the bottom of his disappearance. She supposed she should be elated to know he was alive. To know she would once again be able to look into his devilish dark gaze. Eyes that bespoke a sharp mind and a lust for adventure.

As much as she was drawn to him, a fearful, nagging thought lingered. A worry that had never quite left her mind or her heart. Perhaps it wasn't possible to settle down with a man like Phaeton Black. Perhaps it might be better to move on and try to put him behind her. She swept a few unruly wisps of curl from her eyes and made her way down Pier 12.

Well, she had a great deal more than herself to think about now. She stepped around cargo nets and stacked barrels of stout. Up ahead, through a crisscross of masts and rigging, a blazing red sky framed the eye-catching merchant ship. America shaded her eyes from the low rays and inhaled a deep, cleansing breath. Even with sails furled, her sleek lines and proud stature made the *Topaz* the fairest ship in port. Ned hurried his pace and helped her onto the gangway. Single-file, they climbed the steep ramp.

Halfway up, she stopped and turned. "I caution you, Ned, not a word about my condition. 'Tis a secret between you and I. No one must know—especially Mr. Black."

Ned reached out to steady her. "If you say so, Cap'ain Miss."

She climbed the rest of the gangway stroking her barely swollen belly. "Forgive me, my little pea under the shell. Once we reach London, I fear you might well be fatherless."

"What can one say about you, Mr. Black? You are part devil and angel." The bold beauty stepped closer. Hair a honeyed shade of brown, a lovely aquiline nose, and eyes that sparkled like gemstones—green, he thought. No, blue.

No, green. The color of the seas off Crete.

Phaeton took another leisurely perusal of the young lady's wares. For the sparest of moments, he thought about warning off the intriguing girl. That was before his gaze lowered to her bosom. "I'd have to say largely devil."

Her pale hand swept over the buttons of his trousers. Brazen chit! Delicate fingers found what they searched for. "Largely, indeed." Her touch was light and fleeting, but the very notion that she dared such public foreplay cheered him greatly. Apparently, it also amused the naughty little vixen. Those astonishing aquamarine eyes traced the bulge in his pants. "Rumor has it you are made of wicked wood and when you play the seducer you are so very, very . . ."

A clearing of his throat ended in a grin. "Shocking?"

Her faraway glance about the room returned to him. "Sublime."

He quirked a brow, but otherwise kept his gaze steady. "Are we discussing length and breadth or technique?"

"Not sure." The wily minx tossed a wink over her shoulder and flounced away. "But I mean to find out." He watched the bob and sway of her bustle as she wove her retreat between chattering passengers.

They were nearing the dinner hour. The ship's salon swelled with first-class passengers swilling aperitifs. Phaeton drew in a breath and exhaled slowly. Miss Georgiana Ryder turned out to be a most charming ingénue with a saucy, hoyden-like quality about her. Quite irresistible, as were her siblings Velvet and Fleury, a delightful sisterly trio—each one as lovely as the next. He scanned the salon and found Velvet standing among a cluster of oglers. Her gleaming dark eyes and sultry pout beckoned without words. He met her gaze and lingered for a brief flirtation before he caught a blur of Fleury. The fey, dancing, wisp of a girl instantly distracted. Phaeton watched the youngest sibling flutter about the room, much like a hummingbird hovers and flits from daisy to delphinium.

"Are you enjoying the voyage, Mr. Black?"

"My return trip to London grows more diverting by the hour." Phaeton tore his eyes off the pretty chit and nodded a polite bow to the young lady's mother. "Mrs. Ryder." He feigned a pleasant expression. "Most especially since I have been fortunate enough to make acquaintance with you and your family."

If truth be told, he found the cloying mother barely tolerable and Mr. Ryder, the stout man slurping sherry in the corner, to be a degenerate troll who conducted himself as more of a procurer than a father anxious to see his daughters well-spoken for. In point of fact, the entire family was odd. For one thing, they were inexplicably interested in him.

He had dressed early for dinner and entered the main salon in hopes of finding a tumbler of whiskey. The Ryder clan, which included the mister, missus, and assorted lovelies, had singled him out from a number of wealthy, titled gentleman aboard the *RMS Empress of Asia*. He considered the obvious question—why?—and decided it could wait for later.

Yes, the voyage home was going to be interesting. The ocean journey that had once been tedious and despairing quite suddenly brimmed with intrigue. Phaeton nodded perfunctorily to the mother's ramblings, as the woman found it an unnecessary bother to pause or think between sentences.

He perused the room looking for his evening's distraction, Georgiana. The young lady's mother might indeed be a harpy in disguise and the father no better than a common pimp, but the eldest daughter? The bewitching dream of a young woman stood between two heavily whiskered gents whose eyes never left her astonishing assets.

Phaeton took another look for himself. There was nothing overly voluptuous or buxom about any part of her. It was just that all parts of her were so very . . . luscious. Aware of his attention, she turned and made eye contact across the crowded salon. Gazes locked, the little vixen opened her mouth ever so slightly. A pink tongue swept the underside of a peaked upper lip. The room, for a second, collapsed in size around them. The gesture caused a number of his vital organs to rush a surge of blood to his favorite extremity.

Phaeton tipped his glass for a last swallow.

A white-gloved steward entered the salon and rang a melodious set of chimes. The dinner bell. Another attendant, also liveried in a brass-buttoned jacket, opened a double set of doors. Georgiana turned to leave, but not in the direction of the dining room.

Peripherally, his gaze took in the delicate laces and bright colored silks of the fashionably attired as they drifted into supper. He dipped a nod, here and there, as the beau monde passed in a blur. A few oddly familiar faces, but for the life of him, he could not place the familiar spirits. He set his empty glass on a silver tray and wound his way through the room, in the opposite direction of sustenance. This evening his appetites lay elsewhere.

Phaeton stepped through the hatch onto the promenade deck. The night was clear and warm with a bit of moisture in the air. A sparkling carpet of stars swept across the sky overhead. He strolled toward the front of the ship and thought about a cigar, then thought better of it.

He found her standing near the starboard bow. He could have pressed close, but instead, kept some distance between them. She turned and struck a sultry pose with her back to the rail.

They were alone. He did not know how he knew this, for he made no inspection of the deck. And frankly he did not care. Her gown rippled with the breeze. "Lift your skirt."

She tilted her head and rolled her eyes in the prettiest fashion. Not a refusal, but more of a flirtation. Her hand caressed a curve of hip and lifted her skirt enough to expose a dainty turn of ankle. His arousal was prodigious, yet he continued to trifle with her. He used two fingers to gesture upward.

Inch by inch, her skirt and petticoats rose. A delightful show of calf. A pretty knee. A silk-flowered garter. And above the top of her hose, a hint of peach-colored flesh.

With the slightest measure of control left, Phaeton closed the distance between them. He pressed her against the ship's rail. Not too hard. Certainly not as hard as his burgeoning need. "Georgiana?"

"Mr. Black?" Droplets of perspiration, like tiny diamonds, sparkled across her nose and cheeks.

"Please, call me Phaeton." He kissed the bridge of her nose and tasted salt—and a whiff of something spicy. The stubble of his beard brushed her cheekbone as he worked his way toward an earlobe. He reached under her gathered skirt and felt her body shudder. "Kiss me, Phaeton."

He lowered his gaze to her mouth. "And if I kiss you, what is my reward?"

He enjoyed the playful squint in her eyes and saucy turn to her chin almost more than her words. "As if a kiss is not reward enough? What do you desire?"

He slipped his hands under her bustle and rubbed gently, as softly as a balmy breeze off the East China Sea. "More."

The corners of her mouth lifted. She wrapped a limber leg around him. Good girl. "Then I shall see you snuggly sheathed."

He found the ribbon on her lacy undergarment and pulled. Silk fabric slipped over a rounded cheek, exposing a lovely derrière. Firm with just the right amount of jiggle. He moved inbetween her thighs and slipped the tips of his fingers along the sensitive inside flesh of her limbs. She spread her legs wider.

Phaeton smiled. He didn't even have to ask.

He caught a flash of scarlet in her eyes and caught his breath. Just a ripple of color, but even a hint of suspicion was bad enough. He quickly lifted silk pantalettes and retied the bow. "Arousing to see you again Georgiana, or should I say *Mademoiselle Gorgós*?" He stepped away.

Deep crimson swirled behind midnight blue eyes. Her flesh took on a curiously ethereal form as something reptilian materialized before him. Scaly but feminine, with a pale luminescence. Her dress unraveled to lay bare high-set breasts and rounded hips. A gossamer snake of silk swirled over her nude form, entwining itself around voluptuous curves.

"Ah, there you are." Somewhat wistfully, one side of his lip curled upward.

Fully formed, she was feline and serpentine all at once. Her skin glistened with pearl-sized, translucent scales that rippled with each rise and fall of breath. Her new, darker gaze traveled the length of his frame, admiring, exploring. She grabbed hold of his lapels and pressed him back against the ship's rails. Every fiber of this female entity appeared to quake with anticipation. Sweeping aside her meandering skirt she pressed his hand to her Venus mound, but his fingers retreated. In fact, his arm jerked backward. Awkward, even for Phaeton.

Regretfully, he stepped away. "Not that my soul is worth saving, but I make it a point never to lay with otherworld creatures." His *tsk* was more of a sigh. "Pity—you might have saved this for later—crawled into my berth for the suffocating climax?"

A shockwave of energy knocked him down and sent him sliding along the polished wood deck. He lay stunned momentarily, as the female demon swarmed over him, thrusting herself against his manly parts. He groaned. "Such a naughty succubus." Between caresses, this night creature would attempt to mount, then strangle him. There was nothing left to do but feign a struggle.

At some point he would have to extract himself from her sexual alchemy. But not . . . immediately. He rather enjoyed this part of the macabre dance. There would soon come a delightful, helpless paralysis. He would chance a moment or two of pleasure before those invisible bonds took hold and began to choke.

Irises contracted into vertical slits as bulbous orbs swiveled up and down his torso. Georgiana had become decidedly less attractive.

The buttons on his trousers loosed. "Dangerous play, love."

Phaeton lifted his head as his cock sprung to life. It couldn't hurt to ask. "Might the naughty succubus swallow the dragon?"

Her answer came in the form of a pink tongue covered in shimmering scales and a long hiss. Soon, she would genuflect on his chest. With nostrils flared, bearing down hard, the she-devil would squeeze with all her considerable might and crush the air from his lungs, the living soul from his body.

Her scaled tongue lengthened and tickled his earlobe. Clawed fingers wrapped around his brick-hard prick and stroked. Good God, he ached for release.

The vixen's luscious mouth uttered a deep, throaty sigh and moved lower. "Cocks up, Mr. Black."

"Mmm, the pleasure is mine." He reached into thin air.

"Got nothing to do with your pleasure, sir. They're comin' fer ye. Shake a leg now and be quick about it. We made Port o'London last night."

Phaeton's eyelids flew open. The blurry visage of an old seadog squinted down at him. He jerked awake at the sight of the gray-bearded geezer. "Crew sez they lost their share at cards last evening."

Phaeton rubbed his eyes.

His *tête à tête* with a night terror had been a stimulating hallucination—while it had lasted. He blinked again, and brought a wild bristle of chin hairs into focus. "Good God. That you, Mr. Grubb?" He barely recognized the croak in his own voice.

Rummy old Joe Grubb flattened weathered lips into a thin line. "Crew claims ye cheated 'em."

Despite the blistering hangover, he vaguely remembered a card game as well as a good deal of grog guzzling. "Preposterous." Lifting his pounding head, he reached down to scratch his crotch. A rat chewed on a trouser button.

Phaeton hurled himself out of his hammock. "Bloody hell." He caught a swinging length of knotted rope and managed to remain upright. The rodent skittered away into the deeper shadows of the crew's quarters. Listing to one side, he called after the creature. "Georgiana?"

He ventured a squint about his surroundings. "Where am I?" This was no luxury ocean liner but a rat hole in the bowels of a seagoing vessel. A listen to the chorus of snores indicated a number of men slept in the hammocks strung about the hold. He was in a cargo ship. But not the *Topaz*. And what had happened to America Jones?

He recalled making port in Shanghai. There had been a screeching argument, as well as a long, pointed weapon tossed at him. On further consideration—he shook his head—he was quite certain that the altercation between him and America had not been the cause of their separation. Again, Phaeton tried to shake the whiskey fog from his brain.

The gruff old seabird poked him in the rib. "Crew sez ye could see through their cards,"—his one good eye circled about—"as if by magic."

A blast of rotten breath sent Phaeton backward. "Possibly, but—"

Something surly and imposing stepped through the hatch tossing a cutlass back and forth between clenched hands. Good God. The ogre-sized sailor did seem familiar. Phaeton struggled to recall last evening through a cloud of smoke and spirits.

"Now see here—" He straightened up and backed away from the angry seaman. "Let me assure you, I have no peculiar ability at cards—luck of the draw." A broad swipe of sword took out several hammocks, which fell onto a cold damp floor. Phaeton grimaced. More rudely awakened sailors with pockets lightened by grog and card play.

His heart rate and blood flow elevated to the correct level of alarm. He feigned a left and tilted sideways, barely avoiding the next slash of blade. Phaeton retreated as a number of rousted seadogs fell in behind the hovering thug with the menacing sword. Air buffeted past the end of his nose from yet another swing.

No time to lose.

Using a bit of potent lift, learned from a man full of such unearthly tricks, Phaeton flung himself into the air, banked off the ceiling, and landed atop a sleeping sailor. Arms out to his sides for balance, he grabbed hold of an overhead line and pushed off the grunting chest beneath his boots. He aimed straight for the seamen in pursuit, swinging across the barracks, head down, balls out, he struck the lead man. The rest of the crew toppled over like ninepins.

Phaeton released the rope and landed near the main hatch. He grabbed his hat from a nearby hook and scooped up the loose cutlass sliding across the floorboards.

Joe Grubb broadened a toothless grin. "Cut and run, Mr. Black."

Phaeton flicked the brim of his bowler. "Pricks to the wind, Chief."

He bolted down into the cargo hold, removing belaying pins as he ran. A flurry of cargo net enveloped, then whisked him up into the air above the cargo hatch. Several good swings of the blade loosed the web of rope and he dropped onto the wooden deck. Halfway across the gangplank, Phaeton glanced back. Christ.

He teetered precariously at the sight. The whole bloody lot of them were following on behind. He turned and made a dash along a pier stacked with cargo and crowded with dockworkers. Vaulting over large bales of cotton, he squeezed through stacks of tea chests and skirted cartloads of whiskey. A sprint over a footbridge led him away from the chaos of the docks and into the refuge of a covered alley.

He ducked into a dank niche off the lane and waited for his pursuers to pass by. Once the seamen were well ahead, he darted back into the lane and made his way toward the cab stand on Westferry Road. Trotting along behind a loaded drayage cart, he was steps away from the bustling thoroughfare when one of the seamen gave a shout from behind.

Phaeton pivoted toward the surly bloke who came at him hoisting a belaying pin. He drew a pistol from his coat knowing full well the chamber held no bullets. The sailor lunged just as a fast moving carriage passed between them. The brief respite afforded him the opportunity to abandon all sense of propriety. He wrenched open the door of the passing vehicle and tossed himself inside.

From the floor of the carriage, amid a flutter of pretty lace ruffles and petticoats, Phaeton perused shapely legs covered in pale stockings. "My word, things are looking up."

Chapter Two

Tossing up skirts, Phaeton grabbed the cabin door and slammed it shut. He settled into the empty seat opposite two young women. "Good morning, ladies."

Eyes wide in horror, the distressed damsels' cries merged into a shriek. Phaeton tilted the pistol up and waved it in front of his lips. "Shhh." He unbuttoned his jacket. "Perhaps you might like to suck on this."

When both females recoiled in unison, he studied the attractive pair. "Do you lovely ladies do everything together? I hope so." He removed two peppermint sticks from a pink and white striped wrapper inside his pocket. "Been saving these." He leaned forward. "Open."

Pretty lips slammed shut.

"Open your mouths." He waved the gun. "Or your legs." Eyes wide in horror, the women complied. "That's right, darlings. No sense in disturbing the driver." He inserted a candy stick in each little bird's mouth.

Phaeton sat back. "Now, if you would allow me to share the ride, I will gladly pay the full fare into town."

Whether from shock or the ghastly cold weather, it seemed both women could not quite register exactly what was happening to them. Without much argument, their whimpering appeared to ease as each young lady swirled a candy stick between puckered lips. Phaeton watched the in and out motion with considerable interest. "You can't imagine what sort of favors a peppermint stick earns for a man in Bora Bora."

The boney-shouldered female withdrew the confectionary with a sucking slurp. "Most indelicate." Her lips remained stuck in the pursed position.

Phaeton resisted an eye roll. "You're quite right. Out of the country for a miserable few months and look what happens?" He placed his revolver on the seat beside him. "I've forgotten my manners."

From a waistcoat pocket he withdrew a calling card and smoothed out a dog-eared corner. "Phaeton Black." He passed over his credentials. "I was shanghaied in Shanghai—of all places. Lost everything, I'm afraid, including my fiancée."

It occurred to Phaeton he had escaped his captors, quite spontaneously, without a scheme of any kind. Although Captain Bellamy had never directly discussed the reason for his abduction and removal from China, it was a good guess they hadn't brought him aboard ship for his skills at sitting a yardarm and taking up sail. Someone wanted him back in London. Badly.

Phaeton glanced out the carriage window dockside. London was as gray as ever. Wisps of fog crawled through a cobweb of masts and rigging. He pulled his coat closed and hunkered down in his seat. "What is it they say about the Isle of Dogs?"

In the most provocative fashion possible, the young lady of pleasant expression removed the peppermint from her pouted lips. "Fit for wolves."

His heavy-lidded gaze moved slowly over watered silks and traces of lace to admire ample curves. He determined this one to be the prettier of the two. And without a doubt, the more promising.

"Violet du Bois." Her eyes darted sideways. "And, this is my cousin Clara."

He shifted his attention to the paler relative. "So pleased to make your acquaintance." His most ingratiating smile had little effect on the stiff woman, who sat upright with her shoulders back and her lips in a sphincter. "Where might we drop you, Mr. Black?"

Phaeton shook off a shiver. "21 Shaftesbury Court."

He waited for the dainty arch of brows. Mrs. Parker's house

of ill repute was one of the most recognized addresses in all of London; he'd place it somewhere between 10 Downing and 4 Whitehall Place.

"Been at sea for some months now." He lounged against the upholstered bench seat and stretched his legs. Violet's gaze turned sultry and shifted up and down his frame. Phaeton wasted no time returning the interest. He tilted his head. "So tell me Violet, are you fun?"

"Fun by whose standard, Mr. Black, mine or yours?"

Phaeton squinted his eyes. "Mine, I think. And I believe I asked the question. Which puts me in the position to judge what is fun and what is not."

Violet flashed a pretty smirk. "I take your meaning to be risqué, or am I wrong?"

"Very indecent, but also scientific. I picture you and me on a swing, Miss du Bois. Wearing little or nothing, you ride my loins up and down gently assisted by the gravitational forces of nature." Phaeton grinned. "Science at play, if you take my meaning."

"Get out." This time, the shriek stopped the carriage. The thin, shrill woman had turned an alarming shade of purple. "Get out I say, or I shall have the driver throw you out on the street where you belong."

He caught a glimpse of Lloyd's Bank on Waterloo Place. "Just a few more blocks, Clara."

The woman raised her umbrella.

"Very well." With a wink to Violet, Phaeton was out the carriage door. He tossed several pieces of silver up to the driver—generous by any standard. As the carriage sped away, his trousers received a splatter of gutter slop. He tipped his hat. "Ladies."

Just past Drake's gaming hell, his tread lightened. He was almost home now, if one could call a basement flat beneath a brothel home. He knocked on the door of London's most talked about bawdy house. A scullery maid opened the door and bid him enter. "You're a bit early sir; none of the girls is up yet."

Phaeton retrieved a coin from his pocket. "Might I ask you

to rouse Mrs. Parker?" He held the tuppence between two fingers. "For your bravery."

The girl set down a pail of murky water, rubbed her hand on a grimy apron, and accepted the copper. "Who may I say is calling, sir?"

"Phaeton Black."

She bobbed a curtsy and hurried upstairs.

The house was deadly quiet at this irregular hour. Phaeton removed his hat and paced the foyer, poking his head into a parlor filled with gilt-edged furniture and velvet flock-work wallpaper. An appealing young woman descended the staircase and greeted him with a nod. As she ventured closer, the brown-skinned doxy lowered and raised sultry eyes in a brazen inspection of his person.

At the very moment he recognized the saucy chit, she halted midway down the stairs. "Mr. Black?"

He grinned. "Layla?"

She flew down the steps and threw her arms around him. "Oh, Mr. Black, it is you." She stood on tiptoes and inspected each side of his jaw.

He drew a hand over close-cropped whiskers. "The beard is new."

"A Van Dyke suits you—though you could use a trim." Layla's coffee-colored eyes were the large, limpid type. She glanced into the parlor. "And where is Miss Jones?"

His smile flattened, slightly. "We appear to be estranged for the moment. Rather a long, unflattering story."

"We've missed you so, Mr. Black." She reached an arm around his neck and pulled him close.

He kissed her softly and the buxom harlot used a swirl of tongue to ease up a bit of arousal. "We, or you, love?" His answer came from the foot of the stairs.

"I'd have to say we, Phaeton." Mrs. Parker descended the stairs.

He straightened. "Esmeralda." Shrugging on a soft green wrapper she pulled the ties into a bow. The lovely madam held out her hands, and he reverently kissed one then the other. "My word, you are as lovely as ever."

She withdrew both hands gently. "Layla, ask cook to make up a tea tray, perhaps some toast and berry preserve. Anything else, Phaeton?"

"I could do with a rasher or two and a boiled egg." He grinned. "Scraped my way out of a tight spot this morning—beastly chase through the Isle of Dogs."

"Eggs and bacon it is." Layla winked and disappeared down the servant's stairs. Madam rolled open the pocket doors to the dining room. "I mean to hear all about your adventures abroad, Phaeton."

Over his first cup of tea, he gave a travelogue of Alexandria and Upper Egypt, including the partial excavation of the Sphinx. He shared a few escapades in various ports of India and Burma while shoveling rashers and eggs. By the time he poured his second cup of Earl Grey, the *Topaz* had dropped anchor in Hangzhou Bay.

"We delivered our cargo and acquired a consignment of dry goods bound for France. Everything went along swimmingly, until our last night in Shanghai. America was feeling a bit under the weather." Phaeton cleared his throat. "A few shipmates and I went off for a bit of pipe." He shrugged when Esmeralda frowned. "It was our last night and opium is cheaper than whiskey." He left out the spat he and America had, which culminated in an aboriginal spear being ripped off the cabin wall. He recalled jumping through the hatch as the weapon's tip shattered a hole in the door.

Esmeralda sipped her tea. "And so you were shanghaied?"

Phaeton settled back in his chair. "A little joke of mine, used to obfuscate what really happened. A few puffs on the pipe and I woke up in the hold of a strange ship, bound for home."

She lifted a corner of her mouth. "I take it they didn't need an extra shipmate?"

He snorted a laugh. "Hardly."

Twisting his teacup around in its saucer, the soft grating of china against china helped to break the silence. He met her gaze over the table. Soft auburn tresses fell over ample mounds wrapped in silk. Lovely woman. At one time he had lusted after her mightily. But her interest lay elsewhere. "And . . . how is Exeter?"

Her eyes shifted away briefly. "Troubled."

Phaeton leaned forward. "About?"

"I cannot say." She sighed. "He does not wish to burden me with his difficulties. Or so he claims. But I am worried for him." The lovely madam stirred her tea. Abruptly, her lashes raised. Normally her eyes were a clear blue, filled with light and quick to tease. But much like a sudden storm at sea, they clouded over with worry, or worse—fear.

He exhaled. "I believe I was captured and brought back to London for a reason. Exeter no doubt will have some ideas on the matter." He missed the enigmatic doctor, whose strange inexplicable powers and scientific machinery had proven invaluable on his last case. "I shall visit him straight away—this evening, if that would ease your mind."

She brightened. "I would be greatly relieved if you spoke with him, Phaeton. And he will be delighted to see you."

"I intend to take up sleuthing again. Private assignments. An occasional contract with Scotland Yard." He might even hang out a shingle. *Phaeton Black, Investigator of the Arcane and Unnatural.* He thought perhaps the first case he'd solve would be his own.

He slurped a last swallow of tea. "My old flat below stairs, is it by any chance—"

"Occupied, at the moment."

"Bollocks. That is disappointing."

"By a number of odd apparitions." The light had returned to her face. "We have no idea where they came from. They just . . . appeared recently. Nearly gave the old gentleman who rented the flat an apoplexy. Packed his bag and left yesterday."

Phaeton sat up straight. "Apparitions or entities? There's a difference."

"Not sure. They appear to be a family. A father, mother, and three daughters—all quite charming." Esmeralda rose and moved to exit the room. "Shall we explore?"

Stunned for a moment, Phaeton slumped back in his chair.

Good God. The coincidence was too great. He caught up with the madam near the stairs in the foyer. Esmeralda tightened her wrapper for the descent. "And what of Miss Jones? Should we be expecting her, Phaeton?"

He stared into the dark aether below. "I managed to bribe a cabin boy in Marseilles—sent a wire care of every port in France. At the moment, I can only surmise she believes I am dead or have abandoned her."

He trailed behind Esmeralda. "A family of apparitions . . ." Phaeton ran a hand through his hair. The word *family* usually implied flesh and blood. Frankly, he preferred demons from the abyss. "Their name wouldn't be Ryder, by any chance?"

Esmeralda paused on the landing. "You've met them?"

Phaeton gazed around the old flat. "In a manner of speaking." Everything looked disturbingly the same. "Don't tell me—the old pimp offered his daughter's services." Every square foot of these rooms were suffused with memories of America Jones. "I do hope you didn't take him up on it."

"What? And scare the stiff right off my gentlemen callers?" Esmeralda opened a street-level window to let in air. She brushed a layer of dust from the sill. "Shall we say two and six a week, Phaeton?"

Even the chintz-covered overstuffed chair held memories. He had made love to America Jones on every stick of furniture in the room. Phaeton's gaze lingered in the pantry. He hadn't had her on top of the breakfast table. But he'd wanted to.

"Phaeton?"

He swung around. "Sorry, woolgathering. Two and six it is." He dug in his trousers and came up with a pocketful of metal and a wad of banknotes. "Won a great deal of coin last night at *Vingt-et-un*." He righted himself for a moment. "At least I believe that is what we were playing." He counted out a month's rent.

Esmeralda smiled. "You've been sorely missed, Phaeton."

His gaze moved over her softly. "By Madam in particular?" He placed a banknote and a few coins in her palm.

She pocketed the rent money. "I have a hot bath waiting." He could not help but notice the sway of silk across her bottom. So much more arousing than a bustle. "Room enough for two?"

Esmeralda snorted a laugh and climbed the stairs. "Shall I have Bertie make up your bed and heat water for a bath?"

"This afternoon." Phaeton yawned. "I mean to nick a few hours sleep." He lifted a seat cushion off the chair. "Georgiana?"

After a quick check into dim corners and pantry closets, he flopped onto the chaise. "Velvet . . . Fleury?" He opened an eye and perused the familiar surroundings one more time. "Girls?"

Chapter Three

HAND OVER HAND, toe behind toe, America shimmied down the bowsprit of the *Topaz*. Far below, the basin waters of Isle of Dogs rushed beneath the ship's bow. Millwall docks lay just ahead. The tinge of sulfur in the yellow-brown air sent blood and thrills racing through her veins at the very thought of home.

Without warning, a recurring vision overtook her. America grabbed hold of the jib line to steady herself. Phaeton drifted in a sea of madness. In the vision, they were both in London, but somehow—it was not London. Phaeton was by her side, yet she was but a ghost in his world. America's eyes rolled back in her head. A memory of something her mother, a Vauda witch of great power, had once advised. "Embrace that which haunts you—draw strength from its power—take it in and make yourself whole again."

Wave after wave of uneasy thoughts invaded her mind. Darker times were still ahead for both of them. A shiver ran up her spine, jolting her back to reality. "I fear we are in for a nasty adventure," she sighed aloud. Layered into the sound of rushing water came a series of low-pitched clicks. Something like the vibration heard from the island dragons off the coast of Sumatra. "Edvar?"

Agile as a monkey, the gargoyle slid down the jib sail and landed on the ship's railing. America laughed at the creature's antics. After months at sea, she had finally begun to understand the unusual mascot. "We're about to make port." She looked for the slinky gray gargoyle whose visibility faded in and out at whim.

"Dun-lon?" The query floated up to her. She thought Edvar meant London, though one could never be sure.

America pushed off the rail. "Best finish packing." She wound a path through a busy crew tossing dock lines ashore to her cabin below deck.

Her portmanteau sat on a captain's chair, just where she had left it earlier. She removed a stack of unmentionables from the great chest on the floor and set them inside the satchel.

"Edvar?" America held the bag open. A pale shadow skittered along the floor and landed in the bag. A shifting around of petticoats and stockings indicated the small beastie boy had settled in. Not that the elusive creature needed to be packed for traveling, he just had an affinity for luggage.

After months at sea, she was beginning to decipher a few traits of the little fiend's. Not just his odd clicks and hisses, and his funny attempts at speech, which were often upside down and backward. It was more like she could fathom Edvar's intentions. The scampering imp was more magical dog than gargoyle. From the first, her sensory faculties had perceived an aura of protection—and it was stronger than ever now that Phaeton was gone.

When her errant lover had vanished in Shanghai, the great paradise for adventurers, Edvar had stayed with her. It seemed the gargoyle's umbrella of protection now applied to her and the little pea in the pod.

America recalled the days and nights spent searching Shanghai's most notorious pits of depravity. Since Phaeton had likely gone chasing after the dragon, she checked the opium dens first, then the red lantern districts brimming over with expensive courtesans and short-time whores. Nothing. And those women would have remembered Phaeton. Her heart ached at the very thought, just as it had then.

When it became obvious he hadn't gone after a bit of pipe, nor had he been whoring, her fears had led her to a very dark place. Thoughts of him falling prey to the thuggery of Blood Alley had crept silently into her mind—images of him floating facedown in the Yangtzu river. Then, finally, after days of rummaging about and innumerable bribes, she confirmed Phaeton had booked passage on a steamer bound for Ceylon.

What a relief—he had abandoned her.

After a good cry and an incident of teacups crashing against walls and the feathers of a pillow being—well, feathered about—she had sat up straight and made up her mind. By her order the *Topaz* had set sail early that evening. She had chased the scoundrel halfway around the world, and she would have it out with him—this very night if possible.

A patter of irregular heartbeats danced in her chest at just the thought of seeing him again. She could almost feel him now. They were that close—and yet, she also felt estranged. She wondered, frankly, whether she would kill him on first sight or make love to him. There was such appeal in both, a smile tugged at the ends of her mouth.

"I suppose I'm ready if you are, Edvar."

A whiny snuffle answered from the depths of her luggage.

Early in the voyage, Phaeton had taught her basic gargoyle speech, beginning with the little monster's *yuk-yuks* and *nuh-uhs*. Apparently there was a whole range of nuanced whines and hissing noises that took years to interpret with any accuracy. "You have to understand." Phaeton advised. "He is contrary by nature. There will always be a little bit of no in every yes from Edvar."

She leaned over the travel bag. "You're looking forward to seeing Phaeton again—aren't you?" Edvar's rattle and hum sounded like a harrumph followed by a snort.

"Ha! Thought so—you miss him as much as I do." Golden eyes blinked at her. The gargoyle whimpered a soft *nuh-uh*. America grinned. It seemed there was also a bit of *yes* in every *nuh-uh*.

A sparkle of light outside the porthole caught her eye. Rather bright for dockside torches. Perhaps it was just harbor light reflecting off raindrops on the glass. She leaned over her berth for a better look. Only blackness—no, wait. An oval face emerged from deep shadows. Luminous gray eyes, as small as pearls, gazed at her without blinking. Below flattened nostrils a gaping orifice opened. A thousand needle-sharp teeth, webbed with viscous threads of drool, glistened in the dark.

America jumped back with a shriek.

"Anything wrong Captain, Miss?" America ran to open the hatch door. Her chief mate stood in the passageway.

She turned back to the porthole, but the face was gone. "Be right with you."

She shook off a tremble, closed the satchel and handed the bag to Ned.

"Are you sure you want to be traveling at this late hour, Miss?"

She had a bee in her bonnet to face and have it out with Phaeton Black—then perhaps a nice long session of making up. Where did that lusty thought come from? Mentally, she slapped herself. "I'll just toss and turn all night—best get this over with." She tugged on gloves as she stepped ahead of Ned.

"And you're sure Mr. Black will return to Shaftesbury Court, Miss?"

She was on deck and across the gangway before she answered. "A house full of willing tarts? Where else would the blackguard go?"

She took the shortest way out of Millwork docks, setting a blistering pace over the footbridge that crossed the boat basin. As they passed the cooperage, something slithered into the shadows of the barrel maker's doorway. America turned onto West Ferry Road. Even at this late hour, the Isle of Dogs enjoyed a bustle of activity.

"I'll take care of the Port Authority, contact MacLeod—see if he's got a captain for us. Then I'll have a look about for shipment—" Nate rattled on, unaware of the wraith-like something that had scurried ahead of them—at least that was the impression in her head. Whatever it was had followed them from the ship to the cab stand.

A solitary hansom waited at the cab stand—lucky break at this time of the night. London Docks were busy around the clock, but cabs were often a scarcity in the small hours. Ned opened the door of the hansom and placed her bag inside.

A shiver ran down her spine just before she turned to

her chief mate and boatswain. "Once you hire the rat catchers, wire me."

A sudden gust of evil wind knocked the chief down. America felt something tug at her innards just before she was lifted into the air and tossed into the coach. Her head hit the side of the cab as the door slammed shut. She hardly had time to blink before they lurched off.

America tore at the sharp icicle fingers that gripped her throat, straining to see her attacker. She focused at the edges of her peripheral vision, just as Phaeton had taught her—where the shadow creatures lurked. It seemed a certainty that her attacker wasn't human. "Let me go!" Her voice was a barely audible croak.

And whatever held onto her had to be stick thin, as the inside of a hansom was a cramped space, and she felt as if she sat alone on the bench. The long, thin claws coiled around her neck and turned her scream into a rasp.

She was being abducted—but why?

America shook her head and the claws clenched, cutting off her wind again. Panicked for air, she yanked at the vice-like fingers with both hands. "What do you want?" she choked. "I have money, and I can get more—just tell me what you want."

From the corner of her eye, she could just make out a bulbous oval-shaped head and two very small, pale gray eyes that swiveled about oddly.

"I 'ave mince pies for eyes, but no name. No need—got a dickie from the lath-n-plaster who tinkered me, and many more like Skeezicks."

A monster who dropped his *h*'s and spoke in rhyming slang. America raised both brows. "From the East End, are you?"

"Stop yer gob miss and give me no troubles."

America swallowed, not an easy task with claws wrapped around your neck. Once again she tried to loosen the creature's hold. "I'm not sure what sort of creature you are—but humans need to breathe in order to live—you *do* want me alive don't you? There could hardly be any point to an abduction if you just wanted to suffocate me."

She was beginning to wonder how clever this odd, skeletal

creature was and thought to put it to the test. "Tell me . . . Mister . . . Skeezicks, this wouldn't have anything to do with Mr. Black would it?" She continued to wrench and squirm away.

"Skeezicks wouldn't know, we 'ave our directives—" The creature halted mid-sentence. The carriage had stopped. Bit by bit, icicle fingers released her neck. Feet first, her abductor was swept up through the trapdoor in the ceiling. Something above pulled the rail-thin frame through the hole in the roof, all except for the bulbous head which got stuck and rasped out a warning. "Keep yer shoes on."

Whatever that meant. America wasted no time deciphering the creature's speech, and tried lifting the latch of the cab door. Stuck or jammed or purposely blocked. Up above, the scratches and snarls of squalling alley cats caused the cab to rattle and shake. The hansom door flew open but before she could step out, it slammed in her face. What in heaven's name was going on out there? Again the door flew open and she grabbed her travel bag and jumped out.

Locked in combat, a blur of gray shapes rolled about on the cab roof, growling and snarling. The driver was nowhere to be seen. She was sure the smaller faster shape was Edvar. The valiant little scamp was fighting that nasty Skeezick creature.

Edvar leaped away with a high-pitched yelp as the horrid creature crept after the gargoyle. America narrowed her eyes and recited an ages-old incantation of her mother's. The Helping Hand—something one could never invoke for oneself but could use in the aid of another. As she conjured, something warm moved from her heart to her palm. A phosphorescent ball of energy swirled to life and grew to the size of a melon. Mentally, she gave the energy a push and it flew to the top of the cab. The glob of relic dust and champagne sprouted fingers and slapped the skeletal menace repeatedly—away from Edvar.

The entity cringed at the edge of the cab roof. Beady Skeezick eyes swiveled from the gargoyle to her. With a harsh shriek, their attacker dissolved into small particles and slithered off into the night.

America shook her head. "What was that?"

Edvar licked a few scratches, looking more like a cat than a gargoyle. An eerie chorus of clicking noises echoed along the quay. Her gray protector wrapped a slithery tail around himself and hissed.

She peered into the darkness. "He's coming back—with more."

Edvar sprang from the roof to the driver's seat at the back of the hansom. The gray imp gathered up the reins and motioned her back inside.

She hesitated, then climbed into the cab and opened the trapdoor. Looking up at the little demon she raised both brows. "You're sure you can do this?"

Chapter Four

A DIM GASLIGHT SPUTTERED ABOVE THE STAIR LANDING. America steadied herself and waited for her eyes to adjust to the darkness below. The hansom ride from the Docklands to the West End had been one of the most harrowing in her life, with the possible exception of a ride in a rickshaw pulled by a Zulu in Durban, South Africa.

She squinted and a few details emerged from the flat below, including a shadowy figure in the overstuffed chair. A soft snore rumbled its way up the stair—it was Phaeton, all right. She ventured farther into the room for a better look.

He lounged in the chair with his pelvis forward, legs spread. America angled her head, studying him. There was a rough of whiskers on his chin; could he look any more dashing? She exhaled a sigh. Only if he opened those liquid brown eyes.

"A little lower, darling." He mumbled, still asleep. It suddenly hit her. He was safe. He was healthy. The bilge rat.

"Darling, is it?" she whispered. Her gaze trailed down his open waistcoat to the buttons on his trousers. As if in answer to her own lascivious thoughts, the buttons began to open.

She grinned at first—was this some new kind of power emerging? Something ancient and primal fueled by lust? She had noticed a marked increase in her abilities these last few months; there was no question they were getting stronger. She reached out and her hand was slapped away—by what she had no idea. She tried again to reach out and was flung across the flat onto the lumpy old chaise longue.

America sat up and stared. Something tugged at Phaeton's trousers—something powerful enough to manipulate the physical world and yet remain unseen. Rising to her feet, she strode across the floor and slapped Phaeton hard across the face.

He groaned, still in a deep trance. "Just the tip, Georgiana."

She slapped him again. "Snap out of it!"

Jarred awake, Phaeton pushed away from her and blinked— several times. She slapped him again. This time he rubbed his jaw and his eyes watered. "America?" Gradually, between squints and blinks, he came around.

Her fists landed on her hips. "Who is Georgiana?"

Phaeton eased back into his chair, though he regarded her with some wariness. "A rather persistent succubus. And you certainly aren't one of those—thank God." If it was possible for a man to have sultry eyes, Phaeton had them. Dark lashes lowered over liquid coffee orbs, that weren't sleepy—just seductive. He tilted his chin and studied her. "Though, I must admit the nasty little vixen has me in some discomfort—would you mind?" He gave a nod to the bulge in his trousers.

"Stuff it, Phaeton."

"Exactly." A slow grin twitched on the devilish mouth. "I'm just asking."

"Goodness, how long has it been?" America rolled her eyes upward, calculating. "Separated for less than two months and already I'd quite forgotten how exasperating you can be."

"You followed me—rather sweet of you. I wasn't sure you would. I thought you would think I jumped ship and sailed off—abandoned you."

America's eyes narrowed into cat slits. "According to your wire, which I received just yesterday, you were shanghaied— in Shanghai."

Phaeton shrugged. "Old joke, not particularly amusing anymore."

She stared at him. "You must trust me when I say that it was never comical—in the least." America shook her head and moved to the pantry area of the flat. She braced herself against the table edge. "I chased you halfway round the world, Phaeton. I want the truth this time, and not a crafty as-you-please answer." She swept an errant curl back into her topknot. "I believe I've known eels less slippery."

Phaeton wore that cajoling half smile. "You're angry with me."

"Mad at you? No Phaeton, I'm not angry with you. I'm . . . I'm furious." America choked on her own words—or was it the painful and growing lump in her throat that stifled her breath? "I searched for you in every opium den and every back alley of Shanghai. Only after a great deal of money changed hands was I able to find out you'd cut and run—aboard the *Boomerang*. Do you have any idea how I worried?"

"I've caused you great torment, but I swear to you none of it was my doing. Yes, I was on that ship—in leg irons for more than half the voyage. I was cracked over the head in Blood Alley, stuffed in a sack, and taken aboard ship." She must have appeared unmoved as his eyes fluttered and rolled a bit. "Turns out the captain was a regular chap, with a good supply of whiskey—nightly card play."

America shook her head. "How lovely for you. I don't suppose there was any chance to escape—or any way to get word to me?"

"But I did get word to you, darling—my love." Phaeton appeared rather stricken.

The tears that had welled up began to stream. "And while we were separated, did you . . . think of me?"

Phaeton rose from the chair. "Every minute." He strode toward her slowly. "Of every hour." He caught her up in his arms. "Of every bleeding day." His gaze fell to her mouth, and her lips parted. Good God, what a hussy—she was sending him an invitation.

"Have I ever told you I love you—outside of the throes of passion?"

America shook her head.

"I love you."

"Too late, we're in the throes of passion." America pressed her hands to his chest, but he held on—drawing her lower body against the hardness of him. "The duke appears happy to see me," she sniffed.

He rubbed gently. "So much so, he asks for a private audience—something quick right here on the table," Phaeton crooned, gathering her skirt with one hand. "After two months at sea, this won't take but a minute, I promise." He nuzzled her cheek and kissed the place below her ear that made her tingle. Still.

Phaeton lifted her skirts higher. "And if I promise to place my finger on your little pink pearl?"

America slanted her eyes. "And?"

The sly grin was back. "And . . . if my finger strokes and circles round and round?" Excitement bubbled in her as his hand went between her legs. His fingers played lightly over the slit in her drawers—teasing her—making her want more. When his hands brushed the inside of her legs she opened her stance.

His blistering gaze moved to her lips, but he did not kiss her. "Don't cry, America." His mouth was nearly upon hers. "Punish me." Slowly, he moved his lips to her cheeks, and kissed a tear away. Then another. And another . . .

His finger moved past the slit in her pantalettes and sensation fluttered through her body as moist folds flooded with arousal. More than anything right now she needed that great cock and those magic fingers of his that swirled and teased. She opened her eyes and met his deep brown gaze. "You may enter—but you may not withdraw until I say."

Easing her back onto the table, Phaeton slipped both hands under her skirt and brought her buttocks to the edge. She uncovered his manly cock, which sprang to life and twitched impatiently. He spread her legs and pressed into her with a groan of pleasure. His eyes closed briefly. "Good God, how I missed this heavenly sheath."

"Stop." She murmured, then used her hips to circle, taking his prick with her. She flexed the walls of her passage and knew he ached to thrust in and out, but she shook her head.

Phaeton reached for her small, slick pink nub. He circled slowly, pausing to tap lightly, sending spikes of arousal through her. "Now may I withdraw?"

America's eyes narrowed. "The tip must stay inside me."

His eyes nearly rolled back in his head and his breathing was harsh, but he withdrew—all but that beautifully shaped head. Hard muscular thighs pressed against hers, opening her wider— shuddering with his own pent-up desire.

She unbuttoned her jacket and blouse. Arching her back, she pulled the ribbon on the edge of her camisole. "You may look, but you must not kiss them—yet." All his eyes had to do was widen slightly—and her nipples hardened. He kept a finger on her growing pleasure spot and massaged—circling over and around.

"You're so wet for me," he murmured, "You must have missed me—just a little."

Her gaze remained steady with his. "So much more than just a little."

She wanted him to go faster, harder—but she resisted the command. She wanted so much more . . . writhing . . . before her climax came in shuddering waves. It was his own fault. Phaeton had taught her how to prolong her pleasure.

"You may kiss them now." She met his hungry gaze as he leaned over her breasts and licked. He circled a nipple gently— and when it was hard and tight, he took the whole of her areola into his mouth and suckled with a kind of animal ferocity. Her body trembled with arousal. "I need to be inside you, America." He gasped.

"Slowly then—and stop when I say so." He eased his cock in slow. Inch by inch, until she growled and lifted her pelvis. Only then did he plunge deep inside her. "He kissed and nipped the flesh of her body as he pulled her farther to the edge—enough so he could do something very naughty. Phaeton wet a finger and worked it around the tight little sphincter muscle—coaxing it to relax.

"Come for me, America." With one finger on her clit and the other on her anus, he pushed into her deep—still unhurried, a measured thrust that made her rise up to meet him, to answer his motion as her pleasure climbed.

"Deeper," she ordered. And he disobeyed. He rubbed her with the crown of his cock—the place inside her sheath that loved to be rubbed. The place they had discovered together one balmy night in paradise.

"Harder," she moaned. And still he defied her. His finger slipped into her anus and pleasure ripped through her body.

"Faster," she begged, on the edge of climax. And finally, he complied, pumping his cock into her. His velvet shaft—thrusting deep as his fingers worked every orifice, every sensitive spot—filling her up until her entire body peaked with ecstasy.

The room blurred as reality fell away. He held her at the precipice of pleasure for an eternal moment, until she could stand it no longer. Her body bucked and shuddered as he took her over the edge.

Phaeton, as well, bellowed like a bull in an explosive rush of gasps and groans. She felt the intensity of his climax, as if it were her own—which it was. Lost in bliss, America drifted back to earth with a sigh. Still breathless, she pushed herself up on her elbows and stared at him. "You're so . . ."—she chewed her lower lip—"good at that."

Phaeton smiled down at her. "Hard to stay mad at me, isn't it?"

Tucked into a favorite corner of the Cheshire Cheese, America sliced into a thick lamb chop. "Why would someone shanghai you, Phaeton? For what possible reason?"

Phaeton leaned back in his chair. "Oh, I don't know—I can trim a bit o'sail."

A smile formed as she chewed. "I admit you push the tiller hard."

"Made you come about, quick enough." He took a pull of his pint. "It would seem a mysterious someone wants me back here in London. Badly." The crowded pub was familiar, even comforting, yet his gaze darted about the smoke-filled room somewhat warily.

America thought about his words. "A horrid creature attacked me tonight, on my way to the flat."

He stabbed at a slice of chop. "What kind of horrid creature?"

"Bulbous head, beady gray eyes, skeletal frame—moves about in a sort of mist of particles—quick-like." As America related the tale of her near abduction, a third entity perched itself on a stool nearby. She glanced at the yellow-orange eyes that blinked at Phaeton. "Edvar fought him off and drove me here—quite a thrilling cab ride."

He winked at the gargoyle. "When I was a lad, he rescued me from a nasty goblin or two."

"What is going on, Phaeton? Something doesn't feel right." She set her knife and fork on the plate. "There's a malingering— I don't know what to call it."

"Foreboding in the air?" Phaeton's grin turned thin and rather strained.

America nodded.

Phaeton tipped his chair forward and sat upright. "Exeter."

America blinked. "What about the doctor?"

"Esmeralda seemed worried this morning—says he's not himself. I told her I'd pop in on him. Care to join?"

Chapter Five

THE GENTLE FLICKER OF GASLIGHT ON HALF MOON STREET waxed and waned an unnatural luminescence. Phaeton squinted out the window of the hansom. "Sense a bit of malingering miasma?" He turned back to America.

Her bright eyes grew wider. "There is a definite disturbance in the atmosphere."

He opened the trapdoor in the roof. "This is far enough." He handed several coins up to the driver. "Wait for us here."

He grabbed America by the hand and proceeded down the quiet, mostly residential lane. Nearly all of the unsettling aether appeared to emanate from Doctor Exeter's stately Georgian townhouse.

A layer of ephemeral whispers echoed through the air. The auditory disturbance swirled around Phaeton. Something akin to the hiss of a steam vent mixed with a peculiar effervescent clicking noise—much like the sound of a thousand pairs of scissors all snipping at once.

The signals strengthened with each step. He paused to focus his attention on the front of the residence. Like an ocean tide in moonlight, the facade glimmered with pinpricks of light. Cautiously, he moved closer.

"Look Phaeton, there—in the shadows on the wall." America pointed to the dark side of the residence. He could just make out a number of small metallic objects moving over the facade of the house. Craning his neck to take a better look, his mouth fell open. He stepped off the curb and into the lane for a better view. Thousands of rat-sized devils swarmed up the edifice of the manse. Phaeton squinted. More like spiders, actually. No, they were rats, with long spindly legs.

Each metallic, multi-legged minion cast a strange glow from under its belly, as if each creature's shadow illuminated the way. The pale lights shifted, making the legion of crawling objects appear to undulate. Like foam in an ocean wave, the creatures washed over the residence. He experienced a fleeting sense that the drone-like horde was being directed by something, either by light or sound frequency. The unnatural fizzing chirps from the pests quickly grew annoying. Phaeton plugged his ears with his fingers. "Better."

America covered her ears and nodded her agreement.

The large palladium windows on the second floor of Exeter's townhouse crawled with hundreds of metal rodents. The glazing buckled as one by one each small pane of glass shattered in rapid succession. A salvo of glass slivers flew through the air.

Phaeton ducked under a neighboring portico and slipped America behind him. A knife-shaped fragment of flying glass landed inches from his feet. From the shelter of the covered entry they watched a few nasty scavengers break from the mob and rush inside the residence. If memory served, those large windows illuminated the doctor's laboratory.

Something caught his eye. He detected movement—high up on the roof. The tall dark specter of Doctor Exeter. Phaeton felt a tinge of relief. If circumstances weren't so grim, he would have hailed the doctor with a shout and a wave. Exeter moved with stealthy precision across his own rooftop. Running from or battling back the swarming minions?

No time to waste, he turned to America. She narrowed her eyes. "You're going up there, aren't you?"

Phaeton stepped out into the street, and swiveled back. "Stay put, darling—I shan't be long." Shards of broken glass crunched underfoot as he took a step back and leaped into the air. He landed beside a chimney stack not far from the doctor who had taken up a piece of drainpipe in an admirable but futile attempt to beat off the approaching hordes. With a rather impressive swing he whacked one of mechanical beasts off the roof. "Creeping, low-life, anthropoid devil."

"Esmeralda misjudged. Said you'd be overjoyed to see me."

Exeter whirled around, a spark of recognition in his eyes.

Phaeton leaned against the brick chimney and grinned. "A bit large for rodents—even the Underground variety. Have you sent for a rat catcher?"

Exeter broke off another piece of pipe and handed over a length. Phaeton took aim at a column of creatures crawling up the slate shingles. He held one of the buggers down with his foot and swung the pipe like a croquet mallet, sending a row of them sailing off the roof.

Exeter stepped up beside him. "Good to see you, Phaeton."

He swung at a few more. "If you don't mind me asking, what are we involved with here?"

"Hordes of mechanized rodent-like spiders."

Phaeton lowered his bat. "I'm not blind. Something of your own invention gone rogue, or is this rabble dangerous?"

At the edge of a steep incline, one of the multi-legged creatures sprang into the air. "Careful, they can jump."

Phaeton jerked upright. "Clever of them."

A hundred more crested the rooftop. Exeter sent a swathe of potent energy across the roof and cleared the lot of them. "Relentless might be the word for them."

The shriek of a police whistle sounded from the street below.

Exeter peered over the roof edge and frowned. "Not sure we need the Westminster Police sticking their nose in this."

Phaeton joined him. "Shall we?"

"Been practicing, Phaeton?"

"A long ocean voyage is conducive to polishing any number of skills, including the manipulation of the physical universe."

They landed in the street behind the officer on duty. The trembling neighborhood patrolman nearly backed into them. The doctor sidestepped the man.

America stepped out from the doorstep. "Phaeton?"

He gestured her over.

Exeter nodded a bow. "Miss Jones, always lovely to see you, no matter the circumstances."

"Doctor Exeter." She bobbed a curtsey. "What are those things?"

"A temporary nuisance—let's see if we can't run them off." Exeter turned to the neighborhood patrolman. "Officer Willis, might I borrow your whistle?"

With his eyes bulging, the bobby nodded blankly. Exeter blithely removed the whistle from his grip and used a pocket square to wipe off the spittle. "Please observe, gentlemen—and gentlewoman."

Exeter blew as though he was playing a musical instrument. "I'm modulating the air pressure using my tongue." Exeter paused between blows. "Some of the commands are no doubt beyond ear range." He struck a barely audible note and all at once, every crawling creature froze in place.

Phaeton grinned. "Though not all, apparently."

"Blimey." The officer scratched his head. "Ye mind me asking sir—"

"Don't ask." Phaeton stepped between the two men. "So, the little bastards are being controlled by sound frequency?"

Exeter nodded. "Radio, perhaps. As Hertz has recently proven, electromagnetic waves produced by a radiating conductor can be transmitted and received at a distance of up to 200 feet."

Phaeton quickly scanned every doorway and niche of the lane. "I'll put my wager on that carriage just past the mews entrance."

The moment they all made for the vehicle, the coach moved off. Exeter and Officer Willis chased after the carriage until they reached the corner. By the time Phaeton and America caught up, nothing on four wheels was in sight. A left turn would lead them to Curzon Street. A right would put them on Bolton Place.

"Bollocks." Phaeton sucked in a breath. Sensing something, he turned along with the other men. They were surrounded by Westminster Police. "About time you blokes showed up."

Officer Willis grumbled. "Have ye seen the creatures crawling all over the doctor's house?"

"Been drinking again, Willis?" The bobby shook his head. "All's we've seen is a number of busted-out windows. The street's a right shambles—broken glass and all. We'll have to cordon off the block—call out the street sweepers, first light."

"My laboratory." Exeter started back. Phaeton and America jogged alongside the doctor. When they reached the house, they stopped short. Not a single iridescent creature crawled about the premises. Except for the broken windows, the residence was back to its old self again. Quiet, peaceful, exactly how this posh street of exclusive clubs and stately homes should appear in the wee morning hours.

Phaeton noted Exeter's furrowed brow and thin-set lips. "What do you make of all this?"

"Whoever or whatever was behind this attack used a strange combination of science and pseudoscience—likely some form of potent energy."

"Relic dust and champagne. In-between matter. Potent energy." Phaeton checked a few window boxes for laggards. "One of these days you must school me in the vernacular."

He sniffed around the service entrance and mews before joining Exeter and America upstairs. At the laboratory entrance, Phaeton could only stand and stare. The workspace looked exactly like one would expect a room to look after being ransacked by a swarm of eight-legged rats. He stepped over piles of debris, and picked his way through shards of glass. "Couldn't find a single straggler."

Leafing rapidly through one journal after another, Exeter looked up briefly.

"No permanent damage to your experiments, I hope?"

"I've lost several weeks' work."

Exeter set down his notes. "As I suspected, they used the rat fiends as a diversion. They were after only one thing."

A cold spark of trepidation ran up Phaeton's spine. "What one thing?"

"They've taken what is perhaps the most powerful and dangerous object in the world. So powerful, in fact, it was hidden away for nearly two thousand years. You of all people should know of what I speak. The object was given to you as a gift by the consort of the great Anubis, God of the Underworld."

"Not the orb?" Phaeton snorted a low throaty laugh. "*That* strange egg?"

A glassy-eyed Exeter appeared to be enthralled by the very thought of the odd globe. "Long ago, your gift was known by another name. It was hidden deep inside a Greek *pithos* and guarded by all the evils of the world. When Pandora broke the jar, its powers were released, but for one at the bottom of the vessel."

"Hope." Phaeton blinked. "Of course I know the story."

"And what form might hope take?" A grin edged up the corners of Exeter's mouth. "An egg is the most primal of all containers—a stone the most impenetrable. Fables and myths were often created around ancient objects of power to obscure their purpose."

Exeter braced himself against his worktable. "What Qadesh gifted you with was a massive energy source." Absently, he picked through broken glass beakers. "And now they've taken the stone . . ."

"I dislike the term *they,*" Phaeton complained. "It's not specific enough. Have you an idea who *they* might be?"

Exeter's stare narrowed. "Gaspar Sinclair would be first on my list of suspects."

"Mine as well." Phaeton turned to America. "Are you up for more adventure or shall we drop you at the flat?"

"I'm not tired in the least." America checked the watch pinned to the waistcoat of her dress. "In fact, I'm more than curious as to what is taking place here in London. Correct me if I'm wrong, doctor, but there appears to be an assortment of horrid creatures about." An unexpected smile brightened her face. "And I should like to call on Julian Ping—if he's about."

Exeter raised a brow and Phaeton stared at her. "Ping told you about Gaspar?"

"Mr. Ping and I got on very well, the night you and the doctor were off at the British Museum after the jackal-head Anubis."

Phaeton straightened. "Right. Cab's waiting—shall we go get the damn egg?"

Phaeton pulled America onto his lap to make room for the doctor. "Comfortable, darling?" The driver snapped the reins and turned the hansom down Piccadilly, rocking them all side to side. At this rate the trip to Limehouse wouldn't take long.

"Did you tell the driver to avoid Covent Garden?" America asked.

Exeter slipped his finger into a waistcoat pocket and fished out his watch. "It's nearly midnight, there won't be much theater traffic."

"For argument's sake"—Phaeton tilted his head—"mind telling me why it's so important we retain possession of Pandora's . . . whatever?"

"Shall we give it a nineteenth century moniker—say, Phaeton's Orb?" Exeter asked.

He glanced out the window. A drizzle of rain caused the paths along Green Park to glisten under lamplight. "I prefer . . . Moonstone."

"Moonstone." America echoed in a soft faraway voice.

"Rather romantic of you, Phaeton." The doctor grinned.

"Bugger off."

"As long as Miss Jones approves." Exeter chuckled. "Moonstone it is."

America nodded enthusiastically. "Oh yes, it's a lovely name."

Phaeton turned to the man sitting beside him on the bench. "You haven't answered my question."

"The Moonstone's exact powers remain a mystery, and very much in demand it would seem." Exeter shrugged. "Tell me, what brought you to London so suddenly?"

Exeter had neatly evaded his question. Again. "Did I just fall down a rabbit hole?" Exasperation flooded through Phaeton. He clenched his teeth to control his temper. "I was shanghaied in . . ."—he rolled his eyes and exhaled— "in Shanghai." The joke had definitely lost its luster. "Abducted might be a more accurate description. At any rate, the crew

seemed eager enough to get me back to London and collect
their ransom."

Exeter's inquiring gaze moved to America. "I was able to
track his ship back to London."

"She arrived just hours after me—quite a crafty bit of sea-
manship."

Phaeton exhaled. He may indeed have been taken against his
will, but he had also abandoned America. The thought gave
him pause as his musings conjured a sultry night in Polynesia.
They had dropped anchor in Cook's Bay and the crew had
gone ashore . . .

America sang a Polynesian tune and danced about the deck.
She had worn a thin cotton nightshift, her body silhouetted by
moonlight. She hadn't known he was watching—not at first. A
panoply of erotic images swept through his mind. He untied a
pale blue ribbon and slipped the nightgown off her shoulder.
His tongue circled the tip of her breast. They had made love in
the widow's net under the bowsprit. Afterward, she had lain in
his arms, her leg curled around his thigh. He remembered the
sound of gentle waves lapped against the hull.

America's jab in the side jolted him back to the present.
"We're here, Phaeton." He dipped his head to look out the cab.
A carriage wheel splashed through a pothole as they entered
Pennyfields. At two in the morning, the party was just getting
started on High Street.

Exeter opened the trapdoor and paid the driver. "Drop us off
near the Silver Lion."

Out on the street, Phaeton inhaled a mélange of pungent
scents, burning opium layered with joss-sticks and tobacco. The
sidewalk bustled with a crush of West Enders diverting themselves in the East End.

The doctor grimaced. "One can always find something
morally reprehensible and unhealthy to do in Pennyfields."

"Do you have an entertainment in mind?" Phaeton lifted a
brow along with a lopsided grin. "Or would you like me to
suggest something?"

America spoke up. "I must say I'm suddenly rather thirsty."

Exeter studied the street scene. "No hurry I suppose. The

world is quite safe for the time being. Whoever has the stone can't do much with it. There is only one person in the entire world who can unlock the powers inside the Moonstone."

A prickly tremor moved through Phaeton's body. His eyes rolled upward in a moment of silent prayer. "And that person would be—please don't say—"

Exeter's smile was radiant. In fact, he had never seen the man look more pleased with himself. "You, Phaeton."

Chapter Six

"SHALL WE HAVE A PINT AT THE SILVER LION?" America noted the look exchanged by Phaeton and Exeter. "Must I remind you, gentlemen, I've hauled crew out of the lowest, scum-ridden sinkholes of humanity?"

Phaeton swept her away from a tottering drunk. "Might be worthwhile to formulate a strategy before we meet with Gaspar." A colorful assortment of soiled doves draped themselves against the doorway of Madame Chaing's, a brothel famous for its exotic whores and accomplished flagellators. A rouged-up doxy gave a wink. "Have a good swish, sir—half a crown."

"Another evening, love." Phaeton steered them down the narrow row. Looking back, America rolled her eyes. Doctor Exeter trailed behind for one last ogle at the imported prostitute. A motley collection of foreign scents and sounds greeted them—two Orientals deep in argument. The acrid stink of lime and ash wafted out of a Chinese laundry. She twitched her nose.

"About this Moonstone legacy . . ." Phaeton wove a path through a crowd of pleasure seekers. "Assure me this is nothing more than a theory of yours, Jason." He shook his head. "I examined the Moonstone extensively—to little or no effect."

Exeter caught up in a few long strides. "Think back, Phaeton, to the day we packed our Egyptian gods into the sarcophagus. I thought Qadesh's message was—"

"Cryptic." Phaeton muttered.

Exeter raised a brow. "She could hardly have been more clear."

Slowed by the ever-present gawkers surrounding the British and Foreign Medicine Shop, they sidestepped their way through the milling onlookers. The strangely respectable storefront was a popular East End freak show. The doctor craned his neck for a look through the murky, multi-paned windows. "The usual apothecary jars stuffed with an assortment of horrors. Nothing new—the two-headed fetus of course," Exeter reported back, "as well as the small dragon excised from the bowels of a sailor."

America waited with Phaeton to one side of the crowd. "I could have sworn it was vice versa, a miniature sailor taken from the innards of a dragon." Amused, Phaeton nodded to the tall gray-haired man in the doorway clad in a loose chinoiserie dressing gown and silk opera hat. The proprietor's name was Magister Swinbourne. The man exuded fakery.

Exeter harrumphed. "Wax figures, suspended in mineral oil." The wily Swinbourne pointed his long stemmed opium pipe at them. "Dare ye to come in and have a look—I did most of these extractions myself."

"Not bloody likely," Exeter scoffed, as Phaeton grabbed hold of the doctor's arm and headed them all down the cobbled lane.

Away from Swinbourne's ghastly shop of horrors, Phaeton confessed. "The last time I looked in that window, I'd had a bit of pipe. All those specimens opened their eyes and began to speak."

America shuddered at the thought. Her overactive imagination made a sudden inexplicable shift to the pea in the pod. She experienced a fleeting vision of Phaeton in conversation with the unborn child. Phaeton was intuitive in the extreme, he would sense the life inside her. She squeezed his arm to steady herself.

"Here we are." Phaeton hesitated at the entry to the pub. "All right, love?"

America nodded. "Nothing a bit of refreshment can't cure." She wondered, frankly, how long she would be able to keep the child from . . . talking . . . so to speak. Or better yet, how she might break the news to him.

A favorite of sailors and dockworkers alike, the Silver Lion was as much a casino as a public house, featuring a variety of entertainments that could make a Portuguese sailor blush. For years America had half listened to a string of colorful stories told about the pub, and she was rather curious. It appeared the proprietors had converted the private dining rooms into a gambling hall, with a small space adjoining known as Cat's Meat Shop.

Phaeton gave a nod to the backroom. "Peep shows, two a penny, featuring photographs of a depraved and indecent character." He pulled out a chair for her. "Leastwise that was what the arresting officer reported to the Manchester Guardian the last time the shop was raided." Phaeton leaned close and whispered, "Nothing you and I haven't tried once or twice, darling."

A shiver curved down her neck and spine. Suddenly it was as if they were alone in the casino. Her whole body, every nerve ending, tingled. She sensed his arousal spark to life. This mutual excitation they experienced had always been mystifying. It was as if they each felt the other's pleasure as their own.

"What'll it be?" Exeter cleared his throat and waited.

Phaeton broke the spell. "A pint for me."

"Ginger ale," she breathed, her words barely loud enough to hear.

The doctor went off to procure their drinks, and Phaeton settled in to watch two young women dance on mirrored tabletops. The clatter of coins on the looking glass encouraged the dancers' skirts to rise ever higher.

"Seems like a great deal of money to get a peek at a girl's quim," America huffed.

"Actually, my dove, it's more of a disappearing act." Just as Phaeton spoke, a well dressed West Ender positioned a bottle right side up beneath the dancer. America tried to keep the blush away but heat flooded her cheeks.

Phaeton stretched his legs out and scanned the smoke-filled room. "Something isn't right." He nodded to a darkened corner and shifted his line of sight. He was concentrating on his peripheral vision—exactly as he had taught her to do on board the *Topaz*.

America concentrated as well, and a figure emerged from the

shadows. A hooded entity stood like a sentry. Might there be more? She thought so, but couldn't be sure. Human life forms, at least partially so, but what were they waiting for?

The clink of whiskey glasses returned her attention to the table. Exeter set down a bottle and two pints. "I sense four of them," the doctor warned. "Two more, possibly, in the back." He nodded to the gaming room behind their table. He uncorked the ginger ale and poured a glass.

"I find it oddly comforting that you see them as well, doctor." America drank thirstily.

Exeter grinned. "So, you've both been practicing?"

Phaeton sipped his bitters. "My life has been idyllically unadventurous these last few months, leastwise with regard to the extramundane."

Scanning the corners again, America caught a flicker of light—a glint in the shadows. A familiar feeling licked up her spine and unsettled her stomach. Terror. Phaeton had lived with these kinds of apparitions since he was a child. Growing up, he'd faced down any number of wily phantoms and snarling trolls. She marveled at his composure, as even now he paid little heed to the hooded figures lurking in the corners.

"They know that we know." Phaeton flicked an eye roll toward a corner.

Exeter studied him for a moment. "Well then, shall we let the scenario play out?" The doctor angled his chair so that they could each cover two corners and the entrance.

Two pints and four shots later, Phaeton appeared well on his way to a state of blissful intoxication. America turned to Exeter. "We both sense . . . a different energy about in the city. Perhaps you might bring us up to date?"

"Since you've been gone, there have been . . . disturbances." The doctor leaned across the table. "Attacks by strange entities, as well as missing persons—abductions perhaps—are popping up all over London. According to reports in the *Weekly Dispatch* and the *Guardian,* packs of strange, ungodly creatures roam the streets at night." Exeter referred to newspapers popular with the lower classes. The papers often published wildly speculative stories, which included grisly reports of violence written in lurid detail. The doctor drained the last of his pint. "The entire East End is in a hysteria over it."

Indeed, even here in the Silver Lion things were slightly askew. She sensed a giddy sort of madness among dancers and patrons alike. The laughs were louder, the women wilder—and though she couldn't be sure, even the whiskey appeared more intoxicating. But perhaps the strangest counterpoint to all this heightened merrymaking was the pall that hung heavy in the air, as thick as a black fog.

Exeter related a few of the yellow press reports which included skeletal-like creatures sighted rummaging in dustbins, and various other unspeakable abominations carrying off living beings wrapped in rags—like mummies in the British Museum.

America's eyes widened. "The Skeezick."

Phaeton and Exeter both rocked their chairs forward. "The what?"

That horrid creature I told you about—the one that attacked me in the hansom. He called himself Skeezick." Nervously, America moistened her lips. "Skeletal body, bulbous, nearly hairless, head with beady gray eyes that . . ." America twirled her index fingers in opposite directions.

Phaeton drained his glass. "One eye is on London while the other is winking at Paris?"

Exeter grinned. "The medical term is *extropia*."

America sighed. "The thing implied there are many more like him."

The doctor spoke in a low tone as he scanned the room. "I don't believe the city has ever experienced a metaphysical assault of this magnitude, at least in recent history."

Phaeton rubbed the stubble of new beard on his chin. "I'm sensing something older. Who might have recorded such things in the ancient past?"

Exeter poured another dram. "We might consult the runes of druids."

Absently, America turned the base of her empty glass and stole another glance at the wickedly provocative table dancers. She experienced a touch of vertigo as both young women widened their stance and flung their arms out to their sides.

Phaeton sat up straight. "Is it my state of inebriety, or is the room moving?"

Exeter, as well, readied himself for what none of them could fathom—yet.

Yes, she was quite sure of it. The room expanded and contracted, as though it was trying to breathe or collapse. An eerie cacophony of moans and whispers blew open the doors like gale winds, and swept through the pub. Terrified patrons fled or hid under tables. A chorus of hisses hovered just outside in the street. The rustle of leaves, or the rattle of serpents?

"Shall we retreat now, rather than later?" Exeter stood and backed away from the table. Phaeton reached for her hand. The doctor nodded toward the entrance. "Harpies?"

Phaeton shook his head. "More like . . . snakes. Fiver it's a Gorgon."

Exeter checked the gaming room behind them. "Place a wager with the house, perhaps?" They all fell back into the gambler's den where they found a reasonably defensive position and waited. Phaeton's arm went around her waist. Calming, even though the quiet meant the storm was surely coming.

A second blast of whispers and shrieks swept drinks off tables and rocked a few stragglers out of their chairs. Phaeton lunged forward to rescue a rolling whiskey bottle.

Amid fearful shrieks and a jostle of retreating customers, balls of light—a swarm of them—flew through the pub's doors and into the hall. As the hovering globes traveled farther inside, the orbs appeared to grow tentacles. The elongated, rope-like snakes crawled over and under tables, stopping now and then to examine a bleary-eyed rummy.

Mesmerized, America observed a number of delicate filaments—feelers of sorts, stretched out from the ends of each serpentine appendage. The slightest twitch from the slender threads caused a vibration in the air already crackling with the aether of the supernatural.

Phaeton took a last swig and tossed the empty bottle.

A worm-like tentacle slithered across a *vingt-et-un* table, stretching its antennae in Phaeton's direction. The closer the appendage came, the farther he withdrew.

Fay-ton.

America distinctly heard Qadesh speak. *Fay-ton you have returned my husband to me.* She recalled a strangely beautiful goddess with blood red lips and kohl black eyes. The troublesome goddess had wreaked havoc all over London before Phaeton and Exeter had restored Anubis and reunited the love-starved couple. Yes, she was quite sure the voice was the Egyptian consort of Anubis. But that was impossible. All this had happened months ago. Phaeton and Doctor Exeter had seen the two powerful gods safely ensconced in their roomy stone sarcophagus for an eternity. The coffin had been buried under the sands outside Alexandria. Phaeton had seen to the services, personally.

"Do you hear her?" America whispered.

Both Phaeton and Exeter nodded.

What was this strange voice of Qadesh that they all heard in their head? *I leave you a gift, Fay-ton. Entrust its power only to those who would never abuse it.*

An orb of pulsating light floated into the gambling hall. Like shadows on the moon, shapes formed inside the globe—the face of the Gorgon. Beautiful—but for the eyes, which had been cruelly sewn shut. The freshly stitched eyelids dripped red stains over pale cheeks.

Instinctively, Phaeton pushed her behind him. "I don't wish to alarm, but she's headed our way."

The she-devil's pale lips opened and she gasped for breath, as if she was being born into the world.

"Don't let her get too close. These vicious females have sharp fangs and the tentacles may be venomous." Exeter kept his voice low. "Gorgons predate the written myths of Greece; they are the protectors of the most arcane rituals and secrets."

"Exactly what's needed at a moment like this—a refresher course in ancient mythology." Phaeton picked up a chair and pointed its legs out at the creature. "Stay where you are," he ordered, distancing himself from her and the doctor. He skirted the room, taking refuge behind a tipped-over table. The luminous sphere tracked with him. Phaeton winked in their direction. "She wants me."

The Gorgon spoke. "Those who have stolen that which you

call Moonstone will now seek its protector." More glowing orbs joined their sister. Maidenly heads marred by unseeing eyes encircled Phaeton.

He lowered the chair. "Surely, you can't mean me?"

There was something smug about the way Exeter lifted a brow. "As previously discussed, you're the stone's appointed guardian."

"More than a protector—Phaeton is the spark," the Medusa hissed softly. "The power of the pithos must be returned, or this world will end. Gods and myths exist because—" The beautiful grotesque visage sighed.

"Because humans exist." Phaeton swept back his frock coat, resting his hands on his hips. "Tragic indeed. If we go who will be left for the gods to rule over?"

Tentacles slashed about the globe. "We do not rule—we serve."

A wistful smile tugged at Phaeton's mouth. "Exactly how Victoria puts it."

The beautiful, tortured faces paled as the spheres grew more luminous and withdrew. Phaeton launched himself out of the gaming annex and into the public room. "Hold on—might there be a clue? A suspect, perhaps? A suspicious troll in the Underground?" The orbs whirled up into the air before he finished his query.

Cautiously, America and the doctor joined Phaeton, scanning the untidy room for signs of life. The shadow figures in the corners appeared to be on the move. Pivoting in place, she could plainly see the sharp edge of four swords. The blades glowed just before they discharged a swathe of potent energy. Nothing overly destructive—more like a warning. The hooded sentries emerged from their respective corners, each directing a pale blue ribbon of light at the retreating Gorgons.

The faceless, hooded monks appeared to use just enough energy to put the press on the snake-headed goddesses. The globes withdrew from the room, and presumably, back to wherever Gorgons come from.

The cloaked figures sheathed their weapons. The largest sentry crushed a piece of furniture underfoot and kicked it out of the way as it approached Phaeton. The hood hung low over the face, hiding its eyes. She could just make out a strong mouth and chin—chiseled with a bit of stubble. A whisper of smoke curled away from the glowing ash of a cigar. Male, certainly, but she suspected this entity wasn't entirely human. There was a faint metallic scent—she sniffed again just to make sure. Rusted iron, the smell of blood mixed with something from the bestial realms.

The hooded stranger clenched the butt end of the cigar between his teeth. "I don't believe we've met, Mr. Black. Captain Jersey Blood, at your service."

Chapter Seven

"CAPTAIN BLOOD." Phaeton sized up the man under the cloak. Slightly taller and a bit more brawn, but he could take him in a fight, he was sure of it. "Out of your regimentals this evening, or is your rank self-styled?"

A sardonic grin released another wisp of smoke. "A visitation from Gorgons will draw Reapers or Grubbers—you must leave this place."

Phaeton cocked an ear. "Reapers and what—?"

"Scavengers. Outremer dregs." The captain quite deliberately gave America an up and down look. When his gaze moved over her again, Phaeton blocked the man's view.

During introductions, the captain's cohorts had closed in, surrounding them. Another large male stood between two smaller framed sentries—females, he was sure of it. A series of rhythmic, low-pitched whirs and clicks emanated from the shadows of the sentry's hood. Phaeton tilted his head to see better. The man wore some kind of mechanical apparatus that wound around his throat and over one side of his face.

Phaeton motioned Exeter to close ranks, and a lithe and lovely arm slipped out from the cloaking garment to escort the doctor. Exeter nodded toward the brute of a claymore the self-styled leader held in his hand. "Impressive swords, as well as your cadre."

The captain spoke again in a husky whisper. "Follow us."

Phaeton swept a loose bottle off the floor. He used his shirt sleeve to wipe off the lip, and knocked back a shot. "Why?"

The man named Blood stopped and turned. Eyes Phaeton could feel but couldn't see studied him. Then Exeter. Then America. He felt a tentative probe into his thoughts. "We will see you safely to Pennyfields."

This strange band of monks obviously fancied themselves protectors. The captain nodded to a side exit.

Phaeton narrowed his gaze. "You first."

Outside the Silver Lion they found themselves in a blind court full of hysterical pub crawlers. The piercing shriek of police whistles could be heard as far away as Commercial Road. One could only assume, after a disturbance of this magnitude, the Metropolitan police were about to converge on High Street.

Capes flew up into the air and formed a cloaking veil that hovered above and around them. The atmosphere under the canopy stifled, but he could see clearly in all directions. America's exotic golden-green eyes sparkled with adventure. Phaeton curled his hand around hers and she returned his wink with a smile.

Captain Blood removed his cigar and placed a finger over his lips. "We move out fast and quiet." As they made their way through Wapping Basin, the only sound to be heard was a faint wheeze in the air and a whir of clockworks. Phaeton checked on Exeter and finally got a good look at their two female escorts. One was ivory skinned, raven-haired, and stunning. The other was tall and Nordic—a Viking beauty with ice blue eyes. He also caught a better look at their rear guard. Wheels turned within wheels—just above the man's ear—the mask appeared to be a mechanical engine of some sort.

They turned onto a forgotten row known to opium eaters as Dragon Alley. No names, no numbers—just a riot of differently colored doors, with one exception. The lane ended at a black door with brass numbers mounted at eye level.

They were about to arrive at No. 55 Pennyfields.

Exactly the spot he, Exeter, and America had set out for earlier this evening, had they not been waylaid by a pint or two and a few testy Gorgons. Better late than never, he supposed. And if they were going to find the Moonstone, they could not avoid the nefarious Gentleman Shade himself. "Gaspar Sinclair, self-anointed dark underlord of Limehouse," Phaeton muttered under his breath. Besides being the titular head of an arcane flock of psychic talents, the man was connected to every lowlife operator in London. And there were so many reasons to find Gaspar irritating. The man's jocular familiarity and excessive curiosity about Phaeton's business, for one thing. The de facto leader always had a better scheme, a cheaper rate, a less risky approach, a faster route, and exactly the right talent for the job. He also happened to have thousands of contacts who all owed him favors. Whenever Phaeton was around Gaspar he purposely obfuscated and muddled about with the facts of his cases. It was perverse, but pleasurable.

The sweet musky smell of opium was in the air. Phaeton sniffed again. Something else was about in the alley—the miasma was subtle but rather putrid. He noticed the doctor scanning the rooftops as well.

Just ahead, Edvar made a sudden appearance, as he scurried up the crooked lane—more pedestrian walk than alley. The gray imp often materialized when least expected, or as a warning. Edvar shinnied up a gas lamp, and turned back, adding an impatient hiss. The gargoyle was right, of course, that they must seek shelter, and as quickly as possible.

The sooner they were inside 55 Pennyfields, the safer they would be. Phaeton could not shake the feeling that the hordes were coming. He tossed out an adviso—just to see who received his message. *Watch the gargoyle.* Now and then, Edvar would stop to sniff about and whine. At a turn in the lane, a commotion could be heard at the dark end of a connecting yard. Picking up the pace, the captain glanced back at them. "We're almost there—stay close."

Edvar climbed a downspout and brilliant, orange-yellow eyes blinked into a veil of darkness. From the hollow echoes and terrible thuds, it sounded like a number of dustbins were being rummaged in—perhaps even turned upside down and rolled about.

America turned to him. "What is that?"

Something like the whistle of a whip moved through the air, easily piercing the cloak and wrapping itself around America's ankles. Phaeton grabbed for the slippery bindings that flipped her upside down and into the air. America reached back for him. "Phaeton!"

She was being carried away by a hulking shadow. An unseen puppet-master who walked along on the rooftops above. Her dress fell around her waist, exposing a great deal of leg and pantalettes.

"A bit of relic dust and champagne, if you will?" Phaeton yelled as he sprang ahead of the monkish minions. He had not gotten a very good look at this new enemy, but suffice to say it was large and dark, and it was dragging America back toward those nasty dustbins . . .

"Would somebody please get me down from here!" America dangled precariously above head and was picking up speed.

Phaeton jogged beneath her. Glancing back he could see the cloaking device was gone and all four swords were upright and glowing. A blast of energy shaped like a comet flew past him and up into the air. The bolt of energy slashed the ties that bound her.

America cried out as she fell through the air. Phaeton used a bit of potent energy to break her fall and land her softly in his arms. Phaeton smiled. "Hello, love."

She opened her eyes and exhaled a sigh of relief, before her brows crashed together. "Why are they picking on me, Phaeton?"

He knew the answer, but didn't share it.

"This way—quickly." With weapons trained on rooflines, their protectors swept them down the alley into a small brick-paved yard. Phaeton set America down and spun around, searching for the unseen devil that had tried to abduct her.

They stood in the small court outside 55 Pennyfields and waited for someone to open the black door with the brass numbers. The hooded male with half a machine for a face pounded on the door. They were surrounded by buildings with few windows—just a myriad of colored doors. He steadied America while she straightened petticoats and skirts.

The enclosed court felt rather desolate this evening. Not a single dragon chaser staggered out of one of the nearby dens.

Nothing but the distant crash and clatter of dustbins echoed up the lane. Phaeton raised a brow. "Earlier you mentioned Reapers and Grubbers?"

"Those are Grubbers," the cigar-chomping captain grunted. "They're like dogs. They sniff out energy residue—scraps of fuel in the aether." Silently, Blood used forked fingers to direct his minions, who spread out and formed a protective circle around them.

The shaking and banging about of dustbins grew louder. Phaeton dipped his head for a better look at the large wheezing bloke with the clockwork face. "Might try banging on the bloody door again."

"Please, come in." They whirled around en masse. The black painted door was open and a young man stood in the entry. Exotic silver eyes peered over the rim of spectacles tinted with dark glass.

Phaeton grinned. "Good to see you, Ping."

"A joy to see you, as well." The enigmatic Julian Ping dipped a bow. "And Miss Jones." Ping's faintly Oriental appearance contrasted greatly with his dark frock coat and high-pointed collar. The exotic creature nodded to Exeter. "Doctor."

Jersey Blood pushed past the strange, unearthly young man and ushered them inside. "Quickly." The door slammed shut behind them. Without the aid of moonlight, 55 Pennyfields was darker inside than the alley. Phaeton waited for his eyes to adjust, sensing Ping skirted the edges of the small ante room. If memory served, there was a stair that spiraled downward in the middle of the foyer.

He checked on his lovely companion, whose eyes were large and wide. "I'd give you another smile and a wink," he murmured, "but I've been hellishly cheery all evening."

A small indentation formed on her cheek. She pulled him close and whispered in his ear. "Helps to trim the sails now and then."

He kissed her behind the ear and waited for the tingle to move through her body into him. Phaeton shivered. Yes, there it was. Mechanical spiders, Gorgon visitations, and attempted abductions aside, America had been wonderfully resilient throughout it all. Just having her near tonight was stimulating. He nuzzled her cheek. "Did you know that a lovely translucent blush colors your nipples just before I kiss them?" His whisper brushed the wispy hairs at her temple. "They peak, ever so slightly in antici—"

"Gaspar will see you now." Their pale young greeter stood at the curved brass railing of the stairs. "Make your way downstairs. Seventh door on the left. Please be sure to count. It is dangerous to open any of the others by mistake."

Phaeton had met with the man on several occasions and once attended a soiree of sorts in the upper reception chambers, but he had never been invited into Gaspar's inner sanctum. They descended the stairs and made their way down a long corridor. Between doors, a number of gallery portraits greeted them— Grand Wazirs of the Gentlemen Shades—with eyes that followed a person down the corridor. All of these characters had no doubt fancied themselves powerful sorcerers, going back how many centuries? The end of the corridor featured a near life-size painting of their current leader. "Gaspar Sinclair, fakir of the highest order," Phaeton grumbled.

A chuckle from Exeter drifted up from the rear of the column.

"And what exactly do you find so amusing, doctor?"

"You dislike Gaspar because you're so much like him, Phaeton."

The doctor rarely grinned, so it had an impact. Even the ends of America's mouth twitched upward. "My word this should be interesting."

Their escorts assembled around the seventh door, presumably. Phaeton reached for the knob. "Was that seven doors total—or seven on the left side of the passage?"

The door swung open revealing a spacious room—part library, part gentleman's study. He stepped onto an intricately patterned carpet. Nothing too outlandish about the place. No doubt the most exotic thing in the room was the swarthy, rather handsome man who reclined against the arm of an oversized chair.

A silk robe hung open over a formal tuxedo shirt and his tie was undone. Black trousers and a hint of white braces peeked out from under the deep blue dressing gown. His shirt was open down to the navel and exposed just enough chest hair to be provocative. As annoying as it was, Phaeton admired the man's style. "Sorry to disturb, Gaspar. Did we wrest you away from a liaison? I certainly hope not."

"It's about time you returned home, Phaeton. London hasn't been the same without you." The man's somnolent, heavy-lidded gaze landed on America. "My informants have extolled your looks Miss Jones, but . . ." Gaspar shook his head. *"Vous êtes une grande beauté, mademoiselle."*

A peachy blush colored America's cheeks. *"Merci, monsieur."*

His gaze lingered a little too long before returning to Phaeton. "My congratulations, little brother, she is exquisite."

Phaeton's eyes narrowed. "Just hand over the Moonstone, and you can go back to seducing the Marquess of Bath's wife, or whomever your latest conquest is."

America mouthed, "Little brother?" and she raised a brow to underscore the question.

Phaeton pulled her aside and spoke quietly. "I thought he'd given up the notion. By some deluded faulty thought process he believes we are related." He rolled his eyes in the leader's direction. "Pay him no mind."

A spark of amusement brightened Gaspar's gaze. "Tell me about this Moonstone you believe is in my possession."

"It is the source hidden deep inside the pithos," Exeter offered.

Gaspar's eyes remained steady, unfaltering, almost bored. Exactly the kind of deadpan expression Phaeton expected from the leader of the Gentlemen Shades, whose heart had accelerated at the mere mention of Pandora's jar. This close connection he experienced with Gaspar had always been disquieting—but it certainly wasn't brotherly.

Gaspar blinked, ever so subtly. "Just to be sure—you speak of the quintessence—the substratum that encompasses all things. The indefinite substance to which all things are born and to which all things will return."

"It has been described many ways." Exeter shrugged. "The

quintessence—what Aristotle called the fifth element. The Spirit of God moving upon the face of dark waters." The good doctor nodded his way. "The Moonstone was gifted to Phaeton by an Egyptian goddess. Several months ago, he left the stone in my safekeeping—"

"Not quite so safe, it would appear." Gaspar narrowed his gaze and turned to Phaeton.

"It was taken from Doctor Exeter's laboratory by a horde of spider-legged rodents—man-made is my guess." Phaeton related the evening's events including the Gorgon's message and the hooded sentries behind him. "These—whatever you call them—encouraged the Gorgons to leave and escorted us here."

"The rodents who took the Moonstone were mechanical—radio-controlled locally—but they also disappeared into the aether," Exeter added.

A number of ticks and clicks stirred behind them. Gaspar nodded to the man with the machine strapped to half his face. The sentry spoke, "Most likely RALS built by Lovecraft. It is a surety the professor has allies in the Outremer, which explains the sudden disappearance of the RALS."

"RALS?" Phaeton queried.

"Rat Ass Little Spiders," the mechanized voice answered.

Gaspar shook his head. "Lovecraft would never undertake such a great risk—not unless he was forced to do it. It is one thing to shift an object this powerful into the Outremer—but to recover such a stone?"

America appeared to be bursting with questions. "You speak of—*a terre au delà de la mer*—a land beyond the sea."

"I refer to an alternate London, Miss Jones. A parallel, coexistent realm much more unstable than our own. And this world goes by many names—mostly we use the term Outremer." Gaspar paused, as if evaluating how much to reveal to her. "If the Moonstone has been hidden in this adjacent domain it must be retrieved as quickly as possible."

She swallowed. "May I ask why?"

Gaspar leaned forward and raised his voice considerably. "Because we are being infected with the same instability that is tearing apart their world."

Chapter Eight

"I SEE." America opened her mouth to speak, then hesitated.

"Have a seat, Miss Jones." Gaspar gestured to all of them. "Please make yourselves comfortable—sit, sit." America was quite sure she detected an accent when Gaspar spoke. Old Spanish, perhaps Catalan or Basque?

And the man was tenacious. "You must feel free to speak up Miss Jones—share what is on your mind."

Stunned for a moment, she caught her breath. When Gaspar smiled, a deep dimple ran down one side of his cheek. So much like Phaeton.

America swallowed. "The first creature who tried to abduct me called himself Skeezick and spoke in a funny patois of rhyming Cockney. He referred to his 'lath-n-plaster.' "

"Likely means master," Phaeton mused aloud.

"Master or maker," America agreed. "The creature claimed his master 'tinkered him' and many more like him."

Phaeton steered America over to a comfortable settee, while Gaspar asked about refreshments. "Tea? Whiskey? Absinthe?"

The Shades' leader reached for the bellpull on the wall. "The Outremer has been decimated by a pestilence twice. The unadulterated human species is rare over there—and London is becoming a rather desolate place. Someone—the maker, presumably, is popping out these strange ghouls and shifting them here."

Exeter had settled into a wing chair. "And how is it you've accumulated such knowledge?

"We've caught and interrogated a few." Gaspar's gaze shifted to his small army. "And we've followed many more."

Phaeton asked the question they were all thinking. "You've all been over there?"

Gaspar evaded Phaeton's question. "During your absence, I recruited a small army of my own." He nodded to his warrior specimens. "I don't believe you've been formally introduced."

"Captain Jersey Blood." Gaspar nodded to the imposing man, who snubbed out his cigar stubb. "Captain Blood is related to General Sir Bindon Blood. Comes from a long line of military men—as you may have sensed he is not entirely of this world. But I leave it to you to get to know one another." Gaspar turned back to Phaeton and Exeter. "I have assigned the Nightshades to your protection—"

"Is that really necessary?" Phaeton complained.

"Think of it as a temporary inconvenience." The cigar-chomping captain grinned.

Gaspar pivoted to the fair-skinned female sitting close to Captain Blood. "The very lovely and dangerous Valentine Smyth. Miss Smyth in on permanent sabbatical from the Sisters of Mercy Convent in Mayfield. Suffice to say she began her unusual avocation by identifying priests as demons. She managed to scare the church hierarchy enough, and they ran her off before she finished the job. We are lucky to have her." Gaspar's smile was cagy—measured. "Though she makes Ping nervous."

She nodded politely. "Gaspar took me in after I chased down and eliminated a red-eyed devil on his doorstep."

Captain Blood crossed booted legs at the ankles. "When this is all over, I expect Valentine will try to liberate my head from my shoulders."

Despite the blush on her cheek, Valentine Smyth's answer was almost chilly. "I have sworn my allegiance—for the duration—to Gaspar's army."

"A very small army." Phaeton snorted. "More of a squadron."

A tap at the door brought several servants into the study carrying tea trays and other libations. Gaspar waved off the help and set about pouring Darjeeling for himself and the ladies, while Phaeton, Exeter, and Captain Blood all opted for something stronger. The young man wearing the mask helped serve refreshments.

"I plan to stop this invasion with talent, not numbers." Gaspar sat back with his saucer and cup. "Cutter Coppersmith is a master shinobi trained warrior. He and Valentine are also our best trackers. They can sense where the portals move, and can facilitate a disruption insertion if necessary."

"Do you mind if I ask what happened to you?" America bit her lip, hoping she did not offend. "I only thought that perhaps it would be best . . ."

"Yes, why not?" Coppersmith's mechanical voice clicked and gasped. "Get the whole bloody story out of the way. My fifth trip over, I was captured and tortured. They took an eye—crushed my voice box. I lost hearing in this ear," he banged his finger against a sculpted metal ear. Above the curve of the brass ear plate a small conical-shaped horn vacillated back and forth—picking up sound, presumably.

"Mr. Coppersmith's hearing has been enhanced tenfold beyond the human range." Gaspar balanced his cup and saucer on his knee. "Professor Lovecraft's handiwork. His science has advanced well beyond our time. So much so, he has now become a liability to our world."

America's heart bled to think of young Coppersmith's painful ordeal, but the apparatus he wore on his head fascinated her. "Do you see as well—out of the . . . ?" The pupil of the mechanical eye dilated wide, then slammed shut. It looked very much like a wink . . . in fact, it was a wink. "Well enough, Miss Jones."

America laughed and Cutter Coppersmith pressed full, rather sensuous lips together, his one remaining intact feature.

She had once attended a demonstration of the Edison Speaking Phonograph, where a person's speech might be copied and played back. It reminded her of the raspy voice that came out of his throat mechanism.

What remained to be seen of Coppersmith was a shag of golden brown hair, a strong cheekbone and jaw line, and one dazzling green eye framed by dark lashes. The unadorned half of his face was startling proof he had at one time been an extraordinarily handsome man.

Jersey Blood drained his glass. "Cutter has shifted over as many times as Gaspar. And he is the only one who has ever been close to the one who keeps popping out these Outremer vermin—Skeezicks and Grubbers—Reapers as well.

Cutter removed a large key and inserted it into a slot behind his mechanized ear. In a matter-of-fact manner, he turned the key, just as one might wind a mantle clock. "Reapers are the worst—they're strong and deadly quick—they punch in and out at will. Meet a large group of them and they're nearly impossible to overcome." Cutter returned the key to his waistcoat pocket. "It is likely Miss Jones's attacker was a Skeezick or a Reaper."

She recalled a fleeting moment of terror. Thin, claw-like digits wrapped around her throat. A brief shudder brought Phaeton close. "All right?"

America nodded.

"One last introduction . . ." Gaspar looked up as he absently stirred his tea. "Please meet Ruby Darling." He nearly crooned the attractive blonde's name. "Because she is our darling from down under."

"Don't moon, Gaspar." The statuesque young woman returned the man's obvious interest with a piercing blue gaze. "I know you don't mean to be demeaning and insulting—you just can't help yourself." She shifted her gaze. "My name's Ruby Nash."

Phaeton winked at America. "I like her already."

Gaspar ignored the remark. "Ruby is a seer and translator. She also trained in Japan in the stealth warrior arts with Cutter. In fact, while Cutter was being rehabilitated from his injuries, it was he who recommended Ruby." Now it was Gaspar's turn to mock Phaeton. "She became my bodyguard . . . so to speak."

"Do you two always spar like this?" America shook her head. "All the artfulness, and the outfoxing one-upsmanship—"

"Bloody tedious, if you ask me," Ruby chimed in with a snort.

America had just met Gaspar, but she almost sympathized with Phaeton. Then again, Phaeton had done nothing to help his cause. He had acted the perfect hell-raiser to Gaspar's charming, tolerant older brother, which no doubt goaded Phaeton no end.

Gaspar set his cup down with a clink. "There is another you will soon meet. His name is Tim Noggy. More of a practical man—a specialist who helps us get in and out. We're going nowhere without him and he's missing at the moment."

"And *where*, might I ask, are *we* going?" Phaeton's query brought America to the edge of her seat.

Even as Gaspar's eyes narrowed, a slight curl lifted the ends of his mouth. "To find and recover the Moonstone, of course."

Exeter swallowed a last sip of whiskey in his glass. "It seems evident you and I forced Lovecraft to hide the stone in this alternate world."

"What if . . ."—Phaeton straightened—"the mechanized rodents made it over, but for whatever reason the professor didn't?"

Jersey Blood placed his elbows on his thighs and hunched forward. "That would mean the RALS are mindlessly scurrying around on the other side—with enough power to rip the universe apart."

"Or put it back together?" America offered.

Gaspar studied her, to the point it made her uncomfortable. "I sense you have abilities—but they are not yet reliable skills—very much like Phaeton."

"The aether is strong in them. All they need is training." Blood's grin was less sardonic without the cigar.

She had to ask. "What is it like in the Outremer?"

"The other side is neither above nor below us. It exists in a sea of potent aether, more vision than dream. It is most likely an extra-dimensional plane of existence." Gaspar's distant gaze darkened. "A reality much like our own, only starkly different. And their world is unraveling."

"And I was hoping for Wonderland," Phaeton mused aloud.

Gaspar stared at him. "You will weep for wonder." The clock on the mantle chimed three times. "It is late. We will assemble here tomorrow at dusk. Before bed this evening, you will think of an everyday object. Something you hold on your person or might find in a gentleman's study. Next, as you think of this object, you will drink a few sips of liquid from the backside of a glass."

Phaeton rose from the settee and stretched. "Whiskey?"

Gaspar eyeballed him. "Preferably water, but in your case . . ." The man shrugged. "Just stay away from absinthe."

"Why?" Phaeton rolled his shoulders. "Just . . . out of curiosity."

Gaspar stared. "I'd advise against it—unless you want a pestering green fairy about. Your first experience in the Outremer will be distracting enough."

Jersey Blood nodded. "I sense this will not be an ordinary crossing. Such a concentration of aether will not go unnoticed. There will be more patrols about." The captain turned to Phaeton. "They will use any device or amount of force to find and coerce you into unleashing the stone's essence, including and most especially the abduction of Miss Jones."

"Think of our worlds as two sides of a single coin," Gaspar explained. "If the powers that be in the Outremer don't restore equilibrium, their side of the coin becomes more and more unstable. As it is, I believe they have already begun to drag us into a dangerous dance."

Phaeton appeared a bit dazed as he swallowed a last dram of whiskey. "Lovecraft has to be linked to this—I'm sure he was the one who had me shanghaied."

Gaspar reclined against the arm of his chair. "Let's play Professor Lovecraft carefully. He is more knowledgeable about the goings on over there than he lets on. Perhaps we can learn something."

Phaeton exhaled loudly. "For the record I'd just like to state I have no idea how to unleash these powers in the stone." His scan of the room landed on the Shade's leader. "For the record."

"I believe I know someone who can help with that." Gaspar's attention moved to the shadow standing in the open door. "Ah, Mr. Ping."

Chapter Nine

Phaeton was pleased to see a comfortable-looking carriage waiting in the yard outside Pennyfields. Cutter jumped on back, taking the footman's station, while Ruby climbed up beside the driver.

Ping handed America inside the large town coach and turned to him. "Behind the boxwood planter." Almond-shaped, mercury eyes caught a flicker of gaslight. "He's asked for a minute of your time, Phaeton."

He made his way over to the tall, imposing man in the shadows. "Zander Farrell—I might have known Scotland Yard would be curious."

"Secret Branch is more than curious." Zander stepped forward. "I had no idea you were back in town."

Phaeton eyeballed the two officers standing behind the detective. "I arrived just this morning—was I supposed to check in with you?"

Zander sent the two men farther down the alley. "I'm told there was quite a breach of the peace in the Silver Lion this evening. Care to tell me about it?"

He saw no reason to obfuscate. "It seems I have a role to play here in London—not particularly pleased about it."

A gust of cold mist swirled into the lane and settled along the pavers. Likely wisps of fog, but then one could never be sure. Zander turned up his coat collar. "Mysterious goings on since you've been gone, Phaeton."

The understatement caused a grin. "So I've heard."

"Like to tell us about it, say—in Chilcott's office?"

Phaeton backed away. "Two o'clock, tomorrow afternoon." He climbed into the carriage and settled himself cozily between America and Valentine. As the carriage lurched off, Captain Blood took one side of the carriage, while his female cohort watched the other. Not wishing to distract them from their duties, Phaeton settled his gaze on Doctor Exeter. At Pennyfields tonight he had been uncharacteristically taciturn and appeared inordinately preoccupied. "Esmeralda is worried about you."

Exeter shifted his gaze away and back. "There was an incident at University—something of an occult nature took place near the house where Mia is boarding. Whatever happened frightened her terribly."

Exeter spoke of his ward, a very lovely young lady who was off attending lectures at Oxford. "What kind of incident?"

"She won't speak much about it, but suffice to say, what appears to have happened is so unlike Mia, I am at a loss as to how to help her." Exeter's expression was grim.

"Might I be of assistance?" America edged forward on the seat. "Mia and I got on well together at Roos House."

Exeter blinked several times before a wave of relief shone in his eyes. "I would be very much indebted to you, Miss Jones. She has decided to take a break from her curriculum and will return home by week's end."

"America and I shall pop by for a visit. You and I will slip away, some sort of errand—leave the ladies to their heart-to-heart. We might pay Lovecraft a visit—something bruising and informal." The mere mention of the inventor's name brought Captain Blood's attention back inside the cabin.

Phaeton met the captain's gaze. "What? Can I not have a private conversation—"

"Nothing is private," Blood bluntly interrupted, "not if you want to live."

Even as he narrowed his eyes, Phaeton stifled a yawn. He looked forward to being back in the flat with America alone. He did not relish the thought of these large hooded sentinels posted about the brothel or the flat. On the other hand, he would sleep easier knowing they were on watch.

"You realize my flat is situated below a brothel—you can't go barging in there wielding swords."

"I expect the ladies are used to men flashing swords." Blood's gaze moved to Valentine. "This is likely to be a withering change from the nunnery."

The lady raised a brow. "Because I come from a convent you think I am easily shocked." Her gaze locked with Blood's. "Women in service to their benefactor—providing a path to heaven . . . ?"

America nudged Phaeton. "I like her."

Outside 21 Shaftesbury Court, Jersey Blood assigned Cutter and Valentine to the flat. "Ruby and I will see Doctor Exeter to the residence on Half Moon Street. Depending on how secure he is, either one or both of us will return here to guard the upper floor and roof."

It was obvious he and America were considered targets of value by Gaspar and his band of Japan-trained stealth warriors. They'd received an impressive demonstration of stealth, and seen something of their weaponry—but the warrior part? Time would tell, he supposed.

Inside the house, Esmeralda appeared to be in excellent spirits, especially after he conveyed a rather sweet message from Exeter. Phaeton introduced his guests. "Gaspar calls them Nightshades." Phaeton sighed. "It seems London is in need of rescuing and America and I require protection."

Esmeralda gave the hooded guards an interested once-over and turned to Phaeton, "Would that be Gaspar Sinclair?"

Momentarily stunned, Phaeton nodded. "That name—the one you just spoke. Pretend you never heard it." By the look on Esmeralda's face, she knew Gaspar all right—in the naked, rolling around under the sheets, biblical sense of the word. He cleared his throat. "I promise you won't know they're around."

In answer to Phaeton's pledge, Cutter faded into the staircase banister and Valentine merged into the flock-work wallpaper pattern. "My word." Esmeralda gasp was more of a whisper. Both Nightshades reappeared. "I might like to borrow one of those cloaks." The madam rolled a pocket door closed with a wink. "Do a bit of checking up on the girls."

Phaeton gestured downstairs. "After you, ladies."

The moment Cutter and Valentine entered the flat they spread out and checked every room, closet, and window for the dregs and other lurkers. Phaeton stoked the stove, and helped America put on several pots of water. "I want a bath and bed—in that order." A lovely sigh escaped her lips. He wrapped his arms around her waist and nuzzled the sensitive spot behind her ear. "And if I bathe the pretty lady, what favors might I receive in return?"

America leaned against his chest. "Will there be a back scrub?"

"With a Turkish towel," he murmured.

"Heels and toes?"

"I think I can do a fair approximation of a Mandalay foot massage."

"Help me get the tub." America opened the pantry closet and Phaeton pulled out the copper bath. He glanced at their new roommates. "America is going to have a bath and I plan to wash up as well." He pointed to the overstuffed chair. "She can stay," Phaeton said, then pivoted toward Cutter. "You station yourself above the flat."

"Upstairs? With the doxies?" Though he couldn't see Cutter's expression, the faint whirs and clicks picked up tempo. The strapping lad backed away and climbed the stairs.

Valentine called after him, "Take care you don't catch the pox."

"What me? Hardly a chance of that, Miss Smyth with a y." Cutter's rasp was more of whisper.

The female Nightshade's gaze followed him up a few steps. "The balmy machine head doesn't know how utterly irresistible he is."

"I find I am drawn to Cutter in spite of the mask." America grunted as she helped Phaeton position the tub near the stove.

"His body has healed—but not his pride." Valentine sighed. She sank into the comfortable overstuffed chair and put her feet up on the nearby stool. "I sense apparitions—female energy."

America turned so Phaeton could unbutton her dress. "Phaeton claims an entire family has been following him about."

Phaeton folded her dress over the back of the chair and unbuckled her bustle. "Succubi. Three daughters—each one a siren in her own right. And a mother and father."

Valentine snorted softly. "Do succubi often travel with chaperones?"

"These do." Phaeton held onto America as she stepped out of her petticoats.

Valentine's gaze moved to the side table by the chaise. "And the gray creature in the corner who follows you about everywhere?"

America poured two large kettles of warm water into the tub, adding room temperature water until the bath was comfortable. "That would be Edvar—he's Phaeton's. I like to think of the two as a boy and his dog." America smiled at the gargoyle. "I've grown quite fond of him, myself." Her travel bag sat on the seat of a kitchen chair. She opened it, removed a flagon from the satchel, and poured a few drops of its contents into the steaming water.

"Mmm, oil of lavender and rosemary." Valentine inhaled deeply, then rose from her chair. "I believe I'll join Cutter . . . for a while." She climbed the stairs.

"I was rather hoping for a bit of trim with a nun looking on—or even better, a *ménage à trois*." Phaeton stood by the bath with a towel and cake of soap, unable to take his eyes off America. She removed her camisole and pantalettes, and leaned over the tub mixing the oils into the bathwater. The sight of her nude form was breathtaking in the flickering gaslight. His gaze moved over the exquisite curve that ran along the back of her thigh, up over smooth, rounded buttocks.

He caught the prettiest, stolen glance from her. A narrowed eye and the dimple of a smile she held back. "You're staring at my bottom, *Mr. Ménage.*"

"Yes, I believe I am." Phaeton thought she had never looked lovelier. "I daresay you have filled out in some wonderful places these past few months apart." Phaeton walked up behind her, cupping both his hands on the roundness of her buttocks and then moving them over her hips and belly. "There is something voluptuously curvy about you."

She responded by leaning back against him and wrapping her arms around them both. His skilled fingers ran down her rounded belly into the soft curls below. He waited for her quiver.

"You're tingling, Miss Jones." She took both his hands up to her breasts and he felt her knees buckle. Holding her tight with one arm while his free hand massaged a nipple, he whispered senseless utterances of desire, including lewd, indecent promises to endlessly arouse her.

"Goodness, do you think we can both fit in the tub?" America unbuttoned his waistcoat then backed away to watch him shed his clothes.

Phaeton stepped into the bath and pulled her between his legs. She settled back against his chest, with her knees in the air. "There is something wonderful about being naked with you in a hot bath filled with fragrant oils and soap bubbles. Luckily for us, you're flexible."

"I believe I was promised a back scrub?" She handed off a cake of soap and cloth, and he worked carefully over her anatomy starting with those firm, plump breasts. He made them slippery with soap and tweaked her nipples until they were hard and erect and she wriggled her bottom against his cock.

"Phaeton?"

"Hmm?" He kissed her shoulder.

"I believe you about being shanghaied in Shanghai."

"Is that so?" He moved up her neck to nibble an earlobe.

"Mmm," she murmured. "I have missed your kisses." She ran a finger over full moist lips. "Here." She continued down her torso until the finger disappeared under milky bath water. "And here." Angling her head, she looked up at him. Her eyelids were heavy and sensuous and she opened her mouth just enough to send his ever raucous penis thumping against her bottom.

Phaeton smiled. "And might this kiss involve my tongue?" Gently, he tugged on her nipples. "So clever and talented," she moaned the words.

It was her throaty sigh that did it. He pulled America out of the tub and watched sudsy rivulets of water meander down her torso. He'd missed her nude body—the shape, the feel of her—

just to touch her caused his cock to harden painfully. He hadn't seen her this way in months, yet he remembered every curve—in particular those plump breasts with high set nipples. "Hold still." He rubbed the bath sheet over every inch of her then wrapped her in the towel and carried her down the hallway. "Get the knob, darling?"

"The knob tickling my bum or the one on the door?" The little minx referred to his twitching member. Her eyes gleamed with mischief and something akin to lust.

Phaeton narrowed his gaze. "Careful, young lady. As I recall, your bottom turns a lovely shade of pink under my hand."

She reached out and opened the door to his bedroom, and he lay her out on top of the coverlet—all tawny skin and round curves. With the ducal cock ready for penetration, he crawled over her. "Shall I make you whimper or scream in ecstasy?"

"Must I have one without the other?"

Using a fingertip he stroked softly along her inner folds. Barely rubbing—circling the place that made her shiver and arch upward, she thrust her breasts toward his mouth. Dipping his head, he was happy to nibble. Intimately acquainted with the place that made her writhe with pleasure, he used two fingers and circled gently.

"Yes?"

"Oh, yes."

A flood of slippery arousal invited his fingers deeper, but he stayed light and played at the edges of her opening, leaving his thumb to circle and tease. Her thighs and belly trembled as her arousal climbed to yet another level. "*Mon Dieu, mon Dieu, je suis excité pour vous—n'arrêtez pas*, Phaeton." French, whispered in a husky voice, was America's code for "I am close—whatever you do, do not stop. If you stop I might have to kill you."

"Come for me, darling." Phaeton crooned.

Her expression moved from that of a joyful lover to complete surrender and pure pleasure. At her apex, he sucked one of her nipples into his mouth. The strong tremor of her climax surged through her loins into his body. The shot of arousal nearly sent him over the edge.

He released a beige-rose nipple. "Wrap your legs around me."

Grabbing her buttocks, he pulled her onto the top of his thighs and pressed her down on him. His excitement mounted one inch at a time as she took all of him into her warm slick sheath. She was tight, and wet, and oh so ready for him. All he could do was groan. "You're killing me, darling." He withdrew inch by inch, and then returned to her just as slowly, gradually increasing the speed and depth of his thrusts. Holding onto her hips he rocked her up and down—faster and harder until his own pleasure was dangerously close to its peak, which reminded him—he needed a condom. "I sense that was rather good for you, my goddess of love." Breathing hard, he slipped out of her.

America's face, still flush from his pleasuring, was half-buried in a pillow. She peeked out of soft folds to smile at him. "Mmm," was all she managed, but it was a post coital lullaby to his ears.

The banging on the bedroom door sent Phaeton upright in bed. "Who's there?" The door swung open and a towering specter stood in the threshold. He squinted at the faint orange glow under the hood. "Captain Blood, your timing is most . . . untimely."

Another Nightshade stood behind Blood. Aware he was stretched out on top of his bed, stark naked and erect, Phaeton tossed a sheet over America and a pillow over his privates. "And Miss Valentine."

"We waited for the moans and cries to cease," Blood snarled. There was something awkward and rather comical about the way Jersey described *la musique de l'amour.* Perhaps more than his hackles were up.

Phaeton narrowed his gaze. "If we're going to be rooming together, there's something you should know before barging into my bedchamber. When America and I are engaged in . . . private matters, there will first be a series of moans and cries—perhaps a few naughty demands in French—hers. Those lovely utterances will be followed by a second set of grunts and bellows. Those . . . would be mine." Phaeton raised a brow. "Did you hear any grunts and bellows?"

"Apologies for the interruption." Valentine stepped around the captain and strode into the room holding a container of clear liquid. "You must both choose your inklings and drink—from the backside of this glass—before you sleep." Her hand trembled as she handed him the water.

Curious and amused by her discomposure, Phaeton had to inquire. "Does this bother you, Valentine? All the nudity, body hair—the scent of sex in the air?"

"Stow it, Phaeton." The captain puffed a bit harder on his cigar.

Holding the sheet around her, America sat up. "We think of an everyday object, then we drink."

Valentine nodded. "I know this must seem nonsensical, but you'll understand soon enough." In a most provocative manner, the female shade rubbed her way past Jersey Blood. "Ready for the grunts and bellows?"

The captain followed her out the door. "If you can stand it, I can."

Chapter Ten

"91 TOTTENHAM COURT ROAD." America read the address to the driver and climbed into the carriage. She took a seat beside Ruby across from Valentine and Cutter, who tapped on the roof and they moved off. His gaze dropped to the message in hand. "Anything else in the wire?" Cutter asked. The telegram had been delivered moments before Gaspar's town coach arrived.

Phaeton had left for Scotland Yard, accompanied by Captain Blood, and now she was suddenly off on a mysterious errand with the three remaining Nightshades.

The carriage made a hard turn onto High Holborn and rocked them side to side. America opened the telegram and passed the missive to Ruby who, in turn, handed it across the aisle.

Cutter reached above his mechanical eye and swiveled a lens into place. "Pitt Brothers London Machine Works," he read aloud.

America furrowed her brows. "Phaeton and Captain Blood are going directly to Pennyfields from Scotland Yard. If Gaspar is changing the location of our meeting—"

"If the location changes, Ping will let them know where to meet us." Cutter took a second look at the wire.

America curled up into a corner of the seat and glanced out the window. Phaeton had dutifully rolled on the rubber goods last night. He didn't know as yet, but it wouldn't be long before the little pea in the pod quickened, then he was sure to sense the new life in her.

But how to tell him? The last time they had discussed children, he had made it perfectly clear he wished no child of his brought into the world. One who might suffer the same fiendish terrors and aberrations of his youth. Or his life.

"America is a beautiful name—of course you must be American?" Ruby's question brought her back from her worries.

She nodded. "American mother, British father."

"She doesn't sound American." Ever vigilant, Cutter dipped his head to see more of the street on his side of the carriage. "She sounds . . . British, with a hint of island in her. Barbados, possibly?"

America smiled. "French Creole. I was raised in New Orleans, until my mother handed me off to my father; he was a sea captain. Eventually, he started a merchant shipping business— we were quite prosperous until he died last year. A nefarious business partner schemed to steal his ships away. Phaeton helped get them back." How fearless and heroic Phaeton was, when he wanted to be. The thought caused a smile. "It's rather a long story."

In daylight the Nightshades' robes actually had the appearance of long traveling coats. America noticed the split in Ruby's cloak and had to ask. "Please forgive my rudeness, but I must know what you wear under those robes."

Ruby blushed at the question but she unbuttoned her cloak. "I suppose you'd call these ladies' trousers—a bit less fabric than pantaloons." Underneath she wore a gray waistcoat over a dark, high collared shirt.

America leaned closer. "My word, those trousers look wonderfully comfortable."

"I miss dressing up in gowns." Ruby shrugged and closed up the robe. "Sometimes."

"But not the corsets and bustles," America teased.

Valentine and Ruby laughed, and Cutter winked. "You won't hear much complaint from Jersey and me—especially during martial arts practice."

"You train together?" Just as America asked the question, the carriage pulled up alongside a notorious shooting range establishment called Fairyland. Cutter studied the buildings to each side. "Pitt Brothers Machine Works can't be far off." He pulled his hood down and exited the carriage. "Wait for my signal."

Ruby kept a lookout street side, while she and Valentine watched Cutter disappear inside the building next to the shooting range.

A sudden downpour of spring rain broke the silence inside the coach. The patter of drops on the roof was soothing somehow—something natural and real in her increasingly unreal world.

America squinted at a sign in a third-floor window. "Pitt Brothers—patentees and manufactures of the . . ." She wiped a bit of condensation off the window. "New and improved 'Princess' lock stitch sewing machine."

Ruby snorted. "Not bloody likely."

The sky had darkened considerably during the cloud burst. There were few passersby on the sidewalk—just one man, standing under a shop awning. America eased back from the window just as a bolt of lightning flashed past the carriage and struck the lone man full force, knocking him back against the building.

Horrified, America stared openmouthed as the poor bloke slumped over. A black cloud of particles, much like a swarm of bees, drifted up out of the body. So, he wasn't an ordinary man—and that bolt of lightning had been deliberately fired at him. A shadow of movement raced toward them—Cutter was running for the coach.

"Take us round to Star Yard." She recognized the raspy shout to the driver as the carriage lurched off. A loud thump and dip in the back meant that Cutter had jumped onto the footman's perch of the town coach.

The carriage quickly picked up speed on Holborn, but slowed on the turn down Chancery Lane. They came to a jerking halt in front of Ede and Ravenscroft. "Legal outfitters . . ." America turned to the women in the carriage. "Are we picking up a barrister or do these gentlemen make your cloaks?"

The door of the carriage opened without sight or sound of

anyone. Although, if she listened carefully, she could hear the whir and click of Cutter's headwork.

America leaned forward. "Stay back!" the invisible Cutter hissed. "Here he comes."

Ruby craned her neck to see down the row. "Good Lord, if it isn't Tim Noggy."

She sat back in her seat and waited. She heard footsteps and panting, just before a large man leaped inside the carriage.

"Make room, ladies." The portly young man tossed a satchel into the carriage and squeezed through the door. He fell onto the seat beside Valentine and the carriage lurched off, quickly picking up speed—much too fast for this narrow lane. They had not traveled far when something large and heavy struck the roof of the coach.

All America could think about was the horrid creature that had attacked her in the hansom. Only this time she had with her three rather formidable Nightshades and this new chap, who continued to huff and puff.

"Where's Cutter?" America cried. "Cutter? Where are you?"

Out of nowhere the machine head appeared outside the coach window, upside down. "Be right with you."

"Not to worry." Ruby winked. "He's likely finishing off the Reaper that was after Tim."

America did her best to ignore the high-pitched shrieks and thumping noises by focusing her attention on the round-faced young man across the aisle.

He also appeared curious about her. "Hello."

"Hello, Mr. Noggy."

He gave her a strange sort of military salute and dragged his portmanteau onto his lap. Digging inside, he removed a metal pipe about the length of a foot ruler. He pointed the object at the roof and followed the thumps and screeches back and forth.

Valentine stared. "What are you doing?"

Something hit the window next to America and she drew back. Large dark eyes stared into hers—black orbs with no whites. Strange waving tentacles, like long thick locks of hair, undulated around the creature's head. So this was a Reaper.

The jaw dropped down and a cavernous mouth opened, revealing layers of pointed teeth and something else. She caught a fleeting glance of a tongue curled up inside the mouth like a snake ready to strike. As suddenly as the creature had appeared, an arm reached down and yanked it out of sight. Her gaze tracked a bloodcurdling cry and a number of thuds back to the roof.

Tim Noggy pointed the pipe toward the mêlée above. "Hold on, I think I know which one's which." The moment Noggy toggled the lever, the screeching stopped—and the pounding. All that could be heard was a sucking and gurgling noise from the pipe-like object and the occasional patter of raindrops. Coincidentally it seemed the cloudburst had passed.

America swallowed. "What did you just do, Mr. Noggy?"

The moonfaced young man lifted his brows and shoulders simultaneously. "I shifted the Reaper back to the Outremer."

America felt a bit dizzy—much like Alice must have felt plunging down the rabbit hole. "Is the Reaper gone or is it not?"

A shy smile broadened. "It's gone."

Cutter poked his head in the window. "Gone but not out for the count. We'll likely meet up with him again on the other side—right Tim?" He unlatched the door and swung himself into the coach, feet first. He plopped down between America and Ruby.

America marveled at the peculiar new man. Noggy was obviously gifted but appeared to have little confidence in his expertise. He was also an assemblage of unsightly features. Stringy hair—much too long and shaggy, and a massive rough of beard, all in need of trimming. America's nose told her the generous sized lad was also in very great need of a bath. But he had a sweet smile and that odd metal pipe was . . . impressive.

Cutter stuck the key in his neck and cranked. "Damn fine work. That one was a tough little bugger."

Noggy's eyes flashed upward. "Spot o' luck, mate—all I did was open this tube and it sucked the Reaper in." He gave America a shy glance. "Seriously, it doesn't work half the time."

Cutter grinned. "Tim gets us into the Outremer and back out. In fact, he's in charge of training you and Mr. Black. Your first time or two can be tricky."

America managed a tightlipped smile. "Lovely."

Phaeton reached up to knock and the door opened. It was Chilcott himself and standing behind him, Detective Zander Farrell. "Mr. Black, about time you arrived. And you've brought a friend." The Scotland Yard director gave a once-over to Captain Blood, who had dressed in proper street clothes, sans cloak and dagger—or sword.

Phaeton quickly made introductions. "Elliot Chilcott, this is Captain Blood, my . . . bodyguard."

Chilcott gave his muttonchops a nervous tug. "Good God, Phaeton, has it come to this?"

"Things . . ."—Phaeton shifted his gaze between Zander and Chilcott—"are pretty bad out there."

"Yes, we've noticed," the director grumbled.

Phaeton might have shared more, but why disturb Chilcott any more than necessary? Scotland Yard was fairly useless against the darker forces of the fey world. But on occasion, they were awfully handy to have around.

Chilcott turned to his bodyguard. "You wouldn't by any chance happen to be related to General Sir Bindon Blood?"

The captain stared, then nodded, reluctantly. "Quite closely related, as a matter of fact. Unfortunately, we're estranged."

"Indeed," Chilcott grunted as he stepped past them. "We were just on our way over to the mortician's office. Join us."

Phaeton rolled his eyes. "What's this all about?"

Zander fell back beside him. "Prominent men have been dying in their beds. Heart failure was at the top of the list for a few weeks. But after several postmortem examinations we're beginning to believe they were suffocated."

And here, Phaeton thought he was being called in to be interrogated about Grubbers and Reapers. "The bodies are intact. No missing parts?"

"Just dead." Zander led the way downstairs. "By some form

of asphyxiation. We thought you might know what's lurking about town these days."

"Have you consulted *Reynolds's Weekly*? I'm told there have been reports of strange creatures about." He caught a raised brow from Jersey Blood and quickly added, "your victims sound like they might have suffered an encounter with a succubus."

Chilcott grunted. "Succubus—some sort of she-devil?"

"A demon in female form who has carnal intercourse with men in their sleep." Zander recited as though he was reading out of Underwood's *Dictionary of the Occult.*

"Salacious, ghastly idea." Chilcott stopped at the bottom of the stairs. "But how is this life-threatening?"

"Succubi drain the life force from men while they're asleep." When Chilcott blinked, Phaeton painted him a picture. "The man dreams of a beautiful naked woman making love to him. She slips between his legs—a hand slides under his nightshirt and up the inside of his thigh. Her breasts sway just above his face. Perhaps she dips down and lets him taste. Caught in a reverie of desire, he feels a bit of pressure on his chest, a touch of sleep paralysis. Then when he is fully immobilized and at her mercy, the she-devil takes his life with a kiss."

Chilcott's mouth dropped open. "Might you know how we go about . . ."

"Catching the perpetrator?" Phaeton evaluated the two Yard men in front of him. "Rather dangerous work chasing down these wily women—they take on many forms."

"Any leads you've got would be greatly appreciated. I can put a man on them straight away." Zander offered.

"I may have a few names for you." Phaeton grinned. "Georgiana, Velvet, and Fleury."

Chapter Eleven

"MY WORD YOU LOOK RAVISHING. Might I ravish you, Miss Jones?" Phaeton slipped in beside America at Gaspar's library table.

"You and Captain Blood made it here just in time," she harrumphed

"Apologies, we should have traveled by river this time of day. Had a miserable time finding a cab."

The slight eye roll and tilt to the master's chin smacked of impatience, still it appeared Gaspar was curious. "And how is Scotland Yard these days?"

"Unnerved. And rather occupied chasing after succubi at the moment."

Gaspar nodded. "Good."

Phaeton made a cursory scan of the study. "Where's the doctor?"

Gaspar settled into a wing chair. "In a few minutes we will be traveling to a location on Fleet Street, where we hope Doctor Exeter will join us." The Shades' leader gestured to a wild-haired young man with plenty of flesh on him. "Phaeton Black, meet Tim Noggy."

"Your reputation proceeds you . . . all good, mate." When Phaeton glared, Noggy backed away. "Good in a bad way?"

"Tim keeps track of the dregs," Gaspar explained. "And, on occasion, gets cornered by them. This afternoon, while you and Jersey were consulting with Director Chilcott and Zander Farrell, the lovely Miss Jones and the remaining Nightshades managed to rendezvous with Tim and bring him safely in." The

Shades' leader waved Valentine and Ruby over to the table. "Tim also happens to be an excellent instructor. He will act as supervisor for this expedition." Gaspar gave him the nod. "Make your briefing—brief, Tim."

Phaeton sized up their otherworld guide. "Will you refresh my memory as to why America and I need to embark on this maiden voyage?"

Tim stared. "Because you're the Moonstone man. If anyone can get us close to the stone, it's you, mate." Tim rolled his eyes, "Nobody on either side can get a drop of aether out of the stone without you." The large man's gaze shifted to America, "She's vulnerable in this whole deal because of you . . ."

Phaeton nodded. "I understand she needs protecting at all times."

"I couldn't agree more, but it is also imperative that America is familiar with the basics. How to get in, how to navigate the city, and most important, how to find her way home." Gaspar winked at America, which irked Phaeton no end. "After she completes her training, we can likely spare a guard to remain here with her. Reapers patrol in much greater numbers on the other side. It is always advisable to bring as many Nightshades as possible with you.

Tim cleared his throat and broke the silence. "Right. So . . . does everyone remember their inkling?"

"Inkling?" America asked.

"Insertion. Reentry. Inklings. Terms we use to describe things that defy description," Jersey Blood explained. The captain rested an elbow on the curved arm of the chaise longue.

"The everyday object you selected last night is your inkling." Tim raised his hands, palms out. "Whatever you do, don't speak your inkling out loud. But I do ask you to write it down."

"Why can't we speak it out loud?" Phaeton queried.

"It weakens the charm." The cherub-faced young man passed out strips of notepaper. He pushed a canister full of stubby pencils into the center of the table. "An inkling is a kind of trigger or recall device which allows us to pass between worlds."

Tim Noggy swept around the library table, completely agile for a young man of such bulk. "When you first start to—slip in and out—there's a kind of an adjustment period. Your inkling is like a clue—it points the way out. We can get you in there, but everyone has to find their own way back."

"Eyes to yourself—no peeking at each other's papers." Tim leaned over Phaeton's shoulder. "Sorry, mate, you'd better print those letters—I'll never be able to read that."

Gaspar leaned back into his throne-like wing chair. "The task for your first tour will be simple. You will be given the name of a hotel to locate. Once there, you will ask for a room and you will be given a key. Inside the room, you will search for your inkling. If you do not find your inkling, look for a related object. Be acutely attuned for clues and use all of your senses. The hints to your reentry can be a whisper or something so obvious a person can't readily perceive it." Gaspar grinned "These inklings can also take the form of a riddle or puzzle, which when solved will be your way out."

Phaeton twirled his pencil between fingers. "Why was I expecting something more . . . scientific?"

"More like Jules Verne." Tim Noggy circled a chubby finger at the group. "A person's ability to move from one field to another has more to do with perception than reality."

Phaeton stared at Tim.

Tim returned the stare. "Best not to get too deep in the weeds. And I don't expect you to have any problems."

"Why not?"

"Because the weirdness is strong in you, mate." The stout young man continued his stroll around the table. "Now turn the sheet over and write your inkling again, only this time write it backward."

Phaeton finished in a flash and glanced about the room. He noticed none of the other males in the room were scribbling. Jersey and Cutter were stretched out on settees and wing chairs. "Why aren't they writing?"

"Rather a long story—just consider yourself fortunate you need a trigger," Gaspar replied. An entirely unsatisfactory answer and typical of the Gentleman Nightshade who clearly had something to hide.

Tim collected the strips of notepaper and handed them to Mr. Ping. "Ping will be the keeper of the inklings."

Ping's pale silver eyes dilated into large black orbs, like a cat's eyes in a dark room. "Should one of you not return—I will go in after you." He turned to Gaspar. "The hour between light and dark approaches. We must get ourselves to 16 Wine Office Court."

The only good thing about being stuffed into Gaspar's town coach was having America on his lap. Phaeton settled her into the crook of his arm. "That narrow little pedestrian walk outside the Cheshire Cheese is the entry point? We were just there the other night—for chops and a pint." He snorted at the thought.

Tim Noggy opened the satchel on his lap and passed out pocketsize mirrors. "Expect some disorientation at first. Don't be surprised if you have trouble reading street signs, storefronts—left to right becomes right to left. The mirrors can help, especially if you have to read."

Tim dug back inside his bag. "Or—you can wear these." He pulled out a pair of strange looking spectacles. "Noggle Goggles. They enhance vision and there's also a listening device."

Phaeton reached for the glasses. "I've used these before." He buckled on the goggles and adjusted the eyepieces. Outside the carriage streetlamps glowed the most lurid chartreuse color.

"Yeah, you have. These are based on one of Doctor Exeter's original designs, but they've been modified to pick up on Grubbers and Reapers." Tim looked around the cabin. "I have another couple of pairs, who wants them?" When everyone reached out, Tim had to choose. "Ruby—you already have enhanced vision. Miss Jones—stick like glue to Mr. Black." He gave the goggles to Valentine and Jersey. "Take good care of these, you don't want to know how much they cost Gaspar."

Tim studied the goggle wearers and grinned. "Adds a bit of swagger. You'll find that most of the perception issues go away in time."

The carriage pulled up outside the Cheshire Cheese so they could watch the pedestrian traffic down the narrow court off

Fleet Street. "Jersey and Cutter, you need to make the jump now—give the Reapers something to chase."

Cutter hopped down from his footman's station at the back of the carriage and opened the door. "Ready?"

Tim caught Phaeton's eye with a wink. "Watch this." It was near twilight—they all hunkered down inside the carriage and watched Jersey and Cutter turn down the passageway. They both had their capes on and hoods up. With the goggles everything was seen, including a fleeting glance at the strange, tentacle-haired creature just ahead of the two Nightshades.

"A Reaper—and he's a big one. The simplest way to pass through is a disruption insertion," Tim whispered. "Which means one person disrupts while the other slips through quietly. But it is also the most dangerous way in. All the Reapers near the insertion point will be alerted to your presence and there are patrols of those things over there."

The creature passed under a pedestrian bridge, and Cutter sprinted ahead. A flash like a sheet of lightning illuminated the struggle—Cutter tackled the wiry devil, while Jersey slipped past and disappeared. Cutter swung around, leaped into the air, and kicked. His foot connected and the Reaper was tossed backward. Cutter turned and made a dive under the bridge and was gone.

Phaeton nodded at Tim. "What's with the strange hair?"

"The Reaper gets a hold of you. One of those tentacles goes into an orifice—any entrance will do—you're dead."

Phaeton tilted his head toward the narrow lane. "Is this passage always here? Not Wine Office Court, but . . . the rabbit hole, or whatever you call it."

"You can call them whatever you want. Everyone else does. Cutter calls them loos." Tim continued, "Most insertion sites are shut down once the outsiders find out we're coming through. We only keep track of a few in and out points as they constantly change."

"How many times have you been through?" America asked.

Tim counted soundlessly on his fingers. "Not that many—a dozen maybe. Gaspar has gone through more than anyone except for Ping. But then Ping really isn't . . . human." Tim squinted at the rest of the crew in the carriage. "I probably shouldn't be telling you this . . ."

Phaeton and America leaned across the aisle, as did Valentine and Ruby. "Gaspar is sick from it."

Phaeton straightened. "Sick how?"

Tim lifted and dropped his shoulders. "Nobody knows—too many trips, possibly. He doesn't talk about it much." Their young instructor dipped his head to see down Fleet Street. "I think I have a sighting. Two more Reapers."

Phaeton flipped his goggles down and they all prepared to exit.

Tim reached for the door latch. "One more thing—their time frame is different from ours—by a century. So if anyone asks—just say you're going to a costume party."

America dragged a plump bottom lip under pearly white teeth. Tim smiled at her. "The safer kind of insertion is one where we let them show us the way in. We follow the dregs across, stealth-like, using this." Tim dug around his satchel, and retrieved a length of metal pipe.

America blinked at the object. "You used that this afternoon, to eliminate the Reaper on the roof of the carriage,."

"My *objet éstrange.*" The round-cheeked youth toggled his brows with a grin. Tim Noggy had an infectious smile all right, but there was also something else about him. A lost boy—out of place and time.

He held up the tubular device. "I ripped this out of the Praed Street Reaper station. I've no idea how it works. It seems to be able to form links with the Outremer as well as hold the way open—long enough to get us through." Tim grimaced. "I hope."

Chapter Twelve

AMERICA DIDN'T FEEL ANY DIFFERENT. And she certainly didn't see anything different. In fact, as she looked around she felt a little silly. Even the oval sign that hung above the pub was the same. She wrinkled her brow and stepped closer. Strange, the lettering was muddled. *"Ezzich errsitch dlow aye."* She whispered, sounding out the foreign words.

"Hold on." She reached into her coat pocket and retrieved the small hand mirror. Angling it up at the overhead sign, she smiled. Ye Old Cheshire Cheese.

As she lowered the looking glass she caught sight of a man on its surface, waving. She whirled in a circle. "Phaeton?"

"Come have a look!" Phaeton was standing out on Fleet Street. America picked up her skirts and hurried down the passageway. He opened his arms and she leaped into his embrace. Holding her tight, he soothed her fears. At the same time he excited her senses, by just being . . . him.

He kissed her cheeks and the tip of her nose. "We're down the rabbit hole, love." He was exasperating at times, but the truth of it was—he was exactly what she needed at this moment. Fearless and comical.

A great swathe of red swept past them on the street. America jumped back as the double-decker omnibus hurtled down the road at a frightening speed—only there were no horses pulling the transport. Nor were there any carriages or horses about. A number of vehicles sped past, all of them under their own power.

"Everything is so fast and . . ." America stared at the vehicles going here and about in a blur of motion and color. She swayed slightly and Phaeton held onto her. "It does appear the horse-less carriage has caught on here."

Suddenly aware of people on the street, she spun around. "Where are the others? Have you seen Valentine or Ruby? Where is Jersey? And Cutter and Tim?"

"They're not in the pub; I searched it the moment I arrived." Phaeton was staring at something. America followed his line of sight. A young woman strode down the sidewalk wearing tall boots and a chemise—nothing more. The flesh of her thighs was exposed, and her hair was down, flowing behind her shoulders—a Greek goddess come alive on the streets of London.

America's mouth dropped open. Vaguely aware her eyes were popping out of her head, she checked the other pedestrians on the street. Everywhere she looked women wore trousers, or—nightshirts. Those couldn't possibly be dresses, could they? Nearly breathless, she made the silliest observance. "Not a single person is wearing a hat."

Phaeton turned to her a little dazed. ". . . Hat?"

Across the street, between blurs of noisy engines, another young lady wore an unbuttoned coat, which flew back revealing what she could only assume was a skirt underneath—and bare legs and spindly high-heeled shoes. "Phaeton, this couldn't be the fashion—could it?"

He tore his eyes off the second young woman and smiled. "I do hope so."

"Look, there's St. Paul's." America exhaled a sigh at the sight of the cathedral at the end of Fleet Street. The familiar dome was comforting, somehow. And yet, the image niggled her memory—a task set by Tim Noggy.

"Our first checkpoint is in St. Paul's Churchyard." He stepped out to the curb to peer down the block. "Shall we explore?" Phaeton took her arm and they started down the street.

Suddenly her mind flooded with directives. In the carriage, just before they had turned into the bustle of Fleet Street, Tim had given them all a number of directives. They were to meet up at St. Paul's and travel en mass to an apartment in Whitehall Court—their reentry point. But could she remember her inkling—the key to her return?

Phaeton stopped abruptly and pulled her over to a chalkboard on the street.

"*Spihc dna hsif* . . . fish and chips." Phaeton appeared to be wonderfully clever at reading backward,until he read the price. "Nine pounds."

She frowned. "That can't be right." They continued down Fleet Street, stopping here and there to read jaw-dropping menu prices. As instructed, America had worn a long duster coat. Phaeton had on a sporty hunting jacket, instead of his usual frock coat. The idea, she supposed, was to try to dress to blend into any London they might encounter. And it seemed they attracted stares but nothing they weren't already used to when out together in public.

Just past the Old Bailey the small hairs at the back of her neck caused a furtive glance back. At the edge of perception, she caught a smattering of particles. Tiny specks of gray all moving in unison, like a swarm of bees. The small bits swept in and out of the niches in storefronts, passageways between buildings. Even though it was clearly evening in this world, it still appeared to be dusk. The entire city was bathed in a perpetual twilight of electric street lights and vehicle lanterns.

Phaeton sensed them as well, and picked up the pace. "The Churchyard is just ahead. When we make the turn, get ready to pick up your skirts, my dove."

Those horrible clicking and hissing noises started as they turned into the yard near St. Paul's. The quiet lane featured a tea room and a number of solicitors' offices. "Run, America." At the end of the court, they turned down a narrow row and ran toward a busy connecting street. Phaeton came to an abrupt stop waiting for a break in traffic. Out of breath, they both turned back to see a wraith-like creature with a head full of tentacles leap off the side of a building and gallop toward them.

A black vehicle pulled alongside the curb. A man in a suit climbed out of the back. Immediately another bloke carrying a leather case and wearing a tan coat climbed into the vehicle. He spoke to a man in front. "Eighty-eight Curzon Street."

America turned to Phaeton. "A horseless hansom?"

Phaeton grabbed her hand and they ran down the street. "There's another up ahead." As they ran for the cab, the door opened and two hooded beings emerged.

A moonfaced young man stuck his head out the door. "What are you doing out there? Get in, we haven't got all day." Phaeton helped America inside and leapt in behind. As the cab moved out into traffic, America landed on his lap between Valentine and Ruby.

Almost in unison, they all turned to look out the rear window. She could just make out Jersey and Cutter running down an adjoining alley. They had successfully distracted the Reaper now breathing down their tail.

From his pull down bench seat, Tim yelled instructions to the driver. "Take us around St. Paul's and back down Fleet Street."

Alarmed, America turned back to Tim. "We aren't going to leave them here—are we?"

"They've been in tighter spots before. They can get back on their own if they have to. That Reaper will alert others—Jersey and Cutter will likely double back—" The cab rounded the corner at high speed then screeched to a halt. America nearly flew off Phaeton's lap.

"I've got you, love." The door swung open and Jersey and Cutter flung themselves onto the floor in a flurry of capes and boots. They were all tossed back into their seats as the cab sped off.

America dipped her head to look out the front of the vehicle, and then wished she hadn't. They were traveling at breakneck speed weaving in and out of slower moving traffic. She closed her eyes and tried to ignore her lurching stomach.

Phaeton consulted his watch. "I'm still on pre–rabbit hole time, but I believe we have an appointment at Whitehall Apartments."

"Good recall, mate." Tim angled his hulking frame so he could yell instructions to the driver. "Did you hear that, Singh?"

Their driver wore a red turban and presumably carried a curved, jewel-handled blade on his person. It seemed to America that everyone in this vehicle was rather lethal.

She pressed her nose to the window. Strange. London appeared to be a great deal less muddy, and the sky was—clear. The familiar dark curls of smoke from thousands of chimneys all over town was missing. "What year is here? Are we seeing our own future?"

Tim Noggy's eyes darted around the cabin of the cab and finally returned to her. "Two distinctly different—but mirrored—worlds, affected by a survival scenario that involves both realms." Changing the subject, he nodded out the window. "Trafalgar Square." He yelled instructions over his shoulder. "Take us round to the embankment and drop us off."

The moment the last person stepped out of the vehicle, the cab sped off down Horse Guards Avenue. "Psst!" Tim Noggy motioned them up the block. "We're heading out this way. Stay under the cloaks while we're in the park."

Jersey Blood led the way down a meandering path through private gardens to the imposing multi-spired residence. The structure was edged by the river on one side and the government offices of Whitehall on the other.

They all crouched behind a tall clipped hedgerow on the grounds of the Whitehall Apartments. Lights ablaze on the ground floor, muted strains of music and the tinkle of laughter could be heard behind a bank of French doors overlooking the park. Just inside the paned frames, a cluster of champagne guzzlers clinked glasses.

"Rather lively for a stuffy government official's apartment, wouldn't you say?" Phaeton commented without taking his eyes off the festivities. "Look, mate. It's a hotel now." They all followed Tim's eyes to the large brass plaque alongside the entrance: Horse Guards Hotel.

Cutter's wheels whirred. "You're sure we've got the right place?

Tim turned to Cutter. "Crank up your clockworks, you see another giant residential complex attached to Whitehall?"

"Right. All we need is a room key." Phaeton gave the Nightshades a once-over. "Anyone dressed for a soiree under those cloaks?"

Jersey snorted. "I say we pick a floor and jump the first person entering or exiting a room."

Phaeton nodded. "Good plan."

Stealth-like they moved up a grand set of stairs and then spread out. "Tenth floor," Jersey called out, as he and Valentine disappeared up the servants' entrance. She and Phaeton started up the main stair with Tim lagging behind.

"Hold on." Tim was puffing. He waived them down the hall and pressed a button by a set of gleaming double doors.

"Lifts?"

Tim nodded. "A good deal better than the steam elevators back home." A bell dinged and doors opened. He motioned them inside. "Trust me—you don't want to miss this."

She and Phaeton stepped inside, and Tim pressed the number ten, in a row of buttons next to the sliding doors. He turned to them wearing a grin.

"How is it that numbers aren't backward, but letters are?" America asked.

"The letters aren't backward anymore—you read Horse Guards Hotel didn't you?" As the elevator ascended there was a sensation of climbing rapidly. She looked from Tim to Phaeton, who winked.

"I suppose I did read the hotel plaque." As the lift slowed, the bell dinged again and there was the oddest, momentary floating sensation. The doors opened onto the tenth floor corridor. Tim swept his hand forward. "Ladies first. The longer you're over, the easier it gets to read stuff."

They met up with the Nightshades in the west wing of the hotel. Cutter slipped the pass key into the lock. "Liberated from an unsuspecting maid, currently confined to a linen closet." The Nightshades fanned out into the rooms, checking bedchambers, then the armoires in the dressing areas. The suite chosen appeared unoccupied. Quickly, they all collected around a writing desk at one end of the parlor

Tim pulled out a chair and settled his gaze on America. "Ladies first."

She took a seat, and the Nightshades drew closer. "Do you remember your inkling?" Tim asked.

America nodded.

"Good. You'll need a sheet of writing paper from the drawer, and you can use the pen from the desk."

Scanning the desktop, her heart beat erratically. "But . . . there's no inkwell."

Tim straightened. "Is that a problem?"

She frowned. "I suppose I chose inkwell because of inkling."

Phaeton raised a brow. "Inkling—inkwell? Not very original, but as I recall we were rather . . . spent, last evening."

Tim stared at Phaeton. "What did you choose?"

"Ink pen."

"That's certainly original." Tim's eye roll landed on Valentine.

She swallowed. "Ink spot."

"Uh-huh." His gaze shifted to Ruby. "Don't tell me, ink . . . blotter?"

"Afraid not." Ruby shook her head. "Ink bottle."

Tim hunched over and nodded slowly. "Great."

"Actually, I pictured a quill in an ink bottle," the tall blonde clarified.

A grin broke out on the chubby-cheeked face. He dug a fountain pen from his pocket and placed it on the notepaper. "I guess you'll just have to draw one, then."

America uncapped the stylus and leaned over the secretary. "Should I draw an ink bottle or an inkwell?"

Tim shrugged. "Your choice. Just make sure you picture a desk in this same room . . . back home." He waved the troops in closer. "Ladies and gentlemen—important point. If you can't find your object, you can always draw it."

America tilted her head. "Quite a good likeness." She took a moment to admire her drawing of a crystal ink bottle sitting in an inkwell. Looking up, she realized she was alone, and the room was dim. So dark in fact, she could hardly see her drawing on the desk. Pushing away, she opened her mouth to call for help—for Phaeton.

"Don't." A quiet voice came from the corner of the room.

America was so startled she lurched away from the secretary with enough force to send her chair flying—only someone caught it before it clattered onto the floor.

"I'm here, America."

She whirled around. "Ruby. Did you—?"

"I came across with you."

Gradually, as her pounding heart slowed, the snoring from the bedchamber grew louder. "Where are we?"

"You are in the Whitehall Apartments—same room. Different time and place." Gaspar stepped out of the shadows. He laid a finger across his lips. "Slight inconvenience, the room you chose over there is occupied over here." The Shades' leader did not approach them but moved to the door. "I've rented a room just across the hall where we can debrief." Gaspar nodded to Ruby. "You stay here—and direct our people across the hall."

Gaspar opened the door a crack and waved America over. "Besides, I'd like to have a few words with Miss Jones alone."

Ruby frowned. "I think I should stay with America."

"The man in the other room is dead drunk, passed out on the counterpane of his bed and still in his tuxedo. Stay quiet and send the others over as they arrive." Gaspar escorted her across the corridor and closed the door. This room was dark as well, lit only by a single wall sconce. "I am always thirsty when I return from the Outremer."

America nodded. "I'm parched."

Gaspar poured a glass of water and handed it to her.

She drained the glass. "Thank you."

The man had hardly taken his eyes off her since they entered the room. "Would you like another?"

She used her tongue to moisten her lips. "I'm fine."

Gaspar stood close, and suddenly moved closer. "When are you going to tell Phaeton?"

She tried stepping away, but he caught her by the arm, and placed his other hand on her belly. "When, America?"

"Take your hands off her."

Chapter Thirteen

PHAETON GRABBED GASPAR BY THE NECK and backed him up against the wall.

"I was just. Asking. A simple. Question." With each head bang, the leader of the Shades gasped out another word or two. "That is all." Gaspar held up his hands in surrender.

"Phaeton, please don't choke him," America said as she ventured closer.

His grip eased on the man's throat. "Don't touch her again." He released Gaspar and backed away. "Ever."

Phaeton took her hand and opened the door. "And no matter what your question, the answer is no."

Outside the building, the doorman ushered them toward a waiting hansom. Phaeton helped her up into the cab and jumped in after. He placed both his arms around her and pulled her close. "Now, what was the simple question?"

America sighed. "I know he is an irritant, especially to you. And I know you believe that Gaspar was being seductive and inappropriate, but I can assure you he was not, exactly."

"Exactly?"

She finally looked at him. "He asked me when I was going to tell you."

Phaeton stared at her. "Tell me what?"

America hesitated. "Perhaps, when you're acting less belligerent."

"I'm not angry, damn it." His eyes narrowed.

She met his flinty look. "We might have waited for our

bodyguards. The ones who know how to fight off those creatures."

Phaeton snorted. "They spend as much time running away
from them as fighting them."

Her smile cheered him some, even though she continued to
evade his question. "You know very well, they were leading
those Reapers away from us."

Fine. If she didn't want to talk about it, he could wait. He
had come to know all her little quirks and a great deal about her
temperament on board the *Topaz*. She was a very private person in some ways, almost secretive, while he was curious and
probing. When they argued, which was rare, he had learned to
let her come to him, instead of niggling at her.

The months they had spent together sailing around the
world had been some of the best in his life. Phaeton's exhale
swept gently through the fine hairs at her temple. "The Nightshades are an odd bunch. Jersey Blood with his cigar stubs and
Valentine with her ready barbs."

"A fallen nun and a half-breed demon." She snorted softly. "I
don't suppose a pairing can get more opposite. And the other
three—Tim, Ruby, and Cutter."

"Two Australians and a machine head." Phaeton yawned.
"Cheers, mate."

She muffled a laugh against his tweed sporting jacket.
"Mmm, I rather like them, though." The hansom pulled up in
front of Mrs. Parker's, and she lifted her head off his shoulder.
"I'm worried about Exeter and Edvar."

Phaeton helped her down. "Edvar plainly wants nothing to
do with the Outremer, and I can't say I blame him." They made
their way down into the flat and straight into the bedroom.
"Come here, Miss Sleepy Eyes." Phaeton undressed her and put
her to bed. Minutes later he crawled in and spooned up against
her. He was half hard just rubbing up against those sweet,
plump cheeks. "Would you mind a little midnight love visit
from the duke?"

She turned to him with her eyes closed and raised a brow.
"Only if you promise to do naughty things with your fingers
between my legs."

* * *

Snippets of muffled conversation and a great thirst awoke Phaeton in the middle of the night. He opened the door and distinctly heard low-pitched voices. He looked about the room for his trousers. Orange eyes blinked from the top of a tall chest of drawers.

His trousers were folded over the chair back next to the highboy. He pulled them on and buttoned them as he made his way down the hall. The voices turned out to be Jersey and Valentine. Their speech was low and intimate, in much the same way lovers talk in bed.

"The last time I let you arouse me, I nearly killed you."

"Don't flatter yourself, Jersey. I aroused you for a reason."

"Ah, yes, to exorcise the demons within."

"Afraid of me Jersey?" she taunted. "Afraid of how I make you feel?"

There was a long pause. "Do you remember our first and last time?"

Phaeton couldn't see much in the dark, but the two Nightshades were fully clothed, each one in his or her respective corners of the chaise. "It isn't the way you remember it, Jersey."

"I have no memory problems. I remember that things got . . . rough."

"I guess you forgot that I liked it."

Jersey straightened. "What is it with you, Sister? You want a little of the strap for all those bad thoughts you're having about me? Ask God's forgiveness for sucking my cock two years ago?"

Valentine rose up from her end of the chaise. In the dark Phaeton could just make out that she wore men's trousers. She placed a booted foot between Jersey's legs and encouraged him to open. She sank down on her knees and ran both her hands up his legs—from his knees to his groin. "Has it been that long?"

Phaeton deliberately cleared his throat. "Sorry to disturb." In a few steps he was in the pantry. "But I'm in desperate need of a glass of water." He poured himself a glass of water, which he guzzled. Then he uncorked a new whiskey bottle. "And a dram of this—care to join?" Phaeton held his glass up. He received cool stares from Jersey and Valentine, who had returned to her end of the divan. "Sure?"

After a long silence, Jersey finally answered. "How much of that did you hear?"

Phaeton tossed back the whiskey and enjoyed the slow burn of amber liquid down his throat. "Where are Ruby and Cutter?"

"Checking to see if Doctor Exeter returned from his trip to Oxford."

Phaeton returned the bottle to the cabinet. "Not that it is any of my business, but where is Tim?"

Valentine answered. "At his workshop." When Phaeton raised a brow, Valentine elaborated. "He's got a workshop somewhere in town. He keeps moving it."

"That's one explanation." Jersey muttered. "The other is that he has workshops in several locations."

"Rather an awkward moment for you two." He sauntered back toward his bedroom. "Have you ever played 'who's got the power'? It's one of America's favorites."

Valentine's brows crashed together. "Would you not mention any of this—to anyone?"

Halfway down the hallway, Phaeton paused and turned back to her. "Try telling Jersey you'd like to smoke his cigar. You might also mention you like to swallow the smoke." He turned and continued down the passage. "Christ, now I've got this enormous erection."

Phaeton closed the door to his bedchamber and removed his trousers, taking care to hang them over the back of a chair— exactly where Edvar had left them. Slipping under the covers, he made sure he warmed up sufficiently before touching his lovely bedmate. Icy cold fingers would never do. Snuggling against her, he let his mouth wander along her smooth shoulder, licking now and then to taste her salty essence. Dipping under the covers, his index finger flipped back and forth against her nipple. When it peaked, she moaned in her sleep.

He swept lower, down her torso—past ribs, barely felt, and lower still, to cup her belly. "My darling, girl."

Her belly trembled, and Phaeton smiled, encouraging her legs to open as she rolled onto her back. Inching over her, he took a nipple in his hand and the other in his mouth. He would wake her gently—so that her desire would first occur in a dream, before the growing arousal would finally cause her eyes to flutter open.

His tongue traveled down to her navel and circled. Again, a sleepy moan and her belly fluttered. He was about to grin but something stopped him this time. The tremble had come from deep inside her. As he retracted his tongue, a sudden image of Gaspar with his hand on her flashed. "When are you going to tell him?"

Phaeton sat up straight and tossed back the covers. Beautiful of course, and curvy in all the right places. His gaze went straight to her midriff. Rounded as always—perhaps a bit more so than usual. His hand shook as he reached out to sense the life within her—a fish in a warm pond . . . swimming. A cabbage in a patch . . . laughing. Phaeton removed his hand and placed his ear to her belly.

"Hello?"

Phaeton tossed and turned all night, at least until a bleak gray dawn finally gave him permission to wash, dress, and join the others in the pantry for a cup of Earl Grey. Valentine was heating several large pans of water. Phaeton buttered a piece of toasted bread. "Looking forward to your bath?"

Valentine looked up from the copper tub and smiled. "Very much."

Phaeton angled his chair so he might gain a better view of the tub. "Don't let Jersey and me stop you."

Valentine laughed. "Oh, I'm not. You and Jersey are off to meet with Doctor Exeter this morning, while America and I bathe and primp." She winked at him. "We might actually cook a nice leg of mutton for dinner with roasted vegetables and a custard tart for dessert." Valentine's eyes were smiling; in fact, he had never seen her in such good spirits.

She wiped her hands off with a dish towel. "If you get home in time for supper—you can join us."

Jersey unfolded a wire message. "This must have come last night—one of the doxies brought it down this morning."

"Not convinced the Moonstone is in the Outremer. Stop." Phaeton read aloud. "Meet me at Tower of London Station tomorrow morning at nine."

Phaeton checked his watch and slurped the last of his tea. "I take it you're coming?"

Jersey struck a lucifer against the matchbox and lit his stub of a cigar. "Wouldn't miss it"—he puffed—"for the world."

Phaeton climbed the stairs, and nodded to one of the girls in the parlor. "Morning, Layla." Exiting the brothel, he led the way out of the terraced court to Drury Lane, where they hoofed it down to the Embankment Underground station. His ever vigilant bodyguard scanned the station for tentacle-headed predators. "I'd rather you not report this meeting to Gaspar for the time being."

The cigar glowed in the dark shadows of the hood. As the platform crowded with travelers, Jersey received a number of wary stares. "I can keep quiet, if you can."

Phaeton stepped toward a car already loaded with passengers. "Ah, you're referring to last night. Did your evening improve any? By the look on her face this morning—"

"Nothing happened." Jersey tossed his cigar butt onto the tracks. "Valentine and I took turns on watch."

They rode the circle line to Mark Lane in silence, which gave Phaeton plenty of time to recall last night. He had resisted the urge to wake America and stuffed his rage. And who exactly was he angry with—America? Not possible. At himself for not using a rubber johnny? Very possible.

Around three in the morning, his anger shifted to remorse which lasted but a few minutes. He would never regret his time spent with America. Eventually he settled on the real problem. He didn't want to be a father. Being a father meant . . . reading bedtime stories.

Then, after another hour or so of tossing and turning, he had a kind of epiphany. His reluctant feelings about fatherhood were a small part of the problem. He was concerned about something far more important than either himself or America.

He worried for the child.

The train doors opened and he followed Jersey upstairs. He remained in a haze of distracted thoughts; they walked over to the Tower of London. They spied Doctor Exeter near the gates to the Tower entrance.

Exeter's overall appearance was troubling. He seemed agitated and his eyes darted about, as if he was concerned with other matters, and yet anxious to get on with the duties at hand. He greeted them both cordially, taking an extra moment to stare at Phaeton. "You look worried."

"I was just about to say the same to you."

The doctor's gaze drifted toward the rising mist off the Thames. "I *am* worried." He exhaled a vocal sigh.

Phaeton grimaced. "Well then, that makes two of us."

Exeter stuffed his fists in his coat pockets and turned to Jersey. "This can't be shared with Gaspar—not yet."

Jersey nodded. "Agreed."

Phaeton spoke up, perhaps a little too loudly. "You were missed yesterday."

The doctor returned to him. "I was dealing with something of a crisis. Sorry I couldn't be there. I trust your first expedition to the Outremer went well?"

Phaeton's nod was a bit iffy. "I believe I have seen our future and it is fast, noisy, and alarmingly expensive."

Chapter Fourteen

AMERICA LEANED BACK and let the warm, clean water rinse her hair. Valentine squeezed out the excess water and wrapped her head with a towel. "Jersey and I were having a rather private discussion last night, which Phaeton happened to overhear." Valentine sat back on the kitchen chair. "Did he happen to mention it last night or this morning?"

"He didn't wake me last night—I must have looked tired." America rose out of the tub and wrapped herself in a bath sheet. "If you don't mind my asking, what did Phaeton hear?"

The faintest blush colored Valentine's cheeks. "Jersey and I rarely cross swords, but when we do, it is always the same argument. We would both like to be closer physically, but he is worried about hurting me."

America settled into a chair and studied Valentine. "He is very brave. And devilish handsome, even with that cigar he's always puffing on. I imagine he is also an accomplished warrior?"

"Deadly." Valentine leaned close to the stove and ran her fingers through lengths of her own damp, raven black tresses.

"Jersey is not completely . . . of this world?" America unwound the towel on her head and fluffed out her curls.

"When we first met, I tried to kill him." Valentine's gaze flicked upward. "Love at first sight."

America continued to dry her hair. This kind of intimate conversation was obviously difficult for Valentine, being a former novitiate and all, but there was no way to get round the question. "When you do attempt to get close, what happens?"

"He turns into a beast."

"When I got up this morning, you were just stepping out of your bath." America bit her bottom lip. "There was a crescent-shaped scar above your left nipple."

"Jersey's mark." Valentine met her gaze and looked away. "He didn't mean it—he got carried away, but in those few moments, before he pushed me away, he held my arms above my head and . . . I tried to explain last night." Valentine shook her head. "Until he lost all control . . . I rather liked it."

America draped her towel across the back of a chair to dry. "As long as there is trust between partners, being dominated can be very stimulating."

"Exactly." Valentine's nod grew enthusiastic. "Phaeton mentioned something about 'who's got the power'? He said it was one of your favorites."

America laughed. "Did he really?"

Valentine dipped her head to make eye contact. "Would you mind . . . explaining?"

"Perhaps I could be talked into it—over another cup of tea." America stood up and let the bath sheet fall away. She buttoned on her camisole and stepped into pantalettes.

"You have a lovely body," Valentine said, then hesitated. "You do realize that you are starting to show?"

America's hands immediately went to her belly.

Valentine's gaze traveled up from her middle. "Does Phaeton know you are pregnant?"

"He does not." Nervously, America moistened her lower lip. "At least, I don't think he does."

"I sensed a great worry on his mind this morning." Valentine added new leaves to the teapot and poured in the steaming water. "America—you need to tell him."

She met Valentine's gaze. "Gaspar knows."

"I'm not surprised. He's an intuitive—a very talented one at that."

America removed a jar from her portmanteau. The travel bag still sat on the pantry counter unpacked. "Liquid gold from Morocco. It gives your hair shine."

America poured a few drops into Valentine's hand. "Rub

your hands together and then run your fingers through the strands." Studying the lovely female Nightshade, she had to ask. "Do you believe Gaspar and Phaeton are related?"

"There's no brotherly love on Phaeton's end, but I do sense a protectiveness from Gaspar, as if he can't help his feelings." Valentine frowned. "I should tell you that nothing about our leader is in good trim. He cannot be wholly trusted, as he is dealing with his own mortality."

America stopped smoothing the golden liquid over her own curls. "Is his health failing?"

"He is fighting for his life."

Valentine must have seen her mouth drop open, because she explained. "Too many expeditions into the Outremer. He is unraveling."

Phaeton followed Exeter down into the bowels of the old Tower Underground Station. "It is my understanding that Professor Lovecraft has leased this property from the Duke of Astor for the sum of one pound a year."

In disuse for many years, the station below ground was dark and vaporous. At the bottom of the stairs they turned down a corridor lit by a single sputtering gaslight. Phaeton could just make out a heavy iron door guarded by fanged sentries. Drawing closer, both mechanized cats sat up and snarled. Jersey Blood reached inside his coat and drew out a dagger which immediately unfolded into an impressive claymore.

Not to be outdone, in a series of clatters and clicks, the guardian cats transformed themselves into larger beasts, their snarls deepened into growls and their claws lengthened.

Phaeton raised his gaze above the door. A circle of brass letters spelled out "*Deus Ex Machina*" with a large cursive *L*— for Lovecraft—in the center. Haloed by light, the plaque was otherwise rather industrial in appearance. "God out of the machine." Phaeton's growl matched the cat beasts. "Self-aggrandizing blowhard."

"Lovecraft is developing a number of different engines, some of which he manufactures below." The doctor tapped on the door using his umbrella. A small door within a door opened. A man wearing a battered opera hat squinted out of wire framed spectacles. "Who goes there?"

The doctor cleared his throat. "We wish to speak with Lovecraft."

One of the large feline creatures took a swipe at Phaeton. "Could you call off the pussycats?" From the other side of the door he heard the sound of a toggle switch being thrown, and with it the fangs and claws retracted.

"Who should I say is calling?" The queer man squinted out of spectacles dripping with condensation. Phaeton removed a pocket square from his waistcoat and wiped a clear spot on each lens.

"Much better." He stepped away from the door. "Tell the professor Doctor Jason Exeter, Captain Jersey Blood, and Phaeton Black have come calling."

They waited. "We could use Jinn right now. Where's Ping when we need him?" Minutes ticked by like hours, while Phaeton paced and tried not to think about America's delicate condition. Exeter appeared to have his own set of worries and Jersey leaned on his broadsword like it was an umbrella. Phaeton double-backed. "Is there something you can do with that magical tool of yours?"

Jersey pointed the weapon at the door and a blast of pale blue energy traveled into every crack and crevice. The cigar-chomping Nightshade stepped forward and pushed the door open with his index finger.

A man stood in the doorway. Rather nondescript, actually, except for the pale eyes protruding out of his head. One set of eyes never blinked; the other set was more of a mechanical pair of irises attached to heavy spectacles. The mechanical eyes tracked up and down, and side to side with the real eyes below. He wore the goggles perched on top of his head and the effect was rather disturbing, as though he had two sets of eyes, and all of them were . . . spying.

"Gentlemen, welcome to my world." The man's tight-lipped smile felt a great deal less than welcoming. Of course this had to be Lovecraft, though he did not introduce himself and quickly disappeared through a hatchway and down a length of corridor.

"I am Hudson and I will be your escort." The butler with the fogged eyeglasses ushered them inside. "Professor Lovecraft will see you in his laboratory."

Their tour of the factory was rushed, but dazzling. Sitting in the middle of the barrel-shaped tunnel was an immense armored engine, at least three stories tall. The machine rested majestically on train tracks, as wisps of gray smoke curled out of two massive smokestacks. Phaeton was sure the long spear-like objects that protruded from the front of the vehicle were some kind of weapon, as well as the large blade that angled into a v-shape at the base of the engine.

A combination of live workers and automatons on scaffolding worked at riveting the craft's armor plating. Whatever this was, it was formidable. It also seemed obvious by the number of workers standing about that tests had been postponed while the Lovecraft's Machine Works entertained visitors. Phaeton glanced back at Exeter who answered with a raised brow.

"We expect a certain amount of stopping and gawking—but you must try not to fall behind." Hudson led them upstairs and across a metal catwalk to a narrow room of long tables. Each table displayed an assortment of tools, gauges, and a plethora of odd gadgetry in various stages of development.

Lovecraft rotated a helmet-like object on a turnstile in front of him. It looked something like the mechanized headgear that Cutter wore, except this was more streamlined and aesthetic in appearance. When they were all duly assembled around the object, Lovecraft looked up. "How is Cutter Coppersmith?"

Phaeton was in no mood to let Lovecraft dally about. "I have a better question. Where's the Moonstone?"

He distinctly saw a flash of anger in Lovecraft's real eyes, then a tepid smile. "Is that what you call it? Rather romantic of you, Phaeton."

"The one you stole from Doctor Exeter's laboratory using a swarm of eight-legged rats to do your bidding."

Lovecraft gave the helmet one last turn. "All right. I admit the RALS were mine, but they were there to stop a band of Reapers from stealing the stone." Lovecraft's four eyes moved to Exeter. "Unfortunately your trusted sidekick Phaeton Black shows up and you jam my signals with your police whistle. The Reapers opened a hole in the membrane and herded my army of rats along with the Moonstone—as you call it—back to the other side with them."

Exeter stepped forward. "Just so we're clear—we don't exactly believe that."

The professor shrugged. "Have it your way."

"How did you know I had the stone?"

All four of Lovecraft's eyes narrowed. "A little birdie told me."

Phaeton stepped forward to throttle the smarmy little bastard, but Exeter caught him by the sleeve. "Not yet." The doctor narrowed his eyes at Lovecraft. "Why did you have Phaeton shanghaied?"

"Touch me, and I'll have security up here in an instant." Lovecraft's eyes worked in unison to make sure they all got the message. "It doesn't matter who is in possession of the Moonstone—you know as well as I—we need him to unlock it."

Exeter nodded. "So all these disturbances are because the powers that be on both sides are looking for Phaeton Black?"

"They're also interested in my aether collector." Lovecraft beamed. "I have built a machine not too dissimilar from the machines they use in the Outremer to produce limited quantities of aether. This energy is not unlike the stone's but with a fraction of its force or half-life."

"If they had the Moonstone they wouldn't be interested in your little invention." Exeter leaned on the man. "So what happened?"

Lovecraft's four eyes shifted slightly. "The Reapers must have thought they had the stone, but in the crossing, the RALS somehow got the upper hand and secreted the stone away."

Jersey had wandered off, pretending to be enthralled with Lovecraft's gizmos. Phaeton suspected the ever vigilant Nightshade would come away with a few valuable observatons—at least he hoped so. Lovecraft was a brilliant inventor, but he was also sly, tragically motivated—and very insane. Phaeton pressed the mad inventor hoping for an angry response and a slip of the tongue. "Since your little rat bastards are single-minded and not very bright at that," Phaeton mused aloud, "Are we to assume they're wandering the streets of the Outremer carrying the Moonstone around on their backs?"

Exeter kept the press on. "That's quite an effort. How long before their half-life runs out?'

Lovecraft appeared uncomfortable, boxed in. "Three more days, at most. Until then, they'll just keep moving."

Phaeton recalled the mindless, relentless hordes of spider rats. One wave after another, never stopping, persistently pushing forward. In its own way it was a spot of luck; the Reapers likely couldn't get a bead on the RALS unless they just happened to run across them.

"Will that be all, gentlemen?" Lovecraft signaled his butler, who toggled switches. Presumably the man was calling in re-inforcements, in case they didn't leave.

"One more question." Phaeton thought of the engine down in the lower tube. "Wait—two more questions."

All four eyes narrowed. The effect might have been comical, except that the net result was so sinister. "One question."

Jersey had worked his way around the room. He was not sure how he got the message because the man's expression never changed, but Phaeton was quite sure Jersey was telling him they were being watched. He weighed his question options. The professor was not a man to be easily discomposed— in fact, the man hadn't made a move thus far that wasn't calm and calculated. At least, that was the effect. Phaeton was beginning to think he couldn't rattle him. "Are you and Gaspar working together?"

Lovecraft's real eyes—the pale blue watery ones—met his gaze. "Not at the moment. But I believe we have common goals with regards to the Moonstone."

Phaeton nodded. "Good. Because I'd hate to have you both fighting over my services—your Jinn in a bottle, so to speak." It was a calculated risk to play one off the other, but worth it if it exposed any part of their plans. Phaeton backed away and turned toward the door.

"Say hello to Miss Jones for me."

Phaeton pivoted back, his expression as blank as he could make it.

Lovecraft smiled the sweetest smile. "I understand she is expecting a happy event. My congratulations."

"Bloody bastard!" Phaeton yelled the moment they were aboveground. "Over here." He motioned Exeter and Jersey to an outcropping of wall that surrounded the Tower of London. They stuffed themselves into a battlement niche, most likely an old Beefeater post.

"Why are we hiding in a wall?" Exeter asked.

"Let's see who might emerge from the inventor's den," Phaeton snarled. "He dragged America into this, the bloody bastard."

Exeter managed to pivot in the tight spot. "Is it true—the news about America?"

Phaeton stared, then nodded.

"Congratulations, Phaeton, you must be pleased."

"As a matter of fact, I am not at all pleased."

"Give yourself time to adjust—" Exeter's annoying grin faded. "Look what emerges from the depths." The doctor nodded to the door on the boarded up station marked DO NOT ENTER.

Gaspar Sinclair exited the Underground and jogged off toward a waiting carriage.

Phaeton sighed. "I take this to mean Gaspar and Lovecraft are in this together—how did Lovecraft word it?"

"They have common interests," Jersey offered.

Exeter walked them to the steps of the Underground at Mark Lane. "Just remember you hold the trump card, Phaeton."

"Oh Mr. Black! Doctor Exeter—Captain Blood!" Lovecraft's man, Hudson, ran after them waving a piece of paper in the air. "The professor wanted to make sure you received this straight away."

Phaeton opened the handwritten note and read aloud. " 'I have a machine that is able to track the RALS. I can also get us very close to the correct portal in the Outremer. Our time frame is limited. If you wish to put a stop to these creature intrusions and return the Moonstone to responsible guardianship, meet me at dusk tomorrow evening.' " Phaeton exchanged a look with Exeter. "There is a postscript that advises the location will be wired by noon tomorrow."

Phaeton refolded the note. "What does he mean by 'our time frame is limited'?"

"Closer to what both sides fear the most." Jersey's frown seemed deeper than usual. "The end game."

Chapter Fifteen

AMERICA STIRRED A ROUX OF FLOUR and water into the pan drippings. "The moment you feel uncomfortable or that things have gone too far, you remind Jersey that you've got the power."

Valentine circled the table setting down plates. "If only he would trust me enough to allow such a thing."

America whisked the gravy with the wooden spoon. "You must agree on the ground rules ahead of time—when he feels as if he is losing control, that is his signal to give you the power. Likewise, when you feel that things have gone too far, you remind him that you've got the power."

America moved the pan away from the heat, but left it on the stove to keep warm. Valentine smiled. "The roast looks and smells delicious. I do hope they return soon."

"Oh I dunno—just leaves more of that tasty leg for us ladies." Ruby pulled a short military-style jacket over a ruffled blouse and a smart, narrow skirt. She looked wonderfully radiant and relaxed from her bath. Her flaxen hair hung in long loose waves down her back. As she reached the pantry, Ruby leaned to one side to fluff damp tresses.

"Where's Cutter?"

America wasn't exactly sure how to answer the question and looked to Valentine, who appeared doubly absorbed in place settings. They had moved the copper tub into America's old room so that Cutter and Ruby could bathe. Cutter washed up with Ruby's help, then had gallantly carried fresh water in for her bath. While Ruby was in the tub, he had excused himself and disappeared.

Ruby studied both their faces. "No doubt getting his gears greased by one of the doxies upstairs."

Valentine looked up from her table duties. "You don't know that for a fact, Ruby."

America wiped her hands with her apron. She almost felt a bit dizzy from these Nightshade women and their prickly male counterparts. Then she thought about Phaeton, and decided that all relationships were needlessly complicated.

The tall blonde slumped into a chair. "Ever since his capture, he has let me get only so close—but no closer." Ruby held up a black velvet ribbon. "Would you?"

Valentine scooped up her hair and tied the ribbon. "Cutter's injuries are healed, but his heart is still wounded."

America sank into another chair. "Do you find it oddly coincidental that we are involved with men, who for very different reasons, are all reluctant in one way or the other to fully—for lack of a better word—engage?"

Valentine was the last to sit. "But it is not as if they aren't devoted to each one of us. Jersey plays the stoic role—the aloof leader. Cutter the wounded warrior."

"And Phaeton?" America raised both brows.

Valentine smiled. "My God, are you aware of how he looks at you, America?"

Ruby grinned. "As if it were a hot summer day and you're a lemonade on shaved ice." The lovely blue-eyed girl sighed. "What I'd give for a look like that, and one night with Cutter."

America's heart did a bit of hopping about in her chest. Even though Phaeton had never said the words, exactly, she knew he loved her. He had said as much—at least in the throes of passion. Now she prayed he would love their child.

A deep cleansing breath improved her smile. "I say we work together." America swiveled toward Valentine. "The next time a bit of closeness presents itself, you say to Jersey, 'I have the power. And when I say stop—I mean stop.'"

Valentine nodded.

"Then you kiss him. Start slow and open your mouth. Lick the underside of his upper lip and when he comes out to play—tell him to stop."

Valentine's dark eyes took on a lovely golden glow.

"Do this several times—until he trusts the idea that he can stop—that he is in control. But take it slow. Kisses only for a few days."

Mesmerized, Valentine nodded. "How do you know all this?"

"Phaeton says men are beasts when it comes to intercourse. They need to be trained."

Ruby sighed. "Cutter and I were friends—we met during training in Japan. They isolated me at camp and did not allow me to train with men, but he would come and work with me at night, in secret.

"Gaspar was our first assignment after school. I didn't realize how strong the bond was until Cutter was captured."

America nodded. "Do you desire him?"

Ruby's lovely blue eyes watered. "More than ever."

America looked to Valentine. "I think she should jump him."

Valentine snorted a laugh, and Ruby joined in.

"I'm serious!" America looked from one to the other. "Pretend it's practice—get him in some kind of wrestling hold—be sure it's a hold he can't easily get out of—then rub against him, until he is very hard—but don't touch him anywhere else—just make sure he's got a big veiny boner on him."

Ruby's large blue eyes grew even wider, if that was possible.

"Then you tell him you've got the power. And if he lets you unbutton him, you will suck his cock dry." America smiled sweetly at both women. "Phaeton loves it when I talk dirty."

A smattering of gray matter swirled down the corridor and settled on the chaise longue. America lowered her voice. "I believe we have visitors."

Ruby and Valentine pivoted in time to see a stylishly dressed young lady materialize on the couch.

America blinked. "Can we help you?"

The young woman turned her head and stared. "I have a message for Phaeton Black." Several other apparitions—mostly particles of gray matter—swirled about the room, but never quite materialized.

"Let me handle her." Valentine whispered and rose from her chair.

"I've got this, Valentine." Phaeton stood on the landing with Jersey. The beautiful creature smiled as he took a seat beside her on the lumpy couch. He certainly appeared familiar enough with the dangerous apparition. "How can I help you, Miss Georgiana Ryder?" At least his eyes didn't roam when he returned her smile, America bit her lip.

There was a flutter of eyelashes and a pretty pout as the succubus trained her wiles on Phaeton. "If you are willing to cooperate, there is a person in the Outremer, a man of influence, who is ready to offer you something you cherish highly in your world."

"As you already know, I am a man of simple pleasures. Who is this person of influence and what could he possibly offer me?"

America caught a flash of storm in Miss Ryder's blue-green eyes. "The Orchid Lounge, off Tottenham Court Road," the young lady stated, quirking her head as though listening to an unseen, unheard directive. Quite suddenly, she disintegrated in a gray haze, and whirled up through the ceiling.

Phaeton lay back against the arm of the chaise and looked around the room. "Has anyone the foggiest clue what that succubus gibberish was about?" He rose and headed for the pantry cabinet. "Whiskey?" He glanced at Jersey.

"Be right back." The Nightshade leader was already headed back up the stairs. Presumably, on the trail of the disappearing apparition.

Phaeton lifted the cover on the roasting pan and sniffed. "Succulent roast lamb and gravy as only Miss Jones can make it." He poured himself a dram and sidled close to America. He slipped an arm around her waist to pull her close. "You and I, darling—in my bedchamber, immediately after dinner." It must be windy outside, his hair was tossled and his eyes glistened with something that caused her to shiver.

Footsteps on the stairs indicated Jersey was on his way back down and Cutter was with him. America nodded to the small table set for six. "Are we ready to feast ladies, gentlemen?"

They cleaned the leg of lamb down to the bone before anyone made much conversation. Phaeton and Jersey took turns relating the high points of their meeting with Lovecraft, the Gaspar Sinclair sighting, and the professor's invitation to hunt RALS in the Outremer.

Jersey tipped his chair back. "Gaspar is either in this with Lovecraft or it's some kind of ruse."

"I wager they both think they're using the other." Phaeton swirled a last sip of whiskey in his glass.

Jersey puffed smoke through a grin. "Gaspar will let this new scheme of Lovecraft's play out—see what develops. And if we come back with the stone . . ."

America moistened her lips. "We watch the two of them kill each other over it?" She stared at Jersey. "And what of Phaeton?" She sighed, feeling agitated and frightened for him—and for her. "No matter who's got the stone—"

"That's where we come in." Cutter scrapped the last bit of gravy off his plate with a piece of bread crust. "Our job is to protect the both of you—as well as Doctor Exeter. Anyone who might be vulnerable in the event the maker or Lovecraft get churlish. Gaspar was clear about that." Cutter looked about at everyone. "What?"

"You're not using the voice box." Ruby grinned. "When Cutter eats he removes the rubber choker that keeps the amplifier pressed to his throat."

"Husky, with just the right amount of breath in it." America winked at Ruby.

Her wink caused the Aussie Nightshade to laugh, and flash her bright blue eyes. America made eye contact with Phaeton whose gaze kept returning to her.

How beautiful and desirable you are. And how pregnant.

America sat bolt upright. Phaeton was speaking in her

head—but that was impossible. Or was her mind playing tricks? A wave of trepidation swept through her.

Phaeton rose from his chair. "Bodyguards get kitchen duty. If you'll excuse us, America and I have a bit of business to discuss, don't we darling?" She looked up at him and was sure he recognized the dread in her eyes.

She hesitated. "I should probably stay and help."

He leaned close and whispered in her ear. "I've got the power." He took her hand and led her into his room. The modest bedchamber was all they had left of any privacy in their lives.

America stood facing the door even after she closed it. If she ruminated for long she'd never say it. "I'm pregnant."

She heard the bedsprings creak and pictured Phaeton stuffing a few pillows behind him as he stretched out on top of the counterpane. An eternity of cool silence passed before she turned around. He was staring at her.

She cleared her throat and began again. "Did you hear what I—?"

"Have you seen a doctor?"

She swallowed. "You don't believe me?"

"Of course I believe you. I just thought, isn't that what women do? See a doctor, just to—" Phaeton exhaled and stared at the ceiling.

They fell into another long, deadly silence. America walked in small circles, with her arms crossed over her chest.

"When were you going to tell me, America?"

"Is that what you're angry about?"

"I am not angry," he raised his voice. "And if I was angry, which I am not," he yelled, "It would not be at you." He caught himself mid-shout and spent a moment collecting himself. "I am angry at myself—for not using protection."

America relaxed a little; at least he was being his brutally honest self. "We were rather lax with the rubber goods." She was quite sure he glared at her stomach. "Please don't do that."

"Do what?"

"You're glaring at the baby."

Phaeton's eye roll accompanied a tilt to his chin and a lop-sided frown. He inhaled a deep breath then exhaled. "America, I'm not ready."

"Neither am I."

"Oh yes you are. I expect you're already planning to convert that large closet across the aisle. Paper the walls with elves and fairies, purchase a cradle and—" He lifted beseeching eyes to the ceiling and ran both hands through his hair.

America had to turn away. A smile from her would only serve to irritate. She peeked at him and realized he hadn't taken his eyes off her for more than a second or two since they had entered the bedroom.

"Months ago—before you decided to take an ocean voyage with me, you expressed the worry that any child of ours would be special, as you were growing up. While other children suffered nightmares that could be soothed away, the trolls lurking under your bed were real. I can't imagine how terrifying that must have been for you."

Phaeton cut in. "Thank you for reminding me what a cruel and wretched life we'll be imposing on our child."

America shook her head. "Not such a terrible life with a mother and a father who can guide, nurture, and protect. If you think about it, you've had quite a good life—full of thrills and adventure." She dared to venture closer.

Phaeton exhaled loudly, but he patted the bed beside him. "And what about these creatures from the Outremer, the ones who threaten us?"

"We have the Nightshades—and I suspect even more powerful forces protect us." America sat on the edge of the bed. "We'll do the very best we can to shield our son or daughter. Phaeton, you're the bravest man I've ever known."

"Reckless perhaps, hardly brave." Phaeton yawned. "I barely slept a wink last night after discovering the little bundle. And I'm not done being—"

"Crabby, peevish, curmudgeonly?" America allowed a small grin to surface.

Phaeton narrowed his gaze and started over. "I'm not done being ill-tempered about this."

"I would expect not. That is why I'm giving you a week to adjust."

"And if I'm not ready?"

"The pea in the pod and I are shipping out."

"Out of the question. Those creatures will follow you wherever you go—if only to get to me. You can't leave now, not until we recapture the stone and end this intrusion . . . invasion . . . whatever it is." Phaeton adjusted a pillow. "Besides, I have the power." He added a half smile to a dark, brooding gaze. Those heavy-lidded, somnolent eyes nearly always caused a tingle to run through her body. Like now.

America met his gaze with something sultry of her own. "And the duke's pleasure this evening?"

He leaned back against a pile of cushions. "I believe the duke would enjoy the lady to disrobe for him—slowly—and he'd appreciate that little island song you used to sing aboard ship. The one you rock your hips to."

America turned her back to him. "Undo me?"

"That would be my pleasure." His fingers swiftly undid buttons, and the dress fell around her waist. He ran his lips down the slope of her shoulder.

America stood and stepped out of her dress and petticoats. She pivoted sideways and slipped a camisole strap off one shoulder, then the other. Slanting her gaze, she rocked her hips gently back and forth, and moved her torso in such a way that her camisole fell to the very tips of her breasts.

Phaeton's gaze fell to her pantalettes. "Bottoms off."

Just the way he looked at her caused her body to tremble and her cheeks to blush. America pulled the ribbon on her pantalettes, and sang her native song. *"I want to learn to speak Tahitian, then I can say the sweetest things to you . . ."*

Phaeton smiled. "Turn around—the duke wants to see that lovely bum."

She turned a slow circle as her hips swayed. *"I want to learn to sing Tahitian, so I can thrill you through and through."* America swung her hips back and forth, inching the pantalettes over one curve then the other, until they fell in a puddle at her feet.

She heard the bedsprings move. "Don't look back. Just keep

that lovely rear moving." His hand slipped between her legs. "Open." She widened her stance. His fingers explored her moist folds, stroking the sensitive place that made her knees tremble.

He pushed her camisole up. "Off." His kisses started at the small of her back and moved lower, as he explored deeper— readying her with one, then two fingers that were slippery with the evidence of her arousal.

"Bend over." His tongue delved into her opening, while his fingers circled and teased her pleasure spot. "Please Phaeton— may I touch myself?"

"You may circle your nipples, but you are not allowed to touch them."

She felt the hard thick length of him slip between her legs. He rubbed her with his velvet cock until she moaned from the building pleasure. He pressed into her and planted himself deep. He bent over her and kissed each shoulder blade. She felt his hot breath on her back. "Rock against me, love." She swayed against him and he moved with her.

Holding her against him, he lifted her off the ground and lay her across the bed, keeping her buttocks at the edge. He reached around her, and played with the tips of her breasts— rolling them into hard points. An unexpected pinch sent her to new heights of arousal. "Not yet, love—you will come with me, and not before."

Her heightened arousal threatened to engulf her at any moment, and he knew it. He thrust into her and pumped hard— his balls slapping against her flesh. In a fury of ecstatic cries and gasps of pleasure they came together.

Sated and fully pleasured, America sighed. It was as if Phaeton knew her body better than his own. He remained bent over her, and did not withdraw, but held on tight. Her insides continued to quiver and his cock pulsed in answer to her. He rubbed the stubble of his beard against her back, affectionately.

He kissed each buttock cheek as he slipped out of her.

He lay down beside her, and scooped her up in his arms. "As much as I adore taking you from behind, Miss Jones, I miss these." He kissed her mouth several times.

America opened her eyes. "And was the duke pleased?"
Phaeton smoothed the curls off her face. "Very."
"And how is Phaeton Black?"
"I believe he's been given a week to adjust."

Chapter Sixteen

THE NOISE REVERBERATED THROUGH THE FLAT and woke America first, then Phaeton. She raised her head off the pillow. *Thud-swish, thud-swish*. It almost sounded as if someone was dragging a large sack of turnips downstairs. A chattering of low voices could be heard outside the bedchamber, as well as more thuds and swishes.

Phaeton groaned. "Three more winks, love, and I'll get up."

America gently removed the arm curled around her body and slipped out of bed. She glanced out the window. First light—one of those misty gray London mornings. Pulling on a dressing gown, she tiptoed down the hallway into the pantry. Valentine was on watch, along with Jersey and Cutter. They stood in a circle with their heads down. Was this some sort of group prayer? She ventured closer. "What's going on?" She looped the ties of her robe.

"Cutter caught one on the roof." Valentine stepped away so she could see.

A dark, leather-skinned body lay splayed out on the floor. Gangly limbs were wrinkled and emaciated. The familiar multi-tentacled head was positioned at a disturbing angle.

"I snapped its neck—at least I think that's what killed it," Cutter rasped under his breath.

America clapped her mouth shut. "But—why is it . . ."

Jersey shook his head. "We're not sure why it remains here."

She nodded. "I've seen them shrivel up into a mass of gray

particles and swarm off. I just assumed they return to the other side."

The eyes were huge oval-shaped black orbs. Dark lenses appeared to cover over some sort of vision mechanism. Or might they obscure another feature? America lowered herself down onto her knees. "Is it safe to—"

"Don't touch it." Phaeton stood behind her bare-chested. Lowering her eyes, she breathed a sigh of relief. At least he wore trousers.

Jersey Blood withdrew a pair of leather gloves from a coat pocket and pulled them on. Descending onto his haunches he turned the creature's head face forward. "It's almost impossible to get a good look at them—besides being wicked fast these tentacles are always whipping about." Jersey placed his hands on each side of the head and pulled. There was a sound, but not of bones or sinew. Something clicked.

Jersey looked up at Cutter.

A mechanized arm attached to a clear lens lifted above Cutter's right eye. A rather expressive substitute for a brow, even if it was made from brass. "Likely a helmet of some kind."

Phaeton strode over to his coat hanging on a hook by the stairs. In two strides he was back with his gloves on. "You get a grip on one side—and I'll take the other."

Using a combination of jiggling and tugging, the helmet popped off.

America gasped.

Phaeton looked up at her. "It's the cockney rhymer who attacked you your first night in London."

"Skeezick," she whispered, and reexamined the creature. The body frame seemed right—rail thin. And that horrid mouth and spiked teeth! Small milky-gray eyes stared straight up at the ceiling. "Do you think it followed me here and has been lurking about the whole time?"

"One thing is certain, they know we're here." Phaeton straightened, rubbing the back of his head. He tilted his head left, then right to pop his neck. "I'd kill for a cup of coffee right now."

America beamed. "I bought coffee yesterday." She pulled a bag of roasted beans from the pantry shelf and took down a grinder which she attached to the counter with a vice. "Anyone for some very rich Belgian coffee?"

Her old bedroom door opened and a groggy-eyed Ruby shuffled into the pantry area. She stared at the creature. "I'm going to need a good strong cup of coffee if I have to look at that thing all day."

Phaeton placed the helmet on the kitchen table so they could all examine the strange tentacled headgear. In no time, she was very pleased to note, they were all wide awake, thanks to pressed coffee steamed with milk and sugar.

"A stroke of luck, wot?" Cutter studied the helmet. "I'd like Tim to have a look at this."

Jersey stirred another lump of sugar into his cup. "It might be luck, or . . . it could just be a trap."

"Or a tracking device." Phaeton sat back and sipped his perfectly made *café au lait*. "If Lovecraft has a gadget that tracks RALS, why wouldn't his otherworld counterpart have a machine that tracks—me?"

America set down a platter of rashers and thick slabs of buttered toast. "Well I for one don't believe any of them have the foggiest clue where the Moonstone is." She wiped her hands on her apron. "Perhaps they're hoping that Phaeton will lead them to it, and they're giving him—and us—just enough of a leash to do so."

A deadly quiet silence was broken by a remark from above. "Miss Jones makes an excellent point." Phaeton recognized the gentle voice of the speaker. Julian Ping stood on the stair landing. Actually, it wasn't Julian, it was Jinn Ping—in all her glory. Ping's long hair, normally tied neatly at the nape of *his* neck was flowing around *her* face—as though a magical creature controlled a special breeze that wafted gently around the decidedly feminine *Miss* Ping.

Phaeton had to ask, "Did Gaspar send you?"

Ping descended the last set of steps. "Gaspar doesn't know I'm here. The Moonstone must be restored to whom it was entrusted. It is neither Gaspar's nor Professor Lovecraft's legacy. It is yours, Phaeton."

He grimaced. "So I've been told—*ad nauseam.*" Phaeton studied Ping whom he knew to be a talented empath. One who could stretch his consciousness into other beings—criminals in particular. Still, he wasn't sure how much to trust this wily creature. "America makes a lovely cup of Belgian coffee—the secret is the piece of chocolate at the bottom of the cup. Care to join?"

Jinn Ping halted at the body of the Skeezick. "This poor devil unraveled." She removed kid gloves and placed two fingers at the creature's temple. The corpse appeared to be rapidly decomposing.

"Can you sense anything about the maker?" Phaeton asked.

"There are many more like this one—row after row of them." Jinn's eyes closed briefly. "And there is a face in the shadows . . ." The clairvoyant jerked away. She removed a small square tin from a coat pocket, and a pen knife. Angling the blade, Jinn shaved a layer of gray matter off the corpse.

Sure Jinn had seen something in that brief vision, Phaeton's eyes narrowed. "Out with it."

Femme Ping straightened and approached the table. "The creature was wearing this?"

Phaeton sighed. Jinn was being evasive. "Assuming the Reapers have known where we live all this time—why did they not storm the flat and abduct us?" When Jersey glared at his remark, he tilted his head in apology. "No offense."

"None taken." The Nightshade answered.

"Miss Jones's theory is essentially correct." Jinn's eyes focused on something far away. "I understand it has already been revealed to you that there is not much time before the RALS begin to weaken. As they lose power they will begin to malfunction. The more hunters we have out looking for the Moonstone, the quicker it will be found."

Phaeton frowned. "A very big risk, wouldn't you say? Every bloody player in this game must believe they can snatch it away from whoever ends up with the stone."

Jinn scanned the flat and leaned close. "For tonight, the women will stay with Doctor Exeter. I will return well before dusk and accompany you on your search for the RALS. Lovecraft will be annoyed and believe Gaspar sent me along because he doesn't trust him—which is true." Jinn flashed a sultry look at the men around the table. "You must all insist I come along."

Phaeton tilted his chair back. "If Gaspar is so interested in the Moonstone—why isn't he in on the hunt?" His question yanked Jinn back into the real world.

"He already suffers the ill effects of too many trips to the other side. In fact, his condition grows more serious by the day."

Jinn's gaze moved to America. "The Outremer is known to have deleterious effects on natural beings. Once the particle degradation begins, the unraveling is very difficult to stop. Because of your expectant condition, as a precaution, you will no longer participate in expeditions to the other side." Jinn's sultry gaze made contact with every one of Nightshades. "This is by Gaspar's order."

Phaeton might as well have been punched in the gut. The news that America, and the life she carried within her, might in some way be impacted by her trip to the Outremer affected him beyond reason. Even the idea that Gaspar was unraveling and might soon disintegrate was disturbing.

The Shades traveled light, even the women, and in no time the ladies were packed and on their way to Exeter's townhouse in Mayfair.

Cutter and Jersey wrapped what was left of the Reaper in a sheet and dropped the remains in a dustbin behind Mrs. Parker's. Phaeton set a number of cups and saucers in a large basin filled with warm water and soap flakes. "Now what?"

Jinn's hair was collecting itself behind her ears. Soon the exotic silver eyes would be hidden behind dark spectacles. She wrapped the menacing helmet in a towel and knotted the corners to make a bundle. "We pay a visit to Tim Noggy's workshop."

He rather liked this new take-charge Ping. Was he off the opium? Or was it the change in gender that made the difference? Phaeton grinned. Jinn to the rescue.

As though she could read his thoughts, Jinn looked up. "No one saves us but ourselves."

Phaeton craned his neck to see the third floor of a rookery tenement on Cecil Court. "I thought the Board of Works was supposed to tear down this rickety slum months ago."

Somewhere between Drury Lane and Charing Cross Road, Mr. Ping had returned to them. At the moment, his pale silver eyes were hidden by dark spectacles. "Likely Salisbury's doing—our slumlord Prime Minister."

They found the stairwell to the flats between two booksellers. Watkins Bookstore, Specialists in Mysticism and the Occult and Ellis Peters, Tarot and Psychic Readings. Ping hurried them up the narrow flight of stairs to 18-F Cecil Court.

An eyeball in a peephole looked them over.

The door opened and Tim Noggy ushered them into a flat that was decidedly more workshop than residence. Besides the cast iron bed frame and mattress shoved into a corner, there was scant evidence a human being lived there. The large chap moved the kettle off a Bunsen burner, filling a chipped teapot. "As you can see, I don't get many visitors." Tim's gaze moved from Ping to Jersey to Phaeton and Cutter. "Where are the ladies?"

"They'll not be with us tonight."

Tim grunted. "Sounds serious."

Ping found a spot on the worktable and unwrapped the bundle. "Cutter finished off one of these boys before it had a chance to slip away."

Tim blinked several times. "Dog's bollocks," he whispered. Wiping his hands on a dingy lab coat, he pulled an oversized pair of tweezers out of an apron pocket and a magnifying glass from a drawer on the worktable. "Reapers punch in and out which takes a good bit of energy. If this guy was, say, close to petering out . . ." Tim looked up from admiring the helmet. "This is extreme, Cutter. I'm in awe, mate."

After a lengthy inspection, he probed around the inside of the helmet. "Look here." Tim touched the end of his tweezers to the lining and it crackled to life—even the tentacles twitched.

Jersey tilted his head to look inside the helmet. "Electrical?"

Tim tilted his head and continued to poke about. "Some kind of force field. This might explain how they are able to punch in and out at will, whereas we have to kind of trick our way in and out."

"And how is it we are able to do any of this? The forces that be in the Outremer created these entrances and exits between worlds, did they not?"

"That's part of it." Tim nodded. "The other is like a trick of consciousness."

Phaeton stared. "Which . . . does what?"

"Look here, mate." Tim opened a notebook to an empty page, and drew a dot at the top and bottom of the paper. "It's like—how do we connect one dot to the other?"

Phaeton shook his head. "Not very likely—when the page is bound into the book. Tim grinned. "Exactly right. What the Outremers have done—by punching holes in and out—is something like this." Tim tore the page out of the book. "It's up to us"—Tim curled the piece paper, bringing the two dots at opposite ends together—"to do this."

Ping grinned.

Jersey grunted.

Phaeton changed the subject. "Those thick tentacles, I've never seen them used aggressively. They look mean, but— maybe all they do is latch onto things. Perhaps they're sucking up energy, or maybe they're trying to read your mind—your fears."

Tim picked up the helmet and shoved it on. "How do I look? Fearsome?"

Phaeton chuckled as did everyone else, including Tim. After seeing the helmet on the rail-thin, gangly-limbed Reapers it was startling to see it on Tim and his twenty-stone frame. A large number of thick tentacles waved gently around him.

And they were moving—but only slightly. Not the whip crack, stabbing snakes they were used to dealing with. What-ever energy Tim had in his body was obviously fueling the feelers.

"Do you feel different?" Phaeton asked.

"Nothing." Tim pressed the helmet lower. "Wait." He held

an index finger up to his lips. He appeared to be listening to something, because he nodded his head.

"Tim Noggy." He spoke aloud.

Phaeton looked to Ping. "You hearing—seeing this?" Tim's eyes had glazed over and he was answering questions. "In my workshop." Tim looked around the room. "With my colleagues—friends." Tim nodded. "Who are they?"

Phaeton shook his head. "No names."

Phaeton and Ping took one side, Jersey and Cutter the other. Tim opened his mouth to answer and they each grabbed a tentacle and pulled the helmet off.

Dazed and confused, Tim shook his head. "It was him—I'm sure of it."

Ping leaned close and checked Tim's eyes. "You spoke with the maker?"

"He seemed . . ." Tim gazed at the men around him. "Nice."

Cutter released a curtain and backed away from the window. "Just to be safe—we'd best be leaving here. Have you got another lab in town?"

Tim nodded. "Several."

In seconds they had the helmet packed and were down the backstairs, which let them out at Charing Cross Road. While they waiting for the Underground train, in the midst of the noontime rush and bustle, Phaeton turned to Tim. "Study that thing to your heart's content—but don't put it on again."

"Don't worry, mate. There's some kind of homing beacon inside."

Ping opened the telegram they had received from Lovecraft, and handed it to Tim. "We need your help, to make sure Phaeton gets across tonight."

Their cherubic consultant raised both brows. "Sure you don't want me to go with you?"

Ping shook his head. "We've got the professor with us."

"Why does Lovecraft hate me so much—just because I won't work for him?"

Ping's silver eyes peered over the rim of his dark lenses. "Because you won't work for him."

Tim read the wire. "Hanway Yard, the usual time."

Chapter Seventeen

AMERICA SLIPPED INTO DOCTOR EXETER'S STUDY and quietly closed the door. Valentine sat at the library table reading. She tilted her head to read the spine. "*The Strange Case of Doctor Jekyll and Mr. Hyde.* That might keep an ordinary person awake nights—but not you, Miss Valentine Smyth."

"No, we have Phaeton Black and America Jones in the adjoining room for that." The female Nightshade's grin quickly went lopsided and curious. "Is that a hint of a blush, I see, Miss Jones?"

America felt her cheek with the back of her hand. "Were we the least bit inspiring—I hope?" She sat down beside Valentine and poured herself a cup of tea from the tray on the table.

Soft snores from the parlor indicated a Nightshade male napped on the divan by the window. "Jersey's back?"

Valentine nodded. "Phaeton and Cutter are tucking Tim Noggy into a new secret location."

America nodded. "Where's Ruby?"

"She's up in her room having a bath." Valentine quietly stirred her tea. "Doctor Exeter tells me you once worked for Phaeton."

America found a ribbon in the pocket of her dress to tie her hair back. "Rather a long story, but first . . ." She lowered her voice to a whisper. "I want to hear about you and Jersey last night. Any news?"

A rap at the door brought Mr. Tandi, Doctor Exeter's manservant, inside the study. Dressed in a white caftan and trousers, the elegant dark-skinned servant wore many strands of glass beads around his neck and wrists.

Valentine laid a finger over her lips and nodded toward Jersey.

A soft-spoken man, Tandi hardly needed to lower his voice. "It is my pleasure to serve you and make certain your stay with us is as comfortable as possible. Might there be anything more you desire this afternoon?"

"Plenty of cakes and biscuits left and the tea is still warm." Valentine smiled. "Thank you, Mr. Tandi." They waited for the exotic man to leave the room.

"Any progress?" America prodded.

Valentine slipped a finger between pages and shut the book. "I do believe all those moans and grunts from the bedchamber last night had their effect," she spoke quietly. "He agreed to a test."

"And?"

Valentine whispered in her ear. "Three kisses—each one longer than the last."

America nodded. "He wanted more, but also learned he could stop."

Valentine rolled her eyes over to the sleeping Nightshade on the settee. "Shall we take a walk about the garden?"

The afternoon sun warmed paths that meandered through neatly trimmed boxwood hedges. They found an iron bench, between flowerbeds filled with red poppies and delphiniums.

Valentine took a seat, angling herself toward America. "Next lesson?"

"It's important not to rush things. That lovely hunk of a man curled up on the settee wants you, badly. If you move too fast, and he looses the beast inside, you risk a setback." America smiled. "Make him come to you this time."

Phaeton entered Hanway Yard and checked his surroundings. Even though the uneven pavers were enough to trip a person up, gaslights had been replaced by electric lampposts, and shop windows blazed with light. He was definitely in the

Outremer, and it was nearly dark out. Phaeton strolled past chic boutique windows with smart looking togs on display and racks of clothing for sale inside. The future—if indeed this was the future—appeared ready-to-wear.

He stopped short near Tottenham Court Road, mesmerized by a shop window filled with ladies' unmentionables. The delicate undergarments lay scattered about in front of large photographs of statuesque women, nearly all of them nude, except for a tiny string, running between the cheeks of their buttocks.

Christ, he was instantly hard as a stone.

The fragile, lace pantalettes on display came in every shade of pastel, cream, and black. Tiny pieces of cloth and string—and all he could think about was how they might look on America.

One of the life-size women in the photographs looked over her shoulder. She cupped bare breasts with her hands—like there was something to be modest about when your buttocks were jiggling in the breeze? Still, he enjoyed a quick fantasy.

Phaeton scanned the yard behind him and entered the shop. A pert young woman with bobbed hair popped up from behind a pink and white striped counter. She looked him up and down. "Love your outfit—going to the Anti-Christ?"

"Pardon?"

"The nightclub in Whitechapel? Steampunk theme night?"

A bit slack jawed, he nodded. "Right."

She pointed to the goggles around his neck. "Nice touch."

Phaeton cleared his throat. "Might I inquire about the cream colored lingerie in the window?"

"Oh!" The shop girl gasped. "One of my favorites—did you notice the strategically placed little rhinestone? Adorable!" The enthusiastic young woman opened a shallow drawer in a display cabinet. "We have them in every color!"

Phaeton picked out the cream with the rhinestone, a violet lace little nothing, and something in transparent black with a velvet bow at each hip.

"Is this a gift? Wife or girlfriend?"

Phaeton noted a flash of pale light out in the yard. No doubt his comrades were arriving. "More of a gift for me, actually."

He picked up the delicate undergarments and stuffed them in his pocket. "How much?"

"Thirty-one and six." When he stared, she added, "Including VAT."

Luckily, he still had a money clip full of his gambling winnings. He counted out nearly a half year's rent.

"Phaeton—we've been looking all over for you." Jersey swept through the doorway, goggles resting on top of his head, his cloak swept back off his shoulders looking for all the world like the adventurer he was.

The shop girl's mouth dropped open as her gaze moved from Jersey to Cutter, who stood in the doorway—whirring and rasping. "I could call a few friends . . . meet up with you blokes later in Whitechapel?"

Phaeton stepped away. "We're off to a . . . costume party. Perhaps later, love."

"After hours, then." She winked.

They joined Ping and Lovecraft outside. "Shopping, Phaeton?" Despite the annoyed look, the professor stole another glance at the display window. They all did. Phaeton deciphered the sign above the pink striped awning and snorted. "Of course the queen would want to keep this shop a secret— what year is this exactly?"

"Outremer years don't parallel ours—and their reality may or may not be our future." Lovecraft led the way to the center of the small yard. "One of my scouts spotted a horde of RALS in this vicinity last night."

Phaeton stared at the boxy device in the professor's hand. Lovecraft toggled a switch and pivoted slowly in a circle. A quiet chime sounded at regular intervals—but as the device swung toward a main thoroughfare, the dinging increased to more frequent intervals. Lovecraft headed straight for the Underground entrance near the intersection of Oxford and Tottenham Court Road.

Jersey and Cutter spread out into the first level of the large Underground station and waved them onto a moving staircase which took them down into the lower tube and train platforms.

Phaeton and Ping hovered around Lovecraft's device, while

Jersey and Cutter swept up and down the platform for any visual sign of the rats. The detector had begun to chime repeatedly—much to the curiosity of those waiting for the train.

"Can you turn that thing down?" Phaeton inquired. The sickly, yellowish-green light that illuminated the platform began to flicker, then cut out entirely. Lovecraft looked up furtively and clicked the locator off. A few more flickers and they were plunged into darkness.

He sensed the Nightshades hovered close by. "The Noggle Goggles help." Cutter's rasp cut through the dark. A spark of illumination and a buzzing noise accompanied something Lovecraft called "emergency lights." Red bulbs encased in a metal mesh flashed at regular intervals along the stairs, enough light to evacuate the station.

Ping gave his goggles to Lovecraft. "Now that we have the station to ourselves, why don't you switch that machine back on?"

The device led them off the end of the platform and through a series of service tunnels. All of them ended at a hatch which, when opened, led to yet another passage. And all the while the device chimed faster or slower, depending on the direction they headed.

"Shhh!" Jersey held up an arm and they halted at once. The noise was familiar. Something akin to the hiss of a steam vent mixed with the sound of scissors snipping. Cutter pivoted in a circle, and then slowly tilted his head upward. "Try pointing that thing up."

The device sounded like an alarm clock going off. "Where are they?"

"Hiding in air vents, storm drains—basements. Whatever is between here and the surface," said Lovecraft.

Phaeton signaled Ping to accompany him back down the service tunnel. They stopped at the first air shaft they came to. A series of numbers and letters were stenciled in the rim of the shaft cover. "17–19 TCR."

Ping mused aloud. "TCR . . . Tottenham Court Road."

Phaeton squinted up through the louvers of the vent cover.

He reached up, found the latch and twisted. The cover swung down and a gray metallic object fell out of the shaft and into the floor, toes up.

"Cheerio." The clatter brought the others down the passage. Cutter jabbed the expired rat's underbelly and its spindly spider legs contracted. "One Rat Ass Little Spider down—hundreds more to go."

Phaeton exhaled. "Without a transit diagram that includes the service tunnels and vents between the tube and the surface—we could be down here for days. What say we try our luck from the surface down?"

Up on Tottenham Court Road, they passed a number of dark shop windows and a boarded up shooting gallery. Phaeton jogged down a closed courtyard to do a quick nose about. At the end of the row he discovered a narrow set of stairs. A flashy sign buzzed and glowed a lurid shade of fuchsia. "The Orchid Lounge." Realizing his goggles were on, he lowered the protective lenses.

A deep throbbing beat thumped away at regular intervals. Not the whispered clicks and snips of the RALS, but intriguing nonetheless. Phaeton hesitated on the top step. A door banged open at the bottom and the sound blasted up the stairs and down the alley. The disturbance brought his cohorts out on the street, running down the alley.

A large chap wearing a shirt stretched across a bulging chest and arms took a seat outside the door of the . . . Phaeton read the sign again.

"Blimey, The Orchid Lounge—" Jersey spoke the words out loud. "You asked about the maker and the succubus uttered the name of this place."

"I believe I called it succubus gibberish." Phaeton grimaced.

Lovecraft's watery bug eyes shifted back and forth. "I wouldn't disappoint the maker, if I were you, Phaeton. You were sent an invitation."

The door below stairs banged open again as two young women exited The Orchid Lounge. The girls wore breathtakingly short gowns that sparkled when they moved. Phaeton's gaze moved from ankles to calves to thighs.

As they reached street level, he couldn't resist a nod. "Good night, ladies." Up close, they wore face paint and very unusual hair. The one with straight pink tresses gave him a wink. "Sorry boys, we've got an early shift in the morning."

Both young women halted dead in their tracks and blinked. They were both staring at Cutter. Phaeton remembered what the shop girl said. "Been out . . . clubbing. Just came from Whitechapel—The Anti-Christ."

Both girls exhaled a knowing, "Ahhh," and one even batted her lashes at Cutter. "Hot."

Phaeton tore his eyes off the two lovelies. "Shall we, gentlemen?"

"Welcome to The Orchid Club." A young man inside the door took gobs of banknotes off them and stamped the back of their hands with something invisible.

Phaeton led the way, winding a path through a crush of dancers, everyone dipping and moving in rhythm. He wanted to call whatever it was music—because he could not for the life of him think of what else it might be. The vibration of the low notes thrummed up through the floor and permeated his entire body. He approached a throng of drinkers standing two deep at a bar lit up like a Christmas window at Harrods.

Exotic, colorful drinks were in everyone's hands—Phaeton's gaze meandered through a bevy of scantily clad women and landed on the absinthe fountain. Cold water dripped out of four spigots, dissolving lumps of sugar, and flowing into glasses gone milky green with . . . he turned to his compatriots. "Name your poison—I'm buying."

Perhaps it was the throbbing beat or the lovely bodies—everywhere—but Ping was turning into Jinn. His hair flowed around his face, and his features had suddenly gone all luscious and feminine.

Lovecraft sidled over close and shouted in Phaeton's ear. "If we meet with the maker—we should offer a deal. Promise anything—whatever he wants, if you take my meaning." He rolled his eyes in that weirdly diabolical fashion—a signature look of the professor's.

"You need a drink, Lovecraft—in fact, you could use a good

tumbler full." Phaeton hadn't taken his eyes off Jinn who was rocking her hips against Cutter. The exotic *homme-fille* took Cutter's hand and pulled him onto the dance floor.

Phaeton shouted after them. "Just remember she's got a love stick between those legs." He worked his way up to a bartender with a brilliant blue streak in her hair and hard nipples that bounced about under a tight shirt. "Two glasses of absinthe and two whiskeys—large. Do you happen to have any Talisker's?"

Wary bartender eyes moved up and down. "Twelve, eighteen, or twenty-five year single malt?"

Phaeton stared.

"You think about it." She started two glasses of absinthe and poured a number of pints before she returned to him.

"Make it eighteen."

She smiled. "Won best in the world last year."

Feeling like a finalist in a whiskey connoisseur contest, he tried his luck with a bit of investigating. "I'm looking for three women—sisters, actually. Velvet, Fleury, and Georgiana. You wouldn't happen to know them?"

She nodded to another set of stairs through an alcove. "There's a private dancer in the back of the club named Velvet. Not sure that's her real name."

"Perfectly all right, I'm not sure she's real—period." Phaeton glanced at the stairs. "I'll pop in later, say hello."

The bartender poured the whiskey and collected two glasses of the absinthe. "I hear she's expensive."

Phaeton counted out several months' rent, plus gratuity. "What isn't?" He grouped four glasses together and winked. "Cheers."

Chapter Eighteen

PHAETON SHOUTED OVER THE DIN. "I believe they refer to these places as clubs—not casinos. And if anyone inquires about your costume, just say we're back from The Anti-Christ in Whitechapel." Jersey, who was never interested in having any fun—ever—actually sipped the absinthe he'd ordered for him.

Phaeton tipped his glass and let the pale green liquid slip down his throat. He hadn't had an absinthe in months and it tasted like heaven.

One throbbing tempo slipped into another of similar rhythm with little or no pause. Phaeton found his body moving to the pulse of the music. A lovely tall thing with legs that inspired lustful thoughts approached him from the dance floor. "Bootie rub?" Not sure how to answer, he leaned toward her and tilted his ear. She dipped closer. "Dance?"

He handed his glass to Jersey. "You had me at rub, love."

Somewhere in the midst of a crush of dancers, they faced each other. She moved up close, as the beat pulsed absinthe through his body. He rolled with her, hip to hip—bodies in motion, rocking with the beat. She raised her arms above her head, in a kind of sultry surrender, the motion of her lower body swung her around and she backed up against his crotch, rubbing her buttocks against him.

Phaeton placed his hands on her hips and rocked with her—then against her. He exchanged looks with Cutter, Jersey—even Lovecraft looked like a fish out of water, gasping for oxygen. From the corner of his eye he caught something wild, dark, and sultry on the move.

Jinn was dancing his way.

America made her announcement at dinner, between the turtle soup and filets of cod. "I shall open a sleuthing firm specializing in mysteries of an odd and unexplainable nature. And I have every intention of exploiting all the talent in this dining room."

"Any riddle in need of solving?" Exeter lifted a wine glass and sipped.

"I believe America means to pursue matters of Phantasmagoria," Mia exclaimed. America smiled at Doctor Exeter's beautiful charge, who had recently blossomed into a sophisticated, young woman.

Valentine grinned. "Demons are my specialty."

"We could expose all those horrid séance charlatans out there," Ruby enthused.

Her gaze scanned the table, Doctor Exeter to Valentine, Ruby, and Mia. "Very discreet investigations, of course. The calling card shall read: Moonstone Investigations. No uncommon psychical disturbance refused, no matter how perplexing."

Surrounded by a bevy of beauties, Doctor Exeter looked pleasantly amused. "What about the shipping business?"

"I shall run the shipping office and the detective agency out of a workspace near the flat—I shan't need a very large place," America enthused.

"It would seem advisable that you remain in London, at least until the happy event." A gentle smile tugged at the ends of Exeter's mouth. The upward tilt gave America a lift. She hadn't seen him this relaxed since arriving in Port of London. The doctor had been rather occupied with pressing matters and had all but withdrawn from the pursuit of the Moonstone.

"Moonstone Investigations," Mia contemplated aloud. "Has a lovely ring to it."

America studied the very capable young women at the table. "I'd like to be able to call on all of you to assist on cases. Depending, of course, on your availability—particularly once the pea in the pod arrives."

Valentine sliced into a succulent piece of roast duck. "Of course we will help in any way we can; that little pea is very special."

"Feel free to call on Scotland Yard, as well." All eyes strained in the same direction. Zander Farrell stood in a dim alcove of the dining room entry. "Sorry to intrude. Mr. Tandi asked me to announce myself. Something about a small grease fire in the kitchen."

"This seems to happen whenever the cook serves duck." Exeter stood up. "Please join us; I shall return as soon as I am assured the house isn't going up in flames."

Farrell sat down beside her. "I might have just the unsolved problem to get you started, Miss Jones. And, I've assigned Inspector Dexter Moore to the case, someone you've worked with in the past—and quite successfully I might add."

America's heart raced at the idea of Scotland Yard being her first official customer. "I'm a bit overwhelmed, but of course your offer is welcome, indeed!"

The fact that she would be working with Inspector Moore made it all the more comforting. Moore had helped bring Yankee Wilhem to justice and had seen her stolen ships returned to her. Phaeton did not get on well with Moore—but she was perfectly capable of smoothing that over.

She met Ruby's gaze across the table. "Looks like you have your first case." The cheerful blonde winked. "It will be nice to have something to do with the men off—"

Valentine cleared her throat.

Ruby stuffed a forkful into her mouth.

Farrell caught the exchange.

"Where is Phaeton by the way?" The inspector looked around the table. "I ventured here this evening with the hopes of having a quick consult. I need to know if he's uncovered anything on the Ryders, or sisters succubi, as we've come to call them. Perplexing case. Investigation's got us buggered."

"Can I offer you anything, Inspector?" Exeter was back and

took his seat at the head of the table. "Dessert and coffee—perhaps a brandy."

"Coffee would be very much appreciated, as well as a brandy." Farrell gave a wink. "Phaeton passed on an important lead and we've gone nowhere with it. We need specialized talent, and I'm afraid we don't have the right manpower at the Yard.

America raised a brow. "It sounds like you need woman power, Inspector Farrell."

Farrell grinned. "You read my mind, Miss Jones."

"That was the most fun I've had with my clothes on." Phaeton returned from the dance floor, over stimulated and in great discomfort.

Jersey gave him one of those stone cold grins of his. "Sandwiched between the leggy blonde and Jinn—that's gotta make you feel—"

"Thirsty." Phaeton whipped his empty absinthe glass out of Jersey's hand.

A double shot of whiskey seemed to have little or no effect on Lovecraft. Phaeton took a moment to study the men in his strange coterie. Two of them were magnificent specimens of manhood, who were socially inept. The other two were—well, Jinn was Jinn, or Ping, depending, and Lovecraft was . . . Just looking at the poor man caused Phaeton to exhale. "How long has it been since you've had a bit of trim, professor?"

The question caused those weird watery eyes to vibrate. "My wife died several years ago—just before my son . . ." The professor drifted off in a haze of memories.

Phaeton almost felt sorry for the poor bloke. "If it makes you feel any better, I'm working a lead. One of the Ryder sisters works here."

His news did seem to perk the professor up. "Perhaps . . . I'll have another double."

At the bar, waiting for their second round, Phaeton surveyed the passage that led to what the bartender had called the private rooms. A female dressed in nothing more than a corset and skimpy panties descended the backstairs with a paying customer. The glowing overhead sign read: STAIRWAY TO HEAVEN.

Phaeton counted out his remaining cash and turned back to face the bartender. "How much?" He narrowed his eyes. "For one of the private dancers?"

"Forty quid for a ten minute lap dance." The female bartender looked him up and down.

Phaeton needed details. "And . . . what exactly happens in ten minutes. For forty quid?"

"You want me to talk dirty to you?"

He dropped his gaze to those unrestricted, bouncing breasts and leaned across the bar. "Would you please, love?"

Phaeton returned to his comrades, his head swimming with lusty images. He passed around the drinks. He clinked a toast. "Drink up gents, we're going to call on Velvet." He led the way downstairs into yet another sub-basement covered with padded walls and plush furniture—the throbbing beat from the dance floor, though muffled, still filled the room.

Phaeton's gaze meandered though a sea of gyrating . . . booty. The word for buttocks in the Outremer. He tried to remember what the Ryder sister looked like and got distracted. Everywhere he turned there was a near naked female grinding on a customer. He wasn't sure his brain was functioning—but he was sure his cock was.

"Mr. Black—is that you?"

Phaeton pivoted. "Velvet." She stood with her hands on her hips wearing something resembling string with small pieces of fabric covering her nipples and triangle. "You're looking wonderfully . . ." He forced himself to make eye contact.

"Naked?" She grinned.

"Yes, indeed. Is there someplace we might go to talk, briefly?"

The baldheaded bloke with huge bulging muscles appeared out of nowhere. "You gentlemen have had your peep—now pay up or get out."

Phaeton tossed the last of his banknotes at the man. "There's a tip in there for Velvet."

"Tip her yourself." The hairless bruiser handed a tenner back and walked away. "Ten minutes." He tossed over his shoulder.

Velvet took him by the hand and led him to a chair in the corner of the room. "How are your sisters?"

"I don't see them very often—I don't crossover much anymore." She looked over her shoulder. "Sit down and keep your hands at your sides."

"Ah yes, the most titillating part of this brief entertainment—I can't touch you." Phaeton leaned back into the armless, upholstered chair and watched. Deep violet eyes and raven hair—he had forgotten exactly how attractive she was, for a succubus.

Phaeton cleared his throat. "I'm looking for an unusual object of power . . ." She bent over—shaking her bum in his face. Phaeton swallowed, ". . . Melon sized."

Velvet shot a curious look over her shoulder. Turning to face him, she raised her leg in the air and placed her foot on his shoulder. She pressed in close, and her little triangle dropped to eye level. She rocked into him. "Would it be black, and shaped like a very large egg? With some kind of substance fluttering about inside?"

He kept his eyes on hers. "You just described it perfectly."

She pushed off him, and smiled. Legs spread wide, she snapped the strings at her hips as though she might suddenly remove the small bottoms. Velvet turned her backside to him and slid down his knees. Phaeton gripped the underside of the chair with both hands and hung on for dear life. She lay back against his chest and kept that booty grinding against him.

Phaeton was overcome with the most mysterious image—it was that tawny colored booty he'd come to know so well—jiggling at him. Even though his cock was about to explode, he leaned his head back and closed his eyes. The lights flickered, he was almost sure of it. The fusion of strange music and rhythmic thumps stopped so abruptly the silence actually hurt his ears.

Quite suddenly the spell was broken and Phaeton lifted his head. "What's going on?"

"The power is about to go out. The club has a generator—enough to clear the rooms and lock up the cash registers." Velvet climbed off him and shrugged. "Blackouts are happening with greater and greater frequency—several times a day. There was one earlier this evening." She looked him up and down. "You all right?"

He nodded, recalling the incident in the Underground. Most of the customers were headed back upstairs. He staggered to his feet and glanced around the room. Up above the sound of whips whizzed through the air, punctuated by eerie shrieks and chirping.

"Reaper patrols can sometimes cause blackouts. You'd best be gone," Velvet advised. She grabbed him by his coat lapels and kissed him. Warm soft lips with just a sting of tongue. "I'm not like my sisters." She released him.

The billowing cape of a Nightshade caught his eye. Jersey was headed straight for them. "The others have gone—we'll meet up across the river."

Velvet pointed to a dark corridor. "There's another set of stairs through here." At the door, she turned away.

"Wait a moment." Phaeton lifted the flexible string at her hip and slipped in a large banknote.

She looked up and smiled. "Most blokes would complain, they'd be wanting their full ten."

"Velvet—I have to ask." Phaeton connected with violet eyes. "Where did you see the orb?"

She bit her lip. "It wasn't there the last time I looked."

"Can you find out where it is?"

She glanced over her shoulder. "I'll try to get word through Georgiana or Fleury."

Phaeton raced up the stairs after Jersey. Somewhere below, tentacles whipped the sides of the narrow passage. The Reapers couldn't be more than a flight of stairs behind them. Phaeton and Jersey surfaced just below street level.

"Hold on." Jersey took out his dagger and ran a white hot light down the side of the industrial door. "I'm fusing the lock mechanism," Jersey explained.

"Practical as well as deadly," Phaeton rasped, breathing hard.

He and Jersey made their way through the blacked out streets. The closer they got to the river the more devastation they saw. Things were literally falling apart—unraveling as Gaspar put it. They jogged past a double-decker bus turned on its side, riddled with bullet holes. The buildings behind the omnibus were blackened and burned out.

"Rebels." Jersey frowned. "This is what happens when the power runs out. People go crazy."

Oddly, there were districts of the city that appeared almost untouched, but as they came upon the river, the devastation grew worse.

A jog across the Vauxhall Bridge revealed the Thames was gone—or nearly so. Just a small muddy stream running along the bottom of a wide, dry gully.

They met up with three sober looking comrades across the river. Stunned, Phaeton took in the ruin as far as the eye could see. The only bridges left that still crossed the river were the Vauxhall and the Tower Bridge down river. Looking north, Phaeton was aghast at the sight of a ravaged Westminster Palace—Big Ben was still standing, but God knows what was left of the Abbey.

Phaeton's eyes narrowed. "Someone please remind me that this is happening here, not at home."

"Their reality is only one possible future of ours." Lovecraft wore that tiny smirk on his face—the one that Phaeton often had the urge to wipe off with a slap.

Cutter moved between them, mumbling something.

Still dazed and dumfounded by the sights around him, Phaeton finally looked up. "What?"

"I said—how was the lap dance?"

"Stimulating." Then, he said something shocking. "Almost the entire time I kept thinking about America." Phaeton brightened at the thought. "Not in a guilty way. More like——I kept seeing her lovely round bum."

Chapter Nineteen

AMERICA ACCOMPANIED DOCTOR EXETER and Inspector Farrell to the foyer. "I know Phaeton will continue to be most helpful on the Ryder case, Inspector Farrell."

"I'm counting on all of you. Eleven deaths, nearly all of them suspicious; it is a certainty there was some kind of foul play." The inspector brushed off the brim of his bowler. "This has become an embarrassment and a scourge that will eventually reach the press. Ever since the Ripper, it's been nonstop. A never-ending stream of unusual sightings, and I'm afraid the Yard is woefully lacking in expertise when it comes to the occult."

"I shall ring you the moment I have a shingle up and a telephone installed." America smiled. "I see no sense in half measures—I intend to run a modern enterprise."

"Then, my worries are soon over." The inspector tipped his hat. "Good night, Miss Jones—Doctor."

The moment the door closed, Exeter turned to her. "Are you really going to the expense of having a telephone line installed?"

America blinked. "Is it that costly?"

Exeter walked her back toward the parlor. "Depends, I suppose, on the distance they have to go."

America smiled. "Not far at all—Drakes had a telephone installed last week, no doubt for some nefarious gambling purpose, but that brings the line close, does it not?"

"The bold and beautiful Miss Jones. I have never for a moment questioned Phaeton's attraction to you." The doctor smiled. "It's so brilliantly obvious."

America hesitated outside the parlor door. "Might I have a word alone, doctor?"

Exeter seemed pleased. "I was just about to request a similar favor." He gestured to the grand stairs and they made their way to the upstairs parlor.

America settled herself in a corner of a comfortable settee and waited for the doctor to poke a few coals about in the hearth. A tall, elegant man, everything about Exeter exuded intellect and confidence. He also had the loveliest green eyes that never missed a trick. And there was that dashing Van Dyke beard which suited his golden skin, an exotic gift from his Persian mother.

"Now, how can I be of service, Miss Jones?"

"America, please?"

The doctor took a seat on the settee. "Only if you call me Jason." There began a very long silence between them until Exeter finally cleared his throat. "Are you feeling well, America? Any morning sickness?"

"The morning sickness is gone, happily." Her smile was brief. "Phaeton, on the other hand, did not take the news well."

Exeter raised his chin and struck a thoughtful pose. "Despite his devil-may-care approach to most things, I believe Phaeton worries too much about the people he loves. Give him time, America."

She felt a pout coming on. "I gave him a week."

The doctor's eyes sparkled. "And, how long ago was that?"

"Two days ago."

Exeter reached across the divan and took her hand in his. "Over the next few months, and even after the child is born, you're going to be more emotional, for a time."

She nodded, eyes wide. "I cry at the drop of a hat—it's . . ." Drat! She blinked back tears.

"It's natural." He patted her hand.

She exhaled a deep sigh. "He has five more days."

Exeter laughed. "I doubt that he will need more, but if he

does—do give him a few more." He dipped his head and winked. "I know an excellent midwife—very experienced and decidedly more skilled than the average doctor at birthing. If you'd like, I will be there to administer a bit of ether. Not too much but enough to ease your pain."

America was suddenly overcome by his kindness. She threw her arms around him. "Thank you, thank you," she blinked through the tears. "I know, in his heart, Phaeton will be pleased."

"It is a gift to be present at the birth of a new life." He opened a pocket square and dabbed her eyes. "Shall I ring for something? Mr. Tandi makes a sweet tea with hot milk, cinnamon, and clove."

"Sounds lovely," America sniffed.

Ever the consummate host, Exeter ordered the special tea and a brandy for himself. The moment the servant closed the door, he returned to her. "Might you be feeling well enough for a consult?"

"Of course," she said. There was a storm brewing behind the doctor's intense green eyes. "Phaeton and I have both noticed that you are not yourself. Something is troubling you, Jason."

Another deathly quiet silence permeated the room. "Mia has recently experienced some frightening episodes. Quite extraordinary really." His brows furrowed. "Has she mentioned them to you?"

America shook her head. "Mia and I have yet to speak privately. Whatever you can tell me tonight might prove useful, should she bring me into her confidence."

Exeter nodded. "The day after the Moonstone was taken, I received a wire from the chaperone of Mia's boardinghouse stating that she had been found unconscious between the campus and the house—and asking how soon I could come fetch her."

He continued. "Of course I caught the first train to Oxford, and was at the residence by late morning. By the time I arrived, Mia was recovered—but far from normal. Immediately I suspected there was more to the tale than was being presented to me."

America frowned. "No doubt the boardinghouse chaperone didn't wish to be blamed."

"Mia wasn't very forthcoming, either." The muscle in his jaw clenched. "Eventually I got most of the story. She was walking home from a musicale, and got separated from her peers. Not clear exactly how that happened. Apparently the area was densely wooded, and she became frightened and started to run—she said she fell down and the next thing she remembered was waking up. Someone—one of her friends from school—found her and helped her back into the boardinghouse. Rightly, they wired to tell me about the incident."

"But they didn't just inform you of an accident, they asked that you come fetch her."

Exeter's eyes narrowed. "There were dark circles under Mia's eyes. She appeared to suffer from exhaustion—her speech was confused, and she was unable to focus her thoughts. I administered a sedative and once she was asleep, I questioned a few more of her friends, who were slightly more forthcoming."

A gentle rap on the door brought Mr. Tandi into the room. He placed a tray beside the settee with the doctor's brandy and her tea. "There is more warm milk and sugar should you desire it, Miss Jones." The tall African man nodded a bow and slipped quietly out of the room.

America sipped the tea. "Mmm, how delicious!"

Exeter's smile quickly disappeared. "Later that day, I met with the dean of the women's study program, a Miss Margaret Twombly, who finally shared the alarming details. Mia was found in the woods unconscious, completely nude—her clothes were strewn about—some of them torn. At first they thought she might have been attacked by some sort of fiend, there were splotches of blood between her legs. By the way, she was found on her knees, down on all fours—in a kind of trance, but not unconscious."

"Frankly, the dean was concerned about hysteria, more specifically, Mia's state of mind."

America nearly dropped her teacup. "But, Mia seemed perfectly herself at dinner this evening."

"She is restored, for the most part." He shook his head. "But—there's more to it than just one incident. These . . . odd behaviors started before she left for University."

America sipped more spicy tea. "What started?"

"She kissed me." Exeter was blushing, she was sure of it. And he certainly swallowed hard enough.

She set the cup down. "More than a peck on the cheek?"

"A great deal more." Exeter's eyes darted a bit. "And . . . I may have lost control for a moment."

"You returned her affection."

Exeter didn't answer, instead he leapt to his feet. "I was greatly relieved when it was time for her to leave for University. It was my hope this adolescent infatuation would soon pass once she became absorbed in her studies."

America tucked herself farther back into her corner of the settee. "Confess all, Jason, or I'll wheedle it out of your charge."

He waged his finger in the air. "That's just it—she is my charge. I cannot . . . feel these . . . I must not . . ." Exeter stopped pacing long enough to connect with her gaze, which was riveted on him. She had never seen him in such a state. The even-tempered, unflappable doctor was . . . in emotional turmoil. There really was only one question she could think of to ask. "Do you love her?"

"I have come to care deeply for Mia." He appeared to struggle for breath, on the verge of some sort of attack of nerves. Still, he was not getting away with that answer.

"Jason, not as your ward, but as a woman." America narrowed her eyes. "Do you love her?"

"I cannot answer such a question. I must not complicate matters for Mia right now. Not until I find out what is happening to her."

America leaned forward to pour a bit more tea. "I'll take that as a yes."

Exeter paced the length of the Aubusson carpet and back. "Please don't speak of it to anyone right now."

Admittedly, she did not know Exeter's ward that well, the young lady was barely past her eighteenth birthday. She did recall a wonderful sense of humor and a carefree girlish manner—

a bit precocious, but then what pretty, doted upon young woman of privilege would not be?

"Valentine sensed something interesting about Mia this morning." Deep in thought, America moistened her lips. "I'm afraid I've forgotten exactly what she said."

"We'll ask her to join." Exeter dipped into the hallway and sent an upstairs maid down to fetch Valentine. Returning to the parlor, he took up a post at the hearth. "Mia was born in South Africa—the Transvaal. Her parents were both killed during the first Boar War. She and Mr. Tandi escaped to a neighboring farm. From there, they managed to make their way to the Cape colony and book passage on a merchant ship to England."

"We're only distantly related by marriage. The de Roos baronage is the oldest in the realm. They must have known the name de Roos and when they arrived in London, they looked up my father. You met the Baron shortly before he died—despite his many indiscretions, he was good at heart. He took them both in, and within months they became . . . a part of the family." Exeter rubbed his beard.

America recalled a terribly disfigured Baron de Roos covered in bandages. A dying man who had committed terrible deeds, in fear for his mortal soul. And yet, as Exeter claimed, there had also been something gentle about his nature.

A brief tap caused Exeter to pivot toward the door. "Please come in."

Exeter's pretty charge entered the room. "Ruby and Valentine are in the middle of a game." Mia's gaze quickly moved from America to Exeter. "This is about me, isn't it, Om Asa?"

Mia backed the door shut. "Valentine approached me after dinner this evening and asked me a number of intimate questions." The color in the girl's cheeks burned and she appeared a bit wild-eyed.

America was suddenly overcome by feelings of loneliness— it was purely intuitive, but she sensed Mia's isolation and terror. "Come and sit by me." She patted the seat of the settee. "Mr. Tandi made a spice tea, which is still warm."

She settled back and let the young woman sip the exotic brew. "Mia, if you were free from worry, about what people might think or say, or how they might judge you—how would you describe what is happening to you?"

"Here at home, it always begins as a dream. In the dream my whole body feels alive, alert—every sense so magnified, so wonderful, I never want to wake up. I am drawn out of my bed, and into the garden where I can see and taste and smell the earth—it is as if all my senses are fully engaged at once, my body tingles all over—but it's worse than a tingle because it doesn't go away. It becomes something that makes we want to—" Mia stared at the tea leaves floating at the bottom of her cup. "The tingling grows so painful I claw at my nightgown."

America exchanged worried looks with the doctor.

"I awoke in the garden last night. Valentine was there. She helped me up and returned me to my bedchamber." Mia looked up at Exeter. "I know you worry for me." Her eyes darted about the room. Her skin seemed paler than normal and the poor girl had a look of exhaustion about her. "That is why you asked for Valentine tonight. She knows what is happening to me, doesn't she?"

"You are a half-breed, Mia." Valentine stood in the parlor entry. "You are part nocturnal creature, and you have just entered your womanhood." The female Nightshade approached the doctor. "Mia is experiencing her first menorrhea."

"This is unusually late to begin menarche—I would have thought," Exeter's brows crashed together. "I'm very sorry Mia—I should have thought to ask years ago."

She raised her chin rather defiantly. America thought the flush on Mia's cheeks gave her some lovely color. "Why ever would you think to ask, when you see me as a child?" Mia's stare was rather cool, and wonderfully adult.

Exeter's return stare was less than parental.

Mia shifted her gaze away and spoke to the women surrounding her. "At first I was frightened. I thought the blood between my legs meant I was ill . . ." The poor girl looked a bit mortified. "When I realized it was the monthly curse I was relieved."

Valentine took a seat close by. "I don't believe I have ever encountered one of your kind. There are many kinds of demigods—or half-bloods. Most are gifted with extraordinary powers. Some are part animal, some demon—some angel. They come in various shapes and sizes—and you are all beautiful to look upon. Jersey is one. If you let him, he can be very helpful during this time of discovery."

Valentine leaned in close and took Mia's hand. "Have you met your other half, as yet?"

Mia's sparkling dark eyes grew large and round. And green.

Chapter Twenty

BLOODY BLUE BOLLOCKS! All Phaeton could think about was his cock buried deep inside America. Preferably in a warm bed, but he wasn't about to be choosey. He had stumbled home through an access portal near the Anchor Pub. His latest, best inkling—*bitters*. Interesting how many of these strange slip-streams between worlds were located in such close proximity to a pint of bitters. Or was it just that London had so many pubs?

No matter, at the moment he was not inclined to think about anything other than his pursuit of carnal relief. According to Big Ben, it was near midnight. Just ahead, along the river, the professor materialized, and not long after, the two Nightshades. He assumed Ping moved in and out of these spatial anomalies with ease, perhaps even created his own. Ah, there he was, up on the bridge.

They made their way across the Queen Street Bridge and waited for a hansom at a cab stand. Lovecraft continued to pester him endlessly about his conversation with Violet and the whereabouts of the Moonstone. "My impression is she is somewhat estranged from Georgiana and Fleury. I pressed the matter quite strongly with her—I expect to hear something soon."

"Did she mention names—locations—anything we could pursue?"

"Rather hard to remember details with a lady's derrière rubbing against one's crotch." Perhaps it was the lateness of the hour, but the professor's eyes were particularly buggy this evening. "Need I remind you, Phaeton, time is running out."

"I understand. We appear to be on a collision course with a world that is unraveling as we speak. A crumbling, debilitated London that just might take our side down with it." Phaeton exhaled, loudly. His pressing cockstand no doubt contributed to his lack of patience with Lovecraft. "I expect Gaspar knows the dangers better than any of us."

He wasn't exactly sure why, but he had begun to feel a kinship with the bloody leader of the Gentleman Shades. He thought it might have a good deal to do with how Lovecraft was acting, as if he was entitled to the Moonstone. "Short of calling up the Metropolitan Police and the Horse Guards, which I wouldn't recommend, we're doing everything possible to recover the stone."

"This is a game that must be played by wits and stealth, not with an army of combatants," Ping added.

Phaeton studied Lovecraft. "What is going on with you, professor?"

"Cutter." Without taking his eyes off Phaeton, the professor called the Nightshade over. "Cutter served under my son—Lieutenant Alexander Lindsay Lovecraft. Please tell Mr. Black what was left of my son after the war."

Phaeton had no trouble reading Cutter's expressions, despite his having only half a face. His bodyguard was clearly in distress. "Not much more than a torso—both legs and an arm taken out by cannon fire. They used shrapnel—nails, balls of lead—cut a swath through our men."

"The very best surgical doctors in London managed to repair my son's internal injuries." Lovecraft's sly grimace was laced with grief as well as anger. "It's been over seven years, and I have perfected the artificial appliances Lindsay will use to lead a reasonably normal life—but I need the Moonstone."

Cutter's one good eye bulged, and his mechanical brow lifted. "Lindsay is alive?"

"Like everyone else you assumed he wouldn't last—and he nearly didn't."

Right, Phaeton thought. The balmy professor was certifiably mad. Luckily a hansom pulled up. "Gentlemen, I'm headed off to a soft bed and warm woman." Now it was his turn to eyeball Lovecraft. "We'll take this back up in the afternoon."

Much to his relief, the ride to Mayfair was swift and silent. Mr. Tandi opened the door at 22 Half Moon Street. "Do come in gentlemen. The household is retired for the evening, but you are welcome to take a brandy in the study—or shall I show you to your rooms?"

He led them through the foyer to a curve of stair. "Mr. Coppersmith and Captain Blood share a room on the fourth floor. I have placed a reasonably comfortable chair near Miss Jones's bedchamber, as I am told she is always guarded—as is the doctor." Exeter's man ushered them upward. "I myself volunteered for first watch, this evening."

Halfway up the grand staircase, Phaeton paused. "Changed my mind about a good tumbler full of whiskey—would you be so kind, Mr. Tandi?"

The manservant bowed a nod and slipped downstairs. Upstairs, Phaeton spotted the chair beside America's room. Glancing back at the two Nightshades, he put a finger to his lips and stole inside the bedchamber. He took a moment to orient himself.

Moonlight traced a faint pattern of window pane squares across the plush carpet. The pale glow illuminated a figure at the window. A tall, masculine silhouette stood just inside the French doors. Out on the balcony, Phaeton spied the shadow of a lithe and lovely figure of a young woman. Could it be America? And Doctor Exeter? A heaviness filled his chest and yet he crept forward.

The ephemeral beauty approached Exeter slowly, in a sensuous, feline fashion. Her hand went to the shoulders of her nightgown. She slipped dainty sleeves off her shoulders and let the silk fall to her hips.

Beautiful round globes. Small and high set.

Phaeton froze. Pretty as they were, those weren't America's breasts.

He stole a quick glance at his surroundings. An elegant

canopied bed, and a few tell-tale masculine furnishings. He had the wrong bedchamber. This was Exeter's room. Phaeton's eyes returned to the trysting couple. The beautiful creature reached out for the doctor's hand, cupping his palm to her breast.

"Mia." Exeter spoke her name in whispered protest even though Phaeton was quite sure the doctor's thumb stroked a nipple. Mia arched into Exeter and murmured the loveliest . . . most unusual love cry. Something between a moan and a deep, throaty purr.

Placing one foot behind the other, he backed out of the bed-chamber. He closed the door with a near silent click and turned around. His bodyguard held out a tumbler of whiskey. "Mr. Tandi left this for you."

Phaeton examined the paltry amount of whiskey left in the glass.

Jersey slouched onto a side chair, and grinned. Phaeton had been slow to warm to the quiet leader of the Nightshades, but the man was growing on him. Phaeton knocked back the last half dram.

Jersey nodded across the corridor. "She's in there."

He found her curled up on a small settee, fast asleep. A book lay open in her hand. The booty rub at The Orchid Lounge had kept him half-hard for hours now. Phaeton shrugged out of his jacket and unbuttoned his waistcoat. For the past few hours all he could think about was the sight of America's naked bottom writhing beneath him. Her moans of arousal from his cock rooted deep inside her.

She awoke to the touch of his arms wrapping around her. "Open your eyes, Sleeping Beauty." He brushed his lips over her throat as he removed the book from her hand.

Her eyes opened, bright with mischief. "Am I in a waking dream?" Her somnolent, sensuous smile only increased his arousal. Phaeton slipped her nightgown off one shoulder. "A dream that has to do with you and me on that comfortable bed over there."

"A bit more room than this cramped and uncomfortable set-tee," she replied. "Mmm," Phaeton murmured. "With those lovely limbs wrapped around me, I could go the night."

"Goodness, that long?" She rose from the settee and faced him. The nightshirt covering her breasts slipped to the floor. Golden green eyes watched him as he took in the sight of her.

Phaeton thought America as strong and fine a woman goddess as he had ever seen. In the dim light and shadow of the room her movements were mesmerizing. The curve of that lovely, high-dimpled derrière, breasts bouncing suggestively—he took a deep breath.

Searching her travel bag, she brought out a flask of essential oil; pouring some into the palms of her hands, she rubbed the fragrant oil onto her throat, breasts, and stomach as she stood before him. She was thin, but she was also immensely fit from the physical exertion of crewing a ship. Her skin glistened, and Phaeton felt his cock throb from his raw need to take her—and none too gently.

"I wish to use our act of love this evening and the passions evoked to focus our will. Using this night of bliss to make both a wish and a prayer for certain happy events to occur." She spoke in a kind of ritual language—her Cajun mother's witchcraft speak.

His eyes never left her. "What is this wish of yours, my love?"

"I have already received my wish. Your healthy return to me from the Outremer." She pulled him onto his feet and kissed his mouth.

"And your prayer?"

She talked to him in a whisper. "That no harm shall ever come to the pea in the pod."

Her kisses moved to his ear and neck. *"Angele Dei, qui custos es mei."* She recited a prayer to his guardian angel as his breathing grew harsh and more rapid. *"Me tibi commissum pietate superna,"* She unbuttoned his shirt. Wetting her lips, she kissed his chest. *"Hac nocte illumina, custodi, rege, et guberna."* Her tongue circled his nipples and she used her teeth to scrape gently. She whispered the name of God along with her own name. She returned to his lips, then his forehead and brushed it with kisses. *"In nomine Patris, et Filii, et Spiritus Sancti. Amen."*

She finished the sign of the cross on her haunches—one

sleek, muscled thigh thrust forward between his legs. She then unbuttoned his trousers and took him in her mouth. Phaeton held onto a nearby bedpost and stretched his frame as her tongue licked and her lips surrounded his shaft. He thrust deeper into her mouth, and she gave him such exquisite pleasure he begged her not to stop. Ever.

Throughout the rest of the night they traded off stimulating each other again and again. The slightest touch or kiss from her, and he easily fell into more lovemaking. Finally they lay still, the air of the bedchamber infused with the scent of intercourse. He had thrown off blankets for they were not needed. America lay naked with her arms and legs wrapped around his frame. The tips of her fingers traveled lightly over his chest hair, then trailed down a narrow strip of fuzz that ran down his torso. It was his favorite place she took her fingers walking.

Phaeton stroked her back, contentedly. "After we find the Moonstone and close the bloody connection with the Outremer, I plan on keeping your belly fat with babies."

Wide-eyed, she lifted her head. "My prayer worked, then."

"I knew I should have paid more attention in Latin." His lazy lopsided grin met her look of amused affection. "Do remember I slipped in a caveat, darling. I used the word *after*."

"After you find the Moonstone," she recited.

He lifted a brow.

She sighed. "And close the inter-dimensional portals."

"Hoo-hoo." Phaeton lifted his head and stuffed another pillow under his neck. "Very scientific terminology, Miss Jones."

"It's in the book I started this evening."

"You mean the book you fell asleep reading." He teased her with a one-eyed pirate grin.

She pushed away to make eye contact. "*A Guide to the Probable Locations of Inter-Dimensional Portals,* by Timothy Noggy." Phaeton scooped her into his arms. "Tell me more."

" 'Tis a book full of hidden knowledge. All about the rabbit holes and time travel and—"

Phaeton cut in. "And some sort of solution to this unraveling business, I hope?" He rubbed the bristle of his beard against her temple. "I saw some frightful sights tonight."

"What kind of things?"

"Not now, darling." Why would he possibly wish to give her nightmares?

America nuzzled his ear. "And I look forward to covering your lap with a squirming toddler while you attempt to conduct business with Detective Inspector Farrell."

Phaeton actually found himself smiling at the thought of bouncing a squalling, raucous babe on his knee. "Are we not to have a nurse or nursery?"

America placed an arm around him and ran her hand down his back and over his buttocks. "I stand ready to volunteer my nipples and since I have already reserved your knee . . . all we need is a cradle."

Phaeton looked at her for a very long time. "I love you, America." He stroked her breasts and moved lower to her belly, which was slippery from scented oil. She shuddered gently from his touch.

"I love you, Phaeton." She kissed him sweetly.

He brushed strands of curls off her face. "When two people are expecting a child together—preferably before the blessed event is large and round and obvious . . . it is customary to . . ." The knot in his throat was palpable. ". . . Marry."

America's lip twitched, as she tried not to look overly joyous or amused. "Yes, Phaeton."

He could not believe he heard himself chuckle. "Why am I laughing at this? This is horrifying."

Chapter Twenty-one

"YOU WERE RATHER WOLFISHLY INSATIABLE LAST NIGHT." America sat on the bed with her legs tucked under her. She had taken him in her mouth, and he had been quick to his release, but Phaeton had more than made up for his hasty climax. In fact, she could still feel the pleasurable ache from his hot-blooded invasion.

He stepped out of his morning bath and slung the towel around his backside. Rivulets of sudsy water meandered through his chest hair and down his torso. America paused to admire a ripple of thigh muscle and that handsome bum as he toweled off. Everything about him was well made, including that mighty sword between his legs.

"What on earth happened over there to put you in such a mood?" She resumed drying her hair. Phaeton had a genuine talent for naughty, energetic lovemaking, but last night had been particularly delicious.

"The expedition began on an interesting note." Phaeton wrapped the towel around his waist. "I arrived in Hanway Yard, and was immediately drawn to an exotic little shop specializing in ladies' . . . unmentionables." Phaeton grinned. "A number of very abbreviated pantalettes and camisoles were artfully strewn about the display window." He had that look in his eye—the heavy-lidded lustful look. "Naturally, I was intrigued."

America blinked. "You went inside?"

"The rest of the team hadn't arrived. I saw no reason not to explore."

America considered feigning a bit of outrage, but drat, she was curious. "And?"

"A shop girl helped me pick out a present for you."

Her heart raced at the thought of little French undergarments. "I didn't see a package." She sat up straight and looked about the room.

"They're in my coat pocket." He lifted his coat off the back of a chair and dug in one of the pockets. "I thought they might unravel on the return trip. It was the first thing I checked upon arrival." He untangled strings and lace and held up a triangle of ivory satin and string. "The shop girl called it a v-string pantie."

America stared. "A what?"

Phaeton raised a wicked, charming brow. "Note the strategically placed rhinestone."

Stunned, she rose from the bed. "Is there anything with a bit more fabric?" Her gaze moved to hints of black silk and violet lace in his hand.

"Think of them as the briefest pantalettes imaginable." Phaeton held up each color. "And as these frivolous little items cost me a half year's rent—I would appreciate a bit of trying on and posing." Despite the cost, his grin was back.

He loosened a corner of the bath sheet and the towel covering her fell to the floor. "It's hard to believe I look forward to putting clothes on this luscious body." He stretched out the tiny pantalettes and bent over. "One foot at a time—hold onto me as you step in."

"I'd hardly call this clothing." America snorted. "In fact, I'm not sure why the ladies bother at all." He slipped them over her knees and up her thighs, angling the strings at each hip. He stepped back and just looked at her. Finally, he spoke. "I think the Outremer has taken the concept of dishabille to new heights of inspiration."

She tilted her head and narrowed her eyes. "Phaeton?"

He continued to study her. "Cross your arms and cover your breasts with your hands."

She cupped her bosom, creating a bursting-out-of-a-corset effect. "Like this?" America looked up. Phaeton lifted an index finger and circled the air. "Turn around—slowly."

She pivoted in a circle and returned to him. Lowering her eyes to the towel covering his manly parts she saw her new undergarment was having its effect.

"Once more, but this time, as you face away, widen your stance and turn your upper body toward me, then give me your best, sultriest stare over your shoulder."

Somewhat amused by his requests, America circled and turned.

Phaeton lowered his chin. "Now think about my finger slipping under the string between your legs."

Arousal fluttered through her body. She opened her mouth and narrowed her eyes ever so slightly.

Phaeton removed the towel around his waist, and the velvet beast angled up hard. "Allow me to rub up against your bottom." His warm breath raised the hair on her neck. He slipped his hand beneath the pale ivory triangle. America lay back against his chest and rubbed her bottom against him. He slipped two fingers into moist flesh and circled.

His lips stopped just under her ear to whisper. "In the Outremer they have casinos called clubs. The dance music is loud—all percussion—and the beat throbs through your body."

Phaeton began to rock against her. "Move with me."

Her lower body swayed with his, and then—playfully, she shook her bottom against him—taunting his cock. He lay her head back on his shoulder. "Tongue me, deep, love." She tilted her chin up and he covered soft plump lips with his mouth.

It was broad daylight, but there was something deliciously erotic about Phaeton's requests—his demands. She licked up through that devilish beard of his to the sensitive underside of his upper lip, until he nibbled the tip of her tongue.

He lifted her up and placed her on rumpled bed sheets. "Open for me, Miss Jones." He moved between her knees. His fingers slipped down the inside of her thighs, and pushed the fabric and string aside. She moaned as his fingers circled and rubbed. He knew exactly what she wanted—what she needed. He moved over her body and pinned her arms.

"The entire house is up and about, darling. A cry from you could bring the maids running."

"Or perhaps one of the Nightshades." Phaeton narrowed his eyes and whispered. "And you wouldn't want that—would you?" Her arousal shot to new heights. She knew what he was doing—he was making her think about being seen. Caught in the act of such scandalous lovemaking.

He nipped at her nipples and caused a shutter to ripple down her body. He licked his way past her trembling belly. Once again, he pushed fabric and string aside as he lapped with his tongue. Slow, long licks that caused her to flood with arousal. His hands moved under her bottom and lifted her up to his face—he sucked gently on her pleasure spot. Within minutes she was writhing in his arms as he took her over the edge of pleasure.

As was his custom, Phaeton waited patiently for her to return to him. His fingers played over her body and with the pantalettes' strings at her hips. When she opened her eyes, he was propped on an elbow, smiling at her. "Last night, we entered a kind of casino off Tottenham Court Road. The dancing, if you could call it that, is everyone for themselves. Women and men, makes no matter, move up to you and rub against you—just as we did together."

America wrinkled her brow. "Do they . . . know each other?"

He rolled his eyes upward. "I received a booty rub from Jinn that was rather memorable."

"Booty?"

Phaeton grinned. "Their slang for bum."

America frowned. "Ping—or rather—Jinn was rubbing her bum on you?" She propped herself up. "I'm suddenly feeling rather cross about that."

"You asked what put me in such a mood. If you'd rather not know what goes on—"

"No." America bit her lower lip. "I want to know."

Phaeton turned his head and lowered his chin. "You're sure?"

"I dislike secrets. I want you to feel like you can tell me everything and anything."

His smile broadened. "All this lovemaking has left me famished. Get dressed and you can interrogate me to your heart's content—as long as it's over kippers and egg."

On their way down the grand stairs, America blurted out her first question. "What is a lap dance, Phaeton?"

He paused on the landing. "Where—how did you hear of such a thing?"

"Something you murmured in your sleep—just before you awoke this morning."

Phaeton slowed his pace downstairs. "A lap dance is done in a private room for male pleasure, primarily. The customer sits in a chair and the dancer does a booty rub all over him—but the man can't touch her—hands off or your arse is out the door."

"And . . . did you . . . ?" America felt the heat rush to her cheeks.

Phaeton paused outside the dining room. "Yes."

Try as she might, she could not hide her vexation. And she thought he looked greatly relieved when he opened the door. Nearly everyone in the house was still at breakfast.

Exeter peered over the top of the *Daily Telegraph*. "Good morning."

Phaeton filled a plate for America and returned to the breakfront.

Exeter lowered his newspaper. "I understand you had an unusually productive and stimulating expedition. Let's hear it Phaeton. Not just the highlights—details, as well."

Phaeton swallowed a forkful of smoked fish. He did a quick scan of the breakfasters around the table. "How much have you been told?" He was fishing for a clue as to what the ladies knew of their adventures last night.

"You missed a lively discussion about The Orchid Lounge," Cutter piped up.

"Wonderful!" America brightened. "It's all out in the open then? Jersey and Cutter mentioned the booty rubs and lap dances?"

Cutter blinked.

Jersey cleared his throat.

Phaeton rolled his eyes.

America smiled. "Phaeton has promised to be uncensored and completely forthcoming about their gentlemen's night in the Outremer. Interrogate him to your heart's content ladies—as long as it's over kippers and eggs." She winked.

The silence at the table was broken only by the clink of Valentine's teaspoon as she stirred. "What's a booty rub?"

As delicately as possible, Phaeton took on the task of explaining. "It seemed obvious to ask about the Ryder sisters—considering Georgiana directed us to the club. As it turns out one of the succubi worked as a lap dancer. Velvet—"

Ruby snorted. "Perfect name, wouldn't you say?"

Phaeton set down his fork. "As it turns out, one can't simply have a conversation with one of these girls, one has to pay an exorbitant fee and gratuity for a ten minute—dance."

America's grin was flat and unnatural. "Naturally, Phaeton volunteered for duty."

Phaeton looked up from his coffee cup and stared across the table. "Tell America what I said at the club, Cutter, about the dancing."

The big raspy voiced Nightshade straightened in his chair. "The most fun you've had with your clothes on?"

Phaeton eyeballed Cutter. "No-o-o."

She was not quite sure what came over her, but she tossed her teacup across the table at Phaeton and missed. The china hit the buffet with a crash and splintered into a million pieces. Thoroughly embarrassed, America rose from the table to flee the room. Phaeton jumped from his seat and beat her to the door. He stood with his back to the raised panels and held his hand up. "Wait."

America raised her chin. "Just let me leave, Phaeton."

A rap sounded at the very door he guarded. "You're not going anywhere—until you hear what I said last night."

America shifted her weight from one hip to another. She exhaled. Loudly. "Fine."

Phaeton opened the door. Julian Ping stood in the corridor—looking as masculine as Ping ever looked—which was at best androgynous.

Ping bowed to America. "I believe Phaeton is referencing the remark he made later in the evening after he questioned the succubus."

America sighed. "All right, Ping, what did he say?"

"He said as pleasurable as the dance was, all he could picture was America's lovely plump booty doing the rubbing."

Heat flooded her cheeks. She didn't know whether to kiss Phaeton or slap his cheek. No doubt he would enjoy either one. He tilted his head and smiled at her. "The thought is so arousing I believe I'll fill another plate."

Exeter gestured to America to come and sit beside him. A servant entered the room to sweep up the broken china. Completely humiliated, she joined their host at the end of the table. "I am so sorry, Doctor Exeter."

"Jason," he reminded her.

"Sorry, Jason." Shaking her head, she grimaced. "I don't know what came over me."

"Pregnancy came over you, America." The doctor smiled. "Remember what we discussed last night—sudden mood changes, emotional outbursts, unexpected tears." Exeter looked up, "Are you listening, Phaeton?"

Chapter Twenty-two

"SUDDEN MOOD CHANGES, emotional outbursts, unexpected tears . . ." Phaeton buttered a piece of toast. "The most fearful trials a man can face in this life." America was avoiding his gaze. He waited for the stunning tawny beauty sitting beside Exeter to look up. Would she glower or grin?

She smiled and once more everything went right in his world. She wore a simple gown with a pretty swath of pale yellow fabric that ended in a bow above her bustle. Underneath the virginal frock, however, he knew for a fact she wore the violet lace v-string pantie.

Good God, she had no idea how much she excited him. What a joy she was to have as a companion. How much he loved her. He had been held against his will on that ship for two months. Despite the occasional evening of cards and grog, he'd had plenty of time to think. About his life. About her. Mostly how much he missed her.

And that little outburst of hers over the lap dance—adorable. She was hot blooded, passionate, and he wouldn't have her any other way. And if things were reversed, if she'd been out half the night, clubbing with Valentine and Ruby—men rubbing up and down her . . . Phaeton swallowed. The prurient, devilish side of him supposed he wouldn't mind it so much as long as he could watch. The side that was about to become a father, however, wanted throw a punch at any man who touched her.

Something hit him out of the blue. In those two months at

sea, they'd missed celebrating her birthday. America had turned . . . twenty-one, or twenty-two?

Phaeton smiled. They really needed a night out together to celebrate.

"So—what do we do now? Do we continue to search over there?" Ruby's question broke into his thoughts.

"We wait for one of the succubi to contact us," Phaeton answered.

Jersey agreed. "The Moonstone is not with the RALS. The rat hordes have been exterminated."

"Or they've run out of steam—aether—whatever they run on." Cutter's eyepiece levered up. "Like the dead one we found in the air shaft."

Phaeton eased back from the table. "Meanwhile, I thought we might call on Tim Noggy. See if he's had a chance to dissect the helmet." Phaeton connected with Exeter. "Would you mind putting us up a bit longer? Your place is a good deal more accommodating than the flat below Mrs. Parker's."

Mia brightened. "Oh yes, please invite them to stay," Exeter's young charge pleaded. "I do so enjoy the female company. America, Ruby, and of course, Valentine." The girl lowered her voice. "Please, Om Asa."

"You are all welcome for the duration, however long it takes." The doctor discarded his napkin and rose from the table. "Might I accompany you to Mr. Noggy's laboratory, Phaeton?"

"I was just going to ask if you could come along—shall we?" Phaeton turned to America. "Are you well, and am I forgiven or tolerated?"

America had already moved her seat to cozy up to her new bosom friends. "Which would you like, dear?" She looked up at him with the most beguiling smile.

"I take that to mean, run along darling, so . . ." Phaeton grinned, "I will."

There was something even more wretched about this latest laboratory of Tim Noggy's. It was situated directly above the noxious fumes of a book binder's guild, in a narrow row south of the Strand. Phaeton jogged to catch up with Exeter's long strides. "One of our old stakeout spots is just around this bend."

He and the doctor turned the corner and ran directly into Tim Noggy running toward them. "Grubbers, two of them coming up right behind me." Large as he was, Tim hid behind Jersey and Cutter, whose daggers were already unfolding into claymore sized weapons. Swords that could cut through a Grubber as if it were steamed pudding.

Phaeton hadn't seen one up close until now, but he agreed, Grubbers did look a bit like a blob of steamed pudding. Jersey and Cutter caught them in a diagonal crossfire. No ball of light this time. No small pellets of energy. This time they used streams of energy to hold the Grubbers in place, until they melted into a pool of sludge.

Remnant energy crackled over the dark stains on the pavers until both imprints vanished completely. "Those swords are fierce." Tim peeked over Jersey's shoulder. "Thanks; if you hadn't come along they would have swarmed me."

"Thank Phaeton." Jersey's sword folded down to dagger size. "He's the one who wanted to check on you."

Tim turned to Phaeton. "Really?"

"I wouldn't read too much into it . . ." Phaeton stared at the husky young man. "I just wanted to stop by and see what you've found out about the helmet."

"Plenty." Tim raised both brows. "I have this fear of Grubbers—ever since my lab assistant got swarmed by one." Tim led the way upstairs. "The worst thing about them is that they have this ability to dissolve into the most miniature of particles—like sub-atomic level, if you know what this is." He looked around at blank faces.

"Anyway, once they're in these trillions of tiny pieces, so small you can't see them with our best microscope, then they permeate a person's body and dissolve their victims from the inside out." Tim fit a rather complex-looking key into the lock. "And here's the creepiest thing about it—for a while, the person with the Grubber inside just walks around—talks, eats, sleeps—until they're drained of all their aether."

Noggy opened the door and gestured them inside. One by one they filed in. A single long worktable filled most of the space except for the customary cot and cold closet at the back of the room. Lined up like heads on pikes outside Bishop's Gate were eight helmets. All in various stages of construction.

"Check this out—after you left yesterday, I removed the helmet lining and examined the fabric carefully. What do you think I found?" He offered a seat to Exeter in front of a large black tubular apparatus. Phaeton recognized the instrument as a microscope; he'd seen one in the doctor's laboratory.

Exeter bent over an eyepiece and made an adjustment. "I see a mass of hexagonal cells, like a honeycomb of bees, only much smaller."

"Miniature energy cells—wrapped around your head." Tim lifted up the helmet. "The leathery tentacles on the original helmet are receptors—like radio antennae, they pick up signals as well as energy." Tim turned to Cutter and Jersey. "When you fought these things, did you ever feel drained? Like you just wanted to take a nap?"

"Knackered." Cutter looked over to the captain. "You, Jersey?"

The Nightshade leader weighed the question. "Not during a fight—but a good amount of fatigue after."

Tim studied Jersey. "You're also part demon, mate. You've got some built-in protection."

Exeter swiveled the stool he was sitting on. "Radio transmission is in its infancy here, in our time—how much more advanced are they in the Outremer?"

Tim's eyes flicked up toward the ceiling. "Your guess is as good as mine, Doc."

Exeter didn't let up. "Take a guess."

"A hundred years . . . maybe more." The oversized young inventor shook his head. "But that doesn't mean that we're going to evolve at their speed. We could go faster, or slower."

Phaeton stared. "So, we could be stuck with steam engines forever."

Tim shook back a mop of hair that had fallen in his face. "I don't think so."

Exeter stretched his legs out. "And why don't you think so, Mr. Noggy?"

"Doc—call me Tim." The young inventor crossed his arms over a broad chest. "Because you've crossed a few thresholds—steam conversion, the internal combustion engine, electricity, the electromagnetic field." A smallish grin surfaced on their affable friend. "You're on your way."

Jersey raised a skeptical brow. "On our way to where?"

Phaeton peered into a basket full of fruit on the worktable. "May I have a tangerine?"

"Help yourself, mate." Tim nodded. "They're from Spain—flown here on an airship. Two crazy Frenchmen Gaspar knows."

"It seems to me we have a big problem with a whole lot of unanswered questions, so let's start with what we know." As he peeled the fruit, Phaeton organized his thoughts out loud. "Are we sure we know the Reapers' main purpose, besides reconnaissance?"

Cutter spoke up. "They also run squads of assassins and patrol the Outremer."

"Who'd they assassinate?"

"About ten of our best scientists, so far."

"Why haven't we heard about it?" Phaeton asked.

"Because they make it look like an accident or a heart attack." Tim suddenly looked a little wild-eyed.

"Reapers strike me as too predatory for that sort of ruse," Exeter straightened. "Detective Inspector Zander Farrell popped by last night. Had a brandy and dessert with us. He mentioned a number of untimely deaths. Gentlemen mostly; he never mentioned their professions."

Phaeton separated a section of fruit. "Let me guess, after a few exhumations and an autopsy or two, they discovered the deaths were from suffocation."

Exeter nodded. "Seems the Ryder sisters are on the job, and Scotland Yard is interested in following up on your lead, Phaeton. Detective Farrell has assigned a Dexter Moore to the case.

Phaeton didn't much care for the idea of Dexter Moore sniffing around, especially since he was so taken with America.

"Why did Zander pick Dexter Moore for the job?" he groused. "He knows we don't get on."

Exeter explained to the others. "Phaeton is a bit testy around Inspector Moore. The detective helped recover two of America's stolen ships, then he indirectly got involved with a case Phaeton and I worked on."

"Gaspar told us—the Ripper goddess, concubine to Anubis, the one who gifted the Moonstone to Phaeton." As Tim spoke he sidled over to Phaeton. "Any left?"

He handed over a few sections. "Let me deal with Moore. I'll find something to keep him busy." Phaeton scratched his beard. "Where was I? Ah yes, the Grubbers. I take it these creatures are ordered to abduct us as well as suck the life out of us. So why are they still around? Why did they attack Tim just now? And who gave us the impression that the maker—or whoever—had called off the Reapers and Grubbers?" Phaeton looked around.

Tim hesitated, and looked to Jersey. "Gaspar might be doing some wishful thinking."

Exeter quirked a brow. "What makes you say that?"

"You're the doc. What happens to a person when they start to unravel?"

Phaeton's gaze narrowed. "Have you ever examined him, Jason?"

Exeter shook his head. "He doesn't let me get very close."

"Has anyone seen Gaspar lately, besides Ping?" Phaeton looked around. "Where is Ping?" He was sure Ping had been with them in the alley—but had he followed them upstairs?

Jersey checked the corridor outside the flat. Nothing.

No one was alarmed, exactly. Ping was a thousand times more capable than any creature he might run across. And he often disappeared, returning minutes or hours later. In that way, Ping was a bit like Edvar, who had made himself rather scarce these days.

Phaeton walked around the end of the workbench. "Time for a big question. Is it possible that we could become infected by whatever is causing the alternate world's demise—this unraveling?"

Curious as well, Exeter looked around the room. "Can any-one here get me closer to Gaspar? I need to do an examination. Study what is going on with him."

Tim exhaled. "Gaspar trusts me . . . I think. I'll see what I can do."

Phaeton looked each one of them in the eye before asking question two. "What makes us so sure that the Outremer isn't us? Our future—a hundred plus years from now?"

"That would mean that the space-time continuum is real, not something H. G. Wells thought up. That it is possible to fold space back on itself." Tim raised both eyebrows and looked to Exeter, whose gaze moved to Cutter, Jersey, then settled on Phaeton.

Tim shook his head. "Nah, I don't think so, mate."

"How is that any less plausible than a parallel London that is forced to cannibalize another London to keep itself alive?" Phaeton exhaled. Loudly. "Perhaps we should label them London A and London B."

Jersey moved to the window and stood behind the drape of a tattered curtain. "Best finish up any business you have here."

Phaeton examined the row of helmets. "Why make so many?"

"For us—for protection." The young inventor picked one up. "These helmets don't do just one thing—they do a lot of things, which will take years, even decades, to figure out."

"But . . ." Tim waggled his brows. "There's about a hundred microscopic layers of the honeycomb stuff inside the helmet. It takes only one or two layers of the stuff to block the dark mat-ter in the aether."

Phaeton pulled Tim aside. "How do you know?"

"Because I tested it last night—on myself." Tim looked about furtively. "Don't tell the Nightshades, but I get seasick when I'm over there. Also there's this buzzing in my ears. Gives me a headache that lasts for days. So, I wrapped a couple of lay-ers inside my bowler and took a quick trip over last night and guess what? Nothing. No nausea. No ear pain." Tim waggled his brows. "No unraveling."

Phaeton stared at him. "A shield of some kind." He sidled close and spoke quietly. "Might you be able to stitch a length of that fabric together—enough to make a shawl to wrap around someone?"

Wheels turned behind eyes made smaller by pudgy cheeks. "I guess so. When do you need it?"

Phaeton grinned. "Tonight, at dusk."

Chapter Twenty-three

AMERICA BLEW A LAYER OF DUST OFF what appeared to be a serviceable desk in the office space for let. "Here it is ladies, 21-A Shaftesbury Court. I'm afraid it's a bit musty at the moment." Esmeralda opened a window to let in some air. "I gave up on rent for this space"—she clapped her hands—"it hasn't been occupied in years."

America thought the lack of interest had a great deal to do with the shop's proximity to Esmeralda Parker's—the most infamous brothel in all of London. She peeked into a closet. "Does our flat adjoin this space?"

Esmeralda pointed to a storage closet under the stairs. "We could easily add a pass through below the landing. At one time, there was a dentist in here—grisly old Drake himself used to have gentlemen dragged in here. The dentist would remove gold teeth—inlays, anything to repay their gambling debts." The brothel madam nudged the brass kick plate and the door creaked open. America led the way outside and up a few steps to the sidewalk.

Ruby squinted at the gaming hall down the street. "Quite a brutal way to call in your markers."

Esmeralda blinked in the bright sun. "And effective."

America paid little attention to the ladies' conversation; rather she pictured a sign . . . hanging just about—there. And a crisp navy blue awning over the door. She whirled around. "I'll take it."

"You're sure?" Esmeralda asked.

America inhaled a deep breath. "Positive."

"What do you have in mind, America? A shop of some kind?"

"Moonstone Investigations. A private agency specializing in . . ."

Esmeralda grinned. "The very unusual?"

"I'll keep the sign small," America added. "I don't wish to scare off your customers."

"Good afternoon, ladies."

All three women turned toward the familiar voice. Shading her eyes to see better, America recognized the face. "Inspector Moore. You've arrived just in time to celebrate."

"Whatever you're up to, Miss Jones, it is bound to be exciting."

"Inspector Moore," Esmeralda greeted the detective without a sign of trepidation. Why should she? According to Phaeton, Mrs. Parker enjoyed special protection in exchange for the girls' services as occasional night crawlers or honey pots for Scotland Yard.

"Come, I shall make us up a nice tea in the flat." America started back. "I believe there is also a bottle of whiskey, if you'd rather."

"Tea would be lovely at this hour." Dexter doffed his bowler.

Esmeralda parted ways at the stairs. "Strange noises coming from down there last night—laughter, and a great deal of moaning and carrying on." The madam lifted both brows. "See what you can do about it?"

Dexter kindled a fire in the stove and put a kettle on. "I take it you and Phaeton are staying with Jason Exeter?" The detective was snooping around for a reason.

America sensed something, a flutter of shadow against the ceiling. Perhaps she'd give him something sensational to report back to the Yard. "No room in this small flat since we've been assigned bodyguards." America added ground leaves to the teapot and set out a plate of biscuits. "Phaeton is working on an important case."

"I see." The inspector frowned. "Dangerous enough that you are also in jeopardy?"

"I don't believe you've met Ruby." America smiled across the table. "I have her to protect me today."

Dexter appeared unimpressed. "And who has assigned these bodyguards? Surely not the Yard—"

"I'm not at liberty to discuss much about the case," she cautioned.

Dexter joined Ruby at the table who was nibbling a biscuit. America added a fourth cup and laid a finger to her lips. "We have a visitor."

Dexter Moore reached in his pocket and set his revolver on the table. America stared. "You can't shoot her."

"Why ever not?"

"Because—she's a succubus and they don't die." Ruby poured hot water into the teapot to steep. "They're closely related to demons . . . I think." She rolled her eyes upward. "Anyway, you have to banish them—send them back to their world. Or trick them, which is hard to do." The challenge in Ruby's eyes seemed to be directed at the detective. "They're clever."

Dexter's gaze lingered on Ruby, before returning to America. "And your idea is to invite her to tea?"

America shushed him. "She must believe it is her idea."

Dexter's gaze moved around the room. "Where is . . . she?"

A quick glance told America that he was watching her eyes track the ethereal young lady circling in the air. "She's—hovering close by?" His voice was soft, husky.

Quite suddenly a fully materialized apparition perched on the back of the kitchen chair. She waited for Ruby to pour, then plopped two lumps of sugar into her teacup. "Is this Deejarling? Deejarling is one of my favorites." The singsong voice belonged more to a fairy than a young woman.

America smiled. "You must be Fleury."

Dressed in a pale blue frock and a white apron overskirt, the young succubus looked perplexed. "I was Alice this morning, but you can call me Fleury if you wish." She stirred her tea. "How do you know my name?"

America caught the look of astonishment on Dexter's face. This one had to be the youngest sister. "Phaeton—Mr. Black mentioned you were a bit of a . . ."

"Flibbertigibbit?" She punctuated nearly every sentence with a tinkle of laugher followed by a low wailing moan.

"What seems to be the difficulty, Fleury?"

"Velvet gave me an address for Mr. Black," Fleury whispered, nearly in tears. "But I cannot find him." She squinted at Dexter. "You are not Mr. Black."

Dexter looked to America and she shook her head. "No, he is not." Without Phaeton present, she would have to be cagey if she was going to wheedle the message out of the little minx. "You might leave him a letter—write it down on a piece of notepaper."

Fleury glowered. "No pens or papers."

She racked her brain. "You could send Mr. Black a telegram. I'd be happy to write the address down. We could walk down to the wire office together if you'd like—send it off to Mr. Black." America smiled sweetly.

Eyelashes fluttered. "I've never sent a telegram," she cooed.

America caught a grin from Dexter.

"Eight and a half Queen's Yard," the pretty girl whispered.

America held out her hand. "Come along, let's send it off to Phaeton." America winked at Ruby and Dexter. "Back in a jiff."

Phaeton rocked along pleasantly inside Exeter's well-sprung carriage. The ride back to Mayfair would at least be comfortable, if a bit silent. Unusually brooding of late, the doctor seemed doubly troubled at the moment. "America asked me if I wouldn't please try to get you to open up about your difficulties." Exeter stared blankly at the blur of shops along Piccadilly. "A man to man chat might be helpful."

"I don't need your kind of help, Phaeton."

"Which can only mean that you believe my advice will be to roger her royally. And not to waste another moment in this ridiculous agony you have imposed on yourself—and Mia, as well, I might add."

Somewhat baffled, Exeter slid a glance his way. "You mean that *isn't* your advice?"

"Of course it is, but I might also have some suggestions for you, until you find out exactly what is going on with the lovely chit—poor girl."

The doctor exhaled. "Even you think of her as a chit."

"Which is why my first assignment for you and Mia is to purchase the young lady a new wardrobe. Box up those middy blouses and demure little frocks and donate them to the needy. You must purchase Mia a new wardrobe—clothing a woman would wear. And gowns that show off her figure whenever possible."

Exeter finally turned to him. "Do you realize how completely exasperating you are, Phaeton?"

"I'm also completely right."

Exeter's mouth twitched. "Yes, I believe you might be." He checked his pocket watch and exhaled a deep sigh.

"You just have to let this play out, Jason. From what I understand, Valentine is preparing her for—whatever she is going to be."

"If only I knew what Mia was facing, I might be able to do more."

Phaeton studied his anxious friend. "Mr. Tandi must know something."

"I've questioned him extensively." Exeter shook his head. "I asked if she'd been bitten as a child, or dragged off. What fevers she suffered. Were there any unusual pets in the house . . ."

"He may be afraid to tell you. He's a servant with no family here. Where would he go if you tossed him out?" Phaeton made a mental note to have a chat with the mild mannered servant. "Jason, you've been an exemplary guardian, but now you need to shift your relationship with Mia to a new place. As ever, you will continue to be there when she's frightened—to reassure her. But you must not be afraid to touch her."

The doctor shifted his gaze away.

"Holding is important—America loves to be held. It makes her feel safe." Phaeton dipped his head to reconnect with Exeter. "Are you holding Mia?" Phaeton recalled the intimate scene he witnessed in the bedchamber last night. Mia had lifted his palm to her breast. "Touch her when she needs to be touched—like a woman."

"But if I lose control—"

Phaeton glanced outside the carriage; they were traveling through Green Park. "Your instincts aren't all wrong—you probably should try to take it slow, at least until you know what may or may not happen when she's aroused." His friend was in crisis—the young woman he loved was going through some sort of transmogrification. She could be dangerous to herself as well as others. "Then again, maybe you need to lose a little control, Jason."

The carriage slowed and pulled up in front of the townhouse. Phaeton waited for the Nightshades to check the street and surroundings before he opened the door. He made eye contact with the doctor briefly. "Do you think Tim Noggy is from our world?"

Exeter seemed grateful for a change of subject. "He says he's Australian—as if that explains everything. But his odd vernacular is as strange as his science. He speaks in a kind of advanced physics I'm not completely familiar with, but . . ." The doctor exited the coach and caught up with Phaeton at the door. "I don't believe much of it is from this century."

Mr. Tandi greeted Phaeton holding a silver salver. A telegraph envelope sat in the middle of the tray. Phaeton opened the message. A grin tugged up one side of his mouth. "It's from Fleury Ryder."

"A succubus sent a telegram?" Exeter handed off his top hat. "What does it say?"

"An address in Queen's Yard." Phaeton folded the cable and jammed it in his pocket. "I'm fairly sure The Orchid Lounge is located there."

Exeter raised a brow. "Shall we all go over? I'll send Gaspar a message—and you'll want the Nightshades with you."

Phaeton shook his head. "The cable wire is quite explicit. Eight and a half Queen's Yard. Stop. Come alone."

Chapter Twenty-four

"MIND TELLING ME WHERE WE'RE GOING?" America held onto her boater as a gust of wind swept through the mews alley.

"It's a birthday surprise." Phaeton towed her around the side of Exeter's carriage house.

"But, my birthday was months ago," she protested.

"You thought I forgot, didn't you?" He had that look of mischief about him. "I am stealing you away for a night on the town together." A breeze ruffled his hair and his smile was so dazzling, her heart danced in her chest.

"But—I'm not dressed for an evening out."

"You will be." Phaeton peered around the corner of the carriage house. "Ps–s–st! Tim—over here!" He turned back to America and smiled. "Tim very kindly agreed to design a little something for you."

The well-rounded young man squeezed into the niche and opened his bag of tricks. "It took twenty layers of helmet liner to make this." Tim unfolded a large square of gossamer cloth. The tightly woven material shimmered in the late afternoon rays of sun. "Here you go, mate."

Phaeton folded the large square into a triangle and turned to her. Holding a corner of the scarf in each hand, he wrapped his arms around her and tied the ends together above her bustle. "There now—you are perfectly protected, my love." He rearranged a few of the folds in front and looked up at her. "As is our little pea in the pod."

She wanted to weep—not just a few sniffs but an all-out

blubbering good cry. Phaeton had referred to their child as *ours.*
And he had placed the apron-like shawl around her in the
sweetest way. Emotional as well as bewildered, she suddenly
thought she knew where they were going. "You're taking
me to—"

"Quickly my dear—I've a carriage waiting in the Hays
Mews." Phaeton whisked her and Tim Noggy down the lane
and into the rented clarence.

Phaeton leaned across the aisle. "I need you to get us across
and help us to return."

"You're going on a date to Outremer?" Tim shook his head.
"By yourselves? No Jersey, no Valentine?"

"America and I need a night out—alone." Phaeton leaned
inside the coach. "What shall I tell the driver?"

Tim thought a moment. "Hanway Yard may still be open."
Phaeton relayed instructions and climbed in as the carriage
lurched off.

Settling in beside her, Phaeton explained. "I'm also hoping
to mix a bit of business with pleasure. This afternoon I received
this wire—just an address."

"Eight and a half Queen's Yard." America peered over his
shoulder to confirm the message.

Phaeton turned to her. "You sent this?"

"Shall we say I assisted Fleury?"

Phaeton nodded. "Note these two words at the end of the
address. 'Come alone.' "

"Yeah, but . . ." Tim's brows collided. "You're not going in
alone."

"I imagine this to be a preliminary meeting—no puppet
masters. Just me and a shadow player. Someone who either has
the stone or knows where the stone is. Perhaps a few terms will
be discussed, after which, I will return to our side of the equa-
tion."

"While I wait to be summoned, I plan on having a bit of fun
with America—a belated birthday party—for two."

Tim's worry-riddled face eased some. "Happy birthday.
So . . . how belated is he?" He rolled his eyes over to Phaeton.

"The nineteenth of April."

Tim's observant eyes crinkled. "Aries. Cardinal. Fire. Yeah, you'd have to—you know—have horns and be hot to keep up with him."

America snorted a laugh. Tim had the oddest way of putting words together. She understood him perfectly, but there was something about the accent.

"Wow. A goat and a ram—no wonder." Tim shook his head.

Phaeton stared. "How could you possibly know what astrological sign I am?"

The amiable man shrugged. "You've got to be a Capricorn, mate."

America grinned. "Phaeton was born the tenth of January."

"Since we are early—pre-witching hour . . ." Phaeton instructed the driver to continue on Tottenham Court Road, to Queen's Yard. "Drive up a ways and park near the mews." As they passed the narrow yard, America glanced into the entrance and blinked. She gripped Phaeton's arm.

"I see him," Phaeton growled. "What the devil is Dexter Moore doing lurking about Queen's Yard?"

Tim dipped his head and peered around. "He's got at least two other men with him—one at the corner and another farther inside the yard."

Phaeton swiveled slowly back to her and raised a brow.

"The Inspector paid a call to the flat this afternoon. Ruby and I went over to collect a few things." She certainly wasn't going to tell him about renting the office space—not yet, anyway. She wanted to surprise him.

"What things?" Phaeton queried.

Frankly, she didn't care much for his tone. "For one thing, you're out of clean shirts and collars. I believe Inspector Moore was attempting to find out where you and I are residing."

"No doubt he's curious to know who is doing what to whom—and where." Phaeton frowned. "Excellent use of Scotland Yard's resources, chasing down our sleeping arrangements. Nosy bastard."

Tim turned to them. "Speaking of ins and outs, your entry point is well down the block on Hanway Place. Where do you want your out?"

"Last time we hoofed it all the way to the Thames—Vauxhall Bridge."

Tim nodded. "The professor likes that one. It's easy and it's always open. Keep that in mind if you ever get stuck over there."

Phaeton stared at Tim. "Whatever happened between you and Lovecraft?"

"You don't want to know." Tim shook his head slowly. "Do you?"

"Why would I ask"—Phaeton bit out the words—"if I didn't wish to know?"

America pressed her lips into a thin, straight line—anything to hide her amusement at Phaeton's aggravation. As exasperating as Tim Noggy could be, there was also something wonderfully gentle and genuine about him. America quite liked him, even though she was sure he was neither British nor Australian.

Tim tugged his pocket watch out of a waistcoat that was bursting at the buttons. "Time to go." America smiled more to herself than anyone. He just didn't fit here—even his clothes were ill-fitting.

Exiting the carraige, they made a slow tour of both Hanway Street and Hanway Place, a complete circle of the yard. Tim's eyes darted back and forth. "You both have your inklings?"

America hesitated. "I have mine from the first trip over—inkwell."

"Don't!" Tim threw both hands up to stop her. "Never mind—it was kind of a lame inkling anyway—everyone had some variation on it."

"Lame?" America pouted.

"Uh—I meant faulty. Just use Phaeton's." Tim never took his eyes off the sidewalk traffic—and there was plenty at the end of the day. Tim wove in and out of a bustle of pedestrians. He rasped over his shoulder. "I'm going to get you through—just follow me."

Tim opened his satchel and rummaged around. "Behind us, there's a man in a purple waistcoat. Phaeton, you need to drop back, get his attention, then follow him, now!" Tim pulled America into the niche of a shop entrance and they watched Phaeton bump into the gentleman.

"Clumsy me—pardon."

Tim pointed his mysterious metal pipe as the man caught Phaeton by the arm, steadying him. Phaeton slipped in behind the gent and disappeared.

America craned her neck.

"He's over." Tim grinned. "Have you ever walked through a cold spot in a room or experienced a brief dizzy spell just walking along—maybe you wobbled a little?"

America nodded. "Of course. Are you saying that the way into other worlds, these rabbit holes are—" America sighed, rather at a loss.

"They're not everywhere, but . . ." He scanned Hanway Yard. "There's quite a few of them around right now." Tim fiddled with the tubular device. "Behind me coming up fast—the lady bobbing along in a hurry? Here you go—" Tim shoved her out into the throng of foot traffic and into the woman who dodged out of the way—but not before their skirts touched—vaguely woozy, America was aware of a brush of fabric and whispers in the air. Carried along, as if on the swell of a wave in the ocean, she looked back over her shoulder.

Tim Noggy faded into a fog of gray.

America looked ahead and the crowded lane was suddenly bereft of foot traffic. "Over here, darling." Phaeton stood in front of a small shop. America picked up her skirt and ran to join him. Phaeton pulled her close and kissed her on the mouth. In public. When he released her, she was out of breath. "Happy birthday, love. And I mean to make it happy."

At this moment, she could not imagine being any happier. "More surprises?"

"Many more."

Something in the shop window behind Phaeton caught her eye. Something so provocative, she was forced to lean to one side for a better look. "Good Lord, Phaeton." She stepped out of his arms and over to the window. Captivated or stupefied, she wasn't quite sure which, America studied the scandalous photographs of women wearing—essentially nothing.

"Bigger than life and for all the world to see in a shop window."

Tiny pantalettes and corsets were scattered about the display in front of the photographs. "This is where you purchased the little undergarments?"

Phaeton moved up behind her. "If I remember correctly, you are wearing the violet lace."

She turned around in his arms. "Do I look like those women—in the window?"

"Better." He nuzzled her neck just below her earlobe. "Because you are sassy and warm. And you jiggle." He took her by the hand and walked her up the block.

"Phaeton, how do you manage all this—purchasing things—using what sort of legal tender?"

"My old banknotes seem to pass for rabbit hole currency. I must admit, I had to withdraw more cash this afternoon; the panties and bar tab drained the wallet." Near Oxford he stopped at a shop featuring menswear. They both studied the jackets in the window. America tilted her head. "Rather plain and short."

"Everything over here seems . . . abbreviated." Phaeton offered her his arm. "Help me pick something out."

The clerk inside approached cautiously. "I'm afraid we traveled all the way into town only to discover the masquerade ball is next week. Still, it would be a shame to waste a night out on the town." Phaeton paused to admire the tailoring. "I could use a new jacket."

The shop clerk smiled, "Right this way sir. My name is Dalton."

They chose a black blazer and charcoal trousers, in what Dalton described as a tropical wool blend. And there was quite a discussion as to whether a cravat was needed. "I assume dinner? Perhaps a bit of clubbing?" the clerk mused aloud. In a sudden flurry of inspiration, he removed Phaeton's waistcoat and starched collar. Then he opened a few shirt buttons, and exposed a hint of chest hair. Dalton stood back to admire. "Lovely."

America sidled up next to the clerk. Phaeton looked breathtaking. "Handsome, indeed."

She found a smart satchel, which Phaeton purchased for their costumes. Glancing at the bill, she nearly fainted. He stuffed a wad of folded banknotes inside his new jacket pocket. "Might you recommend a shop for ladies?"

"Stella McCurdy's on Bruton Street." Dalton studied her as he might a seamstress form—taking in her size and shape. "Or Sylvester McQueen on Bond. I'll call you a cab."

Once inside the motorcar she snuggled against him. "Odd, isn't it? The street names and building are completely familiar and yet so entirely foreign."

Phaeton grinned. "Like a waking dream. Have you noticed the shop signs aren't reading backward anymore?"

She glanced out the window at the flashy shops along Oxford. "At least it doesn't feel like we're in Slovakia."

"Look, down there." Phaeton pointed to a narrow side street in shambles. "Parts of the city are fragmenting, or as Gaspar puts it, unraveling. And yet business goes on as usual." He spoke quietly. "Farther south, around Piccadilly, I saw signs of street conflict. You'd think there'd be mass hysteria."

"Perhaps they're used to it," she said. The bleak looking row was swept out of sight as the cab moved on. "Tim mentioned Reaper patrols—have you seen them?"

"Jersey and I managed to elude one at the Orchid Lounge. We escaped up the backstairs."

America turned to him, eyes bright. "Are you taking me there—tonight?"

Phaeton's eyes crinkled. "Perhaps—if you select a new frock that shows off plenty of leg."

Her smile was permanent, until she took one look at the price tags in Mr. McQueen's shop. She looked up. "This can't be right." The simple sparkling dress—if one could call something this plain and short a dress—was eight hundred pounds. Even Phaeton appeared stunned.

She grabbed him by the arm and they tried the shop next door, Domenico & Stefano. "It would seem the dressmakers in the Outremer are either Italian or Scot." Inside, however, the prices were just as shocking. "How disappointing." America turned to leave but something had already caught Phaeton's eye. "Hold on."

A lovely deep violet dress hung against the wall at the back of the shop. The bodice of dress was cut exactly like a corset, while the skirt was made up of several layers of sheer fabric embedded with tiny glittering stones sprinkled about.

"Isn't it divine?" America whirled around to confront a shop girl, who did not seem nearly as intimidating as the prices in this establishment. For one thing she and America were a similar skin color.

Phaeton cranked up the charm. "We were to attend a costume party that was cancelled last minute. Thought we might stay in town, perhaps do a bit of clubbing. Might you have a frock in the house that doesn't cost five years' wages?"

The shop girl fished for the tag on the purple dress and came up squealing. "Fifty percent off!"

Chapter Twenty-five

PHAETON WAITED FOR AMERICA OUTSIDE THE DRESSING ROOM. He tugged a silver pull on a black leather jacket, with a number of closed pockets angled all over it. The jacket opened. Fascinated, he ran the pull up and down the track of tiny metal teeth. A young man carrying a small stepladder and a new dress breezed by. "Zippers galore!" He winked at Phaeton.

Methodically moving from one zipper to the next, Phaeton pulled each one up and down until he had explored the entire jacket.

The young man arranging the dress on the wall seemed amused. Feeling a bit gauche, Phaeton sauntered over to a table of luggage. *Handbags* the shop girl had called them.

"What do you think?"

He pivoted at the sound of America's voice and swallowed.

He had always loved her in violet. The color seemed to bring out a peachy glow to her tawny skin. But this was stunning. "You are a vision, my love."

She had taken her hair down and a mass of curls fell across her shoulders. The corset fit perfectly, adding just the right amount of plumpness to her bosom. A man could still enjoy the slope of her breasts and, when she breathed, imagine the nipple.

"Phaeton!" America twirled around and the dress lifted high up her thighs. She wore dark stockings that shimmered—and went all the way up—well he wasn't actually sure where the hose stopped. All he knew was, America Jones had legs that went on forever.

"Stilettos." She pointed to her shoes and spun around. He realized she was standing on stilts.

"Aptly named. Can you walk—better yet will you be able to dance?"

She looked up at him, eyes glowing with anticipation. "Oh, I do hope so!"

"I'm not done yet." The shop girl led them over to a counter and dusted America's cheeks with peachy bronze powder, then did something dark and smoldering to her eyes. "Wait, lips!" She brushed glossy substance over her lips.

America turned to him. "You are a goddess, my love."

"You need to kiss him for that," the girl advised.

She quirked a brow.

"If my boyfriend called me a goddess he'd be getting tongue right about now."

Phaeton slid his gaze from the shop girl to America. She stepped into his arms and kissed him—soft, slippery bites that tasted like . . . strawberry. She slid her tongue into his mouth and he was instantly hard as stone.

Distantly he heard the shop girl's voice. "When you're ready—meet me in the front of the store; I'll ring you up."

He broke off the kiss. "Be sure to include some of that strawberry . . ."

The girl already had the items in hand. "No worries, love."

He rocked America in his arms. "Ready for a bit of booty rubbing?"

"Eight and a half Queen's Yard." Phaeton tossed their bag on the floor of the cab and stifled the urge to climb on top of America. Instead, he pulled her close. "I'd like nothing more than to be deep inside you with your legs in the air." He nuzzled her cheek. "But I believe I will let you drive me mad this evening."

His hand slipped over her stomach. "The wrap that Tim made for you and Pea, are you—?"

America smiled, "I'm using it as a kind of petticoat."

"It's very possible we might have a slight interruption this evening."

"You could be called into a meeting, or something worse." America frowned. "A lap dance with Velvet Ryder."

He pulled her close and watched that lovely mouth twist it-self into a pout. "If we have a daughter, she is going to be very beautiful." She slanted her gaze toward him. "Pea will also be strong and wicked smart, just like her mother." His eyes dropped to the dimple emerging on her cheek. "And if Pea is a boy . . ." The cab slowed and made a turn into Queen's Yard. The driver pulled in front of the club.

Phaeton paid the driver, and noticed he wore a red turban. Something oddly familiar—then it struck him. "You were our driver, a few days ago."

The man stared at him.

"You lost the Reapers. Dropped us off in Whitehall . . . near the Horse Guards Hotel."

The driver took his money. "I've done my share of eluding the patrols."

Phaeton nodded. "And if I asked you to come back for us at midnight?"

The man nodded. "Then I'd be here, sir."

Phaeton took up the satchel and met America at the top of the stairs. Already the deep bass rhythm vibrated up through the steps and into every cell of his body. The doorman lifted a velvet rope and waved them in.

"Welcome to the Orchid Lounge," the greeter said.

Phaeton paid the cover charge and checked their bag. "This way, darling." He took her hand and pressed through a crush of dancers. Inching along they passed a man bobbing to the beat in a booth with flashing lights. Phaeton hadn't noticed this per-son before. The chap seemed to fancy himself a kind of master of ceremonies, spouting a nonsensical rhyming commentary. The character eyeballed America. "I see you're lookin' fly tonight. Two more for the dance floor."

Phaeton found a spot at the center of the undulating bodies. He pulled her close and she immediately began to rock her hips with his.

"Feel the rhythm—all fresh and funky," the jabberwocky be-hind the glass crooned.

Adding a few new steps of her own, America ground against

him. Phaeton sucked in a bit of air. He knew she was going to be good at this free style of dancing, but this was truly—inspired. Mesmerized, he watched the sway of her hips as she turned a slow circle.

She bumped into a strapping young male, who turned around and returned the bump only to frighten her away. Phaeton stepped between them and slipped his knee between her legs. "Nothing to fear, darling." He pulled her up against his thigh, and her hips connected with his. Her eyelids lowered with desire, as she arched away. He loved the way her breasts moved within the confines of the deep violet corset.

A lone figure caught his eye—a familiar someone. Phaeton growled. He was aroused. He wished to stay that way for the duration of the evening. Hardly a chance of that—now that Gaspar Sinclair was headed straight for them.

He opened his arms and America stepped into his embrace. "I need a drink—possibly several." He guided her off the dance floor and into a throng of thirsty patrons standing three deep at the bar. Phaeton suddenly understood what the jabberwocky meant by "last call—two for one." A space opened up and he ordered three shots and an iced ginger ale. Leaning against the bar. America was all eyes, as she took in the club. When the music shifted from one tune to another, she moved her shoulders up and down in perfect mimicry of a couple on the dance floor. She leaned in close. "I say this is wonderful fun, but so . . ."

"Decadent?" He handed her a glass of ginger ale and downed his first shot. It was enough to take the edge off—for starters.

"You really shouldn't try to hide from me, Phaeton."

He sighed. "I wasn't hiding, I was avoiding." He turned to face the leader of the Shades. "You're looking dapper Gaspar. I see you're dressed for this world."

Tim had mentioned Gaspar was sick from too much exposure to the Outremer. Phaeton looked him up and down. A bit wan perhaps, but the man's world weary grin and crinkled eyes turned genuinely appreciative when his gaze fell on America.

"The dress is lovely, my dear, and you are breathtaking. I understand you are celebrating a belated birthday."

Phaeton knocked back his second shot. "Belated because you and Lovecraft conspired to have me shanghaied and brought back to London." He shook his head. "Tim Noggy told you where to find us, didn't he? The rotund rat bastard."

Gaspar shrugged. "I had to torture him."

"Not hard. Just take his fish and chips away." Phaeton was livid. "And you're not here to wish America well. You're here nosing about in my business."

Gaspar nodded a bow to America. "Many happy returns."

Phaeton exhaled. "Can I buy you something? They have eighteen-year-old Talisker's here . . ." He swallowed the last dram and nailed Gaspar. "The message said come alone."

The man raised a brow. "But you didn't come alone. You brought your lovely paramour. If you meet with someone tonight, I shall stay with America." He turned to her. "May I call you by your given name?"

"Please." She smiled.

Phaeton eyeballed her, and she eyed him right back. He leaned close. "Are you certain you don't mind?"

She nodded. "I'll be fine."

Phaeton let his tensions ease slightly. He supposed a backup as well as someone to guard America was not a terrible idea, but Gaspar would not have been his first choice. "Right. Shall we find a table?"

"I have reserved a booth." Gaspar gestured to the far wall, where a line of roomy padded seats surrounded small tables with drinks on them.

"Good God." They were all there, stuffed into the large corner banquet. The four Nightshades and Tim Noggy.

Phaeton groaned.

America squealed.

Gaspar grinned. "The more the merrier—this is a birthday celebration, is it not? And should anything go wrong, plenty of protection."

As Phaeton approached the table, Tim shrunk behind Ruby, who looked ravishing in her namesake color. America slid in beside her. He glanced around the booth. "Shouldn't you all be cloaked, or is that too stealthy for this evening?" Phaeton yelled over the dance beat. "Best to give the appearance of being up front—nothing to hide."

Gaspar sat beside Ruby. "Behind you, Phaeton."

Phaeton pivoted. His gaze traveled upward—then farther upward. There was a jutting jaw line, and deep set beady eyes under a heavy brow ridge—gnarlish features. Phaeton squinted. Neanderthal came to mind. Whatever it was, it was large and ugly. Customers in the bar were giving the creature a wide berth. Something vaguely reminiscent about this brute—a character from a childhood fairy tale, perhaps. He examined Phaeton then spoke. "Come." The beast turned back and glowered at the table. "Alone." Phaeton glanced back over his shoulder. America's features were frozen with fear.

The beast stomped up the stairs and out into the courtyard. The damp, cool mist helped sharpen his senses. Phaeton followed the hulking figure, covered head to toe in a long coat. They hadn't taken more than ten brute-sized steps when the behemoth turned and entered a door marked EXIT.

The giant swept down a narrow corridor and into a room at the end of the passageway. The room was small with a gallery of photographs hung on one wall and a number of very comfortable looking divans positioned about.

Something about the placement of the furnishings reminded him of the room below the club—except for the gallery of photographs. Phaeton stepped closer for a better look. The images in the pictures—people mostly—were moving. Viewing another frame, Phaeton recognized the dance floor. "The Orchid Lounge." His eyes took in the entire bank of moving images on the wall. The brute leaned over his shoulder. "That leggy beauty you came in with tonight and your moxy friends are in the second row of screens on the end."

Phaeton squinted at the image—there she was, chatting it up with Ruby and Tim. He turned toward the beast, who looked awfully amused. "What is this? Some kind of magic show?"

"In a manner of speaking." His escort didn't seem so brutish anymore. A third hand reached out from inside the overcoat and unbuttoned the creature's coat. A somewhat disturbing sight, until he studied the hands in the coat sleeves.

"Appendages fashioned to look real but are . . ."

"Lifeless fakes." Something about the brutish man's eyes—seemed familiar. "Velvet, would you mind?"

Phaeton hadn't noticed her standing in a dark corner of the room, but then succubi lived their whole lives in the shadows, and were rather good at making appearances when the mood struck them. Or when summoned.

The coat came off to reveal the large brute was actually a smallish, gnarlish creature . . . on stilts. Velvet removed the long coat with the fake hands and hung it on a wall hook.

Phaeton tilted his head. "This feels a bit like a circus trick."

The smallish brute unstrapped his feet and jumped down from the wooden blocks. "That's because it is a circus trick." Hardy for a small bloke, he gathered the stilts together and left them beside the coat.

Phaeton blinked. "You're a dwarf."

"Thank you for stating the obvious." The small man stepped forward. "Victor Hugo Tennyson. Not related to the writer or the poet. And do not refer to me as Mr. Tennyson." Flopping down on one of the low slung divans, he crossed short legs. "I am Victor. And you are Phaeton Black. Trustee to the greatest power ever gifted to mortals." Velvet returned to stand close to the dwarf, who stroked her arm. "It seems you have quite a cross to bear."

The succubus smiled. "Good evening, Mr. Black."

"You're looking radiant, Velvet." He took a moment to admire the young siren, attractive even in clothes. "Any female, no matter how illusory, who has rubbed her naked bottom against my crotch, can call me Phaeton." He shifted his gaze to Victor. "As for the Moonstone, it is a task I did not wish for—a responsibility foisted upon me by a deranged, ungrateful goddess. No doubt she was glad to be rid of it." Phaeton took a seat opposite the dwarf. "I'd shirk the job in a second if could just find a way to . . ."

"Duck out?" The dwarf raised a brow.

Phaeton glared.

"Ah, the reluctant hero." Victor appeared entirely too entertained by Phaeton's dilemma. "The young Jason embarks upon an impossible quest, fraught with harpies, hydras, and horrible beasts." There was a momentary hint of longing in his eyes before the small man came around. "I understand you drink eighteen-year-old Talisker's."

The lovely succubus brought over a bottle and two glasses. "If you'll excuse me gentlemen, I have to undress and go to work."

Phaeton followed a sultry sway of hip as she exited the room. "A dangerous flirtation, Victor."

The dwarf poured their drinks. "Don't I know it."

Phaeton leaned forward. "Have you found a way to—you know . . ." He rolled his eyes. ". . . That is, without getting the bloody life sucked out of you?"

Victor handed him a whiskey. "We're working on it."

Phaeton sensed a possible kindred spirit, at least in matters involving the penis. "Cheers." He took a swallow and enjoyed the whiskey burn. "I understand that dwarves do not get the short shrift—between the legs that is."

The man raised both brows. "Shall we compare cocks?"

Phaeton grinned. "Hard or soft?"

Victor threw back his head and laughed.

Chapter Twenty-six

"Only I can unleash the secret powers from the stone—or so they keep telling me." Phaeton swirled the amber liquid in his glass. "And here's the rub—I have no idea how to access this amorphous aether. It's rather comic; I control the power but have no idea how to use it."

"Or perhaps it is a kind of perfect genius. The man entrusted with the stone doesn't know how to open it." Victor grinned. "And what if I told you I can help you with that?"

"You can show me how to loose the power?"

Victor rocked his head, equivocating. "I think I can get you close—but there are others with knowledge of the stone. Gaspar and Lovecraft went to a great deal of trouble to have you captured and brought back to London—your London. And the moment you arrive the stone is snatched from under their noses." Victor sipped his drink. "That should tell you something, Phaeton."

"That there are forces on this side, who seek the stone just as desperately."

Victor did not break his gaze. "Powerful enough to punch holes into your world and recover the one thing that could save ours."

"And what role do you play in this game?" Phaeton tilted his head. "Are you puppet, master, or candlestick maker?"

Victor scanned the wall of screens behind Phaeton. "Your lovely young lady is out on the dance floor." He dipped his head to view another screen. "She's with several Nightshades, and where is Gaspar . . . ?"

Phaeton stole a quick glance at America. Smiling, laughing—swinging that booty around. It struck him dumb, sometimes, how much he loved her.

Victor's gaze landed on another screen. "Ah, there he is—snooping around outside in the yard with Tim Noggy."

Phaeton turned back to Victor. "How is it you seem to know everything about us, and yet we know next to nothing about you? We have this cryptic name—the maker—which came from a cockney rhyme. A menacing henchmen gave it up—one of those creatures without the Medusa helmet."

"Those are Skeezicks."

He nodded. "That *thing* tried to abduct America." Phaeton shrugged. "Cutter got close enough to be tortured and left for dead. Whoever captured him took half his face away. Nice characters you've got over here."

The dwarf nodded. "But no names?"

"All we've got—correction. All *I've* got are the names like Reapers and their comrades in arms—the scavengers."

Victor wore that amused look on his face again. "I believe your side calls them Grubbers."

"Whatever." Phaeton glowered. "I need to know at least as much as Gaspar and Lovecraft know about what is happening to your world. I already know their personal reasons for wanting the stone."

Victor raised a brow.

"If I give you this, I want the whole bloody story." Phaeton eyeballed the little man, who gestured for him to proceed. "Gaspar is unraveling and believes the stone can cure him. Lovecraft's son lives in a machine that keeps him alive. Reportedly, the professor has invented something better—sophisticated mechanics that will give his son mobility—but he needs a potent, efficient aether."

Victor knocked back the last half dram and set his glass down. Phaeton closed his eyes and waited for answers. "Once upon a time, there were three brothers. One set of identical twins, and the other, a badly deformed child. All three children were raised together, played together . . . educated together. But when it came time to run the business, the eldest child, eleven minutes older than his twin, was chosen."

"I take it you are one of the brothers."

"Guess which one." A wry grin curved Victor's mouth. "From the moment the torch was passed there began a struggle for power that continues on to this day. We live in a world that is run by a corporate oligarchy. A few wealthy entrepreneurs are in control"—Victor waved his hands in the air—"of everything."

Phaeton blinked. "Then what goes on in Westminster Palace–or Buckingham Palace for that matter?"

"Government as usual—just as you are accustomed to it."

"You're saying there's a shadow government here, in the Outremer."

Victor smiled. "The land beyond the sea. Much too romantic for us, Phaeton." The dwarf straightened. "The eldest twin pushed the younger out, then came to me and asked for my help—it's a long, tiresome story of struggle, which also includes a wizard of science and industry who saw our vulnerability and made his own grab for power.

"Eventually, I led what some call my own bid for control." Victor leaned back into the plush sofa. "I became the de facto commander of a league of insurrectionist rebels; we disbanded months ago. Most of us were forced into hiding—decimated by the first few editions of Reapers, which were very powerful. They are less so now. The second rebellion started forty-eight hours ago, the wreckage around town still smolders from it. We won a major skirmish, but the war is far from over. Hundreds of Reapers roam about largely unsupervised."

Phaeton blinked. "I've seen the overturned vehicles and the burnt out buildings."

"That would be our refuse. The powers that be would have cleaned up any evidence of insurrection by now except we have bigger problems to solve at the moment."

"You're unraveling."

"You noticed."

"And the maker?" Phaeton queried.

"A leviathan-sized aether company run by a twenty-two-year-old cyber geek. He's into creating and manufacturing cybernetic organisms."

Phaeton tilted an ear. "Which are?"

Taking pity on his blank look, Victor explained. "Beings with biological and mechanical parts. The machines this young man builds are programmed to call him their maker. As a matter of fact, there have been rumors of industrial spying recently . . . from your world."

"Professor Lovecraft."

"Very likely." Victor shook his head. "Sorry to disappoint, Phaeton, but I fit in nowhere here."

"I have to ask." Phaeton looked up from his empty glass. "Do you know where the Moonstone is?"

Victor studied him. "And what if I do?"

"Then,"—Phaeton leaned closer—"I might be willing to cut a deal."

Victor stared at the wall behind Phaeton. "Reaper squad—a big one."

Phaeton stood up and whirled around. A screen in the top row showed a number of motorized two-wheeled vehicles pull up and park outside the club.

Victor touched a device that appeared to be hooked over his ear. "Reapers—get them out the back way."

Several dancers—operatives of Victors—approached Gaspar and within seconds America, Tim, and all the Nightshades were whisked downstairs, past the lap dancers and out the secret exit. Phaeton watched their escape until he ran out of screens.

Victor looked as frustrated as he felt. "Unfortunately there is no coverage of the rear stairs; if this lair is ever found, I don't want them to know about the stairs."

Phaeton nodded. "Did they get out?"

"Presumably." Victor shrugged on a jacket. "Where do you reenter?"

"South side of Vauxhall Bridge."

"We'll not only catch up—we'll beat your friends over

there." Victor dimmed the lights and opened the door a crack. "Come."

All hell had broken loose in the yard near the club. Reapers herded a number of detainees into paneled vehicles using some sort of stick; Phaeton flinched at the sharp crack. "Electrical switches," Victor whispered, waving him up beside him. "Straight across the yard there's a covered passage that leads to a mews. Stay to the shadows and circle about, I'll meet you over there."

The sly dwarf turned back downstairs.

"Wait, where are you going?" Phaeton hissed.

"Secret passage—if I showed you . . ."

"Never mind," Phaeton growled. He slipped into the darkest shadows of the courtyard and quietly made his way over to a narrow walk between buildings.

"Who goes there? Stop where you are!" The voice sounded artificial, somewhat like Cutter's voice box. Phaeton thought about running, but slowed and turned. All he could make out was the silhouette of a snake entangled head.

On second thought.

Phaeton did an about face and ran. At the far end of the passage, he paused. This was supposed to be a mews but there were no carriages or stables. He turned toward the street, only to find himself in a blind court with a whip-cracking Reaper bearing down on him. The creature sprang out of the tunnel, leaping from wall to wall. Phaeton forced himself to stop, before he backed himself into a corner.

Something dark and fast rumbled into the alley. Phaeton squinted. An engine on two wheels moving very fast—and it was very loud. The strange vehicle struck the Reaper full bore and sent the creature flying into the air. The tentacled head smacked into the wall and the body slid to the ground.

The powerful engine pivoted in the middle of the yard. Phaeton sniffed the burn and smoke off thick, black wheels. The driver, who wore a helmet and dressed in leather, straddled the vehicle like it was a bicycle. "Climb on back, Phaeton."

The creature stirred. Phaeton jumped on and held on for

dear life. The motor bike took off with such power he thought he might be thrown off the back.

"Hold on tight."

At Tottenham Court road, the bike accelerated to such a speed that it took his breath away. Now and then, they slowed at a cross street, but otherwise blew through traffic lights and stop signs—something he had come to understand was de rigueur in the Outremer.

The power between his legs was like nothing he had ever encountered. Then he thought about standing up on the bowsprit of the *Topaz*—the sea rushing under you, the sun rising over an ocean of blue. Okay, this was the third most exhilarating experience of his life.

The driver slowed as they wove in and out of the wreckage of an old urban conflict. The rebels must have taken refuge behind that overturned double-decker. He wondered absently how long they had lasted.

Several Reapers jumped out at them and made a swipe at the handlebars of the motor bike. Phaeton tightened his grip as they accelerated to a speed that left even the Reapers in the dust— and Reapers, if he remembered correctly, were wicked fast creatures.

As they approached the Vauxhall Bridge, the driver slowed down. They continued along the bridge cautiously—waiting, he assumed, for a sign. There. Near the south end of the bridge, a flash of light. And a second flash.

The driver accelerated. At the southeast corner of the bridge, the driver made a cautious turnabout. "I believe this is my stop." Phaeton swung a leg over and approached the driver.

"Thanks for the—"

Under the streetlamp he caught a better look at the driver. He should say the curves of the driver—definitely female. Taken aback, Phaeton stammered, "Thanks for the—"

The driver took off in a blur of thrust and noise. He stared after the motor bike until it disappeared on the other side of the river.

"Hypothetically speaking, if I were in possession of the Moonstone, I would need Phaeton Black—that would be you—to help do what must be done." Phaeton turned to the familiar voice. Victor sat behind the driver of yet another motor bike. The silence felt odd—the engine had been turned off.

Phaeton dipped to look in the black cab that passed by. No America. No Gaspar. No Nightshades. "If you have a plan, let's hear it, Victor."

The dwarf handed over a satchel—the same one he had purchased earlier that evening, only heavier than he remembered.

"Nested among your clothes you'll find a perfect copy of the Moonstone, complete with a swirl of relic dust and champagne and the occasional quiver." The driver of the motor bike stepped down hard on a metal plate and the engine chugged to life. "Should you need anything, contact me through Fleury or Georgiana. Prepare yourself and your young lady, Phaeton. There are men who will stop at nothing to force you to loose the power in the stone. We're going to flush them out—find out who's against us and who's with us."

"Then what?" Phaeton yelled above the engine.

Victor waved as they moved off. "Then we save the world."

Chapter Twenty-seven

AMERICA STEPPED OUT OF THE CAB LOOKING FOR HIM. "He's not here." A huge red omnibus roared past. "Wait a moment." She smiled. The passing double-decker revealed Phaeton standing across the street. She waved to him, but as her focus took in the backdrop behind him, her mouth dropped open.

"Wait there," she called and ran to join him across the road. He led her to the bridge path. "Good God, Phaeton, what is happening here?" He held her in his arms while she peeked now and again at the ghastly sights. The grand waterway that was once the Thames was a muddy wash, with nothing but a trickle of water running down its center. All along the North bank, buildings were disintegrating—unraveling, including the whole of Westminster Palace. Her gaze trailed the riverbank all the way down to—half of St. Paul's dome appeared eaten away, as though some giant had taken a bite out of the cupola.

Phaeton spoke softly. "I was worried, my love—I wasn't sure if you avoided the Reaper patrols."

She arched back in his arms. "You were worried? Phaeton, you do realize we had no idea where you were? All we could do is hope you made it here, as well."

"I can assure you I was perfectly safe and had my eye on you all the whole time—well, Victor did anyway."

"Who's Victor?"

"Yes, Phaeton, who is Victor?" Gaspar stood a few feet away, eavesdropping.

Phaeton spun away from her to confront the Shades' leader. "I say we trundle on home to bed, and debrief in the morning."

Gaspar studied him, as well as the satchel in his hand. "As you wish, Phaeton."

Tim Noggy approached them, followed by the Nightshades, all of whom were dressed for clubbing in the Outremer. Phaeton found the sight highly amusing. "This must have cost Gaspar a bloody fortune."

"Let me tell you what's not so comical." Tim got out the small device he sometimes used to locate the ins and outs between worlds. "The stream is gone, mate."

"But there are others, right?" America asked. "We could go back to the hotel, again—might that work?"

Tim looked around at the concerned faces. "It's worth a try—otherwise we have to find a new one and they're harder to locate over here."

Phaeton's eyes narrowed. "I'll tell you what I think—I think Lovecraft tampered with this return point."

Tim looked at him. "I was thinking it, I just wasn't saying it."

"I asked the driver to wait." Gaspar did not look pleased. "Let's get to the hotel."

Phaeton pivoted toward the boxy black cab. "I do hope you got the driver with the red turban."

The ride over to Whitehall was taken up by an argument over the hotel room number. America tried a fresh start. "We agree on one thing—we were on the tenth floor."

"I swear we were in room twenty-eight, in the east wing." Ruby huffed.

"She's got a truly remarkable memory for topography as well as a sense of direction." Valentine eyeballed every man crammed into the cab. "We follow her lead first."

"Fine. Agreed. We go to twenty-eight first." Tim rolled his eyes. "Why do you like this guy with the turban?" he asked Phaeton.

"Because he has experience."

It appeared to be a quiet night at the hotel—the lobby was nearly empty as they traversed plush carpets and marble floors.

As they had done the last time, they split up and met on the tenth floor.

"Here it is, room twenty-eight. Tim got out his sensor. "What do you know? We've got an opening."

America walked up and down the corridor. "No maids about."

Cutter removed a key from his pocket and fiddled with the teeth end. "I have an uncle who works as a second-story man now and then. He taught me a thing or two about jimmying a lock."

"The one doing time at Wormwood Scrubs." Ruby rolled her eyes.

America tried to suppress a smile. Cutter had received an inordinate number of booty rubs on the dance floor this evening. He not only had some amazing dance moves, but his clockwork half mask had the young ladies swooning over him in the Outremer. Tim had called it a chit magnet. It was also hard not to notice Ruby's cool, aloof reaction to all the attention he received. She supposed they would quibble and bicker until one day one of them would get up the nerve to jump the other's bones.

Cutter wasn't on his knees for a quick minute when the door swung open. "I thought I might find you all here."

America noted Phaeton's glower. "Not particularly hard when you shut down the main highway out of here, Lovecraft."

"If any of you had thought to check with me . . ." The man's pale, watery eyes swiveled eerily. "I would have told you Vauxhall was down—a few maintenance issues." So this was Professor Lovecraft. The man was not imposing in the least, but he wore a perpetual half smile that was disturbing because of its obvious insincerity.

"If you wish to return to our side of the universe, please join me inside." Lovecraft stepped back to allow Gaspar and the Shades in first.

"Back away quickly," Phaeton whispered and grabbed her hand and made for the lift.

"Phaeton, what are we—?" She had no time to finish the sentence, the elevator doors opened. Phaeton blindly pressed a number of buttons on the panel.

"Step out of there now, or I'll shoot." The professor stood in the corridor brandishing a pistol pointed at America.

Phaeton swept her behind him. "You'll have to shoot me to get to her, and then where will you be?" Jersey Blood rounded the corner and tackled Lovecraft from behind. The gun went off just as the doors closed.

America squeezed Phaeton's hand and moved forward.

"Are you all right?" he asked.

"Well and bravely protected." She examined his jacket. "If you'll excuse me." She leaned close. "I have to check for bullet holes." She opened his jacket and a few buttons of his shirt. She loved the feel of his fuzzy mat of chest hair—sweeping her fingers lightly over his chest she moved lower until his stomach muscles quivered.

"I remember now, danger excites your desire for me." Phaeton grinned, looking up and around. "I've never done it in a lift—might be fun."

The elevator suddenly lurched to a halt. America moved beside Phaeton and waited for the doors to open. But nothing happened. Phaeton checked all the buttons on the side panel. "Ah here we are." He pressed the button marked DOOR OPEN.

"Hello?"

The voice came from a small mesh square above the control panel. America looked up at Phaeton. "Might it be a telephone of some sort?" America stood on tiptoe and answered. "Hello?" She had observed that Outremer denizens either carried or wore strange little communication devices. In the club, Gaspar had explained these gadgets were more important than flesh and blood people.

A face appeared in the flat square above the buttons and America jumped back. "Apologies for the delay, we'll be bringing you down shortly." It appeared to be a photograph of a young man with close cropped hair, near their age. And she distinctly saw the disembodied head animate. The image turned profile and bobbed about.

Just to make sure she wasn't hallucinating she checked in with Phaeton. "Are you seeing this?"

The lighting inside the elevator dimmed, and the panel of buttons flashed.

Phaeton cleared his throat. "Mind telling us where we're going? Just so we don't get the mistaken idea we're being abducted?"

The elevator dropped suddenly, then corrected itself for the trip down. They both anxiously watched the numerical digits above the door, until the word *Lobby* appeared. But the metal cubical didn't stop; it continued its descent, past P1, P2, P3, P4.

Then there were no more numbers or letters. Phaeton caught America around the waist and gave her a reassuring squeeze. Suddenly, the word *Pool* flashed above the metal doors and the lift came to a stomach lurching stop.

The doors opened onto a room encased by glass walls and a rectangular bathing pool. The main plunge was large indeed with two smaller, steaming pools at one end. America reached for Phaeton's hand. The air was sultry, with a tinge of antiseptic in the air.

They walked around the entire glassed-in pool, until they found the entrance. An envelope was attached to the door with a message: *One for each ear.*

"Welcome to Black Box." A young man approached them wearing a dressing robe, over loose fitting plaid pajamas, and bedroom slippers. "My name is Jared J. Oakley. Most everyone calls me JJ or Oakley—take your pick." He pointed to the packet on the door. "You don't need to put in the ear buds unless you want to send or receive messages." His smile was relaxed, affable.

She and Phaeton were a bit slow to answer, since they were so busy staring.

Jared's laugh was gentle. "Look, I know this is a bit overwhelming so why don't I ramble on—stop me if you have a question."

The young, rather handsome man looked them over. "You're Phaeton and America." He grinned. "Cool names." There was something about the way he spoke that reminded her of . . . Tim.

"Where are we exactly?" Phaeton queried, having found his voice.

Jared turned to him. "You are in the guest sector of a very large complex of interconnected underground chambers." His eyes rolled upward. "We are nine stories underground, and the space is hermetically sealed—impervious to harmful gases—and the chambers are lined with fifteen inches of lead, which means this environment is free from the destructive cosmic rays that are about to unravel our world."

He paused to let them take it in. "About an hour ago, Victor called and said he suspected Vauxhall was down and thought you might try the hotel. He asked me to keep an eye out."

"It appears Lovecraft had the same idea," Phaeton said.

Jared nodded. "It's late—enjoy your stay—sleep late. We'll slip you back through in the morning." He showed them to a sort of tropical bedchamber just off poolside. "We have regular rooms down the corridor." Their congenial host rocked his head back and forth. "Maybe four star quality without the turn down and pillow chocolate." He rolled back a glass door. "But since we have no other guests at the moment—you can have the pool and this room to yourselves."

A four-poster bed veiled in sheer white drapes lay cantilevered over a rectangular pond, which featured a waterway that trickled over smooth black rocks, and zigzagged down into the swimming pool.

"There are three pools. The large for a swim, two hot pools for tired muscles, and the other is for bathing. If you decide to bathe—don't get out until you are finished washing up. The bath automatically drains, sanitizes, and refills itself." Jared nodded a bow and backed out of the room. "Sleep well."

America whirled around. "What do you think, Phaeton?"

He set down the satchel. "I think I'm beginning to like it over here." He shrugged out of his new blazer and rolled up a shirt sleeve. Down on his haunches he dipped his hand in the water. He peeked over his shoulder and raised a brow. She knew a signature Phaeton grin was hidden behind his sleeve.

She tilted her head. "Well?"

"Like a baby's bath water." Now she could see his smile.

"Stop! I know exactly what you're thinking, Phaeton Black."

His arm swept back and forth. "Oh no, Miss Jones, you're wrong indeed." He shook off droplets and sauntered close. "You are going to have to seduce me into removing all my clothes." His smile turned into a challenging grin. "So that we might cavort like porpoises in and out of the pool."

America lowered her chin and slanted her eyes. The sultry look that always captured his attention. She reached up behind the strapless gown and found the small metal pull.

And pulled.

The bodice slipped off her breasts, and down her hips. She stepped out of the dress and laid it across a lawn chair near the pool. She turned to him and unknotted the tie at her hip. She let the protective shawl fall away.

"I suppose there is no need for that, with fifteen inches of lead protecting pea in the pod from nasty cosmic rays." He was so taken with the violet lace v-string pantie, he could barely speak the words.

America pulled the strings halfway down her buttocks and she caught a glimpse of him watching her disrobe with unapologetic interest. America began to laugh. "You might attend to the removal of your own clothes."

Eventually, he did turn away, but not before taking a good long side-glance at her. Phaeton finished his undress while she waded into the pool. From a safe position in the water, she watched him disrobe with growing curiosity.

His shirt was off and his torso and arms were taut with muscle. His beautifully proportioned broad chest narrowed down to slim hips and long sinewy legs. America sank lower into the warm pool water. Needless to say, he was a particularly handsome man. But this evening, he could be a seductive stranger. "Shall we have a fantasy?"

"What do you desire, my love? To be captured by a centaur and ravaged in the road?"

She wrinkled her nose. "Too muddy." She dipped her head back to wet her hair. "What about this . . . a lovely pond nymph is taking her bath in a woodland thermal spring, when a hot and dusty warrior comes along, and begins to disrobe . . ."

Phaeton grinned. "Start us off darling."

She looked up at him as though he were a complete stranger. "Don't be shy handsome warrior, show me everything."

Chapter Twenty-eight

PHAETON DROPPED HIS PANTS and America's brows lifted. She pretended that she saw entirely too much of the beautiful warrior. Squealing with laughter, she turned around and did not move until he plunged into the pool.

She circled back as he rose out of the water. "Are you a Greek god? Tell me sir, what is your name?"

"Sir Phaeton." He swept wet hair back behind his ears, and waded straight for her. "And compliments like that will get you ravaged soon enough."

America back-paddled farther away from the swinging sword. "Very impressive, sir."

"Alas, the beauty extols not my intellect, but my lance. Come here, little nymph."

Warily, she swam around him. " 'Tis a very grand and ferocious lance, sir."

Phaeton narrowed his gaze. "I take what I want, pretty one. You will do as I say or there will be consequences."

America shook her head. "I have come to this place to bathe, not to screw."

He waded after her. "Coward."

"Bully," she countered, drifting closer, her head just above the water.

"Beware, my love." Phaeton sank deeper into the pool and soon they were close enough to kiss. "That kind of impertinent speech requires punishment.

Without touching him, she pressed her lips to his. "I feel great love for you, Sir Phaeton." His body stirred.

"As well and as deeply, I hope, as my affection for the ravishing pond nymph."

She gave him another kiss for his endearing declaration.

"Again," he ordered gently, and she complied. "I must see more." With a bit more coaxing he led her to the shallow part of the pool and America allowed him to look upon her. "Tell me what you are feeling little nymph."

She blushed. "I feel beautiful and seductively naughty."

Phaeton remained the strange knight as his eyes roved appreciatively over her body. He experienced the strong rush of desire that swept through her voluptuous frame. She shivered slightly under his scrutiny.

His cock was as hard as a stone. "You are perfectly made, America."

She stared for a moment, then shook her head with a laugh. "What flattery and nonsense." She noted stacks of rugged towels and huge wooden bowls filled with soft brushes and soaps.

Her eyes grew wide. "Look, the pool for bathing." She led him over to the separate bath, and admired his rigid, bobbing lance. She took up a block of soap, and pushed it into his hand. "This will give you a chance to appraise every small detail. Count the beauty marks." America turned her back to him and held her hair up as he scrubbed from shoulders down to the pleasantly curved small of her back.

He couldn't see her expression but he was sure she smiled as he counted her flaws. "Three small moles thus far."

" 'Tis a relief to turn away from such a penetrating gaze, sir."

"And what about you, my dear? I can still see the blush on your cheeks from the sight of my erection—I mean my savage sword."

He pointed out a bruise above America's hip and traced it to the booty bumps she had taken this evening. "Yes, I think my back did ache some after a dance." She turned enough to see the frown on his face. "Phaeton, you must not treat me like a fragile little flower."

The irony of her remark elicited a bark of laughter as he

scrubbed her lower back. "Two perfect dimples above a plump little derrière."

"Too plump?"

The frown in her voice made him chuckle. "Perfectly plump, my love, and very desirable." His hands were full of lather and he slipped them around her hips, to softly stroke her belly.

America shuddered from his caresses, falling back against his chest and into his arms. Her knees had quite literally grown weak from his gentle fondling.

He moved his hands lower, under foaming water, to stroke between her legs. "Open for me."

Catching his fingers in hers, she brought the well-practiced, stimulating hand back up out of the water. "Not yet, sir." She found herself arching back against his chest as she encouraged him to explore her torso. His fingers lightly traced along her hip bones and up past a hint of ribs, to the crease under her breasts. Cupping both mounds, he pressed her against his body and she felt the hard thrust of his erection pass across her buttocks.

Her entire body relaxed, as his fingers moved past her navel, and lowered into the channel below, the one that made her writhe with arousal. His fingers circled the place that made her want more and more of his touching.

"Please, I cannot breathe." Wrenching herself out of his arms, she moved away. She reached out to hold onto the edge of the pool, and took up a cake of soap.

He did not follow her directly, but watched her wade through the pool, a beautiful woodland water nymph in a garden of earthly delights. "You have the most glorious flush of arousal on your chest and neck . . . and cheek."

Lathering her hands with soap she offered to bathe him. "Come here, handsome knight, and let me clean you up."

America washed his unruly hair and brushed the dirt from his fingernails.

"My turn." Phaeton soaped her tangled mass of waves. Wrapping one arm around her waist, he used the other to support her head as he laid her back into the gently stirring waters to rinse the soap away. He kissed her mouth, her neck, her shoulders, and when he reached her breast he covered her nipple with his mouth and tongued until she arched against his arm. She uttered his name in the most erotic and innocent bedding voice.

"Sir Phaeton."

"Let yourself explore, little virgin nymph. I will not hurt you."

Guiding her hand below his navel, her fingers tangled in the mat of wet hair, landing on his erection. She wrapped her fingers around the velvet shaft and stroked. He groaned and encouraged her to soap and stroke some more.

There was something wickedly daring about flaunting their nudity and sexual response to each other in such a potentially public place. The more he touched her—the more she opened up to him. Most provocatively, Phaeton wanted them to be chanced upon. And she could not deny that their possible exposure felt delicious and decadent, as long as she was safely in his arms.

Phaeton lifted her up onto the ledge of the pool. America drew her legs out of the water, and he moved between her thighs, opening her. He remained in the water with his head buried between her legs.

"Phaeton," she moaned, "We've got company."

"What?" He looked up to see two chaps step into a pool across the room. Steam swirled off the circular shaped bath. And there was a low motorized humming and a great deal of foaming and churning at the surface of the water.

Phaeton vaulted out of the bath, pausing briefly to take in the vision of her nude figure as she reclined in repose. "You are a beauty, my love, but you are mine alone." He carried her into the bedroom and lay her down on the bed.

Propped on her elbows, America directed her most radiant smile toward him. She shook her head, and a mass of damp waves descended past her shoulders and down her back.

Phaeton rested on his side, chin propped in hand, enjoying the beautiful picture as she pushed her hips up and tossed her head back. In fact, he watched her erotic undulations with a sinful amount of lust building in his groin.

"She lays beside me naked, not a stitch of clothing
 I cannot fault her body, not a single part
Soft shoulders, lovely shaped arms
 Nipples that invite my mouth, her slightly
  rounded belly
Beneath her rounded breasts
 That comely curve of hip and heavenly thigh
There is not a detail that falls short of perfection . . ."

Phaeton ran his finger along her comely curve of hip. "Ovid—third century poet philosopher—"

"I think he died in prison from syphilis," she interrupted. "And that was rather a mangled recitation." America's eyes had changed into challenging, smoldering pools of desire.

Phaeton was very aware that she had moved her knees farther and farther apart so he might see more and more of her. Pink folds of moistened flesh, framed by close-cropped curls. She moved her fingers through the folds and opened farther, bidding him to enter her. She smiled, a bit dreamily. "Let's see if I can torture a bit of the old Roman poet . . .

"Such wicked behavior—please do save your badness for bed.

 "Strip me naked with no embarrassment—
Your knee between my thighs,
 And vary your passion, sir, thrust that tongue
  between cherry-ripe lips.
Do not hold back your whispers, your moan of pleasure
 Make this bed shake like mad . . ."

America watched his desire grow as she spread her legs. "How long can you stand this?" she whispered.

Phaeton had not far to reach her. He was on his knees and took her up into his arms. She kissed his face and ears and neck and helped him reach her breasts by arching her back. She watched him bring one tight, swollen nipple at a time to his mouth to suckle, then nibble until she moaned with pleasure.

America pushed Phaeton away and moved off the bed. "Perhaps your difficult pond nymph needs to be taught a lesson?" She held out a hand, and Phaeton was on his feet. He ordered her to the tall bedpost. Obediently, she turned her back-side to him and held onto the heavy carved post above her head. Her body quaked in anticipation. He stood to her side, and placed one hand on the flat of her belly, the other on her rear.

He spanked firmly, until her stomach shuddered from arousal. Then he stopped and moved his fingers between her legs and stroked softly until she wet his hand from her pleasure.

"Again," she whispered. Phaeton repeated this punishment several times, moving his hand up her belly, across her ribs and over her breasts. He whispered in a dry husky voice, "I will use my hand as long as it makes you moan in ecstasy."

"Umm, yes, that kind of playful force that goes well with pleasure." America stopped his fingers, and backed away. "Pun-ish me with demands, if you can catch me, sir."

He pursued her around the bed and across the room. Against the wall, she allowed herself to be captured by her ravager and made to do his bidding.

Taking her by the hair—he pushed her down on her knees and presented his turgid cock to her mouth. "Take it—all of it."

They aroused each other against every wall, inside the water closet and on a secretary chair. By the time he cleared the top of the writing desk they were out of breath, skin glistening with sweat and the delicate perfume of America's musky emollient all over their bodies.

Phaeton nuzzled her hair, her throat, pausing above her mouth to recite.

> "Ladies, in fact, love to yield,
>   Even prefer a rough seduction.
> It delights them, the audacity of near rape,
>   And the lady could have been forced,
> Yet she asked . . . for the pleasure."

America took Phaeton by the hand and led him to the end of the secretary where she bent over, laying her chest on the table so she might present her backside to him. Phaeton was so highly aroused he nearly thrust in for immediate relief—but he stopped himself.

He gathered her wrists together and held them down with one hand. "You can't escape from me now," he whispered. With his free hand he gently stroked and rubbed until the lady begged him to stop. "Turn over."

Lifting her up, he set her buttocks on the edge of the worktable. She faced her lover and he gently brought her forward, inch by inch. Slowly. Until she moaned in frustration. He then ordered her to do his bidding. "Open your legs."

"Make me." America had drawn her legs up and she teased him with just enough resistance, until she allowed him to push them open. Then wider still.

"Now for a taste." Phaeton kissed the lovely flesh of her belly, moving down through fleecy curls into moist petals of rose flesh. His tongue found the small throbbing place in need of his attention and teased.

He brought both legs up close, leaving a trail of soft kisses over the inside of her thighs. He understood what she wanted, the pleasure of his gentle, measured force. It was so like his America. In these last days together he felt more certain of her affection than ever, and he had somehow found the courage to love her utterly and completely.

Phaeton guided his tongue over and over the most sensitive places, his face wet with her scent. He felt her legs and belly tremble and heard her gasp for breath, and only when he knew she neared the peak of her pleasure did he enter her.

America threw her legs up over his shoulders and he yanked her closer so that he might have a mouthful of breast. He nipped and bit her nipples harder than he ever had before, and she cried out from both arousal and pain. As he pumped into her, America took hold of his hand and placed it so that his fingers reached just the right place.

All it took was one touch and she went over the edge. Phaeton shook from his own climax and finished loudly, to underscore his pleasure.

America rested, fully naked, sprawled across the desktop. His breath was on her neck—just his breath—he didn't say anything—he didn't have to. They were both completely satiated. He carried her to bed and curled up behind her.

Chapter Twenty-nine

AMERICA LUXURIATED UNDER SOFT SHEETS. She listened to the gentle sound of water spilling over rocks in a brook. A brook? She sat up straight. Then she remembered that she was in an underground facility in the Outremer. "What time is it?" She had an appointment with the telephone company. And the sign maker was coming by to take measurements.

Phaeton rolled over, a sleepy frown on his face. "My watch is in the satchel." He rubbed his eyes and ran a finger from the cleft of her bottom, up her spine. "Why do you need to know?"

"At first, I wanted to keep it a surprise. But then, there was a minor complication. I was going to tell you last night—about the surprise." Feeling every bit the naked little sprite, America leapt out of bed and opened the satchel. She stopped and blinked. "Phaeton . . . ?"

"The Moonstone." Propped on his elbows, he lifted a finger to his lips.

America nodded. "I'm opening a shop, more of an office actually."

Phaeton raised a brow. "A shipping office?"

"That, too." Then she added hastily. "Investigations primarily." She found his pocket watch. "Good God, I've only got half an hour—if this is right." She held the timepiece up to her ear and exhaled a sigh. "Still ticking." America rolled on hose one leg at a time. Phaeton stared. "Are you purposely trying to give me an erection?"

"Whatever it takes to get you up." She winked. "You must

dress quickly. We have a very important appointment with the telephone company—we're—having a line installed."

"We're what?" He sat up straight. "A line? Whatever for?"

"We . . ." she stared at him, "have our reasons."

"According to the *Guardian,* twenty thousand telephones in a city of one and a half million. Why would you—?" Phaeton's gaze narrowed. "You need me, don't you?"

"There's a contract involved." Drat! Her eyes shifted. "I told them Mr. Black was out of town until this morning." She tossed him his shirt and collar. "Quickly darling, we can negotiate favors once we're home." Dressed, with satchel in hand, Phaeton followed her around the pool. "Shall we try the lift?" She tossed the question over her shoulder.

He pressed the button with an up arrow and waited. "How much?"

A ding sounded, and the doors opened. America's mouth dropped open. "You haven't been riding up and down in this all night—I hope?"

The Nightshades stood in the lift dressed in their evening attire. Jersey waved them inside. Gaspar appeared far from well, there were dark circles under his eyes. And his color was . . . colorless.

Phaeton eyeballed Jersey. "Last night you tackled Lovecraft to the ground—so what happened?"

"The professor is tied up in the room upstairs. Tim is watching him." Jersey pressed number ten.

Ruby piped in. "We figured you might try back—so we waited for you to return. A bellboy knocked on the door this morning with a wire. Get in the lift." The blonde shrugged. They spoke between stops and starts. Passengers entered and exited. By the time the lift opened onto the tenth floor, America felt a bit queasy. "If you don't mind, Phaeton and I have an appointment with the Oxford Court Telephone Exchange. Might we hurry it up a bit?"

Inside the hotel room, Valentine drew an ink bottle in an inkwell—she wrote the word *quill* and drew a picture of a quill pen tracing through a spray of ink splats . . .

America looked up from the desk and the room was . . .

filled with people. Strangers all milling about. She had crossed over and appeared to be caught in the middle of a reception of sorts. A table overflowing with breakfast items caught her eye— a wedding reception, perhaps? America stepped around a bustled skirt, poured a cup of tea and gulped. Between tiered crystal platters filled with delectable tarts she spied Phaeton. Quickly, she forked several pastries into a small napkin and met him at the door.

"No more lifts." She took his hand and ran down ten flights of stairs. Phaeton flagged down a hansom on Whitehall Place. Inside the cab she opened the napkin and they shared an iced strawberry pastry and a lemon-filled tart. Cheered by a bite of breakfast, Phaeton inquired about their upcoming appointment. "You never answered my question. How much are we on the hook for?"

"Twenty pounds the first year, but that includes the expense of running a wire to Mrs. Parker's." America braced for the growl.

Phaeton's gaze moved out the window, and she took it as a good sign. Perhaps the cost of living in the Outremer had inured him. She slipped her hand in his. "Sir Phaeton turned out to be a very talented lover."

He winked at her. "And poet."

She thought the worry on his face had more to do with the responsibility of the Moonstone. "I can feel the weight, Phaeton—please know it is on both our shoulders. I understand I am a burden as long as very bad elements scheme to force you to their will."

Phaeton slipped an arm around her and pulled her close. "Last night I met with an odd duck—a very small person by the name of Victor. Fancies himself an insurrectionist—but also seems well aware that the stone is needed to heal both our worlds. The man is quite singular in his *lack* of greed. Victor was also the one who suspected Vauxhall was down and kept an eye out for us at the hotel."

America studied his face, a bit more brooding than usual. "But—you don't trust him."

"Between Gaspar and Lovecraft on our end, and this new

Oakley chap and Victor—I'd be a fool to trust anyone completely." Phaeton exhaled. "And Lovecraft is brilliant but raving
mad; he should be in Bethlem Hospital, poor unfortunate."

"What shall the Nightshades do with the professor? Not
likely they'll be turning him over to the authorities, even
though he threatened us both and fired his pistol." The more
she thought about it, the angrier she got. "He should be locked
up in a jail cell."

"I expect there are more devils yet to come." Phaeton
scanned the street ahead and the traffic to each side of the hansom. She had never seen him so on edge—so vigilant. He
shook his head. "And—who's the maker—still no real answers
there." Phaeton slid back the cab window to see behind them.
"Our self-appointed protectors are following us."

"I must say I've become rather fond of them."

She found the patter of spring rain on the roof comforting.
Phaeton closed the window. "After I sign the papers, I'm off to
Pennyfields. I suspect things may get a bit rough from here on
out, so be mindful, on your guard."

America threw her arms around Phaeton and kissed him.
She even added a bit of tongue, and a nose-to-nose nuzzle.
"You said you'd sign the papers."

Sometimes, when Phaeton looked at her the way he was
now, he made her feel as though she was the most admired and
loved woman in the world.

"And if I repeated 'I'll sign the papers' would you . . . ?"

She kissed him again.

"You look terrible." Phaeton sat at the opposite end of the
settee from the leader of the Shades. Gaspar was losing his
hair—or perhaps the top of his head was unraveling; either way
it angered Phaeton. No matter how much the man irritated
him, Gaspar was too smart, too young and—dare he admit it—
too kind to die.

"And where are the ladies?"

"America put them all to work, scrubbing the new office."
Three bodyguards remained with America—Ruby, Valentine,
and Cutter. Phaeton had left the office with Jersey.

Gaspar added a faint smile to his heavy-lidded gaze. "Miss Jones is a lovely and spirited young woman. I do not envy the road ahead for you Phaeton, but when it comes to America—she is one of those special women."

"I know exactly how special America is—and I didn't come here so you could tell me."

"I'm so pleased to hear it—there was a time not so long ago . . ." Gaspar shrugged.

Phaeton sighed. "I came to ask you one question—but first things first." He opened the satchel and lifted out a large, swirling black egg. He placed the Moonstone on the settee between them.

"Tell me how this might work—if I used the Moonstone to cure you." Phaeton leaned back into his corner of the divan. "Would that be it? One bloody cure and we toss it in the dustbin? The all powerful stone puts Humpty Dumpty together again—but can it also restore the Outremer as well? And if it can do both, why not have it power Lovecraft's son's mechanical parts, as well as the rest of his toys? And why do I believe everything I've been hearing about this bloody egg is a pack of lies?" Instead of kicking something, he ran both hands through his hair roughly.

"You do not seek power, Phaeton—in that respect you are pure of heart." Gaspar finally ripped his gaze off the stone. "Perhaps that is the reason you were chosen. You have an appetite for life, but no wiles or ambitions—you are a lone wolf—"

"Who has found his mate." Strangely, Phaeton felt like taking a bite out of Gaspar. "So, in that sense, I am vulnerable. What if something happens to America? Perhaps she has a hard labor, there is trouble delivering the babe. The stone could make her well—save the child."

"A reasonable fear—there might be nothing left to save your own loved ones."

"Yes—but again it all seems so nonsensical—if the Moonstone truly is as powerful as everyone seems to think . . ."

"The power in the stone is equal to the purity of the request." Ping approached them quietly—at times it seemed like his feet barely touched the ground. His long coat was off and he was in a waistcoat and trousers with his shirtsleeves rolled up.

"Up all night writing, Julian?"

Gaspar was perhaps the only one he had ever heard refer to Ping as Julian. A given name one presumed, but then it was hard to think about Ping having a mother or father—or even being born for that matter. Everyone just called him Ping—or Jinn depending on his gender.

The benevolent, silver-eyed creature peered over wire spectacles. "My kind often sleep for centuries inside jars or oil lamps. We need little rest in the span of a human lifetime."

Dumbfounded, Phaeton clapped his mouth shut. It was the first time he had heard Ping speak of his origins. "So, tell me, Ping, how many wishes must I facilitate—and who shall be granted their wish?"

Ping stared at Phaeton to the point it made him uncomfortable. "You wish for nothing for yourself?"

"I wish to rid myself of this unwanted, thankless task that has needlessly put my family in jeopardy."

Gaspar interjected. "Phaeton did express a concern that should America's labor run into difficulty, he would like to reserve a little protection—for mother and child."

Jinn raised his hand in prayer and bowed.

Phaeton grinned. "Help me here, Ping. Do I have to figure out a way to coax the jinn out of the bottle, or . . . are you already out?"

Ping clasped his hands behind his back and thought a moment. "Let us say—I serve in the capacity of advisor to the Moonstone's chosen guardian."

Phaeton brightened some at the thought of advice. "It has been some years since I read the *Arabian Nights*. I need a refresher."

The young androgyne brought out a packet of opium-laced tobacco and a briar pipe. "Rule number one: the stone can't kill anybody—so don't ask. Rule number two—" Ping held up a safety match and it burst into flames. "Just a guess, but I suspect the stone can't make someone do something that is not in their heart to do—for instance, it can't force someone to fall in love."

He touched the flame to tobacco. After a few puffs on the briar pipe, Ping shook out the match. "Rule number three. No power on earth or beyond can bring people back from the dead, and finally this is not an oil lamp from an Arabian fairy tale. You can't wish for more wishes—elementary you'd think, but you'd be surprised how many try for it." Ping blew circles of smoke into the air. "In your instance, Phaeton, I suspect the powers in the stone will rest when your task is finished, so there may well be no limit."

"Which only makes the bloody stone that much more appealing to nefarious types," Phaeton groused. "So how do I begin? For instance, might I ask that Professor Lovecraft walk into Bethlem Hospital and commit himself?" Phaeton sat back and waited for Ping's answer. "Somehow I don't believe it's that simple, exactly."

Even as his teeth clenched the pipe, there was a slight upturn to the ends of Ping's mouth. "That is because it is not in the professor's heart to do such a thing."

Phaeton rolled his eyes. "Promise me you'll say not a word about this wishing business. Christ, can you imagine if this gets out? They'll beat a path to my door for favors." His eyes felt like they were bulging out. "And just in case someone dares ask—no love, no marriage, no sex—right? I mean, a man could ask that a female would sleep with him, whenever he wanted, as long as this woman didn't also have to love him, presumably."

"You cannot trick, cajole, or manipulate the stone. And there is a strong connection between the heart and the will. So, no games, Phaeton."

He nodded. "Good, when do I start? How do I get this over with?" He looked to both men. "This is not a task that goes on indefinitely—it isn't—is it?" Phaeton leaned forward, "Because if it is, I want out—I want to pass this egg to someone who wants the job."

"It's not as easy as that." Gaspar grinned. "The people who want such a venture, like me for instance, would never be given the charge."

Phaeton placed his head in his hands and sighed. "Why not?

Why can't it just be as easy as me walking up to a chap and saying, 'Here you go, mate—the stone's yours.' "

Ping stepped closer. "Make up your mind who and what needs help—what must be fixed or righted—and put it directly to the stone. No magic words. Then place the stone in the care of a pure-hearted soul."

Phaeton sank back into the divan. "Christ, I'll never get rid of it."

Chapter Thirty

AMERICA STOOD BACK TO ADMIRE THE OFFICE. The windows were washed, and the walls and floors were swept of cobwebs and dust. The floor, desk, and a few leftover furnishings were covered with drop cloths as the painters and paper hangers were coming.

"Fresh paint and a coat of varnish on the door should give the place a lift." Valentine stepped outside and tossed the basin of dirty water out at the curb.

"Shall we see if Cutter and Ruby have a spot of tea and sandwiches ready?" America gathered up the dirty cleaning rags and placed them in the just emptied bowl. "Is it my imagination working overtime, or was Ruby beside herself with jealousy last night?"

"She and Cutter play this cat and mouse game—the advantage constantly shifts between the two. Jersey and I are often amused by their antics." Valentine's eyes rolled upward.

Inside Mrs. Parker's, on their way back to the flat, they stopped off at the kitchen to return the basin and rags. "Speaking of games—how is 'who's got the power' working for the two of you?"

Valentine's sultry dark gaze slid sideways. "Things are—improving. Jersey is beginning to trust me with the game. He is a man of his word and takes his vows seriously—one of his great attractions. Near the landing, America stopped mid-step and placed her finger to her lips. Silently, she bade Valentine stay and descended a stair or two. She crouched down to see below.

Ruby was giving Cutter a bath.

All the face plates were off—as was the mechanical eyepiece. A number of small screw drivers and connecting plates indicated that the removal of Cutter's iron wear was a time consuming, even painful procedure. Drawn in the most lurid, mesmerizing way, she dared to look at his injured face. His ear was missing—nothing left but a semicircular scar and a hole in the side of his head. Crisscrossed with scars—he was not recognizable as Cutter. There was no eyebrow or lid, and what remained of his eye appeared to be dilated. The injured orb also tracked rather well with his good eye. She surmised the lenses attached to the headpiece must have more to do with correction than enhancement.

Ruby gently dabbed a cloth around the eye. "I'm going to borrow a bit of arnica cream from the pantry—it will help the chafing." She stood up and he caught her hand. America could have sworn he wanted to say something—perhaps ask her something, but he didn't. With his chin tilted up, America noted the marks around his throat—as if he had been hung from the neck and had lived to tell about it. He just held Ruby's hand another moment and gradually let go.

America blinked back tears. What sort of a cruel monster could have done such a thing? The very thought of a powerful unseen enemy in the Outremer made her tremble. One who might stop at nothing to obtain the Moonstone and Phaeton. She tiptoed up the stairs and took Valentine by the hand. She continued climbing upward, toward the doxies' rooms, but stopped midpoint.

"Ruby is bathing Cutter."

"In that little tub of yours?"

"I caught a glimpse of long muscular legs, before . . ." America's smile faded.

Valentine stared. "He let her take his helmet off."

She swallowed. "What kind of savage fiend would do such a thing?"

"Men either hungry for more power or terrified of losing it." Valentine's gaze seemed far away. "Gaspar hired us several months ago—not long after you and Phaeton sailed for the Orient." Valentine leaned against the banister. "I suspect that the hunt was on, the moment the Moonstone surfaced—word travels fast among the powerful of any time and place."

"Gaspar named the maker Prospero, and thought he could strike a deal with the fiend. But once he unleashed his stealth army—the Reapers and Grubbers—he used his minions to suck the life out of this world. It seems his plan was to use the aether accumulated from this world to shield himself from the unraveling."

America snorted. "And how is that working for him?"

Valentine joined her with a smirk. "The more aether he removes from here—the more unraveling happens on the other side. The Grubber foraging has lessened, and as you've noted, he confines his attacks to Phaeton or . . .

"Go ahead, you can say it—or me." America exhaled. "Phaeton has always felt a strong connection with the Outremer. Why can't we find a way—" A sweep of pale, silvery particles circled the chandelier above the staircase landing. She met Valentine's gaze and flicked her eyes upward.

Valentine studied her a moment. "It's the flighty little succubus again, isn't it?"

A musical laugh resolved itself into a smile, which balanced on the staircase newel. America smiled. "Very clever Fleury, just like the Cheshire Cat."

The succubus draped herself along the railing beside them. "I have another message for Mr. Black."

America nodded. "Would you like to send a wire to Phaeton—like we did last time?"

The young succubus fluttered an eye roll. "That stuffy old office full of clerks? Would you please deliver the message for me?"

"I'm rather busy today, Fleury," America played hard to get, "but I suppose . . ."

"Oh please Miss Jones, I would be entirely indebted to you."

"All right then, I shall gladly see that Mr. Black gets your message—if you in kind deliver a message to Georgiana and your parents from me."

The juvenile succubus sat up and blinked. "Victor requires a brief meeting with Phaeton. Come alone to Highgate Cemetery anytime after dusk."

America nodded. "Is that it?"

"No, there's more." As lackadaisical as you please, Fleury swept a fey wisp of hair behind her ear. "My sister Velvet says to prepare for an attack."

"What kind of attack?" Valentine rose from the steps. "On this side?"

"Mmm . . . I believe so." The girl giggled and began to fade.

America raised her voice. "Fleury come back—I have a message for you."

The curious girl remerged.

"Tell your parents that they must control Georgiana—for the time being—until we can find a less lethal form of recreation for her. No more sucking the life out of men in their sleep. Scotland Yard is terribly upset and might use their . . . succubus . . . extinguisher on her." America did her best to look anguished and distressed. Not difficult considering the girl's message. "You wouldn't want Georgiana to be extinguished—would you?"

"I might have to think about that," the flighty little vixen mused. Valentine quietly backed down the steps one foot behind the other. "I'm feeling rather cross with Georgiana today; all my green ribbons went missing this morning," Fleury sniffed.

"I'm sure if you ask politely your trinkets will be returned." America also retreated. "Until tomorrow, Fleury."

She flew down the stairs after Valentine. They both landed in the flat in time to see Cutter pull on his undershirt. America gawked slightly at the sight of him. She had never seen a man's chest as muscled and smooth as his. Though she preferred Phaeton's body, it was quite astonishing to see a man who looked like one of the Greek statues in the British Museum.

"We've just had a rather disquieting chat with Fleury upstairs," she stuttered. "There is to be some sort of attack we are to prepare for."

Cutter frowned. The familiar sound of his helmet parts

whirled and clicked quietly. "Pennyfields is the safest place to hunker down in—and there are several Underground passages we can use to escape, should we get overrun."

Valentine fastened on her cloak. "I'll see about a carriage."

"We can take mine." The imposing Doctor Exeter stood on the landing. "I was worried. No one came down to breakfast this morning, so I thought I'd pop in."

America sighed with relief. "You are a godsend, Jason."

On the ride to Pennyfields, America did her best to fill the doctor in on the events of last evening, including Lovecraft's threat to shoot them. "The man needs a good long break in a sanitarium," Exeter shook his head. "He hides his son away—but I wonder if the young man might not be helpful in this matter."

America grimaced. "I'm afraid we may be too late for the asylum. You have yet to hear the worst of it. Just before you arrived we received communiqués from Fleury Ryder."

"One of the Ryder sisters," Exeter remarked. "The succubi Detective Moore is after."

America nodded. "She's rather a flighty, gossipy little thing, but has thus far been both accurate and timely with her messages. There is to be an attack—I surmise it is because Lovecraft believes Phaeton and Gaspar have the Moonstone."

"The fact that an attack is even rumored about in the Outremer means Prospero is involved." Cutter shook his head. He appeared anxious, keyed up, like a soldier ready for battle. America thought about the torture Cutter had been put through—how could he not be ready for a fight?

Exeter frowned. "If the professor is waging war, he will need Prospero's army of minions." The carriage slowed in the lane and came to a halt outside 55 Pennyfields. They all piled out of the vehicle and were quickly escorted down into Gaspar's study.

The Nightshades' leader studied their faces. "So, they are coming."

Cutter tossed off his cape. "A combined attack, by Lovecraft and Prospero. They want the stone—they know you have it. This also happens to be the most defensible place to be. The only other viable strategy would be to cut and run."

Phaeton sat up. "Personally? I'm for cutting and running. What happens if they overtake this place?"

"There are many escape passages below us—tunnels no one knows anything about except for myself and Ping." Gaspar seemed less unnerved than anyone, but then he faced every pitfall, every crack in the walk of the life, the same way. As if all things were possible."

America stepped forward. "There was also a message from Victor. He asks that Phaeton meet him at dusk in Highgate Cemetery."

Chapter Thirty-one

PHAETON STEPPED THROUGH THE EAST ENTRANCE of Highgate Cemetery and experienced a fuzzy moment. Behind him in the strange mist that moved between worlds he heard Tim Noggy's voice saying, "You're in, mate."

Agitated and in a hurry, Phaeton looked around and recognized the entrance to Egyptian Avenue—an old haunt in the cemetery. "Victor," he called out.

Highgate looked more or less like the last time he had been there. A little less wreckage, perhaps. Six months ago he had wrapped up a case at Highgate with Exeter. An irritable Egyptian goddess had wreaked havoc up and down the avenue of crypts until her husband had been restored to her.

Phaeton continued on past tombs and burial chambers, but turned up nothing—just a sly fox that crossed his path. The prick-eared creature stopped and stared before leaping through a bit of tall grass and into the woodlands that encroached on all parts of the cemetery.

After a search of Egyptian Avenue, he decided to jog through the Circle of Lebanon. The crescent row of crypts reminded Phaeton of a curve of pristine terrace houses in Regent's Park— only dead people resided in these little units.

"Victor!" he shouted.

Dusk was turning to twilight—the few minutes of the day when the sky wasn't completely dark, but evening had yet to begin. Whatever Victor had to say, it had better be fast. He

THE MOONSTONE AND MISS JONES 235

needed to return to Pennyfields to protect America and his friends.

Phaeton stopped a moment to consider the word. *Friends.*

He had come to think of this odd bunch of cohorts as friends, people he cared a good deal about. He had never allowed himself the luxury of many friends, and certainly not close ones—bosom buddies and the like. But now he had Exeter and Mia. And Mr. Ping. As well as the Nightshades—Jersey, Valentine, Cutter, Ruby. Tim Noggy—even Gaspar. Christ, he had even begun to think about Victor with a certain amount of . . . attachment. Frankly, this new aspect of his life disturbed. How had he let this happen? He was a loner. A misfit. A tortured soul. Wasn't he?

He cupped his mouth to call out again.

"I heard you from Egyptian Avenue." The voice had a bit of an echo but he was sure it was the homunculus. Phaeton whirled around. No sign of the small man.

"You called the meeting, Victor, and here I am. What shall it be tonight?" Phaeton wandered back in the direction of the voice. "I'm hoping you might be in the mood for a bit more storytelling. Perhaps an anecdote or two about the maker, who currently goes by the name of Prospero in our world."

"You continue to pick the most romantic names for our side—now it's Shakespeare's tortured magician." Victor stepped out from between two pillars wearing a tuxedo.

"Gaspar's the starry-eyed romantic, not me." Intrigued by Victor's appearance, he moved closer. "You're looking dapper this evening."

Victor grinned. "They say wearing all black elongates."

Phaeton remained at the bottom of the steps, which put them eye to eye. "Perhaps your message got garbled—dear Fleury, she does her best—but there was nothing said about a white tie affair . . ."

"The mice are away tonight, but the cat remains at home—hosting a charity soirée, bless the maker's little heart. I'm planning a disruption—something explosive, as a matter of fact."

Phaeton studied him. "Sounds . . . lethal . . ."

"If we are successful, I will very likely have to go underground—for a considerable length of time." Victor dipped into
the shadows and reappeared with a satchel nearly identical to
the one that held the Moonstone copy.

"You've given me hope, Phaeton. With this stone, I believe
you are going to restore my world. And if that is, indeed, to be
the case, we shall begin anew with fewer bad characters in
charge."

"By the way," Phaeton lifted his gaze from the satchel.
"Thanks for the warning; we assume the attack will come
sometime tonight." Phaeton squinted at the dwarf. "What can
you tell me about this unholy confederacy between Prospero
and Lovecraft?"

"They both lie quite effectively." Victor reached inside his
jacket and removed a leather cigar case. "Care for a smoke?"

"No, thank you—not much of a smoker." Phaeton frowned.
"So . . . what's the scheme? What do you believe they're hiding?"

Victor struck a safety match on the pillar. "They both claim
to want the Moonstone for altruistic reasons . . ." He puffed on
the cigar. "But what stops either one from a darker, more prof-
itable purpose? Remember these two are moguls of industry. I
know how these men think, I was raised by one—my brother
runs a high technology company. The other is an inventor."

Phaeton blinked. "A mogul, a scientist, and a rebel—interesting family."

" 'Long Live the Queen' or 'Shoes for Industry'—whichever
slogan you prefer." Victor exhaled pale gray smoke. "Suppose
for a moment these industry tyrants get a hold of the stone, I
suspect they'll keep it in the private sector—so much more efficient than creating another government office. Perhaps they'll
sell subscriptions. Those who can afford it—pay to keep their
house from unraveling."

"Or their brain." Phaeton thought about the vast potential
for profit. "Lovecraft could make a bloody fortune selling pros-
thetic limbs." Victor relaxed against a fluted pillar. "Since I am
a very rich, self-funded rebel, I might decide to add a bit of

height to my stature." He grinned. "Never too old to grow a few inches."

Phaeton picked up the satchel. "Sure you want to give me this? I'm headed into conflict, once I get back." Distressed at the thought of what lay ahead for both of them, he turned to leave.

"Why such a long face?" Victor called from the steps of the crypt.

He turned back briefly to glower at the dwarf.

"Chin up, your darkest hours have yet to come, Phaeton. Just remember—I have faith in you."

"Bugger off, Victor."

Phaeton took the woodland path out of the cemetery—the fastest way to meet up with Chester Road—where he'd look for a pub called the Duke's Head. Though the path was lit by moonlight, he hit a dark patch and ran straight into the North gate, which was closed and . . .

"Bloody locked."

Nothing left but to use a bit of relic dust and champagne. Phaeton gripped the satchel and readied himself for a leap. An easy jump—not more than seven or eight feet at the gate's highest point. Whenever he used this special manipulation of aether, he always felt more of an upward pulling sensation than a thrust from below.

"Careful—the gate's higher than it looks."

The voice was young, female. Phaeton pivoted slowly. Squinting into the darkness, he spied a silhouette—standing beside two grave markers. She spoke again: "You wouldn't want to rip your knickers."

The cloaked figure came forward. A sliver of pale luminescence bathed her face with a hint of dappled shadow from the leaves overhead. The entire effect was supernatural, only this was unearthly in a new and different way.

The ethereal beauty smiled at him. What was it about her—something vaguely familiar. Phaeton studied the flawless skin, the high cheekbones, and the slanted, golden-green eyes. He swallowed.

"Hello, father."

Phaeton suddenly went a bit lightheaded and woozy in the knees. He had never experienced a sensation quite like it before. Perhaps once, when Exeter had taken some of his blood during a transfusion, but this was . . . different.

He ventured closer and quirked an ear. "Come again?"

"You look just like your photographs—only more handsome, if that's possible."

Unsure, puzzled, and slightly pleased, Phaeton tilted his head. "Might I ask . . . your name?"

"Luna Black."

He must have swayed slightly—looked as though he might tip over, for the dear girl reached out and caught hold of his arm. "How did you—know to find me here?" He glanced to either side of her.

"I come here often. The wood is peaceful, and I have no fear of the dead. In fact, I commune frequently with the spirits of the past, as well as the future."

Her mouth was not quite as full as her mother's but she had that lovely cupid's bow, and he assumed there was a dimple as well. His mind whirled at all the possible scenarios that might explain this chance encounter with his grown—or nearly grown—daughter. "How old are you, exactly?"

"Seventeen—I'll be eighteen this fall. I take courses at London University. Ancient Civilization, mostly. One day I will go on an expedition, explore tombs—dig up dead bodies." She grinned a bit sheepishly.

Yes, there it was—she had her mother's dimple. "Speaking of the dead." His heart raced a little. "Am I . . . dead?"

"Mother said you'd be blunt, as well as direct." She hadn't used his name in past tense, but then she wasn't meeting his gaze either. "We lost you a very long time ago to another world. Then we got you back, only to lose you again—you've been gone for some time, now."

"And your mother, is she . . . well cared for?"

"You left us well provided for. And she is a wonderful mother—so very beautiful and cheerful and resilient."

Phaeton nodded. "Yes, she is all of those things."

"But I know she misses you. Will you come home soon father?"

He had never experienced heartache to the depth of anguish that he was feeling in this moment, as though his heart had been ripped out of his chest. When he spoke, finally, he hardly recognized the husky voice that answered her question.

"We are having this discussion through the mists of time, so I don't know how to answer you—exactly." Phaeton tipped up his bowler and scratched his head. "It's rather difficult explaining behavior one can only guess about, yet I want to say that if I am not with you and your mother, then there must be a very good reason. Perhaps, to keep you out of harm's way."

Luna's eyes watered. "Mother has always said she thought you did this to protect us."

"She knows, then—well that is some relief." Phaeton managed a strained smile. "She was always wickedly intuitive as well as brilliant—ahead of me in most ways."

Phaeton sensed she felt a bit awkward, as he did—yet they both marveled in each other's presence. "I was just on my way back to Pennyfields to help defend your mother and friends. There is an attack under way—some dreadful creatures from a parallel London . . ." He stopped himself. "It's a long story." Phaeton studied her closely—she was perhaps an inch or two taller than America. "Might I hold you?"

"I thought I was going to have to ask." Phaeton dropped the satchel. She ran into his open arms and he held her tight—rocking her gently, never wishing to let her go. He kissed the small hairs at her temple. "You even smell like your mother."

Gradually, they both arched away. He kissed tear-stained cheeks and stepped back to fish a handkerchief out of his trouser pocket. "We call you the pea in the pod." He patted her cheeks. "You're in your mother's belly right now."

She blinked, eyes wide. "Mother never mentioned it."

"Impossible, I know." Phaeton grinned. "How could you be as little as a pea? When here you are, my fully grown, beautiful daughter!"

"And here you are, my young and handsome father."

He held up the satchel. "Herein this bag lies the hope of our world and the Outremer—possibly even more planes of existence, but who's counting? I have to find a safe place for this— until the battle is won or lost. A temporary guardian. An innocent personage, who is pure of heart, who will not be swayed by any cause personal or grandiose, which leaves most of us out."

He grimaced. "I'm afraid the two worlds I move to and fro in are greatly troubled. I've left your mother with a band of skilled warriors but I must return shortly to help protect you both." Phaeton moved to the gate. "Walk me to Chester Road?"

Her mother had taught her well. They jumped the gate together and took the wider foot path that angled over to the street.

He couldn't hide a frown. "If you don't mind my asking, what are you doing here in Highgate Cemetery alone in the dark?"

Luna smiled. "I could ask the same of you, you know."

"Sassy, just like her mama." He inhaled a deep sigh. "Good God!" He stopped in his tracks. "You're not seeing any young man right now, are you?"

The dimple came out again. "No." She rolled her eyes.

Phaeton reached out to squeeze her hand, but her image changed rapidly as she began to slip through passages of time. He called after her, "If it is in my power to do so I will return— take care of each other . . . " A fleeting glimpse of Luna in braids with a tooth missing emerged from the mist and disappeared. His heart ached once again before she dissolved into the fog of space and time.

". . . I love you both." It was drizzling—at least his vision was blurred.

Phaeton managed to find the Duke's Head and stumble inside. According to Tim this comfortable old pub was his exit portal. He ordered a dram and a pint and took a seat by a window street side. There was no use trying to fathom what he'd just experienced—but the event, the marvel of seeing his child fully grown, shook him to the very foundations of his being. He felt unnerved and euphoric and cruelly heartsick. He chased the whiskey with half a glass of bitters.

And try as he might, he couldn't remember his inkling. If only he could remember the damn thing, he might have a chance to slip back in, grab hold of America, and make a dash for the *Topaz*. They'd up anchor and clear out of London. To hell with Victor's unraveling world and Gaspar and the Nightshades, and . . .

"Father?"

He looked up. Nothing. Not a soul across the table. Something fluttered and then settled outside the window—a bird perhaps? No, the child with the missing tooth was standing on the sidewalk, her nose pressed to the glass pane. A sweet little voice whispered in his head.

Think back to when you were a little two-penny like me, Father. There has always been someone pure of heart with you.

Luna waved as she faded into the crush of pedestrians on the street.

Suddenly, Phaeton knew who he needed to find.

Chapter Thirty-two

THE FORCE OF THE EXPLOSION at the front entrance caused America's hearing to cut out. In an eerie hush of silence, Jersey cracked open the door of Gaspar's study only to shut it quickly and push everyone back. He mouthed words she could not hear. "They've got more explosives." She shook her head and Jersey's voice cut back in. "Someone get America under the table—now!" The high-pitched grind of a metal device rolling down the corridor proceeded the next explosion. Jersey dove away from the door, just as the blast demolished Gaspar's study.

America coughed—wishing—hoping to see someone friendly through a haze of dust and debris. "Are you all right?" Gaspar tossed off chucks of lathe and plaster. He reached under the library table and America grabbed hold of his hand. Likewise, Jersey, who was covered in gray dust, helped the other Nightshades up.

"Any moment now, Reapers are going to start pouring in from the street level." Jersey lined everyone up behind him near a giant hole in the wall. He drew his weapon as did all the Nightshades. Metal slipped against metal, like a knife being honed, all four devices unfolded to full length. "Cocks up," she blurted out.

Jersey turned and raised a brow.

She swallowed. "The warrior phallus stiffens with resolve?" America mentally slapped herself for such Phaeton-like remarks, especially in such dire circumstances. She grimaced. "Sorry."

Wait a moment—perhaps this was exactly what was needed to stop the terror and muster some courage. Phaeton had a kind of genius at doing just that. America grinned. "On second thought I don't apologize."

Jersey's mouth twitched, "Let's just get the hell out of here." He dipped his head out of the smoldering hole in the wall. The narrow corridor was thick with dust and debris, but the dense cover would last only minutes. America stifled the urge to sneeze. "Who's got the stone?" Jersey croaked, his throat raw from the chaff in the air.

Gaspar held up the satchel. "Right here."

"Follow me—as silently as possible." Jersey led them over and under wreckage until they reached the end of the passageway. Gaspar felt along the bottom of an ornate painting frame and pressed. The entire wall moved like a pocket door. Jersey motioned them through.

As America stepped across, a terrifying growl swept down the corridor followed by a number of shrieks and whipping noises. The tentacle-masked creatures were being attacked by something that had escaped confinement—one of those objects behind the mystery doors in the corridor. What strange sort of grotesque petting zoo was this, she wondered. Or was Pennyfields a sanctuary for creatures too unfortunate or too dangerous to live among the populace?

"I believe that was the dybbuk in possession of a griffin," Gaspar spoke softly. "It isn't like a demon to posses something more tortured and unfortunate than themselves, but it happens. Deadly murderous though."

"Good news for us—hopefully it picks off a few Reapers," Cutter rasped, urging them forward.

The narrow, dank passage seemed to go on and on, with the Nightshades' swords providing their only illumination. Jersey held up a hand, the signal to halt. The silence was broken by the sound of her heartbeat and something else—the unworldly hissing and whipping noises. There could be no doubt what was up ahead. Jersey pointed a finger at Valentine, then forked two fingers forward. He wanted her up front with him, Cutter and Ruby would guard the rear.

"Put Cutter in front as well," Gaspar advised. "We need to clear a path through the Reapers and get to the Underground tunnel before they close in behind us."

"Ruby," Jersey hissed. "Are you all right with that?"

She nodded. "Just get us out of here—where we have some room to fight."

America suddenly understood. They could easily be hemmed in by the Reapers. "What'd wrong with their swords?" she asked. The glow from the blades appeared greatly subdued.

"They can't use much charge," Gaspar explained, "They must fight like Spartans—using short bursts of aether that won't bring the walls down around us. In a narrow tunnel like this, their movement is limited."

"In other words, all our options suck." Cutter squeezed by them. "I learned that word in the Outremer, it means—"

"Things are starting to suck—now!" Jersey yelled.

Screaming like banshees, the first wave of Reapers attacked in full force. Jersey felled the first one and let Valentine take the next. Cutter leapt to one side of the tunnel, catapulted himself off the wall and dove into a thicket of Reapers. The three warriors slashed and thrust and prodded until a pile of the creatures lay dead or dying around them. Gaspar pushed America forward. She climbed over steaming, oozing bodies and leathery tentacles, still undulating with residual aether.

"Press on," Gaspar urged his captain. "We've got to be near the Underground tunnel."

Jersey nodded, "We're going to advance farther ahead of you—follow on as quickly as you can." The three Nightshades took off at a run—and were soon just footsteps in the dark.

Gaspar helped America over the last of the dead bodies. Something slashed and buzzed—the sound of a Nightshade's sword. America glanced back. "Where's Ruby?"

Gaspar shoved America forward. "I'll find her."

"You've got the stone, let me go back." America turned just as Ruby emerged from the darkness, racing toward them. "Get a run on—they're coming fast!"

★ ★ ★

Phaeton finished his pint and looked around the pub—a couple sitting nearby were supping on eel pie—a specialty of the pub. Eels, snakes, worms. He sat up straight. "They're like worm holes," is was what Tim Noggy had said about the slipstream between worlds. He caught a serving wench by the arm. "An eel pie and another pint, if you would, love."

Before the young woman had a chance to blink he was sitting in the Duke's Head pub—again. This time he sat across from an old sot with a row of empty pints in front of him. The bleary-eyed geezer squinted at him. "Where'd you come from?"

"You really care to know?"

"Name's Homer McFee." Homer wore that slightly indignant look drunks get when they insist they're not drunk. "Three pint n' some tonight—feeling a wee bit happy is all. Not bladdered enough to be imagining things. You just appeared before me very eyes, lad."

"Newly arrived from a parallel London." Phaeton looked about for Edvar. "I've been doing a great deal of traveling lately, to and from . . . London." He rose from his chair and tipped his hat. "If you'll excuse me, Homer."

Phaeton jogged several blocks before he found a hansom for hire. Tossing the satchel on the seat beside him he settled in for the ride to Pennyfields. He heard a familiar snuffle, and smiled. "I never got a chance to thank you for staying with America after I was shanghaied. Things have been happening at a whip cracking pace, plenty of danger to go around as well." Phaeton sighed. "Even now, I don't have much time to explain, but I need two huge favors, Edvar."

Large, golden eyes appeared beside him and blinked.

"I know you don't care much for this Moonstone business, can't say as I blame you, but I need you to stuff the stone away—somewhere safe, a place no one goes but you." Phaeton glanced at the gray gargoyle, now fully formed and perched on the luggage. "Perhaps you could take it wherever you go when you disappear."

Edvar shook his head vehemently, and bounced up and

down on the satchel repeating a number of *nuh-uh, nuh-uh, nuh-uh, nuh-uh*s.

Phaeton lowered his chin and made soft eyes at the gray monster. "Please?"

Edvar ceased his bobbing and harrumphed. Phaeton brightened. A snuffle meant the gargoyle would think about it—that he might reconsider.

"The second favor is far more important. Whatever happens to me in these next few hours or days—or years—you must stay with America and the pea in the pod. Always."

The gargoyle nuzzled against him. There were no clicks and rattles, no snorts this time, just a simple *yuk-yuk* and an affectionate rub.

Phaeton scratched behind Edvar's ears—something he hadn't done since he was a boy. "Tuck the Moonstone away for me, old friend? Just until things settle down over here."

"Can't we go around them? Blast a hole somewhere else?" America was nearly bug-eyed with fear and exasperation. The Reapers were determined not to let them break into the train tunnel, and a whole horde of them were closing in from behind. It seemed as though legions of snake-headed foe were lined up and coming at them one after another. The tunnel they were in narrowed even further at this point, which gave them a chance at survival. Even though there were many more Reapers, they had to attack the Nightshades single file.

Jersey fell back and dipped his sword into a slain Reaper to recharge his blade. Cutter and Valentine continued to fight, but each time they advanced they were shoved back by the hordes. "Not much fight in them, but there are so many."

"Why not just bowl them down like ninepins?" America asked. "One big blast?"

Jersey wiped the sweat off his brow. He took a long look at her and exhaled, shook his head and then grinned, of all things. Apparently the man was only truly happy when engaged in battle. At the moment, a losing one.

He smiled even larger. "America wants a big blast? I think we should give it to her."

Gaspar stepped up, concern written all over his face. "What are you going to do? What is your plan?"

"The first thing I'm going to do is stop taking orders from you, Gaspar. Then I'm going to line up all four swords and blast the Reapers down like ninepins." He winked at America. "So we can get out of this small hole in the ground, and into a larger hole in the ground."

"What if you collapse the walls around us?"

"Then we all die ten minutes earlier." Jersey shook his head. "My people are exhausted, we're not going to be able to hold them off much longer."

"One more big push fore and aft," Jersey shouted. "Then recharge your swords and give them to me. This has to happen fast, soldiers—I'll have a few seconds."

All four Nightshades jabbed and sliced and battled back the hordes pushing them back until they cleared a bit of breathing room. Then the Nightshades withdrew from each end, and dipped their blades into fallen Reapers. They each tossed Jersey their sword.

The Shades captain ran straight for the regrouping hordes. A fiery ball of aether-charged energy ripped down the corridor, flattening everything in its path. "Let's get out of here," Ruby yelled from the rear. Dodging a rain of debris and rock, they all ran after Jersey who led the way to the end of the tunnel, where he stopped.

They all crowded around him to get a look into the Underground tube. Nothing. Just darkness and the hiss and whip of a thousand, snake-headed creatures. Using one of the swords, Jersey shot a ball of phosphorescence into the air of the larger tunnel, which burst into smaller particles of light, haloing the abandoned tube. Hordes of Reapers as far as one could see. Stunned, they fell back to regroup.

"We are so fucked," Cutter groaned.

Ruby stared at him. "More colorful use of language, courtesy of the Outremer?"

Cutter tilted his chin and stared back. "Proper word choices don't matter much when one is *fucked*."

Jersey shook his head. "I don't think so—did you see them?

Something else happening here. Like, why aren't they up here frying our brains out?" Jersey handed back their weapons. "If you want to hang back, that's fine—but I'm going out there." He turned and descended into the larger tunnel.

"Wait!" America hurried to join him.

Chapter Thirty-three

PHAETON APPROACHED THE ENTRANCE to Lovecraft's factory carefully. The iron doors looked as if they had been torn off and tossed to one side—run over by a swarm of Reapers, perhaps?

No wonder Edvar had steered him here—and not to Pennyfields. It appeared that Lovecraft had overestimated the alliance and underestimated Prospero's greed. Phaeton kicked bits of debris out of the way, and the sound bounced from wall to wall of the passageway. He took a right turn, which he was almost sure led down to the factory floor. He hastened his pace, fearful he was too late—the battle was over, and the other side had already won.

Entering the vast cavern of the abandoned train station he could not help but notice the imposing landship. Occasional bursts of steam made it appear as if the impressive engine was about to roll down what remained of the old Underground tracks. Phaeton listened to his footsteps echo off the paved parapet overlooking the facility. Other than a great deal of debris laying about, there didn't appear to be any great damage done to either the landship or the manufacturing enterprise.

Phaeton scanned the abandoned factory floor and the platform above. His gaze settled on a rather rotund chap tied to one of the station pillars. He climbed over an upended cart and made his way to the old passenger platform. Tim Noggy rolled his eyes in relief when he saw who it was.

"I thought Lovecraft was in irons." Phaeton removed the gag. "And weren't you supposed to be watching him?"

"The mistake was coming here. The tables turned pretty quickly once a battalion of Reapers arrived."

"And Lovecraft?"

Tim's eyes shifted. "Watch out mate—he's right behind you."

Phaeton pivoted. The professor walked behind a wheelchair that appeared to be propelled by some sort of clockworks. The young man in the chair steered the vehicle by manipulating a large toggle switch.

"Mr. Phaeton Black, meet my son, Lieutenant Alexander Lindsay Lovecraft." The professor's face was a mass of lash marks and bruises. Even those watery bulbous eyes were swollen and near closed from the bashing Lovecraft had received at the hands of the Reapers. The two goggle eyes were back, though, perched above Lovecraft's forehead.

Phaeton exhaled. At least one knew where to make eye contact.

The son leaned forward and offered him his good hand, all other limbs were mechanized. "Call me Lindsay."

"Phaeton." He shook his hand and leaned closer. "It seems I missed the most bruising part of the action. Mind filling me in?"

"The Reapers turned the lab upside down." Lovecraft offered. "When they didn't find what they came for, they decided to believe what I had been telling them—"

"That Gaspar was in possession of the Moonstone." Lovecraft's mechanical eyes shifted ever so slightly.

Phaeton's jaw muscle twitched. "You realize America is with them?"

Lovecraft pulled out a pistol and pointed it at Phaeton. "She's not a priority now that I've got you, Phaeton."

"Quid pro quo, Lovecraft." Phaeton backed away.

"About an hour ago they swarmed down the tunnel heading toward Pennyfields."

"And when do we expect the Reapers' return—or do we?" He felt a charge run through his body as his heart beat harder and faster.

"As soon as the Moonstone is operational, so to speak, these limbs of Lindsay's will make him more powerful than any ordinary man—twice as fast and ten times as strong. Then I will build an army of automatons just as powerful." Lovecraft actually smirked. "And no one from this world or another will ever be able to challenge me again."

If the professor's face didn't already resemble a piece of raw meat, Phaeton would have gladly added a few lashes. He looked down at Lovecraft's son. "Ready to be tanked up with potent aether?"

Lindsay looked weary, ready to die. "This is the last time I will put myself through such a trial. After this, I'm through."

Lovecraft leaned far over the chair back. "You're through when I say you're through."

"You are torturing me!" The son erupted, his anguished voice more of a plea than an accusation.

Phaeton turned to Tim. "Do we know who exactly is with Gaspar?"

Tim shook his head. "It doesn't much matter who all is with him—it's whether or not they managed to dodge the hordes, mate."

"And how is it you're alive?" Phaeton studied Tim's unmarked face. "At the very least, avoid a drubbing?"

Tim shrugged round shoulders "Same way I always do."

"He's our brother." Life-sized images of both Victor and Oakley materialized on top of a number of crushed factory carts. "Don't mind us—we're only projections." They were full sized and made up of many tiny particles. One of those odd grainy images that were so popular in the Outremer, only this was three-dimensional in effect, as if they were both actually standing upon the overturned wagons. "And the fact is he's brilliant, which makes him somewhat indispensible."

"Of course." Phaeton tilted his head. "Victor and Oakley are your brothers."

"We're kind of estranged." Tim's eyes rolled toward his brothers. "You've met them—they're pushy and arrogant and they each have their own weird agenda." He shot Phaeton a pudgy-faced grin. "You kind of remind me of Victor—only taller."

Tim and his brothers might be alienated, but Phaeton sensed

no real animosity, either. "Victor and I do get on, and Oakley reminds me of you—only thinner."

Tim continued to grin. "I'd be handsome, wouldn't I? If I lost a few stone."

Lovecraft waved Phaeton away using his revolver. "I want you over there—next to the transport machine." The professor motioned to his son, who used a separate ramp built for the wheelchair.

"What is this machine exactly?" Phaeton craned his neck as they neared the behemoth.

"Opens portals when and where I want them." Lovecraft flipped a few switches near a large opening. "The portals will eventually have two-way access, powered by enough potent aether."

Oakley snorted, "It's my understanding after you shut down Vauxhall, you couldn't get the machine calibrated again for our world—excuse me, the Outremer."

"Spying, Oakely?" Lovecraft's alternate eyes narrowed. "He steals all of his best ideas here—sends over his little electronic flies on the wall."

"And where are you are sending your guinea pigs, Lovecraft? Have any idea where they might be in the universe? They might never be found again. Lost in the cosmos."

Victor caught Phaeton's eye. "I wouldn't get too close to that door. There's an energy field—a vortex that sucks unsuspecting volunteers in." Victor shifted his gaze briefly to Lovecraft. "I believe that is how you do your recruiting?"

Phaeton shifted away. "And how goes the rebellion?"

Victor grinned. "Remember the big bang I mentioned? We took out a huge aether refinery—powers most of Prospero's machinery. It should have helped some, over here, what with the attack on." The small man looked about. "Ah, here come the mighty warriors."

Everyone swung about—even Tim managed a peek.

Jersey Blood led the way, followed by Valentine, Gaspar, and America. Cutter and Ruby, in their usual positions, guarded the rear.

Astounded to see the Nightshades alive, Lovecraft poked the gun muzzle into Phaeton and urged him forward. He hardly noticed the revolver at his back, because he hadn't taken his eyes off America.

"Phaeton!" She tried to break away, run to him, but Jersey held onto her. Good man. She appeared tired and dusty, and she never looked more beautiful to him.

"So what happened to the Reapers?" Phaeton asked them. "I know you're good but—"

"They were weaker than normal, right from the start. But they just kept coming—by the time we broke into the tube, they were standing around in a kind of stupor. Not dead exactly but—not really responding to anything, either. We walked right through them to get here." Jersey shrugged his shoulders and grinned. "They just ran out of juice."

Phaeton turned to the dwarf. "I believe I owe you a debt of gratitude, Victor."

Lovecraft nodded to Gaspar. "Toss the bag over."

Jersey Blood moved to fire up his sword—but nothing happened. The other Shades tried their weapons. Cutter shook his head. "I'm on empty."

Lovecraft eyed them all. "This machine is an aether receptor—your force has been usurped. Those weapons are useless here."

Gaspar moved toward Lovecraft.

"Stay where you are—just toss it over." The professor moved out from behind Phaeton to catch the bag.

"As you wish." Gaspar flung the suitcase so hard it hit Lovecraft in the solar plexus, and knocked the breath out of him.

Gasping for air, Lovecraft pointed the gun at Phaeton and cocked it. "Now Miss Jones."

"Don't. Stay where you are, America." Phaeton ordered. "He's not going to shoot me—I'm the one who grants the wishes. He plans to use you to manipulate me."

Lovecraft fired the weapon so close to Phaeton's head, a horrible ringing began in his ear. Slightly incapacitated, Phaeton grimaced in pain.

America broke away from the Nightshades and ran to him. The moment Lovecraft had America in his clutches he shoved Phaeton off and backed away.

"Finally—" The sniveling grin was back on Lovecraft's face. Holding onto America with one arm, he opened up the satchel with the other, which proved a greater task than he could possibly imagine. "I have the Moonstone, Phaeton Black, and Phaeton's motivator."

"The miracles inside the stone cannot be forced—let her go." Ping walked through a burst of steam and joined Phaeton who was gradually creeping up on Lovecraft.

Phaeton continued his advance. "And that part about finally having the Moonstone." He sucked a bit of air through his teeth. "Not exactly true, professor. The Moonstone in that satchel is a fake—a very good copy I must say, but alas, not the real stone."

"You'd like me to believe that, wouldn't you?"

"Drop the gun, professor." They all turned toward the new voice in the crowd. Phaeton was relieved to see Inspectors Zander Farrell and Dextor Moore on the platform above them aiming good old-fashioned hardware at the professor.

"Well, the gang's all here—there's a wine cellar below the lab—be sure to remember us with a toast." Lovecraft grabbed the satchel and the stone and dragged America into the pre-chamber of the machine. "Come along Phaeton, you'll cooperate with love in your heart or she goes . . ." Lovecraft's lunatic smile was back. "Who knows where."

Phaeton moved forward slowly. Someone had to wipe that feeble grin off his face. No use prevaricating. Phaeton lunged straight for the professor as bullets flew.

He shoved America out of harm's way, just as Lovecraft took several bullets.

Try as he might, Phaeton could not stop his forward momentum and slid directly into the chamber of the machine—something like hurricane forces whipped up around him as a whirlpool of aether yanked him farther inside.

America flung herself forward and caught hold of his jacket. "You must let me go, America."

"I will not!" As hard as she tried, she could not pull him out. It took all the strength Jersey and Cutter possessed to hold onto America, holding onto him. Her beauty and her bravery stunned even now. "Earlier tonight, I met our child—our daughter."

America's brows lifted. "What did you say?"

"Her name is Luna. You have to let me go, America."

Phaeton did something he didn't think was possible—he used a bit of potent lift to rip the coat off his back, and then he slipped away. The last thing he saw as he was sucked deeper into the machine was her sweet face. She reached out and screamed, "Phaeton!"

America fought and kicked and tried so very hard to go after him, but Jersey hauled her into his arms and held her until she promised not to do anything reckless.

Even after she promised he held onto her wrist with a wary eye.

Bleeding from several bullet wounds, Lovecraft dragged himself up and pointed his gun. "Watch out, he's going to fire!" Lindsay's warning caused Lovecraft to turn the gun on his own son. "You betray me after all I have done for you?"

"You betrayed me years ago. You did all this for yourself." Lovecraft's son nearly choked on his own words. Cutter stepped in front of Lindsay to protect him.

A second volley of police bullets hit Lovecraft and tossed him against the control panel of the machine. Dead-eyed, the professor slid down the side of the door and threw a switch. The engine made ominous noises that sounded as if it had locked up.

"Open the door! We must get Phaeton out!" America tried her best to twist out of Jersey's grip.

Jersey called on both female Nightshades to try to calm her as he and Cutter went to work. Feverishly they tried to open the doors to the machine. The panel on the door had a number that ticked down. Four. Three. Two. One.

The countdown was up.

A low humming noise swelled into a drone that reached ear deafening levels. There was a sudden shift—or sucking noise, then a clunk—then silence.

"What just happened?" she asked.

Lovecraft's son looked up. "He's gone."

America searched faces—from Oakley to Tim. Tim looked to Oakley.

She ran across the factory floor and up the ramp to the platform. Furious fingers unknotted and unwrapped Tim. "But we can find him, right? We can go after him. Tell me we can find him." Panicked, and out of breath, America panted, "Please Tim."

He looked at her for a long time, so long it made her whimper. She waited for him to nod or say yes—something that might deliver a ray of hope, and could stop her heart from aching inside her chest.

Tim cleared his throat. "It's kind of a complicated answer. You sure you want to hear it?"

She sniffed as she nodded.

"I'd like to hear this big guy," Oakley goaded his twin.

Tim sucked in a deep breath. "There are approximately one hundred billion to one trillion galaxies in the universe, maybe more. And each one has, on average, one hundred billion to one trillion stars. So if you multiply those numbers together, you get between ten sextillion and one septillion stars in the universe . . . times . . . nineteen different dimensions—give or take." Tim's eyes rolled upward. "Divided by the number of possible planets with civilizations . . ."

Oakley snorted. "I doubt whether that hulking contraption reaches half the galaxy."

Tim glared at the grainy image.

"Call me when you wheedle the odds down to a needle in a haystack, bro."

She had felt this kind of desolation before in her life. When her mother left her with her father, a stranger at the time. When her father died last year. And this moment—this moment that embodied the possibility of a lifetime without Phaeton.

Ping approached them with his hands behind his back. "Please remember we have more than science, we have the power to influence the course of events by the use of mysterious, supernatural forces." He took America's hands in his and blew a ball of ethereal silver blue light into her palm. "It's called magic."

Epilogue

DOCTOR EXETER AWOKE IN THE MIDDLE OF THE NIGHT in a cold sweat. Nothing unusual about it. A good night's sleep had evaded him for weeks now. He was getting used to feeling a bit ragged during the day. This time, his worried mind had fallen on Pennyfields. His comrades and friends had more than likely been attacked tonight, and it perturbed him to no end. He might have stayed to help Gaspar and the others—not that he would dream of leaving Mia alone.

Phaeton had insisted he return to Half Moon Street. This was more than a rough patch his ward was going through. Mia was sailing in uncharted waters. And he would be there for her, come what may. Whatever she must endure, he would suffer this passage with her. No matter how frightening these changes became, he would guide her through them.

The bedchamber was no darker than usual, yet it felt blacker. He was also vaguely aware of a presence in the room. Sensing movement, he sat upright. His gaze swept the carpet, the drapes—the play of tree branches at the window. Nothing. He exhaled, lowering himself down onto his elbows.

A shadow leapt through the air. Whatever the force was, it hit him and threw him down onto his pillows. Something velvet soft and heavy weighed on his chest, torso, and loins.

His first thought was he was being attacked by a she-demon. One of the Ryder sisters, perhaps? If it was a succubus—she panted. And each breath was sultry, like the warm body sprawled on top of him.

Feeling a bit foolish, Exeter opened his eyes.

A black leopard with green eyes stared at him. A low rumble came from deep inside the large cat—a resonance he felt through his entire body. The animal stretched, and a whiskered nose landed inches from his face. Exeter's heart pounded blood through his body. The cat opened its mouth and bared long viscious-looking teeth.

A long pink tongue emerged and licked.

If you enjoyed *The Moonstone and Miss Jones,* learn how
Phaeton Black and America Jones's adventures began in

The Seduction of Phaeton Black

A Brava trade paperback on sale now.

Turn the page for a special excerpt!

Chapter One

4 FEBRUARY 1889
SCOTLAND YARD, SECRET BRANCH
MEMORANDUM TO: E. CHILCOTT
FROM: Z. FARRELL
RE: AGENT REASSIGNMENT

Believe I have located Phaeton Black. Appears to have let a flat below Madam Parker's brothel. Though the suggestion will undoubtedly cause you pain, I must continue to recommend Phaeton as the best man for this unusual case.

"OH, PLEASE NO, MADAM, HE IS A BEAST," THE HARLOT WAILED. "I beg of you, Mrs. Parker, do not send me down to Mr. Black."

Phaeton Black turned his back on the hubbub, and paced the length of corridor between the foyer and staircase. A sultry sway of hip caught his eye. A luscious copper-colored wench descended the stairs. Her dark eyes lusty, curious, she ventured closer. "Fancy adding another dollymop, sir?"

Slouched against the stair rail, he swept a lazy gaze over her every curve. "Yes, why not? The more the merrier." He ducked his head around the corner and caught a glimpse of the bickering females in the salon. "We are waiting, my timid little sparrow."

The pretty whore beside him tilted an ear toward the clamor and quirked a brow. "Lucy?"

The din from the parlor hardly dampened his grin. "I believe so."

Right on cue, the reluctant whore let loose a shriek that pricked up the ears of every hound in the neighborhood. "I promise I'll work double the number of gents, just don't send me—"

"Hush, Lucy, before you have all the customers in an uproar." Esmeralda Parker stood just inside the parlor, arms crossed under an ample chest.

His stare trailed the baroque details of velvet flock-work wallpaper. "Does my reputation precede me?"

"Oh yes, something the size of an elephant's trunk, sir." The cocotte flashed a flirty smile.

He foraged back in his mind through a blur of absinthe and opium. "How long has it been since I rented the flat below stairs?"

"Near a week, Mr. Black."

He sighed. "I toss up a few petticoats, just to try out the wares, and already I am obliged to face down frightfully depraved and exaggerated rumors."

"Not a bad thing if you ask me, sir. Pay no mind to Lucy. She's a nervous little goose—believes everything she hears. Hasn't yet figured out a girl can pretty much work any size in, as long as she has a bit o' sloppy down there."

He dropped his head back against the wall, angling his gaze at the bronze beauty. He patted his leg. "Come closer."

She pressed against him and rubbed.

"Lovely."

The whining and whimpering from the parlor continued unabated.

"And your name is?"

"Mason, sir."

"What kind of a name is—?"

"Mason." She sucked in a breath and pushed her breasts up and out at him.

Mentally, he undressed her voluptuous curves. Cheeky toffer, this one.

"Named after me da, who was a stone mason by trade—all I know of him." Her deep, coffee-colored eyes brightened. "Mrs. Parker calls me Layla."

"Ah, the ancient Persian tale, Layla and Majnun." The wanton strumpet brushed back and forth across his lower anatomy. "And do you promise to drive me mad, Layla?"

The parlor door rolled open and Madam Parker swept down the hall, dragging the miserable little tart behind her. He noted the vitality in Esmeralda Parker's determined stride, a fine looking middle-aged woman. Truly a shame she had retired early to run one of the more reputable bawdy houses in town.

Things grew wonderfully cozy as two more women crowded onto the stairs. He inhaled the myriad scents of the female flesh surrounding him. "Esmeralda. Care to join?"

"Phaeton, be a dear and assure Lucy you will be reasonable with her."

Blinking back tears, the pretty whore shrank behind Madam's skirts.

He considered her again. Round bosom, tiny waist, lovely hips. Yes, there were very good reasons why he had selected her. "Lucy, might I assure you I am a man of . . . tolerable size, bone-hard." He tucked a finger under her chin and tilted upward. "Though I am not entirely safe to play with, at the moment I am far from dangerous. In fact, it may take the two of you to flog me into a state of excitement."

Esmeralda snorted. "I imagine that will be quick work, ladies."

He held his hand out until Lucy placed a trembling, clammy palm in his. He frowned. "This one has been on the job how long?"

"She has a crippled brother and rummy father. Teach her well, Phaeton—she is their only means of support." Esmeralda stuck him with a fierce look before she turned to climb the stairs.

The sway of Mrs. Parker's bustle captivated him. He had attempted several times to lure her into his bed. So far, to no avail. With each refusal she became more attractive.

He cocked his head. "Any house credits for the instruction?" A faint echo of laughter and the muffled rumble of a door rolling shut answered the question.

Two delectable lovelies stood before him.

"Are you done crying and being afraid, Lucy?" In the darkened stairwell, he could just make out a nervous nod. A terrified doxy just wouldn't do.

"Suppose I make you a bargain. If, at any time during the frolicking and frivolity, you decide things have gotten a bit—"

"Whopping?" The copper-colored vixen offered.

He dipped his chin. "Do try to be helpful Layla." He closed his eyes and inhaled a deep breath. "Now, where was I?" A hooded gaze shifted from one comely wench to the other. "If our interchange gets a bit too impassioned, shall we say? You may call a break in play. Exactly like a game of rugby—not entirely an unlike activity. What do you say, Lucy?"

"Very kind of you, Mr. Black."

"You're sure?"

Her eyes shone with relief. "Yes, sir."

He leaned closer. "Prove it with a kiss." He touched his mouth. "Here."

Tentative, soft lips pressed to his and shyly pulled back. "Charming." He pulled Layla close for a taste. Ah yes, sensuous lips with a bit of tongue. "Delightful."

"I believe this might turn out to be satisfying." Hands pressed to his lower back, he stretched. "Well then, shall we visit my den of iniquity? After you, ladies."

Descending into his flat, he opened the stove and poked at a few coals. The act of love should be something reasonably well-enjoyed by all participants. Even for ladies who made a living on their back. Phaeton bristled at the thought of Lucy's inexperience and terror. Well, he would make it a point to show her some pleasure. Pleasant enough duty.

"Madeira, or perhaps something stronger?" He perused several pantry shelves, upper and lower, and shuffled several packages and bottles about.

He passed through a cold spot and shivered. A low, unearthly vibrating snarl drifted up from below. The ghastly creature's purr was familiar enough. Phaeton took a peak at the girls. Predictably oblivious to his otherworld intruder. A shadow of movement swept past the corner of his eye. The end of a leathery scaled tail slithered around a cabinet opening. Phaeton stomped hard but missed. The fey creature disappeared into the blackness of the cupboard.

"Damned little demon."

"Rats, sir? Mrs. Parker set traps out just last week." Keen-eyed Layla dipped to get a look. He suspected she didn't miss much.

Phaeton kicked the lower door shut. "Harmless as a dormouse. Nothing to fear, ladies."

He decided to pour something stiff. A brief inspection of the young women had him imagining two sweet derrieres. "To a most favored position." He lifted his glass with a wink. "Bottoms up."

At the moment, his informal sitting room featured a single overstuffed club chair and a comfortable old chaise longue. Phaeton flopped onto the divan and reclined against a curvy pillowed end. He opened his arms wide. "I invite you to loose the dragon."

Reluctant Lucy made him grin, for she now eagerly climbed onto his lap. "Ah ah ah." He wagged a finger. "This teasing prelude has a caveat. For every button of mine undone, you must remove one article of clothing apiece."

He studied his evening's leisure through half-closed eyes. A man could be infinitely happy, at least for an hour or two, with a beauty settled on each knee. And the diversion was sorely needed. Purge the jabberwocky from his head and calm the racing thoughts that threatened to drive him round the bend. After a few hours of vigorous love play, he fancied himself dead to the world, thoroughly spent, snoring between two naked lovelies.

An ephemeral breeze bristled the hair on the back of his neck. The subtle shift in air pressure signaled yet another presence. A shadow drifted overhead and the stairs creaked. Just above, in the darkness, something moved. His gaze shifted away from nubile flesh spilling out of unhooked corsets and untied petticoats. "Why, I believe we have a visitor, ladies. Care to join? One for each, I don't mind sharing."

The tall, dark-haired man on the landing frowned and continued his descent.

"Such unfortunate timing." Phaeton nuzzled a supple neck and groaned. "And I so dislike postponing pleasure."

He shifted both doxies off his lap. "I promise you will each have a turn on top of me." An exposed fanny invited a gentle smack. "Off you go."

The pretty trollops gathered a few undergarments and paused for a brazen inspection of the intruder before vanishing upstairs in a clamor of footsteps and twittering.

"Well, well. Scotland Yard's most celebrated agent, Zander Farrell, come calling." Phaeton buttoned his pants and settled back with a grin. "Something desperate has happened to bring you here, below stairs."

"I admit it took a bit of ferreting about." Zander ducked under a sagging floor joist. "You've made quite a comfortable nest for yourself down here." He lifted an aquiline nose and sniffed the air. "A bit moldy in winter, perhaps."

"Due to my recent loss of employment, I have found it necessary, indeed prudent, to conserve resources."

Never one for small talk, which Phaeton greatly appreciated, Zander got straight to it. "We appear to have another monstrous character about on a killing spree. Chilcott wants the case solved before the bloody press clobbers us. He'll not have another debacle like the Ripper."

"I can assure you Jack is gone. I took a stroll through Whitechapel just yesterday. Not a trace of the fiend's miasma."

Zander glared. "Exactly the kind of green fairy talk that got your contract cancelled."

"Chilcott doesn't like me. Never has." Phaeton noted the barely perceptible clench in the man's jaw. Zander seemed strangely unnerved, a rare state of being for him. "Something's got you rattled. What is it?"

"There is some kind of beast or—vampire stalking the Strand."

Phaeton never laughed, a self-imposed rule that had remained unbroken for years. Otherwise, he would have been rolling all over the cold stone floor of his new flat at that very moment.

So he simply grinned. "Perhaps an actor costumed as *Varney the Vampire?* Or an Empusa. Might I look forward to a seduction by a bewitching female bloodsucker?"

Zander's glower gave way to a wide-eyed stare. "I thought you'd be pleased. You claim to believe in fairies and all that undead rubbish."

"My interest in the occult is not a matter of faith, actually." He rose off the couch and signaled Zander to follow. Rummaging through a set of pantry cabinets, he withdrew a bottle of liquor. "Nevertheless, I am honored and amused that Scotland Yard appears ready to consult the fey world."

He sensed darker undercurrents and listened momentarily to a fog of whispers. "The notion of an unearthly murderous evildoer is intriguing." He pulled out a chair. "Why don't you brief me while I *louche* us a glass?"

"Whiskey for me."

He swung back and raised a brow. "Certain about that? A bit of absinthe might help the investigation right about now."

Zander exhaled a bit too loudly. "As you wish, Mr. Black."

Phaeton set up two glasses and poured the dark green distillate. He angled slotted silver spoons etched with the likeness of a naked flying nymph across the rim of each vessel, and placed a lump of sugar on top.

The number two Yard man leaned back in his chair. "Quite an elaborate ritual."

"Hmm, yes. I suppose it falls somewhere between a witches' Sabbath and the Eucharist." He retrieved a pitcher of iced water from a makeshift cold closet. "Just as the water looses the spirit of absinthe, so does the absinthe free the mind."

As the chilled liquid dripped slowly over the sugar cube, Zander's glass changed from deep emerald to a delicate, cloudy swirl of pale green elixir. "Ah, the transformation, when essential oils bloom and the fairy is released. To quote Rimbaud—"

"A meandering, scatological French poet." Zander huffed.

Undaunted, Phaeton poured a last splash over nearly dissolved sugar. "As I was saying: 'the poet's pain is soothed by a liquid jewel held in the sacred chalice, sanity surrendered, the soul spirals toward the murky depths, wherein lies the beautiful madness—absinthe.' "

He settled down and lifted his glass. "I know what they say about me at the Yard. Eccentric, when they're feeling charitable, a menace or madman otherwise."

"That's not true. Gabe Sterling thinks the world of you."

"Then you and he are the only ones."

"Not me, just Gabe." Zander sipped a taste before taking a swallow. "Frankly, I can't say enough about a man who can step into a crisis situation and disarm a Fenian bomb without a care. I don't know where that kind of courage comes from, Phaeton, and neither do a lot of other agents who would rather call you mad than try to understand a man who invites death and fears nothing."

Phaeton shrugged. More pale green potion slipped down his throat. "I miss those small hours of the morning. You know as well as I do, from all our evenings on surveillance, the coldest chill of night happens at the edge of dawn." His hazy gaze landed on Zander. "The time when shadows are not deep enough for spirits and abominations to hide in."

Zander leaned forward. "I need you back on the job. Murdering hobgoblin, vampire—whatever or whoever the killer turns out to be. Take the assignment, Phaeton. But don't do it to prove the other agents wrong."

Taken aback, Phaeton blinked. "Why not?"

"Because they're right."

"Bloody, thieving pirate."

America Jones's gaze fixed on Yanky Willem's every movement as he moved across the polished wood floor of the shipping office. The vile ship snatcher paused between secretary desks and curled back an upper lip.

Up until this night, she had merely been an annoyance to him. A pestering fly he could easily wave aside. But his nonchalance had served only to embolden her purpose. She had picked the door lock, and he had caught her, dead to rights, searching for proof of treachery. Now, quite suddenly, her circumstances had grown perilous. Eyes darting, she calculated the position of Willem's other lackeys stationed around the workplace. His men had not bound her as of yet. No doubt they thought her a helpless, frightened twat. Thickheaded cock-ups.

"Miss Jones." The Dutchman exhaled smoke as thick as his accent. His breath reeked of the black cigar clenched between his teeth. "Words cannot express how pleased I am to have you in my company this evening."

The captain's gaze traveled over every inch of her. "And my great, great grandfather was a pirate, Miss Jones, but not I."

One day she'd wipe that smug grin off his face. Forever.

"I was obliged to take over your father's shipping business because he failed to make good on our loan arrangement."

She bit out a single word. "Liar." Quick as a strike from a snake, his hand lashed across her face. The blow jerked her head back, flooding her cheeks with heat. She licked dry lips and tasted blood at the corner of her mouth. Heart pounding, she blinked aside tears and retreated.

By the look in his eyes and the bulge in his pants, he would have her flat on her back soon enough. Then he would hand her off to his crew.

"I wager you'd all like a taste." She lifted her skirt and lace petticoats above the knee and made eyes at every surly mate. Her sashay about the room revealed more and more leg. When she reached the tops of her stockings, their mouths dropped open.

Seductively, she slipped her hands between her thighs. Eyes wide with feigned surprise, she looked down, then up again with a wink. "Silly me."

In one swift motion, she loosed a derringer from one garter and a bowie knife from the other. Falling back toward the door, she brandished both weapons.

"If you value y'er jewels, I wouldn't make a move."

Chapter Two

"HOLD ON, MR. BLACK." The pretty harlot quickened her steps to match his longer strides. Phaeton grabbed her by the hand and wove a path between the fancy carriages and cabs queued along the Strand. Traffic would shortly become a mangle, as theatres began to let out. A frosty wind blew across the broad avenue forcing them both to squint and hold onto their hats.

"Come along, Lizzie."

He quite enjoyed Miss Randall, whether she was on the job for Mrs. Parker or retained as a night crawler. He often used her for reconnaissance, a spotter who ably worked the streets or public houses.

At the corner of Savoy Row, he parked the tempting doxy by a lamppost. "Right here, love." A fine dusting of snow covered the cobblestone. Not enough to turn the ground white, but just enough to reveal a curious impression of footprints leading off down the row.

He directed his gaze after a diaphanous, almost imperceptible, flurry of snow. "I mean to follow a trace of vapor down the alley. I shan't be far off."

"A trace of vapor?"

He paused to think about his answer. "Do you believe in ghosts, Lizzie?

The girl scoffed. "No, sir."

"Phantasms with fangs who can pierce a vein and drain your body of vital fluids in mere moments?"

Eyes wider. "No, sir."

Phaeton leaned close and brushed her neck with his lips. "You will."

She shivered. "No need to frighten a girl, Mr. Black."

"I need you to keep a look out. Act like a street whore—not terribly difficult. If any gents or goblins get too frisky, you scream bloody murder."

He swept a stray curl off her robust, pink cheek. "Lizzie dear, have I ever ventured into your lovely slit?"

She snorted. "A girl doesn't forget a poke like that, sir."

"Did I pleasure you?"

She batted dark lashes. "Yes, sir."

"I am so pleased to hear it." He tipped his hat and walked into the deeper shadows of the narrow lane.

The trail of impressions appeared cleanly made. Small feet, with steps placed far apart, as if whomever or whatever barely needed to touch ground. He followed the tracks down a curve in the row until the imprints grew so faint, they became all but invisible. He inhaled deeply. Snow and soot and something else, faintly . . . metallic. Again, Phaeton sniffed the air as he scanned the rooftops and lane ahead.

Aware of the faintest shift in atmosphere, he focused his search once more on the bricks below his feet. A tear-shaped drop fell onto the pavers.

Red. Warm. Ice crystals surrounding the drop melted.

There, another drop.

He looked up, but could make nothing out. A sudden spray of crimson drops scattered across the snow as a gust of wind blew off the Thames. A hiss of fine ice swirled into the air and traveled up past shop windows. A ghastly misshapen figure settled onto a window ledge close to the roof.

Phaeton froze. A large, birdlike entity formed out of ice crystals and grey speckled flakes, or were those feathers? Long, spindly legs, tucked against each side of a thin torso. As the creature struggled to gain its balance, a bloody appendage slipped off the window ledge. Pearlescent feathers ruffled as the rare bird retracted the crooked, gangly limb. A protective wing folded over the injury.

So, the owlish harpy appeared to suffer.

He stared hard at the apparition. Would the wraithlike specter ever fully materialize? The pale visage continued to reshape itself until it resolved into something more human than avifauna.

"Ah, there you are." He inched forward, mesmerized. "My high-strung, feathered"—the facial features were feminine, fragile; an enchanting, chimerical bird—"beauty."

The humanlike face swiveled and blinked. *Why do you not fear me?* The voice whispered in his head.

"You might try being more bloodcurdling. Bone-chilling. Hair-raising, perhaps?"

Another ruffle of ashen feathers. *Male, what is your name?*

"Phaeton Black." A wicked smile encouraged him to press forward for a closer look.

I do not like. The white bird hissed and drew away. Phaeton tilted his head to align his sights with her yellow-eyed stare. There, on the rooftop, the dark silhouette of a man gazed down on them.

He had to ask. "Friend of yours?"

A blast of air and cyclone of snow enveloped the harpy. A billow of white particles whirled off the ledge and vanished down the alleyway.

A chill shivered through his body. And a deep sorrow. Squinting through a tempest of frost, he swept the skyline for the stranger. Nothing.

Intrigued, he started after the small twister passing by several basement railings. He paused to stare at an odd finial post. The cast-iron head of a dog. Edging closer, he imagined the canine's upper lip curled back. How long had it been since his last glass of absinthe? Several hours ago with Zander. Any unearthly effects should have passed by now. He reached out his hand and the canine creature snapped.

"Ouch!" He put his finger to his mouth and sucked a very real scratch.

A faint tinkle of laughter. Crimson drops fell at his feet. Were they his? He guessed not. Wavering on the edge of hallucination, he traced bleeding drops of red over street pavers. Light snowfall dampened each footstep to a soft crunch. An icy stillness crept over the lane. Nothing but the sound of his inhale and exhale.

"Over here, lovey."

"Hav'a taste, handsome?"

A pair of street prostitutes stepped out of the shadows and beckoned to him.

"Evening, ladies." He noted a large dustbin just past the huddled women. Inexplicably drawn to the container, he reached for the lid and hesitated. A steady pulse of rapid heartbeats throbbed in his ears.

Lifting the cover, he examined ordinary contents. "Rags."

With a glance around the alley and a wink at one of the working girls, he edged closer. A rat leaped out of the pile of refuse. He dropped the lid, and it clattered to the ground. "Bloody hell."

Wait. Phaeton pivoted.

A presence lurked in the velvet black darkness of a niche between buildings. He leaned into the unknown. The cold steel of a large blade pressed against his neck.

"Do as I say, *mon ami*, and I won't cut your throat."

A feminine voice, with an accent. He swallowed. "I make it a point never to argue with a female wielding a knife." In the blackness, he could just make out luscious plump lips and almond-shaped eyes. Human. What a relief. And a good deal prettier than his recent encounters.

"Back me up—against the wall." She pressed the blade edge deeper into his flesh. A trickle of blood ran under his collar.

"Careful." Adhering faithfully to her instructions, he pressed her to the bricks.

"Any moment now, a number of pirates are going to round this corner. They wish to do me harm. I want you to convince them you are near to completing your satisfaction with a street doxy."

He grinned. He couldn't help it. "Allow me to do my best."

A clamor of hurried footsteps echoed off the row buildings. Racking up her skirt, he inserted a hand between her legs. "Hook a leg around me."

When she complied, he placed both hands under her buttocks and angled her against the wall.

"Oh my!" She cried. "What is that?"

Phaeton paused. "My cock, miss. What were you expecting?"

"But—" She gasped.

A few harried shouts came from several yards away. Quickly, he brought himself under her and worked her down onto his prick. He began his thrusts slowly. Not too deep, as yet, until he knew her body would receive him. "Make much ado, as if you are a pretty whore well paid for a quick tumble."

Buttons loosed, he nuzzled a firm, round breast and tasted salty sweat. He suckled a taut morsel of nipple through thin fabric and bit down. "Ahhh." She gasped. A flood of moisture drew him deeper.

"That's a girl. Louder. Tell me you want more." He drove in. "Do it."

Her words seethed between her teeth. "I will kill you for this."

"Must I remind you"—he gasped—"your blade remains at my throat." Gently, he began to withdraw from her. "In or out, love? Make up your mind."

A low mewl from this luscious alley cat accompanied a bold thrust of hips. Her cries were layered with mockery. "Oh yes, more of that—big man."

"I'll take that as a yes." This woman's sheath girdled him like some kind of heaven. "I have yet to play deep, miss. How much of me do you want?" His arousal was huge and satisfaction precipitous. He pumped into her, closing in on his own finish. "This is going to be fast."

"Deeper, lovey." She cried, urging him onward. Phaeton could just make out the shapes of several men. Her pursuers paused to listen to their heated sighs and muffled groans.

"Yes, oh yes—give it to me." Warm flesh quivered as her words gave way to lusty exhales.

"Happy to oblige." As he growled his lust like some kind of wild beast, his fingers pressed into the flesh of her buttocks.

Heavier footsteps this time and the harsh, exhausted breath

THE SEDUCTION OF PHAETON BLACK   275

of hunters in pursuit of runaway prey. The men circled closer, near enough to make out her features or wardrobe.

"Bugger off." Phaeton barked over his shoulder. "Get your own doxy, mate." Inarticulate grunts accompanied his intensified thrusts as her pursuers changed course and ran off toward the Embankment.

Arousal heightened by their public exhibitionism, the little minx moaned a fiery incantation. "Jesufina, Marianna, Josephina."

He was close. On the very edge of climax. He opened his eyes to view the beauty who had captured him. Her eyelids fluttered. Momentarily, she was incapacitated.

A fierce wave of pleasure slammed through his body. Phaeton let loose.

His prick throbbed inside her. A long moment passed, before he remembered the blade. In one swift move, he grabbed the knife and twisted it out of her hands.

Those slightly exotic, almond-shaped eyes narrowed. "Get off me."

One last glimpse up and down the alley. "Very well." He kept her pressed to the wall and slipped out. "Lovely, unexpected diversion."

Pants buttoned, he looked up in time to avoid the blow of her fist. The ferocity of her swing caused a temporary loss of balance and the lady tumbled into an iron basement railing.

Phaeton leaned over. "Blimey, she's knocked out cold."

He had little choice but to pick her up and throw her over his shoulder. The pirates might double back this way. Pirates? Was she daft, or was he? More likely she was some kind of common street thief. He retraced his steps out of the row and onto the busy thoroughfare of the Strand. Lizzie, dear girl, stood under the streetlamp right where he had left her.

Quickly, he settled both women into a waiting carriage. The coach lurched off, rocking Lizzie back and forth. She tilted her head and studied the young lady. "Who is she?"

"A mystery." Gaslight briefly lit the interior of the cabin. Enough for him to note his little cohort's sallow cheeks and red-rimmed eyes. "Lizzie, anything unusual to report this evening? Perhaps a flying phantasm or two?"

"Nothing much, sir." She hesitated.

Phaeton removed her gloves and chafed icy hands between his. "Tell me, Lizzie."

"Well, sir, a very beautiful woman approached me. Pale she was and stood real close, wanting a bit of warmth." Lizzie pulled at the collar of her dress and began a raspy struggle for air. "I don't remember much after—"

He pulled her onto his lap. Gently, he brushed back loose curls to expose a lithesome neck and two perfectly dainty puncture wounds.

A dull ache of drums nagged at the back of her head. She moved to stretch and found her wrists tied to the arms of an oversized upholstered chair. Her pulse throbbed under the bindings. Assessing her circumstances, she closed her eyes and feigned a long awakening.

"Good morning, my dove."

She sensed the unmistakable power of his essence. He was a channeler. A mortal being haunted by demons, or enchanted by fairies. Hard to say which, perhaps both. Genteel society would likely call him a wretched man afflicted by a mental disorder. Wretched? Possibly. But a rare gent he was, and no doubt gifted in peculiar ways.

Aware of a bubbling tea kettle and the familiar clink of china cups set on saucers, she opened an eye to observe the dark-haired man from last evening. The man who had thrust into her woman parts. Deep inside, she could still feel the effects of his churlish prick.

The shadowed niche of the alley had afforded scant illumination. This morning she revised her assessment of him. A bit swarthy, he hadn't shaved as yet and wore no cravat. His waistcoat remained unbuttoned, but she could see enough to know he was nicely made. Genuinely handsome, if a bit untamed.

His nose was strong and straight, but in profile appeared slightly beakish. His mouth was full and, yes, sensuous and kissable. Hair much too long to be fashionable, but there was something about the mode. Bohemian, perhaps? She examined his body as he moved around the stove. He was a nice size. Large enough but not imposing. And that rude shaft was plenty of male.

"If you are quite finished with your assessment of me, I would like to begin one of my own."

She closed her eye. Blood accelerated through every pathway in her body.

"You must know you have nothing to fear from me."

Still, a throb of alarm surged in her ears. She shifted her head and forced herself to open both eyes. He stood close by, scratching a raised brow.

"If I have nothing to fear, why have you made me your prisoner?"

"Ah, the ties." He tugged a side of his mouth upward. "For my own protection."

She strained against her bindings as he circled the chair. "While the Darjeeling steeps, why don't we revisit our precious moments together, last evening?"

He had a kind of unruffled, arrogant way about him. She squirmed in the chair. "I prefer an Oolong. Or a nice, smoky Lapsang Souchong."

His eyes crinkled, but his expression otherwise remained stoic. "You know your tea, Miss, but I shall not be diverted. Evening last, I was having a chase down Savoy Row after a pesky, flirty little phantasm when I was abducted by an equally trifling, yet forward olive-skinned maiden who put a dagger to my neck and proceeded to abuse me."

His gaze wandered between several undone buttons that exposed much of her flimsy chemise. "Care to explain?"

In the blink of an eye, she moved into a trance. Transporting herself back a few hours, she recalled a whisper of chimera and a tingle of demon. Her eyelashes dropped lower. "I sense unfathomable powers and yet almost unendurable exhaustion. Not death, but a weakness of spirit." She looked up into his eyes. "And great sadness."

He studied her. "You have abilities?

She nodded quickly and shook off the spell. "My mother had gifts. A Cajun witch, powerful, beautiful."

"A *Vauda?*"

She eyed him suspiciously before nodding. "You know the *sang mélangé français* ways?

"Your name, mademoiselle?"

"Why should I tell you my name? You hold me captive, sir. Why should I reveal anything to you?"

"Because I believe in civility." Caught in his own deceit, he shrugged. "Let's just say I prefer a name. If not possible before intercourse, after will do."

"I had no idea a man could get up a shag with a knife at his throat." Was that a smirk or a lopsided grin from him? "That wasn't a compliment," she growled.

"Honestly?" He tilted his head back. "Sounded like flattery."

"You raped me."

"You demanded it." He placed a hand on each chair arm and leaned forward. "Why didn't you cut me ear to ear?"

Her glare faltered. Why hadn't she killed him? The evidence of her knife was right in front of her. A fresh scar slashed across the side of his throat. If she had pressed harder, he would be dead.

She chose not to respond to his question because she didn't like the answer. How could she forget those intense waves of arousal? Pleasure that was both frightening and miraculous. She caught her bottom lip between her teeth.

His gaze lowered to rudely ogle her mouth. "Our first time was rushed, wouldn't you say?" Grazing the curve of her cheek, his lips brushed closer to her mouth.

Weakly, she parted her lips. "You took advantage of me, sir."

"I heard little protest." He held back, his words delivered as a soft caress. "Only oohs and aahs. Your hot, breathless words in my ear."

She curled the tip of her tongue over the edge of her upper lip. With his attention on her mouth, she furtively lifted a knee between them. "How could I complain with a band of filthy pirates after me?"

"Mmm, most taxing." His exhale buffeted softly over her cheek. "But, did you enjoy yourself, miss?"

"Yes." With one swift kick, she shoved him off.

He bellowed a hellish groan, as his hand flew to his crotch. Apparently she had clipped the jewels. Bent over, he walked off his agony by rubbing himself into impressive arousal.

"Happy now?" She braced for a beating. But none came.

Spurning the steeping teapot, he went straight for a bottle of whiskey and popped the cork. She gave him high marks for grog guzzling and pain tolerance.

He sputtered and coughed. "Delighted."

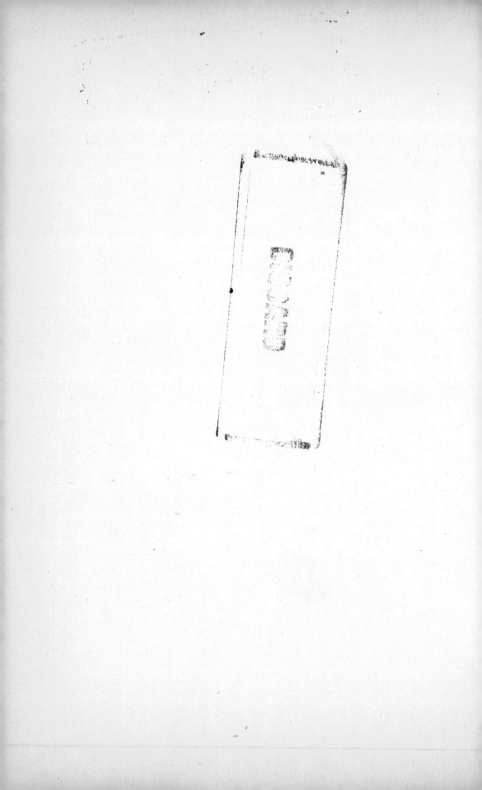